Pompey Hollow Road

OTHER BOOKS BY JULIE OLESZEK

THE FIFTH FLOOR TRILOGY

THE FIFTH FLOOR
JUST LIKE ZIGGY
ALL BUT ONE

Pompey Hollow Road

a novel
by Julie Oleszek

Mockingbird Publishing
Batavia, IL

Published by Mockingbird Publishing, LLC

WalkingBird Publishing™, Walk-a-Bird Publishing™, JulieOleszek.com™ are trademarks of Mockingbird Publishing, LLC.

Printed in the United States of America.

Cover design by Deborah C. Blanc

Oleszek, Julie
        Pompey Hollow Road: a novel/Julie Oleszek. – First Edition.
        ISBN 978-0-9862705-7-4 (pbk)
        ISBN 978-0-9862705-8-1 (eBook)

First Printing, 2023
Mockingbird Publishing, LLC
JulieOleszek.com

For my nieces and nephews,
and great-nieces and great-nephews

Part I
1829-1842

1

Mr. Hyde, a wheat farmer from Williamsburg, walked into the office at 1315 Duke Street in Alexandria. "Hello, sir," he said, tipping his hat to Mr. Franklin. "I'm looking for a Negro at a good price."

Mr. Franklin smiled. "Indeed. A good-looking dozen is right outside. I'm having them transported to Mississippi today. The South's paying a mighty fine price these days with all the cotton fields springing up. But I'd be obliged to sell any of them at a reasonable price just to have one less to manage during transport."

Mr. Hyde, a considerably large man, left by the side door of the building to have a look around. He stopped in front of two girls chained together at the ankles. Mr. Hyde was interested in the younger of the two girls because his wife had sent him here to get a playmate for their daughter. Mr. Hyde pulled the little girl closer with his hand hard pressed around her arm, forcing her around. "Open your mouth," Mr. Hyde demanded. He checked inside to ensure her teeth weren't decayed and her gums displayed a clean bill of health.

James Worthington, a tobacco plantation owner, was headed home after a business meeting in Alexandria's town center when he passed by the slave jail. On the far side of the building, Negroes chained together stood in a line; among them were two young girls standing rigid. James wasn't in the market for slaves, but seeing the increasing fear in the girls' faces and an overweight man tugging at the younger one caused James to stop his horses, jump down from the lumber wagon, and investigate. He wasn't a man to eavesdrop, but if it meant the safety of these girls, then so be it.

A nearby onlooker smirked in Mr. Hyde's direction. His teeth, what was left of them, were yellowed and tobacco-stained. "She sure looks like she'd be a good picker. And I reckon she'd respond keenly to a whip by how she turned at your command." He let out a raspy cough that spewed tobacco juice. "What would ya ask for a puny slave like her?"

Mr. Hyde continued through the line of shackled slaves, avoiding further conversation with the redneck. James figured the yellow-toothed man couldn't have afforded the chains binding the girls, let alone a slave, but the other man, Mr. Hyde, could afford both girls, although he was interested in only one. James worried the two girls, whom he assumed were sisters, would be separated.

Mr. Hyde returned to the front office to make an offer. James followed him inside.

"I'll take the littlest slave girl for two hundred dollars." Mr. Hyde said.

James came from behind Mr. Hyde and offered Mr. Franklin a price he couldn't refuse. "I'll take the two girls for seven hundred."

Mr. Hyde scowled. "Now, wait a minute! I was here first. You have no right—."

Mr. Franklin hurriedly held out his hand to James, and a price he couldn't resist, considering the long journey could kill both girls. He looked at Mr. Hyde. "You understand. Business is business."

The two girls huddled in the back of James's wagon. Rachel hoped her new master might be kinder than the last one.

"Are you sisters?" James asked.

"No, sir," Rachel said. "Don't know who she is."

"Is that so? Do you have a name?" James asked the younger of the two girls.

Simone tucked her head further into Rachel's neck.

"I got a girl at home about your age," James said, trying to comfort the girl. "Her name is Charlotte. She will be pleased to meet you both."

When neither girl spoke, James told them they had nothing to fear, then climbed onto his lumber wagon and clucked for the horses to go home.

"What's your name?" Rachel whispered.

"Simone," the little girl answered.

Rachel recognized Simone's fear and was afraid, too, but she could be brave to ease Simone's anxiety. She pulled Simone closer and told her it would be alright, but Rachel didn't know if this was true. She hoped this new master and the girl Charlotte the man talked about weren't cruel like the last ones.

Not long ago, Rachel lived with her parents in the back of Mr. Sopley's tailor shop, sewing shirts and skirts, but when she was eleven, Mr. Sopley got into terrible financial troubles and used Rachel to pay his debt. Rachel watched it happen almost every day in her head—her mama crying and Papa pleading with Mr. Sopley to let Rachel stay. Master Sopley's eyes looked like he might change his mind, but he only promised to return for Rachel when he had extra money. He never did, and Rachel hadn't seen her parents in the two years she lived with the Browns.

Rachel had known Mr. Sopley since she was born. He was never unkind to her or her parents, but Rachel's new masters, Mr. Brown and Mrs. Brown, were cruel. Mrs. Brown said she wanted a sewing girl, but it was a lie because Mrs. had plenty of delicate dresses bought from high-end stores. What Mrs. Brown wanted, Rachel finally guessed, was a slave for her eldest son's training as an overseer, or something like it, because he kicked her around every chance he got and whipped her for no reason.

Last week, Mrs. Brown told Rachel she was gobbling their food, causing trouble, and was of no use. Rachel thought this meant she was going back to her parents. She was thirteen, and her parents would be shocked to see how much she had grown.

It wasn't like Rachel assumed.

"Please, Mr. Brown. Take me back to my mother. She's waiting for me," Rachel begged, but Mr. Brown ignored her and handed money over to the overseer.

"She goes by the name of Rachel Brown." Mr. Brown told the man.

"My name is Rachel Hess," Rachel spat out in anger. "Take me home."

Mr. Brown slapped her so hard across the face that she fell backward against the wagon's side, hitting her head.

The thought of it made Rachel want to cry, but she decided against it. She must be brave for Simone.

2

James's home was five miles from town. Rosalie and his children, Charlotte, Thomas, and Henry, would be there when he returned. Charlotte was vivacious and would be thrilled to have a girl her age on the plantation. However, his wife was on his mind. Rosalie disagreed with the purchase of slaves. She would follow his decision, but James would still justify what transpired in town to bring these two slave children with him.

James thought back to a decade ago. His father bought slaves, and no one gave it a second thought. But love changed this ideology for James. Rosalie's father nearly refused his daughter's hand in marriage because James was the son of a slave owner.

Mr. George Farnsworth, Rosalie's father, was a wealthy self-made and well-liked business owner of a construction company south of the Erie Canal in Syracuse, New York. His success did not spoil his daughters. George believed Rosalie and Sarah must develop a strong work ethic and a savvy business mind. They were taught business by example, and often the girls returned home with their father, all three dressed in dirt. Their mother met them with a smile at the front door, but it didn't change the fact she wanted her floors to remain clean.

James's dad, Mr. James Worthington, Sr., sought out Mr. Farnsworth due to good business connections. They met several times for business, and trade was crucial to the North. Undoubtedly, the North had its industries, but the South had essential goods. James Worthington met important people through George Farnsworth—those who purchased tobacco by the barrels, and in return, James Sr. sent important people to George.

One evening, young James and his father dined at a fine restaurant after a business meeting.

"Well, will you look at that? Mr. Farnsworth is here with his family."

James looked toward the table, and at that exact moment, Rosalie, Mr. Farnsworth's daughter, looked in his direction. James's heart skipped a beat seeing the girl's beauty.

James stumbled on his words. "Father. Who? Who's sitting next to Mr. Farnsworth? I must meet her. Please introduce me to her. Straightaway, Father."

His son's absurd reaction did not amuse James Sr. "Son, Rosalie is Mr. Farnsworth's daughter. You remember, don't you? Mr. George Farnsworth, the wealthy and powerful man we did business with only hours ago. I will not have you interfering with what is good business." James Sr. dramatized the latter to force reason upon his son.

Young James couldn't help himself. He didn't care about the rich and powerful Mr. Farnsworth or that Huntington Manor Plantation would someday be his. Rosalie was the loveliest girl he'd ever seen. "Look at her, Father. You must introduce us!"

James Sr. kept his gaze on his son. He placed his elbow aside his dinner plate and waggled his index finger at James. "I've met Rosalie, but I will not have you courting a girl who, if in chance, does not go well, will spoil my relationship with one of my most important connections because you've mustered some crazy idea you're in love with his daughter. Furthermore, might I remind you, a girl you've never met?"

James responded as if his father kept serious information from him. "You mean to tell me you've met Rosalie and never thought to mention her?"

"Of course, I've met her. You know I've made this business trip a half dozen times in the last year." James Sr. sighed. "What is this? Am I being interrogated by my only son?"

"Not at all. I'm only asking that you introduce me to Rosalie. What is the harm in that?"

James Sr. forced a laugh and then said in a stricter tone. "You will not talk me into spoiling my business relationship with Mr. Farnsworth. He is a powerful man, and I suspect he would not be fond of any boy dating his young daughter."

James looked directly at his father. "A boy? This afternoon, you alleged what a man I've become. And now I'm a boy again? Father, believe me when I say I have not wanted anything more in the world than to meet the prettiest girl in all of New York and Virginia combined. And she is sitting only a few yards from us. I may lose her forever if I don't act now."

James Sr. swallowed his last bite, but his son barely touched his food.

"Son, this appeal of yours is absurd—."

Young James was growing impatient. "You fell in love with Mother straightaway. How is this any different?"

A waiter delivered dessert to Farnsworth's table. Rosalie offered a quick smile toward James but turned back to her family, engrossed in a conversation. James straightened with conviction. "Father. I am going to meet Rosalie Farnsworth with or without you."

James forced his father's decision. Mr. and Mrs. Farnsworth invited James and his father to a family picnic before returning to Virginia. It was the beginning of an affectionate relationship between Rosalie and James. For the next year, they sent letters, and James visited Syracuse three times. He planned to ask for Rosalie's hand in marriage. However, Mr. Farnsworth would not approve of anyone who owned slaves for his daughter.

George Farnsworth hoped his daughter would court a neighbor or schoolmate. He hoped Rosalie would marry and live in the same town, maybe even on the same street, but those dreams disappeared day by day. His daughter's love for the young lad deepened, and he could do nothing to stop it from happening. If he didn't give in to this relationship, Cecilia, Rosalie's mother, warned him that he might as well lose his daughter to spite.

George was a businessman, so he conjured up a business plan. "I'll tell you what," he told James. "If you truly love my daughter, like I suspect you do, come work for me for a time. It's only fair you know what you're getting yourself into."

"Oh, Daddy," Rosalie squealed when she learned James agreed to move to Syracuse. She swung her arms around her father's neck and hugged him tightly. Rosalie then turned to her Mother, "Can he stay in our guest house?"

"I'm not sure I want that young fellow in my guest house," George Farnsworth explained to his wife that night before dowsing the oil lamp.

Cecilia replied, "We've got to find out what kind of boy he is, George. Our daughter deserves a respectable man. Let's see if James can prove himself."

George huffed. "Our guest quarters are meant for guests. I will confirm James is well aware he is a boarder, and we expect him to act as such."

"Yes, dear. I'm sure you will."

George smiled, thinking James wouldn't last in construction for over two weeks. There were no slaves to dote on him here. George would have plenty of strenuous work for his new boarder.

When James Sr. heard of the business deal Mr. Farnsworth offered his son in Syracuse, he was angry. "I cannot imagine such an absurdity. My only son is willing to leave Virginia and our tobacco crop because of a girl?"

James convinced his father to let him go. "I'll be back, Father. And I'll bring Rosalie Farnsworth with me as my wife. Until then, you have Mother and three daughters to keep you company."

James surprised George Farnsworth with his work ethic and determination. Young James stayed as a guest in Syracuse for thirteen months, working for George Farnsworth and properly courting Rosalie, and would have stayed, but tragic circumstances changed his life. James Sr. died in the tobacco field when his heart stopped. Young James returned to Syracuse soon after his father's burial and again asked for Rosalie's hand in marriage. George Farnsworth allowed matrimony but with stipulations. James was never to enslave or purchase another Negro.

James agreed. He married Rosalie the next day, and together they moved to Virginia.

All these years later, James treasured his wife. James looked over his shoulder at the two Negro children in the back of his wagon. Rosalie would not turn them away even when they defied her father's wishes. James was no longer a boy in love from years ago. After his father's death, he realized his promise to Mr. Farnsworth never to sell or purchase slaves was unrealistic and a precursor for financial ruin. If Huntington Manor was to survive, slaves were necessary, but when James purchased Reedy, one of the plantation's slaves, Rosalie accused him of being a promise-breaker. It was an unexpected blow from the woman he loved, but he adored Rosalie and wanted to make it right.

He concluded if his marriage and Huntington Manor Plantation were to survive, he needed to appease Rosalie and uphold the success of his tobacco crop. Through his good sense and business mind, James managed both. Rachel and Simone were the perfect examples.

James turned the horses toward Huntington Manor. He marveled at his land with the tobacco fields spread across the plantation and his house in the distance, at the edge of his property. But above all else, he loved his family.

Rachel straightened and watched the big house grow larger as they came closer. "Look, Simone," Rachel whispered and nudged the child. Simone pushed herself to her knees and stared with wide eyes. Rachel petted Simone's head and smoothed back the girl's hair.

Charlotte, a beautiful little girl with thick blonde hair, loose curls cascading down her back, and soft blue eyes, did not hesitate to ask the younger girl how old she was. James listened nearby, humored that Charlotte asked for the girl's age instead of her name. He hoped to hear both.

Simone, equally as pretty, with her hair in ringlets and large dark brown eyes, was cautious in her response. "Seven, Miss."

"Me too," Charlotte squealed. "But my name isn't Miss. It's Charlotte. Do you want to play with my dolls?"

11

Simone nodded, and the girls ran off to play, leaving Rachel alone with Rosalie.

"Come with me," Rosalie said to Rachel.

Rachel followed the Mrs. through a hallway, past a beautiful staircase and large dining room, and into the kitchen

Rosalie introduced Hilda and Chloe, two of the plantation's slaves, without specifying one from the other. "This is Hilda and Chloe. I'll let you get acquainted."

When Rosalie was out of earshot, Rachel quietly asked, "Who's who?"

James told Rosalie that evening. "It's uncalled for—Rachel's back scarred like that. And they were scared stiff, and nearly naked, chained at their ankles, gawked at by onlookers like they were select pieces of beef."

"They're safe now. You did the right thing by bringing them here." Rosalie could not utter the word purchase when it applied to the Negroes on their plantation. She knew that James understood this about her. She loved her husband. James was confident and kind, and he was well-respected, with charisma most people adored. He was a successful businessman and a good provider.

James's honesty captured Rosalie's heart. He was a man of his word, and his actions backed what he set out to do. This quality had saved their business over the years when crops didn't produce the expected quantity. Rosalie looked over at her husband as he was unbuttoning his shirt. James was handsome. Brown hair with hints of gray at the temples and soft, blue eyes secured a compassionate appearance. He was nearly six feet, and his sureness added inches.

"How did you find the girls?" Rosalie asked.

James took off his shirt and laid it over the bed's footboard. "I was in the right place at the right time. I hadn't planned to turn onto Duke Street on my way from Hall's Feed, but there I was, passing by Isaac and John's slave house. There were twelve Negroes outside shackled like criminals, ready for transport, and these two young girls were among them. I couldn't get their scared faces out of my mind. What if that was Charlotte? Could you imagine the horror?"

Rosalie hinted at the conflict inside her. "No, James. I could not."

James shook his head, then proceeded without reason to think his wife's mood had altered. "People are selling their slaves south, trying to get a better price. It's not right."

It had been a long day. Rosalie got into bed and read from the Bible. James sat at his mahogany desk and pulled out a ledger to view last week's profits.

3

Huntington Manor, Virginia 1829-1830

Upon his father's death, James had inherited Huntington Manor Plantation. The two-story house was Georgian in style, with a third-floor attic providing plenty of room for a servant's quarters through a back staircase from the kitchen. The big house stood out from where it sat on the edge of the plantation, back a distance from the main road and overseeing the stable and the fields. Eleven large windows cased the front, and around the back, eight windows gave a broad view of the land. Large oak trees shaded the front porch on hot days and blocked the wind from rattling the windows through the winter.

There was a schoolhouse several miles away in Alexandria, and Charlotte had attended for two years, but Rosalie preferred that her children learn at home. She'd wanted to be a teacher, but marriage changed her plan. When some mothers might complain their children were underfoot, Rosalie never minded. She liked watching her daughter and two sons play in the afternoon after their studies.

The front foyer was bright and airy, allowing a lovely view of the curved staircase. A large parlor housing a fireplace opened to the right by large French doors. The drawing room was visible from the front foyer, and beyond was the dining area. A black walnut dining table and chairs seated their family of five comfortably. The kitchen was at the back of the house.

A curving mahogany staircase ascended upstairs alongside a light blue, grand chateau wallpapered wall, and opened to a landing. There a hallway led to four bedrooms and a nursery that three-year-old Henry recently outgrew. Rosalie and James Worthington and their three children slept on expensive feather beds in their rooms. The master bedroom window was above the front porch on the main floor, where the sweet smell of James's pipe below floated into their upstairs room on summer mornings.

James also inherited four slaves upon his father's death: Hilda, Chloe, Zeke, and Lars. Since that time he also purchased Reedy, Willy, Rachel, and Simone.

The four enslaved men labored in the fields and tended the horses. Rachel, Simone, Chloe, and Hilda worked inside, managing the kitchen and other housework, but were required in the field, too, along with tending the nearly quarter-acre kitchen garden. A rear door allowed easy access between the kitchen and garden. Sweet potatoes and turnips, collard greens, beans, snap peas, and onions grew in one garden section. Three rows of corn bordered the west edge, the tall stalks blocking the direct afternoon sun from the more delicate plants, like the herbs, lettuce, and spinach, that would shrink if not for the few hours of shade. Melons and squashes of all colors bordered another edge allowing their thick, long vines to travel clear across the yard.

At a close distance to the big house was a large brown barn with an attached stable. A tack room that linked the barn and stable held bridles, saddles, blankets, and other equipment. Farther still, set away from the house and pasture, were apple trees. And beyond the fruit trees, acres of woods separated Huntington Manor from Mr. Joed's plantation. Reedy, Huntington Manor's most reliable slave, usually accompanied Master James on hunts, shooting mostly possums, rabbits, coons, geese, quail, and turkey. James shot an occasional deer or elk, but the small game was easy to manage and kept the slaves well-fed.

Six months had passed since Simone and Rachel came to live on the plantation.

Rachel whispered to Chloe one afternoon, "Ms. Rosalie ain't never scolded me. It give me the jitters. Likes she's gonna strike like a snake at any minute when I'm not expectin' it."

Hilda, the plantation's oldest slave, stopped scouring a large pot. "Ms. Rosalie don't never scold you cuz you learn from me. It's the only reason she keep you here."

Chloe snapped at Hilda. "Don't do my talkin'." Chloe turned to Rachel, who was chopping celery. "You be fine with Ms. Rosalie. And pay no attention to old maid ove' there," she said, pointing her head toward Hilda. "She ain't mean, but she be wantin' you to think it. Ain't that right, Hilda?"

Hilda, plump and nearing forty, shook her head in contempt. Her hair was full of black and graying curls, like ghosts in the shadows, but her dark brown eyes glimmered, feigning her wretchedness.

Chloe continued the banter. "You like havin' Rachel with us 'cause it lessens the work 'round here. That's what I think."

"Then you'd better stop thinkin' and get back to work." Hilda continued her work, stirring gravy and slowly adding pinches of flour to thicken it. Rachel saw the woman's full lips curl into a tiny smile at the corners.

Rachel looked out the kitchen window before she returned to preparing dinner. It reminded her of the window from Mr. Sopley's sewing shop, where her parents were sewing dresses or mending shirts and wondering what became of her. Simone, Charlotte, and her brothers, Thomas, age six, and little Henry, who warmed Charlotte's heart with his giggle, were chasing each other around an old willow tree playing a game of tag. Charlotte took Henry's hand so he wouldn't fall and get hurt. Rachel watched through the glass and smiled. Simone had outgrown her dress. "I got to find some material to make that girl a new dress before she's in nothin' but her drawers."

Hilda huffed. "We could all use something new, but that don't mean we get it."

The following day before dawn, Hilda entered Rachel and Simone's room. "This is for you," she said, handing Rachel stiff cotton material. "Ms. Rosalie said you could use her needles and threads when you finish your chores."

"Hilda. Thank you."

"Don't go thankin' me. You said yourself Simone is growin' clear out of her dress. I'm sparin' myself the trouble of hearin' 'bout it while cookin'. That's all this is. Don't go askin' for anything else."

By the week's end, Rachel had finished sewing a new dress for Simone. The little girl's reaction was not what she expected.

Simone's eyes bubbled with tears. "I don't want a new dress."

"This is real nice," Rachel reassured Simone. "You're growing too big for the one you got on. Another month and the seams will be comin' undone." Rachel tried again. "This one give you wiggle room."

"I don't care. I don't want it."

17

Charlotte was on the front porch reading when she heard the commotion between Simone and Rachel. Thomas was reading from his reader, and Henry, who couldn't read, was in Mother's lap, listening to his older brother sound out words. Her family ignored the sobbing from around the corner, but Charlotte would not. She sat taller in her chair for a better listen.

Her mother noticed. "Mind your manners, Charlotte. Eavesdropping is vulgar."

Charlotte returned to the page in her book and pretended to read. If Thomas kept to a whisper and stopped asking Mother for help with words, she could maybe hear what was troubling her friend. She wanted to run around the corner of the house and console Simone, but Mother would never allow this of her, even if Simone were her best friend in the whole world.

Rachel, bewildered, asked Simone to come to her. Simone obeyed. Rachel held the dress against Simone's front. "It's perfect."

"I don't want it."

Rachel kneeled, bringing herself slightly below Simone's level, as Mama did for her when she was upset, mainly when watching the white children play outside Mr. Sopley's shop window. Rachel wanted to play with them, but her father told her no. When she sulked, her mother kneeled by her and tried to justify the unjust.

Rachel asked in a gentle tone, "Why don't you want a new dress?"

Tears fell hard and Simone's little body convulsed with sobs. Rachel pulled her into her shoulder. "Tell me, baby girl."

Baby girl sounded odd coming from Rachel, who was only fourteen, but Charlotte couldn't lose her focus.

Pretending to read and grasp what was happening in the garden was difficult. There was a long pause, and Charlotte wondered if the two had gone inside through the rear kitchen door.

Inside the kitchen, Rachel wiped Simone's tears with a cool, damp cloth.

Simone pulled at the side of her dress. "Mama made this for me." The words came with the last remaining sobs. "It's all I got left of her."

Rachel had figured out why Simone was fussing and that's why she led Simone inside. Ms. Rosalie and her children were on the front porch with their schooling. She knew better than to bring problems into the open. Mrs. Brown would have whipped her once and told her son to finish the beating. Neither Rachel nor Simone had received any backlash from Ms. Rosalie, but Rachel never fully trusted the white folk.

"We could put your mama's dress in a special box and place it under your bed. Then, anytime you want to look at it or hold it, you just take it out. Only you and me need to know 'bout it."

A lingering sob gave way to a deep sigh, but Simone agreed.

The next day, Charlotte went to find her friend before breakfast. She found Simone polishing the staircase spindles and wearing a new dress. It was big on her friend, but Simone looked beautiful in it.

"Hi, Simone."

"Hi, Charlotte."

"Your dress looks pretty on you."

"Thank you."

"Do you like it?"

"Yes."

Charlotte wanted to ask her about yesterday—why Simone hadn't wanted the dress, but she wasn't sure she should. Mother would tell her it was impolite to ask such questions, which confused Charlotte. She asked her brother Thomas all sorts of questions and asked Father about the tobacco crop at the dinner table and Chloe about her delicious corn cakes. None of those questions got her in trouble.

Charlotte wore white stockings and a blue dress with a line of buttons on the front. Simone's dress didn't have any frills. Instead, it was simple. Charlotte didn't need to touch the material to know it wasn't smooth like hers. Maybe Simone wanted a blue dress instead of her gray one.

Charlotte sat on a step near Simone. "Why didn't you want a new dress, Simone? I heard you tell Rachel."

Simone stopped polishing. Charlotte was her friend, but would Charlotte ever understand a white man stealing her from her mama and how Mama begged for mercy? Mama told her when she was old enough, people should never be bought, white or Black, but Charlotte's papa had done precisely that. How was she supposed to explain to Charlotte and have her understand?

Charlotte saw Simone was sad and took her hand in hers. "It's okay, Simone. You don't have to tell me."

The two girls scooted closer on the step. Simone doubted she'd ever tell Charlotte about her mother.

That same day, during a geography lesson, Charlotte asked her mother. "Where do you think Simone lived before she came here?"

"I don't know, darling. Simone has never said."

"Did you ask her?"

"Yes, when she first arrived." Rosalie had asked and even tried to coerce the child within the first months. She hadn't known what she would have done with the information. Maybe return Simone home, but even then, there was no certainty. But for argument's sake, she'd reasoned, if her daughter insisted on Simone for a best friend, then Rosalie wanted to know from what kind of family this Negro child had come.

"Charlotte. Some questions don't have answers."

Charlotte scowled. "But you and Father taught us to find an answer." She turned to her brother, who was listening intently. "Isn't that right, Thomas? Mother said when we can't find an answer to a problem, we must keep searching."

Thomas nodded. Henry copied his brother, nodding his head too.

Rosalie could not deny her daughter's inquisition. She and James agreed children needed to learn from a young age to solve problems and to think beyond their reach. It would assure confidence and a successful business. They'd never expected their children to sit silently at the dinner table. They discussed the day's business, school work, and other matters.

Charlotte had a point, and Rosalie was never one to deflect. She either put a stop to nonsense or furthered her children's knowledge. It would be so simple to tell her children not to get into the lives of Negroes on the plantation, but Rosalie saw the bond Charlotte formed with Simone from the first day. It reminded her so much of her childhood in Syracuse. She and her sister, Sarah, tossed balls and played chasing games with the Negroes their father had hired to work in the garden or the house. Rosalie's stomach churned. Her father would disapprove of James owning slaves. She'd only been allowed to marry

James on the condition James would never purchase another man.

Another question broke Rosalie's silence, but this time from her oldest son. "Are you alright, Mommy?"

"Yes, Thomas."

Rosalie looked at Charlotte. "That's enough geography for today."

4

Huntington Manor, Virginia 1833

Charlotte and Simone were the same age, though no one was sure of Simone's date of birth, not even Simone. So, weeks before Charlotte's eighth birthday, she pleaded with her mother that she and Simone share the same birthday. When Rosalie finally agreed, Charlotte squealed and ran around to the back of the house to tell Simone. Since that day in April, the two girls had shared four birthdays.

On their tenth birthday, Charlotte's papa brought each girl a wrapped bag of lemon drops from a candy store in New York City. Charlotte jumped with excitement. Simone was less enthusiastic because Rachel warned her to know her place.

"You're not to eat those all at once, girls," Rosalie told them. And it worked for about three days until the girls sneaked the bags from the dining room chest of drawers and sat in the stable eating their remaining six candies. It would have been seven, but Thomas found them with the stash and told them to each hand over a lemon drop, or he'd be sure to let Mother know what they were doing.

Though Charlotte and Simone had different established roles, the two remained best of friends. Charlotte spent the day being schooled by her mother. Morning lessons included reading classics and learning proper penmanship. After a hearty lunch at noon, she joined her brothers in arithmetic, geography, and history. Simone spent her day cleaning alongside Rachel and in the kitchen with Chloe. However, Charlotte and Simone were allowed to play together in the late afternoons.

One mid-morning, when Charlotte grew tired of her studies, she asked her mother if Simone could join her in learning.

"She has her housework, darling. Simone must know her place. If she studies with us, there will be no time for her chores."

"I could help her with her chores, Mother. I promise I will."

"And what about the chores you have already? How will you plan to do your work and help Simone practice reading, writing, and arithmetic?"

"Oh, Mother," Charlotte smiled with a lighthearted giggle. "I only have my bed to make and tidy my room. There is plenty of time to help Simone."

Rosalie smiled at her daughter's earnest thinking.

"We'll see. But for now, read the next chapter aloud."

By the time Thomas was ten, his mornings consisted of learning the business and accompanying his father to town. Afternoons entailed reading, geography, and history lessons with his older sister Charlotte and younger brother Henry. In the early evenings, Thomas and Henry followed their father to the tobacco fields to survey the land, tend to the season's crop, and bring cool water to the field hands, who shared a ladle and took long drinks.

James questioned Reedy, the man he put in charge while away from the fields. "The work today is good, I presume?"

"Yes, sir," Reedy confirmed.

"Is there anything that needs my attention?"

Usually, Reedy told Master James that everything was good. But on a rare occasion, Reedy reported other matters. This scorching day was one of those occasions. "Lars is mighty sick, Master. He's been hacking for weeks."

"Is that so? What ails him?"

"Don't know, Master James."

James Worthington slowly worked his way over to Lars to avoid appearing eager. He knew men didn't want someone feeling sorry for them. Besides, it was necessary to remain in charge as an overseer, no matter how civil he was. Lars's sickness should be his discovery, and he appreciated Reedy for recognizing it.

"Lars," James said when he approached the oldest field hand. "That cough will kill you if you don't let it heal. I don't want you in the field tomorrow. It isn't worth you dying and me spending hard-earned money to afford another good worker like you. Get some rest. And take care of that terrible cough."

"Yes, sir." Lars headed to the cabin, trying to keep his cough quiet until he closed the door behind him. He fell onto a bed, stared at the ceiling, and praised God for the rest.

That evening, as Reedy figured, the doctor was at Lars's side administering some relieving tonic to heal his lungs. Thomas and Henry learned from their father. "Don't you ever turn your back on a sickly worker," he told them.

The following day, James found Lars harvesting tobacco leaves. "Didn't the doctor order you to stay in bed 'til Thursday? According to my calendar, it's the day before."

"Feelin' fine, Mast'r," Lars said, keeping his eyes on his work. Sweat rolled off Lars's back in strange patterns around his raised scars, and some beads of sweat puddled in enclosed and unshapely elongated hollows.

James used a solid and exact tone. "Lars. You wouldn't disobey, would you?"

"Oh no, Mast'r. Neveh."

"Then why are you working?"

"Don't eveh wanna to be sold fo bein' lazy."

James laughed. "You? Lazy? You are far from lazy, Lars. You're a hardworking man. And I plan to keep you strong and healthy."

"Yes, sir. Thank you, Mast'r."

"Now, give Reedy the tobacco bag and return to bed."

Lars carried his half-full bag of tobacco leaves to Reedy. James turned on his heel, looking over his plantation. His workers and sons were working in the fields. He was proud of his family and his slaves. Many believed it was impossible to show enslaved Negroes respect.

Mr. Joed himself warned against it. "If they know you are unwilling to use the cat-o'-nine-tails occasionally, you're as good as dead."

James knew this was a doomed misconception. Never were there better workers than the slaves he owned. Scars like Lars's resulted from an abomination, and James Worthington would not participate in such a hellish crime.

Thomas and Henry worked in the field, and Charlotte tidied her bedroom. Playtime was not allowed until schooling, homework, and chores were complete. Charlotte quickly attended to her homework, which included reading, writing, and arithmetic; the three R's her mother called the tasks. Then Charlotte gathered dolls lying around the house from the morning. The dollhouse, which occupied the corner of her bedroom, needed tidying. When Charlotte finished her chores, she and Simone rushed through Simone's remaining chores to have time for play before supper. Rachel caught on when she noticed the staircase spindles were not adequately oiled. She marched to the willow tree, where the girls caught the first emerging fireflies.

Rachel stood erect, her hands on her nearly invisible hips, showing her disapproval. "You get in the house now and finish your responsibilities," she scolded Simone. "You too, Miss Charlotte."

The girls were eleven. Charlotte ran ahead of Rachel and Simone to the front porch, where her mother drank tea.

"Mother, can't Simone play instead of oiling dumb old spindles?

"Don't use the word dumb, Charlotte. It's unladylike."

"I won't use it again," Charlotte said insincerely. "But Rachel said we have chores to do."

Rachel and Simone turned toward the kitchen entrance on the side of the house and out of view.

Charlotte sulked. "Please, Mother, the fireflies will be gone before long. Me and Simone want to catch a whole bunch."

"Simone and I." Rosalie corrected her daughter. "You should have considered your options earlier. If you'd done the job well, you'd be catching fireflies now."

Charlotte's posture sank with disappointment.

"If you finish the chores, you and your friend should have plenty of time to catch all the fireflies you can."

Charlotte frowned with a weary side smile, hoping to guilt her mother.

"You will have fewer wrinkles with a lifetime of smiles than a lifetime of sorrows," Rosalie said, her decision unaltered by her daughter's sweet half-smile. "I believe you wanted to help Simone to have more playtime together. It is most commendable, darling, and in times like this, you must follow through."

Charlotte sulkily went into the front entrance and joined Simone, who was standing at the base of the staircase and looking hopeful for good news, but then handed Charlotte an oiled rag when she saw Charlotte's sad face.

"No." Charlotte smiled. "I have a better idea. We have perfect rags right here." Charlotte held out the skirt of her beautiful dress. "Follow me."

Simone dropped both rags and hurried up the stairs after Charlotte. Charlotte then carefully straddled the railing.

Frightened but exhilarated, Simone looked over the railing, first to make sure no one was around and second to comprehend the drop if Charlotte fell from the banister. "Are you sure?"

Charlotte didn't hesitate, and down she went at lickety-split speed, being flung from the end when she got there. She sprinted up the stairs two at a time. "It's your turn."

Simone looked doubtful, but not for the dread of falling. She loved this adventure, but if Ms. Rosalie, or worse, Rachel, caught her polishing the railing in this way, she'd get a whipping from someone.

"Go ahead," Charlotte encouraged.

Simone straddled the railing and slid to the bottom, wanting to wail excitedly on the way down, but if Rachel came running, the fun would end. Charlotte and Simone managed to slide four times before they heard footsteps. They were both at the bottom of the stairs. They grabbed the rags and polished the spindles. The two smiled as Rachel walked past them, unsuspecting of their misconduct, and when Rachel was out of sight, the girls each took one more slide for good measure.

5

Huntington Manor, Virginia 1834

Thomas was with his father when Mr. Worthington happened upon a passerby on the road near town. A thin boy bound at the wrists and ankles slumped in the back of the man's wagon. James slowed the horses. "You stay put, Thomas," he said to his son.

Thomas obeyed. He had seen bound slaves before but never one in such a hideous condition. James climbed from the wagon, and Thomas watched his father approach the other wagon.

"Hello there," James called out.

Tilby opened his eyes to the sound of the stranger. The man was probably another lazy evil-doer like the others. Tilby ran from Mississippi and Mr. Lester, a cruel master, months ago and was captured close to Indiana territory by a man claiming protection but only looking for reward money. Since then, Tilby changed hands three times to men trying to make a quick buck, and Tilby suspected Bols was no different.

Tilby remained motionless, careful not to move the shackles holding him, and lifted his eyes to the stranger for a better view.

Mason Bolsom, Bols, as he was called back in Norfolk, stopped the horses.

"Are you selling?" James asked.

"Who's asking?" Bols snorted.

"I can offer five hundred dollars for his purchase. You won't get a better price in town."

Bols couldn't believe his luck. "You say five hundred?"

Mr. Lester guaranteed two hundred for the boy's return—that's what the flyer read. If this passerby was good on his offer, Bols was about to be a rich man, and with Mr. Lester never the wiser that the boy had been captured.

"Five hundred cash," James repeated.

Tilby cautiously moved his eyes to see the looks of his new owner. He saw Bols snatch the man's money, count it, and push it into his tattered vest pocket.

"What do you want with a no-good slave," Bols asked as if his cash load made him and Mister business partners.

Mister said to Bols. "What does it matter to you? You've accepted my payment. Now unchain him, and we'll be on our way."

"Well now, Mr.—what did you say your name was?"

"I didn't say," James responded.

"Why don't I give you this key here, and you can take the chains with you. You'll need 'em. This good-for-nothing boy is a runner. Only one time, though. I made sure of it." Bols let out an obnoxious laugh.

"You have your money. Now, unshackle the boy and hand over the chains."

"Ah-ha, so you agree. You can see the evil in the blacks of his eyes, can't you?" Bols jumped from the wagon, took the slave by the shirt, and dragged Tilby from the back. He unchained the boy's wrists and kicked him away from his presence. "Git!"

Tilby stumbled toward Mister, his ankle chains tripping him up.

"You ain't my trouble no more. You got a new master, boy. And if he has any sense, he'll ensure you stay put wherever he dumps you."

"Give me the key," James demanded of Bols.

"Tsk! Tsk! Not even a please." Bols tossed the key to James and got on his way.

Thomas's eyes fixated on the disheveled Negro.

James unlocked the irons from Tilby's ankles. "We'll dispose of these later."

Tilby stared at his bare feet.

"What's your name, son?"

"Tilby Smith, sirs." He stood slumped in his weakened condition.

"Good to meet you, Tilby. My name is James Worthington, but sir is fine. How old are you?"

"Don't know, sirs. Thirteen. Fourteen, maybe."

"Are you a runner?"

"No, sirs," Tilby lied.

"I've got a plantation a few miles from here, and it so happens I've been looking for a man to help out." James Worthington pointed to the back of the wagon. "Climb in."

Cautious of Mister's kindness, Tilby did as he was told.

James sat by Thomas, laid the chains at his feet, and clucked for the horses to go.

After minutes, Thomas asked. "What are you going to do with those chains?"

"I have a mind to dump them in the river."

Tilby's chance to run was when sirs clucked for the horses to move, but he couldn't do it. He'd been tired with exhaustion and so hungry. He'd watched Bols eat and drink for three nights and then reluctantly offered Tilby food scraps and only enough water to keep him alive in this heat. His lips were parched. His feet were blistered and swollen, and his mind faded. In one corner of the wagon, his head slumped against his shoulder as he fought sleep, wishing death would come for him.

A half-hour later, the horses and wagon stopped near a stable, which Tilby suspected was where his new master and his boy lived. In the near distance, a big house sat on the edge of fields. Tilby lifted slightly and peered farther over the wagon to scope the area and understand what to expect.

"Reedy," Master called out, and the Negro stopped inspecting the crop and walked toward them.

"Yes, sir," Reedy said.

"This is Tilby," James said, hopping down from the wagon. "Make his introductions among the men and teach him the ropes."

"Yes, sir."

"And make sure the horses have plenty of water."

"Yes, sir."

Reedy waited until Master James was out of earshot before speaking with the plantation's newest slave. "You'll be alright, and you're in no danger here. How old are you?"

Tilby looked up. The man's eyes were warm, but kind eyes could darken in a split second. Besides, Tilby didn't know his age, but he could be tough and make this man believe he was like him. Tilby pulled himself from the wagon and tried to appear confident, but he felt weak from hunger and dehydration.

Tilby took his chances with this man called Reedy. "I is fourteen. Maybe older, but age means nothin' besides."

"You look twelve," Lars belted, coming up behind him.

Tilby startled.

"This here is Lars," Reedy said. "Over there," he added, pointing toward two men. "Willy. Zeke. And over there," he said, turning toward the garden on the side of the big house, "is Rachel. And Simone is the girl walkin' toward us."

Simone stumbled on a rock and nearly dropped what she carried. If Lars hadn't been breathing down his back, Tilby would have gone to aid her. The girl redirected her quick walk toward Tilby. Tilby looked at Reedy, but Lars said, "What wrong wit you, boy? Ain't you neveh seen a girl before?"

Simone reached the men and handed Tilby a shirt, pants, and boots. "These are for you," she said, with a slight smile, and turned away from the men and walked back to from where she had come.

Tilby stood motionless, holding the clothing and watching Simone.

6

Tilby guarded himself around the slaves on Lester's cotton field and planned to do the same here. He trusted nobody. Not Reedy, Willy, or Zeke, and especially not Lars. Tilby got the bed near the cabin's door with a folded blanket, but Lars told him to keep his hands off anything else. The first night, Tilby slept with one eye open until his lids gave in to exhaustion. On his second day, a doctor looked at Tilby's teeth, gave him salve for the blisters on his feet, and told Mister he'd be well with a day's rest.

Tilby had no intention of resting. The other slaves wouldn't appreciate the special treatment and could turn on him if he wasn't careful.

Tilby was a lanky boy with black eyes, blacker skin, and tight black curly hair. After a week when it seemed like Mister had no intentions of selling him or returning him to Lester in Mississippi, Tilby worked himself to the bone proving his worth.

Thomas, Henry, and even Mister helped irrigate the crop, and Tilby didn't know what to think of having those boys work alongside him like they were equals. Back in Mississippi, Mr. Lester's overseers whipped him any chance they got. For not picking enough cotton, Lester unleashed a lashing and, for looking tired, got another. The food portions were inadequate for a small dog, let alone a growing boy, and water was restricted so many times, Tilby thought he'd die of thirst in the cotton field under the hot sun. He supposed he was lucky these days, but only because Mister James was a fair man and not the devil like the ones before him.

"You need a drink?"

Tilby looked up from deworming the tobacco plants. Simone held out a ladle full of water.

"Go on, drink."

Tilby took a long drink, avoiding eye contact with Simone, but he'd do it if he could get a good look without being noticed. He wanted to look at her brown, round eyes like he did when he arrived. He hadn't meant to stare at her then, but it had been barely impossible to unlock his eyes from her beautiful face. And Tilby couldn't figure out how it was possible, but the girl smelled of fresh melon, and if he dared to get closer for a better whiff, he'd do that too.

"Mighty kind, miss."

Simone laughed. "My name isn't miss." Charlotte had said these exact words to her when she and Rachel first arrived, and Simone called Charlotte miss. Simone had been frightened those first months and wondered if Tilby felt the same now. He seemed different from the other enslaved men. Tilby was kindlier and caring, though Reedy was a close second. She'd spied on Tilby tending the horses and overheard him talking to them like they were his friends. Simone stayed hidden behind the barn door, quietly giggling at Tilby's sweet nature and tip-toeing away when she had the chance.

Tilby replaced the ladle in the bucket Simone carried. "Thank you."

Simone turned, and Tilby watched her walk toward Zeke.

The hot weather lingered for another month. Tilby spent a portion of his days draping tobacco leaves on strings in the curing barn to dry, very different from picking cotton on Lester's plantation. Reedy said the tobacco would remain in the barn for forty to fifty days, depending on the wetness or dryness of the air, which Reedy determined by licking his finger and lifting it high above his head. Then Reedy told Tilby to open or close the vents in the barn's roof.

Mister checked in on the progress of the tobacco more than Tilby liked—always thinking Mister might have a whip with him, but it never happened that way. Mister came to inspect the leaves and the work of the slaves. When one of the vents needed repair, Tilby managed to fix it. That time, Mister came to inspect Tilby's work. Tilby ignored the inspection and kept draping tobacco leaves until Mister came to him and told him the vent looked as good as new. Tilby didn't give the compliment another thought until weeks later when Mister asked him to fix the barn's door and, later, a closet door inside the big house.

Tilby didn't know what to think of stepping into his master's house, but he could do nothing but oblige. He worked long, hard hours, like when he picked cotton for Lester, but the blasted heat of Mississippi and the cracking sound of a whip were nonexistent here, and besides, mister offered plenty of water, adequate food, and a few more hours of rest.

By the end of his first tobacco harvest, the days grew shorter, and the slaves of Huntington Manor worked fewer hours, but plenty of work still existed. They toiled the land, cut trees, and uprooted stumps, preparing the ground for the next season of crops. Tilby took to the horses' upkeep and spent most evenings in the stable unafraid Lars or Zeke would appear and find him there with Simone. The other men, especially Lars, were happy to forgo the responsibility of feeding, laying hay, and grooming the horses. Still, Lars told Tilby, pointing in his face one day, "If Mast'r or one of his boys get thinking it's only you mucking out stables, you make sure they believe it ain't true. We in this together. And don't be gettin' lazy about the field either. There's plenty of work."

Tilby wasn't intimidated by Lars as he had been in the first months at Huntington Manor because Lars had his own sorrowful story. If nothing else, the thick and raised scars on Lars's back told Tilby so.

Tilby spent evenings in the stable. He welcomed the cooler weather and enjoyed caring for the horses. He found calmness in brushing their coats and manes, and when he was alone, he whispered encouraging words and looked into their undemanding eyes. These beautiful creatures somehow understood him.

Simone visited him a few times in the stable. Tonight she said she'd try and sneak away. Tilby brushed the chestnut horse, thinking of her—the way Simone held her head slightly to one side when she spoke like she was always thinking of questions in her head. Her bold brown eyes spoke volumes of stories, and Tilby wondered what her life was like before he knew her. Maybe, someday Simone would share her past with him. A throaty noise made Tilby turn. Simone was standing inside the stable's door, black ringlets of hair flowing from her head to her shoulders.

"You came," Tilby said.

Simone picked up a horse brush. "I said I would."

"Looks like a storm might be comin'," Tilby said, combing the horse's mane.

"I believe you're right," Simone responded, brushing the horse's slender legs, her cheeks blushing redder with Tilby's every word.

"I's like you bein' here, Simone."

"I know you do. I like it too, but I can't stay for long, Tilby. Rachel can't know I'm here cuz she'll start asking questions." Simone put her hands on her slender hips, imitating Rachel. "What-choo doing in the stable when you got work to do. The spindles ain't gettin' clean by theirselfs."

Tilby laughed.

Then Simone laughed. "Aw. You know I love Rachel, don't you?"

"I knows you do."

If Tilby could get past the small talk and his shyness, he'd ask Simone for a kiss. He wondered if she'd let him kiss her. If she said yes, he'd do it right now.

7

Tilby had lived at the plantation for eighteen months, through one total crop production and then some. But in the meantime, he grew six inches and filled out between plowing and harvesting and a new spring season. He was no longer a skinny boy. Tilby stood over six feet, and at sixteen years old, he was lean and muscular, and without a reason to prove his toughness, his eyes naturally matched his gentle nature. Black curls sprang from beneath a sweat-soaked bandana Tilby wore on his head, and his stained gray overalls attested to his work, not all of it in the field and stable.

In the last year, Tilby earned respect as a skilled handicraftsman. He fixed legs on beds and tables, replaced pieces of barn siding, built raised watering troughs, and reinforced horse stalls. There was nothing too small or large Tilby couldn't repair or build. He'd been inside the big house a few times, once fixing a broken hinge on a kitchen cabinet door, another repairing a crooked door leading to the parlor, and again hanging new drapery in the dining room.

Northern Virginia's mild winter faded away into a warm spring. Simone and Rachel were out tending to the seedlings that would eventually become plants producing fruits and vegetables for selling, eating, and storing for winter.

Tilby walked toward Rachel and Simone with several long wooden stakes. Rachel asked for them last week to provide a climb for the beans, but Tilby waited until today when he saw Simone gardening. He wished Simone was alone because if his tongue got tied, she'd smile and be patient, but Rachel was there. It would have to do. He was not about to miss an opportunity to be near Simone.

Rachel spotted Tilby coming toward them. "Well, it's 'bout time. What took so long?"

"I is here now. Where do you want these stakes?"

"Over here," Simone said, pointing to several rocks she and Rachel had placed as markers. Simone smiled at Tilby when Rachel was bent over, pressing dirt firmly around each seedling and adding a ladle of water, careful not to saturate because soggy soil could cause mold and pest infestations.

Tilby smiled at Simone, looked at Rachel busy with her work, and smiled again. He hoped Simone could sneak away from the house tonight like she did every chance she got. He'd be in the barn waiting if she did. Last November, Tilby finally asked Simone permission for a kiss, and she allowed him a peck on her cheek. The following week, they quickly kissed on the lips, but under the dark sky of December and Rachel's watchful eyes in the big house, Simone's visits to the barn had been few and far between.

Rachel looked up from the soil to Tilby. "We don't got all day. What-choo standing 'round for?"

Tilby pounded a dozen stakes into the ground, tipped his hat, and returned to the field before Lars gave him an earful.

In the early evening, Thomas and Henry each held a mouse by its tail. They tip-toed toward Charlotte and Simone, who played string games under the willow tree.

"We'll lower them right before their faces," Thomas said.

Henry's grin widened. "Like spiders."

Thomas whispered, afraid he might alert the girls, "You go after Simone. I've got Charlotte."

Henry nodded, happy his older brother included him in such fun.

Rosalie heard screaming and hurried outside the house. Thomas and Henry ran about, chasing Charlotte and Simone with dead mice. It was not the first time her boys played this trick on the girls. Yesterday, she'd seen Thomas head to the barn with a box. Rosalie suspected the two mice swinging in her boys' clutches resulted from yesterday's find.

Charlotte and Simone ran away screaming, leaving Thomas and Henry laughing.

Two days later, Charlotte decided her brothers should have a taste of their own medicine, and Simone should be part of the prank.

"Please, Simone. They deserve it. We'll collect all the beetles we can find and put them in a jar."

Simone listened closely to Charlotte's every word. Her eyes widened with excitement because she could almost read Charlotte's thoughts—it happened to all best friends, like kindred spirits, Charlotte had told her, and Simone believed it was true.

"But what if we don't catch enough beetles?" Simone asked.

Charlotte laughed. "I just thought the same thing."

"We could use currants," Simone suggested. "Last year, Chloe spilled currants all over the floor. When Hilda walked into the kitchen, she screamed." Simone smiled, remembering the incident. "She thought her kitchen was infested with something awful. Chloe and I had a good laugh."

"But currants won't scare them."

"The currants are extra. When they feel the beetles crawling on them, they will think the currants are bugs too."

"Simone," Charlotte screeched. "You're brilliant."

On Saturday, before sunset, Charlotte and Simone, each with a jar, went around the barn and dug in the dirt for bugs. Simone hoped Tilby wasn't in the stable. She and Charlotte were fourteen, and she wondered if Tilby might think digging in the dirt was immature.

When the girls only found a few bugs and one spider, they went to the trees and the grass. They found plenty, including several large crickets.

The following morning, before dawn, Charlotte and Simone entered Thomas's and Henry's room. They spread heaps of currants they took from the kitchen under the boys' covers. Then, they emptied the bugs onto their pillows, quietly sneaked from the room, and hurried into Charlotte's room to wait for her brother's screams.

The anticipation was horrid. The girls stood behind the bedroom door waiting, but nothing came. Ten minutes passed, and they worried every single bug had crawled to safety, but soon, Charlotte swore she heard someone stirring in the boys' bedroom. She put her finger to her lips and quietly whispered, "Shh."

Henry roused slowly, sleepily brushing his face and neck, but when bugs crawled in his ears, Henry jolted awake. He jumped from the bed and pulled the covers away in the dawn's early light. Hundreds of what he thought were bugs in his bed sheets caused him to scream for Thomas. Thomas woke startled, saw the bugs, and shrieked. The boys yelled for their parents and squirmed, desperate to rid themselves of bugs.

Rosalie and James fled from their bed to Thomas and Henry.

"What is this all about?" James asked sleepy and confused.

"Bugs are in our beds," Henry cried, pulling a beetle from his pajamas.

"They're biting me," Thomas screeched.

"What in heaven's—" Rosalie demanded.

Charlotte couldn't hold her laughter one second longer. She sprang from behind her bedroom door and went to her family. "Come, Simone," she said, laughing. Simone came from behind the door, giggling cautiously. Simone played in Charlotte's room many times over the years, but still, Simone knew her place in this house, an unpleasant fact of life her kindred spirit friend didn't understand. To Charlotte, she was equal, and Charlotte always treated her in this way, but Rachel warned Simone often this was not her home, and no matter what Miss Charlotte said, Simone was to watch herself.

James swept a mound of currents into his hand. "What is this? Is this why you're hopping scared," he said amusedly. He spurted a chuckle and roared with laughter.

"That's not fair," Thomas said toward Charlotte and Simone.

"Wait a minute, boys," Rosalie said.

Charlotte crossed her arms over her chest, her eyes wide with amusement, waiting for her mother's response.

"Were you not chasing your sister and Simone the other day?"

Charlotte finished her mother's sentence. "With two big rats."

"They were tiny mice," Thomas shot back.

"Oh, is that so?" James questioned. "Well, then, it serves you right. Maybe you'll think twice before pulling pranks."

James turned to his wife. "Who should clean this mess?"

In unison, Charlotte pointed at her brother, and Thomas and Henry pointed at Charlotte.

Rosalie spoke evenly. "It's the boys' room, and they shall clean the mess."

8

Huntington Manor, Virginia 1836

Reedy was in the field when Henry came running toward him. "You're out of breath, Master Henry. Everything alright?"

The other men looked on, slowly gathering closer for a better earshot.

"Father needs Tilby."

"He's in the stable, tending the horses. You'll find him there."

Henry ran off toward the barn without so much a kind word for Reedy's assistance.

The men looked at each other. Lars slouched. He was in his mid-forties with a lingering scowl. "Which one of you be accusin' Tilby of something? That boy manages the stable on his own and neveh axes us to lift a fingeh. And now, he looks like he in a bad way wit Mast'r."

Lars's anger flared. Upsets like this were an added reminder of how horrible his life was. He was born with a deformed leg, and because of it, he'd been a tragedy all his life. He'd been sold a handful of times and whipped so bad he almost died. Life never got better until he met Stephaney. They had two sons, but Stephaney and their boys were sold long ago, and his heart ached.

Reedy attempted to put Lars at ease. "Could be nothin'."

Lars shot back. "No boy runs like that fo nothin'."

"Heck, Lars," Willy said. "Them boys are protected like a queen bee. Do you think Master is sendin' Henry on a mission for somethin' so severe we should be worried? Nah."

Lars spoke. "Don't be so sure. The minute you think white folks be good, they turn on you. There no such thing as a decent white man."

Reedy turned on Lars. "Are you sayin' Master James ain't a decent white man? You lay in a bed for a week— nearly dyin' after those men in the woods beat you to a pulp—claimin' you were runnin' with a rifle when you got separated from us on a hunt. Your body was so swollen nobody thought you'd live. Master James called for the doctor four times, Lars. Four! Afterward, he gave you the option to stay back on future outings. You've seen a lot of hate. One look at your back, and I know that, but none of those marks come from nobody on this plantation."

Lars swung at Reedy.

Willy intervened, separating the men by the length of his arm span. "Are you both lookin' for trouble? Lars. You always sayin' we in this together."

"What that got to do wit' this?" Lars spat.

"I'm just sayin', we don't know nothin' yet. We got to keep our wits intact 'til we know more. They ain't do anythin' if we say we know nothin'."

Lars snorted, pushing Willy's hand away from its position on his chest.

Willy dropped his other arm to his side. "And you, Reedy. What's got into you? I ain't never seen you like this."

The men separated and went back to work. They looked toward the barn, the hot sun at their backs. Tilby ran toward the big house, Henry's short legs following behind, trying to keep up.

Simone heard the door open and then pounding feet. She yelled for help. "We're in the library! Hurry!"

Tilby followed Simone's voice into the room and found Simone straining to lift a heavy bookshelf off Mister. James lay flat on his back, his shoulders pinned by the heavy furniture, and still, he struggled to free himself.

"Get it off me, Tilby. I'm wedged."

Tilby took hold of the shelf with two hands and lifted it, but only enough for Mister to scoot out from under the frame and all its fallen books. "Is you alright, sirs?"

James brushed himself off and straightened his suit jacket. "For all days to have Rosalie and Thomas at the mercantile." James brushed at his sleeves and combed his hair with his hand. That's when Simone squealed. "Your hand, sir—is bleeding."

Blood gushed from a wound on James's hand. He hadn't even noticed it until Simone nearly fainted from fright. Tilby took a cloth from his pocket and handed it to James. Blood quickly soaked it.

James took the cloth away from the wound to replace it with a clean rag, and blood spurted feet into the air. Simone gasped and covered her mouth. Henry stared in fright.

"It seems I've nicked an artery. Tilby. Take Henry and go for the doctor?"

Simone was serving the family that night at dinner when James said to Rosalie, "Tilby has become a strapping young man. He pulled the bookshelf off me like it was a bed covering."

Simone figured Mr. Worthington fibbed to ease Ms. Rosalie's worry, because Tilby had used all his strength. It took two men to lift the shelf back into place. Simone returned to the kitchen, thinking of Tilby and smiling.

47

"Does it hurt, Father?" Charlotte asked of her father's stitched hand.

"Not at all, darling. It was nothing but a scratch."

"Blood spurted to the ceiling," Henry added, excited now the trauma was over. He hoped their father or Tilby never told anyone he and Simone almost fainted.

"That is enough talk of such unpleasantness at the table," Rosalie said.

Henry was ten years old. He was tall for a boy his age. His blonde hair matched his fair skin, and his eyes were sky blue. He looked like his father, whereas Thomas looked more like his mother, with brown hair, hazel eyes, and a sharp jaw. And Charlotte was a combination of both her parents. However, the three children had rigorously different personalities. Henry was fun and loving with a gentle nature. Charlotte was determined and inquisitive, and Thomas was authoritative with a mind for business.

All three children loved dinnertime because Father spoke of the day's happenings, mostly business, but occasionally he'd tell stories of when he was a boy and of his parents and three sisters.

Huntington Manor had been in the Worthington family for three generations. James had business savvy like his father and grandfather. With a hundred acres of their five hundred used solely for growing tobacco, they were wealthier than some plantation owners with hundreds more. "You can make a living on ten acres, boys, if that's all you've got, but only if you treat people respectfully. Be smart, trust your connections, work hard, and never ..." Father said, "Bite the hand that feeds you. Those Negroes out in the field are feeding you."

"Why did Granddad have so many more slaves than we have?" Thomas asked.

Charlotte spoke before Father answered. She repeated to Thomas what Father had said often. "Don't call them slaves, Thomas."

"That's right, Charlotte." James looked at Thomas. "If you call them slaves within earshot, you have a good chance of losing them to laziness. But to answer your question, Thomas. Reedy and the other Negroes are good workers. We have plenty of help. They're all we need to run this plantation. Besides, you and Henry are growing taller and stronger every day."

James tore a chunk of meat with his teeth from the roasted bird. "And you're learning the business. Tell me, Thomas. What is the best way to grow tobacco?"

Henry was quick to answer to please his father. "You must have well-drained soil, plenty of sunshine, and never use the same acreage for more than three planting seasons." Henry smiled, proud of his quickness.

"Not fair," Thomas said.

Thomas wanted to be like his father more than anything; for Henry, being like their father came naturally. Thomas wasn't sure how he knew this was true. Maybe it was by the way Father mussed his brother's hair jokingly or the way he often crouched to Henry's eye level to give encouraging words. Henry was three years younger than he, but Thomas didn't ever remember his father being so relaxed when he was Henry's age.

Charlotte interjected. "You can't depend on the weather, Henry. What if it rained every day?"

James looked to his daughter with an expression to be still and to let Thomas speak. "Tell me, Thomas? Why should we never use the same acreage for more than three planting seasons?"

"Tobacco drains nutrients, and any fool who planted it in the exact location for another year risks a profitable crop."

"Very good, son." James pointed his fork at each child, "Providing the best tobacco every year will keep you profitable in your worst years." He pronged a potato and popped it in his mouth. "And profits keep food on the table."

Charlotte pointed. "Look, Mother. Your diamond is dancing on the wall."

Rosalie discouraged Charlotte's pointing, but all five family members looked at the lines of beautiful prisms bobbing on and off the dining room wall. The spectacle arose from Rosalie's diamond ring.

"Make them dance, Ma," Henry said.

Rosalie moved her hand. Colors of reds and yellows and blues danced, moving in every direction. Her children laughed at the phenomenon.

"Father, tell us the story of the ring. Please, Daddy." Charlotte insisted

James cleared his throat. "Again?"

"Yes. Please." Charlotte put her fork to the side of her plate, ready to listen. "Tell us exactly how it happened, Father. Don't leave out a single detail."

James smiled at his eager children. "Well. I was living in Syracuse and working for Grandfather Farnsworth."

Thomas swallowed a gulp of milk. "Because you wanted to marry Mother."

Charlotte threw Thomas a sharp look. "Let Father tell the story."

Henry was feeling left out. "You bought the ruby from a beggar."

Charlotte had an abundance of patience for Henry. "It's a diamond, Henry. Rubies are red. And besides, Father purchased the ring from a peddler."

James gave a hearty laugh. "Not quite. It began with Heathrow Tucker. Now there's a fellow I'll never forget. He also worked for your grandfather. One day, I tell Heathrow I'd like to buy your mother a nice gift, so he tells me of a man who sells fish by Onondaga Lake. Well, I give Heathrow a funny look. Fish! I exclaimed. That is a terrible present."

Charlotte, Thomas, and Henry laughed at their father's joke.

Thomas furthered the joke, and it made everyone laugh. "Mother almost got a fish ring."

"Indeed." James kidded. "Heathrow and I also had a chuckle. He tells me the fellow who sells fish has a few jewels he peddles. I was interested, so I went to see for myself. The man was selling fish—that was true, but I didn't see any jewels, so I told him what I'd heard and asked if he knew anything about it. Lo and behold, he pulls that very diamond," James said, referring to Rosalie's ring, "from his pocket. I'd be telling a falsehood if I said I knew what to look for in such a jewel because I'd never seen a diamond. But what caught my eye was the very thing that caught yours moments ago."

"The colors on the wall."

"That's right, Henry. Understand, children, only kings and queens wear diamonds, so seeing such a jewel was astounding. And so I decided, if royalty has diamonds, then so should your—"

"Mother." All three children chimed with excitement. It was Charlotte's favorite part of the story.

"I went home, gathered every dime I had, and returned to the fisherman."

Charlotte wanted to ask how much it cost, but when she had before, her mother scolded her for being impolite. If she asked again, she'd be sent straight to her room until morning.

"The next day, I took the diamond to a jeweler. He told me it weighed 5 carats and described it as flawless.

Henry's face twisted. "What is flawless?"

Charlotte didn't wait for her father to respond. "It means Mother's diamond is perfect."

"That's right. It was then I believed the diamond to be the perfect present for your mother."

"Was it, Mother?" Thomas asked.

"Yes."

"Is it why you married Daddy?" Charlotte added.

"I would have married your father with or without the diamond."

James continued. "I don't believe the fisherman knew the diamond's worth. I had no idea, for Heaven's sake, but I liked what I saw and found a way to get it for your mother." James waggled his finger and leaned forward in his chair while six curious eyes watched him. "Let this be a lesson, children. When you envision what you want, go after it. Stay vigilant, and you will reap your reward."

"Look!" Charlotte motioned.

Everyone looked to the wall again to see colorful prisms pirouetting like dancers.

9

Huntington Manor, Virginia 1837

Simone pulled a sack of flour from under her dress.

"Rachel," Charlotte said, "Look what we managed to confiscate from the kitchen."

Rachel put her hands on her unseen hips. "What exactly do you plan to do with that? You're gonna get yourself in a load of trouble."

"Rachel, don't be such a prude." Charlotte laughed.

"You want to help us?" Simone coerced. "A pulley and a bucket are all we need. When Tilby comes through the barn doors, the flour will cover him, and turn him white like Charlotte."

Charlotte's grin embellished what came next. She lifted her skirt and showed Rachel the long rope tied around her waist. "I sneaked it past Tilby on Sunday."

Rachel huffed. "Tilby's been looking for that rope for two days. Come here yesterday looking 'round this garden wondering if I'd taken a rope for some fool idea I might've had. And all along, you got it tied 'round your waist. Tilby was accusing me of taking his dumb rope." Rachel stood. Dirt pressed into her cotton dress where she had been kneeling. "Deserve him right to go white. No offense, Miss Charlotte."

"None taken."

The two girls, who were too old to play such tricks at fifteen, had roped Rachel into the prank. Charlotte and Simone sported broad smiles behind Rachel's back. Usually,

Rachel wanted no part in their silliness, but if Tilby had gone and blamed her for something he knew nothing about, then she would teach him a lesson."

That evening, when the men were behind the cabin eating dinner, the three crept into the barn. They used sacks of grain as hoists until they finally placed a pail of flour above the door. The plan was when Tilby came to clean the stables and push the door open, five pounds of flour would coat his face and shoulders.

Rachel, Simone, and Charlotte hurriedly climbed the stairs to the servant's quarters and watched through the window. A half-hour passed before Tilby strolled from the cabin to the stable unsuspectingly. The girls held each other close, squeezing each other in anticipation. Tilby opened the barn door, and it seemed like the world stood still. Seconds later, Tilby turned in circles, like a hornet buzzing about a downed nest. He was ghostly white, all covered in flour, coughing plumes of powdery smoke and rubbing his eyes.

Simone and Charlotte busted with laughter. Rachel couldn't help herself either. Tilby coughed his way over to the water pump, looking like a ghost floating three feet above the ground in the dark.

The following day, Simone crept down the curved staircase from upstairs. She needed to speak with Tilby. Charlotte and her brothers were inside with their studies, and this might be her only chance all day. She wanted Tilby to know that yesterday's prank was all good fun. And that she went along with it because Charlotte would be suspicious otherwise. Though she didn't necessarily regret the prank. Tilby's lanky legs and arms swinging about was funny, but she'd never wish anything bad on him.

Simone was almost in the clear when Rachel appeared from around the corner and nearly bumped into her.

Frightened, Simone let out a masked scream. "You scared me stiff, Rachel."

"What-choo doing down here? I told you to dust upstairs," Rachel said, one hand positioned sternly on her hip and the other pointing to the second floor.

"I forgot the polish," Simone hastily lied.

"I do swear, Simone. I wasn't nearly as forgetful at your age. You go and get the polish and hurry it up. We got lunch to serve in an hour."

Simone hurried toward the polish, but when Rachel turned and was out of sight, Simone snuck out the back door.

Tilby was mucking out the stalls with a pitchfork when Simone arrived. He leaned the tool against the wall and walked straight to her before he lost his nerve. He knew Simone was part of last night's prank, and her spunk made him love her more. "Miss Simone," Tilby said, "I's love you, and someday I's gonna marry you. I's knows you is young, but you is the most beautiful girl in the world. I's know'd it the day I's laid my eyes on you."

Simone blushed. "I'm fifteen, Tilby. I'm not a child."

They were the sweetest words Tilby ever did hear. He stuttered. "You—you mean someday you might marry me."

Simone smiled. "Sure, I would. I love you, Tilby Smith."

For the next year, when she could, Simone secretly snuck off to the barn to see Tilby. They mostly talked between feeding and watering the horses. Sometimes, if Simone arrived in the barn after Tilby mucked out a few stalls, Simone spread and raked fresh hay for the horse's bedding. However, Simone carefully tracked her time and stayed only for ten or fifteen minutes before she feared Rachel would take notice. "I got to get back, Tilby," she'd say, and Tilby knew it was a good time to kiss her.

10

An unusually strong northwest wind rattled the windows of the big house. Christmas was days away, and somehow the robust wind made it more exciting for Charlotte, Thomas, and Henry. For the house servants, what happened outside made little difference. There was plenty of housework before the big day, but when Rachel looked out the window and saw the willow's branches reaching out like a dozen angels, she admitted the wind added to the festive mood.

Chloe and Hilda prepared the kitchen in advance. Christmas Day took more pots and pans than any other holiday, but when Master James and his family finished their feast on Christmas afternoon and moved into the parlor for dessert and coffee, the end of the day's chores was in sight. Simone, Rachel, Hilda, and Chloe hurried to wash and dry every dish and put it in its proper place while they listened to the Worthington family sing. It was a joyous time. Mister sang *Silent Night*. Simone wiped at a tear on her cheek. It was such a lovely song, and Mister sang it beautifully like the baby Jesus was in the manger in the center of the parlor.

The women headed to the men's cabin when the kitchen was clean. It would be crowded, but tonight they would celebrate together.

"Come now," Rachel said to Simone. "Button your coat. It's mighty cold outside. I won't be nursing a fever on my only days off."

Charlotte and Henry appeared in the kitchen with their hands full of wrapped presents.

"Why, Master Henry and Miss Charlotte—what's this?" Rachel said, her hands on her hips.

Charlotte and Henry beamed with pride delivering the Christmas gifts.

"From Daddy and Mother," Charlotte said. She handed Rachel all but one of the gifts.

Henry handed his armful of presents to Chloe. "These are for Reedy and Lars. And Zeke and Willy. Happy Christmas."

Chloe thanked Henry.

Charlotte went to Simone. "This one is special. I made it for you. I hope you like it. Rachel helped me with it. She said she wouldn't tell you."

Simone looked at Rachel with wide eyes.

"Oh, Charlotte," Simone laughed. She quickly went to a drawer, opened it, and pulled out a scarf. She went to Charlotte. "And this is for you. Rachel promised she would keep my secret."

Both girls eyed Rachel and giggled.

Rachel's smile broadened. "What? I know how to keep a secret."

Charlotte admired the scarf's perfect shape. "And it's blue. My favorite color. Thank you, Simone. I'll wear it every day." Charlotte wrapped the scarf around her neck. "Would you like to open your gift?"

"Very much," Simone said. She looked at Rachel but saw Hilda's scowl.

Hilda hurried from the kitchen to the fire outside the cabin every half hour, roasting two turkeys from the week's hunt—an annual gift from Master James and a tasty change from river birds and the shoulders and fatback of salted ham. Reedy ensured the fire stayed aflame, but Hilda itched to get on with it. She could roast a turkey perfectly, but not if she stood around waiting for two silly girls to exchange gifts. Without Charlotte and Henry in the kitchen, she would have disappeared outside five minutes ago. A feast needed preparation, and Hilda couldn't waste another second.

Simone let her eyes fall away from Hilda's scowl. She pulled white mittens from the wrapping and put them on her hands. "Thank you, Charlotte."

"Do you like them?"

"They're beautiful."

Simone hugged her friend. They held each other tight.

"Happy Christmas, Charlotte."

"Happy Christmas, Simone."

The womenfolk prepared a great Christmas dinner. There was enough turkey to go around twice, with plenty of potatoes, turnips, and squashes from the root cellar roasted to perfection. Rachel and Simone had dreamed of this moment when they harvested the garden in the fall. Rachel kept quiet about keeping the best vegetables for themselves. She figured they'd never be trusted again if it got back to Ms. Rosalie, but she didn't care. She worked her fingers to the bone in the garden. Her kin deserved to eat like kings every once in a while.

Inside the cabin, the men and women feasted, sang, and danced into the night and early morning. The women returned to the big house, their path lit only by a full moon and stars. The men took to their beds. Tilby checked on the horses, especially the new foal born last week. Charlotte and Simone decided she should be named Summertime. They loved that critter more than its mother.

Rachel was fast asleep within minutes of climbing into bed. She never heard Simone slip away from the room and creep down the stairs and out the kitchen door.

Tilby expected Simone soon. They'd secretly signaled to each other without anyone being any the wiser. A slight tilt of the head and a quick glance was all Simone needed from Tilby to know that he'd be in the barn waiting for her.

"Tilby," Simone whispered when she entered the barn.

"O'er here," Tilby called back. They quickly found each other and wrapped themselves into a tight embrace.

"Come with me." Tilby climbed the ladder to the garret, and Simone followed. The air was cold, but the hay was warm and soft. Tilby and Simone settled under a saddle blanket. Their bodies added extra heat and warmed them on such a cold night. Under the blanket, Tilby took Simone's hand in his. His pulse and breathing quickened. He moved to his side, toward Simone, and leaned in to kiss her neck. Simone's face reddened with warm excitement.

"Tilby," Simone whispered. "I'm a decent lady, you know it, right? Please tell me you do."

"I's do, Simone. I's didn't means to—."

Simone put her pointer finger over Tilby's lips. "I know you didn't.

A long silence hung over the two friends before Simone asked, "When can we get married?"

"We gots no say, Simone, but we will. And when Mister says yes, then we can gets married."

An owl hooted in the near distance, perhaps calling for its mate, like Tilby calling through the barn's darkness for Simone.

Tilby and Simone might have fallen asleep in the quiet, but Simone intentionally stayed awake, knowing she must be in bed when Rachel woke at sunrise. Simone snuggled closer to Tilby. The end of Christmas dampened her happiness. The new year meant changes on many plantations, and a melancholy mood swept over her. "What will the new year bring? Do you think Master will ever sell either of us? I couldn't live if he did, Tilby. I'd run 'til every bone in my body ached from exhaustion. And then I'd run some more. I'd keep running 'til I was dead."

"Stop talkin' like that, Simone."

Simone pushed herself closer to Tilby. "You can kiss me, if you want to—there's no harm in a kiss, Tilby?"

Tilby took Simone in his arms and kissed her tenderly. When it was over, the two stared into the silence, holding each other close.

11

Huntington Manor, Virginia 1840

"Mama! Mama!" Simone screamed into the dark. "Don't go, Mama!" Simone sat straight in her bed with heavy breath. Sweat covered her brow and drenched her nightgown.

Rachel woke and immediately went to Simone. She sat on the bed's edge, cradling her friend. "Shh, baby girl. You alright, Moni. I'm here now. You gonna be fine."

Tears flooded Simone's eyes. "I'm getting too old for dreams. When will it stop?"

"Being seventeen don't mean the good Lord stop you from remembering when you was a child."

"How'd you know, Rachel," Simone said. She sobbed and took in a heavy breath.

"You cried out for her," Rachel said softly.

"I miss her so much it hurts."

"I know you do, Moni. I saw it in your eyes the day we was chained together. I believe the good Lord sent me to look after you."

"How can you believe there is a good Lord, Rachel?" Simone pulled away from Rachel and fell back on her bed. Where was the good Lord when a white man pulled me from my mama's arms? She was screaming and throwing a terrible fuss until—" Simone covered her face with her arm. "It was so awful."

"Tell me again what happened, Moni. Each time you get it in the open, the pain will get less." Rachel coerced. "I promise it will."

Tears dampened Simone's cheeks. "A white man beat my mama to the ground and held her with his foot. She could barely breathe pressed to the ground like that." Simone sucked in the air and let it go, intertwined in a moan that sounded more like an injured animal than a young woman. "It was so awful. How could God let something like this happen?"

Rachel smoothed Simone's hair. She, too, had lost faith in God, but she eventually returned to prayer. When she lived with her parents, they read the Bible every day, and Mama taught her how to pray. Whenever people afflicted Rachel with hatred, her mama chose the right verse. It didn't always make the hurt disappear, but she always felt better. When Mr. Sopley sold her to Mr. Brown to pay his debt, the Bible verses kept her mind from dying.

Rachel petted Simone's arm. "Those men who stole you from your mama has got the devil in them, Simone. We can't do nothin' 'bout that but believe the good Lord look out for us. He's already done it—me from Fairfax, and you, all the way from Kentucky. Then Mister James come along and buy us, thinking we are sisters. That was the Lord's good work. We both want our mamas bad. When I lived with the Browns, some mornings I'd wake thinking Mr. Sopley would come calling to purchase me back like he promised, but it ain't never happened that way."

"Will we ever see our families? Fairfax isn't so far from here."

Rachel wiped a tear from Simone's cheek. Her tone was soft and reassuring when she spoke. "If not on this earth, then in Heaven we sure will."

"I can barely remember what my mama looks like, but I remember that day she was taken from me like yesterday. It hasn't ever left my mind."

Rachel took hold of Simone's hand. She closed her eyes and prayed over her friend. *"Cast thy burden upon the Lord, and he shall sustain thee: he shall never suffer the righteous to be moved."*

Rosalie had heard Simone's initial cries. She presumed Rachel was there, consoling the girl. It had been over a year since Rosalie heard Simone scream at night. A few months back, she'd wondered if it was over for good, but tonight proved that memories never entirely fade away.

When Simone arrived at Huntington Manor ten years ago, her dreams were frequent. Simone had no physical scars, but Rosalie supposed that wasn't worth much. Emotional scars could be and most often were more detrimental to the spirit of a human being, especially a child. And yet, she let Rachel attend to the little girl after she woke from nightmares. Never once had Rosalie gone to Simone in those times of terror. She'd let Simone's kind— Rachel and Chloe—deal with cuts, bruises, and bad dreams because that's what she forced herself to believe a slave owner should do.

Rosalie had accepted James's broken promises to her father, which put her at fault, but her father could not detest purchasing two children chained together. They would have been sold to someone if not James. When Charlotte bonded with Simone, Rosalie was slightly liberated from their wrongdoings. It had been why she'd allowed the friendship to mature so quickly.

James's father had purchased Lars, Hilda, and Chloe. However, it hadn't made Rosalie blameless. The Negroes were still enslaved instead of becoming employed servants, as her father had requested of James before allowing their marriage. There were other slaves on the plantation besides those who remained at Huntington Manor, James had told her, but when his sisters married, each girl received a slave of their own as a gift from their father. Rosalie didn't want to believe it was true. It was appalling, but she kept her opinion to herself.

Rosalie was a plantation owner's wife, and adjusting to James's Southern ways was in her best interest. She eased her mind, reasoning the slaves on the plantation were treated kindly, but still, when she lay awake at night, her mind switched to babies being ripped from their mother's arms or lashes so horrible that Lars's body was deformed.

The moonlight softened the glow of the night sky. Rosalie pulled herself from bed, went to the window, and stared into the starry night. She wondered how often Simone or the others had had sleepless nights reliving their past and fearing their future. Rosalie had allowed Simone to suffer from a nightmarish reality without ever lifting a finger to console her. She had eliminated certain particulars from her mind to live this life, and tonight, Rosalie felt utterly ashamed.

12

Huntington Manor, Virginia 1840

Charlotte stayed late into the evening in the servants' quarters. She'd brought a cake from the kitchen, and the girls and women shared it before Chloe and Hilda went to their room for the night.

Rachel shook her head in disbelief. "Eighteen tomorrow. Time sure does fly. It seems like yesterday you was playing with dolls and chasing boys 'round the old willow tree."

Charlotte and Simone beamed. Rachel was like a mother to Simone for the past eleven years, but she'd also been a surrogate to Charlotte at times. Rachel had made the girls matching dresses when they were ten. She recalled Rosalie's expression. "Look, Mother," Charlotte had said. She and Simone were holding hands. Rosalie had been reading and looked to see two girls, same height, same slight girl shape, Charlotte with a broad smile, waiting for approval. When Rosalie said nothing, Charlotte said. "We look exactly alike, wouldn't you agree, Mother?"

Rachel had wondered about this for some time. Rosalie's expression had shown a glint of curiosity, like she was deliberating how her daughter saw Simone as looking the same as her. Maybe it had stuck with Rachel because it perplexed her too. The girls couldn't look more different. Charlotte was pearly white, with hair as yellow as the sun. Simone was as dark as night. Her skin tone was the darkest on the plantation, but not once in all these years had Charlotte noted their evident differences.

When she was a little girl, Rachel dreamed of playing with the children outside Mr. Sopley's shop. Considering Ms. Rosalie's stare, she wondered if it hadn't been for the parents, would the children have noticed her skin was black?

Rachel yawned as she crawled under her bed covers. "You girls can chat all night long if you wish, but come tomorrow, Simone, I better not find you sleeping with a rag in one hand."

Charlotte and Simone laughed. They chatted about nothing in particular until soft snores came from Rachel's side of the room. This was Charlotte's chance. She couldn't wait to talk about the good stuff.

"Are you sweet on someone?" Charlotte asked in an excited whisper.

Simone's smile faded. "What are you talking about, Charlotte? You can't be saying things like that."

Charlotte looked surprised. "Simone," she whispered. "I'm your best friend. You can tell me anything." Charlotte looked over at Rachel, deeming this the cause of Simone's unease. "Don't worry, Simone. Rachel is fast asleep."

Charlotte tiptoed over to Rachel's bed.

Simone whispered. "What are you doing?"

"Making sure she is asleep," Charlotte whispered.

Charlotte returned, sat on Simone's bed, and pulled her legs to her chest. She pulled her nightgown over her legs so her feet poked out from underneath. "Rachel is sound asleep," Charlotte said in a quiet voice.

Charlotte looked at Simone. She hoped her friend said something about Tilby. Charlotte had seen them holding hands when they thought no one was watching, and since then, Charlotte had observed them twice in the garden, talking. The way their eyes met looked similar to when Mother and Father's eyes met at the dinner table, different from when she spoke with one of her brothers. Charlotte was sure Simone and Tilby were sweet on one another, but that didn't give her the right to ask. It was one of those questions that she contemplated. Her mother would tell her it was unladylike to ask such questions, but she and Simone were best friends, so why wouldn't she pry?

Simone sensed Charlotte's eagerness and quickly deflected what Charlotte was about to ask. "Did you see anything interesting in town today?"

Interesting in town? Charlotte had planned on a different dialogue than this, and if she didn't redirect Simone, then this could be the dullest chat they'd ever had.

"No, nothing in particular," Charlotte replied. "Thomas and Seth Joed ran into each other and bored me with business. Though, he did comment on my hair—said it looked pretty."

"Who?"

"Seth."

"Do you like him?"

Charlotte smiled. "He's not the kind of boy I fancy." Charlotte was not about to go into all the reasons she would never consider Seth Joed for marriage. Mr. Joed, Seth's father, threatened his slaves with a whip. She'd never heard he took to his threat, and honestly, Seth seemed like a decent person, but anyone who threatened actual harm on a person for no proper reason was not for her.

"How about you? Is there anyone you might fancy?" Charlotte said, stretching the words.

"Who?" Simone retorted.

"Tilby, silly."

It was hard to contain her silence, but Simone knew she must for now. Tilby would ask Mister James if they could marry after the growing season. "It's the best time," Tilby had told her. "Profits and worry be done by then."

"Charlotte. Tilby and me are just friends." Simone hadn't wanted to lie, but Charlotte couldn't know. Simone didn't want anyone to know, not even Rachel. Especially not Rachel. Rachel would deliver an earful and perhaps take a knife to Tilby to scare him.

Charlotte's disappointment saddened Simone.

Rachel stirred. Both girls went silent, stared at Rachel's bed, and waited, assuring she hadn't woken.

Simone took a wavering breath. "Charlotte? What is it about a boy like Seth Joed?"

"What do you mean?"

"You didn't say that you don't fancy Seth. You said you wouldn't fancy a boy like Seth? I'm wondering what you mean by that?"

Charlotte was at a loss for words.

Simone could only assume why Charlotte wouldn't marry a white man like Seth. Master Joed lurked over his slaves and beat them more than a dozen times. Every slave within ten miles knew this was true. Seth, though—word got around—was an improved man. Never touched a whip yet, but Charlotte—Simone figured, thought any boy with a father like Mr. Joed would turn out the same. Simone agreed with this notion. In time, boys become their fathers.

Charlotte deflected her friend's question, like she figured Simone had about Tilby. "No reason. Seth doesn't suit me, that's all. There's nothing complicated in the matter."

But it was complicated, and for some reason, Charlotte never noticed. Simone's cheeks burned. "Charlotte. Do you actually think we have the same kind of life?" Simone saw the hurt in Charlotte's face but didn't care. If Charlotte implied everything was so uncomplicated, then Simone would tell her she was wrong.

"I don't care about your skin color, Simone, if this is what your implying. We are friends."

"Then tell me why you wouldn't marry a boy like Seth Joed," Simone asked again, this time with a whispered short fuse."

"You first," Charlotte said. "Are you and Tilby sweet with one another?"

"No," Simone lied. "And now you. Why wouldn't you marry a boy like Seth Joed?"

"I wouldn't marry a boy like Seth because they are unkind to their Negroes."

"By Negroes, do you mean slaves?"

Charlotte stood from where she sat on the bed, crossed her arms over her chest, and stared at Simone. "Why does this matter to you, Simone?"

Rachel woke with Charlotte's heightened tone. She leaped out of bed and swatted at Simone. "Hold your tongue, Simone," Rachel scolded, without knowing what was said.

Simone jumped to the floor out of Rachel's reach. "I'm not only a Negro, Charlotte. I'm a slave. I'm your father's slave."

"Oh, my Lord in Heaven." Rachel moved around the bed and caught Simone by the arm. "You stop this minute, Simone. Do you hear me? God will damn us to hell if He ain't already." Rachel looked at Charlotte. "Miss Charlotte. Please. Simone must be sick with a fever."

Simone thrust her arm away from Rachel. "I am not sick."

"It's not the same, Simone." Charlotte's eyes teared up. "We would never hurt you. My father and brothers don't do the things other folks do to their Negroes."

Rachel quickly spoke. "You are nothin' but kind, Miss Charlotte."

Charlotte looked directly at Rachel. "Do you think you and Simone are in some kind of trouble because Simone is speaking her mind?" Charlotte said. "Have you befriended me because you believe harm might come to you if you don't?"

Rachel's mouth gaped. "No, Miss Charlotte! Lord, no."

Charlotte turned to Simone, tears bubbling in the corners of her eyes. She took Simone's hands in hers. "We are best friends, Simone. Our lives are different, but who we are beneath our skin makes us kindred spirits. Nothing can take that from us. Never be scared to tell me anything. I'll take it to my grave, Simone. I promise I will."

Simone's nose stung as she tried to push back tears, but instead, she let go of the stress she held inside. Tears slid from her eyes. "Charlotte." Simone's voice squeaked. She cleared her throat. "You are my friend forever."

And your father's slave forever. Simone loved her friend, but she couldn't stop the thought from surfacing.

Rachel wrapped both girls in her arms. "Praise the good Lord," she whispered.

13

Simone lay in bed thinking about what had happened between her and Charlotte. She saw more hatred in this world before the age of seven than Charlotte would see in a lifetime. Her black skin complicated everything—her friendship with Charlotte and especially her place on this plantation. How were friends supposed to be kindred spirits if there was an entire race between them? Charlotte lived by a set of different rules in plain sight.

Simone let her thoughts roll off her tongue to Rachel.

Rachel sat beside Simone. "But there ain't nothin' we can do 'bout it, Simone, not unless you want to end up dead. You and Charlotte being best friends don't change nothin'. You still a slave—and it's got to be good enough for you, Moni. Sharing birthdays and playing with Charlotte all these years has done you terrible wrong—cuz you think dreams are possible like Charlotte—but there's nothin' but ungodly cruelty outside these walls for us. You spoutin' off like you did is asking for trouble. You ain't allowed to speak your mind, Moni, cuz bad things will happen—things you never imagine—abuse so bad you beg for death."

Simone sobbed. Charlotte was her best friend, but Rachel had her worried she'd gone too far tonight, and what if it got back to Rosalie? Tears rolled to her chin. "I only wanted Charlotte to understand everything wasn't so simple."

"Don't blame Charlotte for being innocent. Her parents are protectin' her from the worst people, but I believe that girl could change this world."

Rachel wiped teardrops from Simone's cheeks.

"Are you angry with me?" Simone asked in a faint voice.

Rachel smoothed Simone's hair. "I ain't mad."

Rachel's tone was so warm and gentle that Simone couldn't stop herself from crying again.

"Shh," Rachel said.

Simone sniffled, and sobs wrenched her gut. Somehow Charlotte had discovered her and Tilby, and Rachel would know soon enough. "Can I tell you a secret?"

Rachel nodded.

"I love Tilby."

"I know that, baby girl."

Simone looked at Rachel bemused. "You know?" she rubbed at her nose and wiped her tears. "About Tilby and me?"

Rachel half-smiled.

"And you haven't chased him with a horsewhip around the field?"

"No, and I don't plan to either."

Simone sat up, resting back on her hands. "Why not?"

Rachel laughed. "Did you want me to? It'd be mighty worth it, givin' him a fright."

"It's not that."

"Then what?"

Simone let out a long sigh. "I don't know."

"C'mon. Put your head on the pillow, and I'll tell you what I know."

Simone lay down, ready to listen, her eyes intent on Rachel.

"I noticed you goin' to the barn a lot. I thought it was to see Summertime because you love that horse, but nobody spend that much time with an animal. That's when I think you might be sneakin' off to see Tilby." Rachel grinned. "Sound right, so far?"

Simone nodded in agreement. "But that doesn't explain why you didn't tell him to mind his business."

"You growing up, Moni." Rachel paused. "But it ain't why, I suppose."

Rachel put her hands over Simone's hands. "You and me saw enough horrors to last a lifetime. But Mister—he found us. He found Tilby too. Now, I ain't sayin' it's right to be buying slaves, but I got to believe God had a plan."

"So, are you saying me and Tilby are supposed to be together?"

Simone raised her eyebrows. "I ain't sayin' that, and don't go thinking it." Her brows relaxed. "But Tilby is nice. And you are the sweetest, kindest girl I ever did know." Rachel leaned back and crossed her arms. "You know who else knows?"

"Who? Chloe?"

Rachel laughed. "Probably, but I'm speaking of Miss Charlotte."

Simone lowered her eyes.

"You can't blame Charlotte for anything but love, Moni. You ain't a slave to her."

"I want Charlotte as my friend, but what is a friend if you can't say what's deep inside?"

"We ain't got much choices in this world, but nobody can take away love. It's up to you to be Charlotte's friend if you want to. Charlotte ain't got no say in it."

"Do you think Charlotte will tell Ms. Rosalie what I said tonight? What will happen to me?"

Rachel looked at Simone, but her mind was on Ms. Rosalie.

Simone worried. "What?"

"Charlotte will keep quiet."

"But you look puzzled."

"I can't be sure Ms. Rosalie would do much even if she did find out. It's like she's pulled between two worlds."

"What do you mean?"

"I can't explain it, Moni, but it sure is curious."

"Maybe like me and Charlotte—in two different worlds of Black and white people."

"I suppose, but I ain't for sure." Rachel soothed Simone's hair and stood from Simone's bed. "We got lots of work tomorrow. You are fine, baby girl."

Rachel slept almost immediately. Simone looked out the window at the bright stars and thought of Charlotte.

Charlotte lay awake in bed, staring into the moonlit sky and thinking of Simone. She was angry with her friend for spoiling what should have been an enchanting evening, all boy talk, but if Charlotte was perfectly honest with herself, she was at fault too. Charlotte tried to convince herself it was for Simone that she never questioned her friend's position at Huntington Manor. Charlotte cried into her pillow, realizing what a fool she'd been.

If Charlotte imagined the differences beyond their skin color like Simone had suggested, then yes, there were many differences between her and Simone. Charlotte had neither seen a Negro wealthy like her father nor a white slave. Father, Thomas, and Henry worked in the fields with the slaves, but it was obvious who was in charge. But it was because Father was overseeing a plantation and the finances. *There was nothing evil in that.*

There were undeniably instances in her life that would imply Simone was right in what she'd said in anger. Their birthday was a prime example. She and Simone celebrated with lemon drops or played with dolls when they were children, but in the evening, after dinner, Charlotte enjoyed a berry dessert, two if she desired. Tomorrow, Hilda would bake raspberry tarts for after dinner, but Simone would not sit at the table with them to celebrate. And once, Charlotte remembered Mother asking Father if the slaves should earn wages. Her father said he'd spent good money on their purchase and provided food and shelter. *That's a great life for a Negro.* Those had been her father's words. Tonight, it meant something different than when she was a child.

There was also the instance of Charlotte's schooling. She was young when she asked her mother if Simone could join her for lessons. Mother explained why it wasn't possible, and Charlotte had obediently not asked again. But Charlotte had been curious and asked Simone what kept her busy during the day. Her friend responded with a simple answer, but Charlotte pushed further. Then Simone gave a short list, like beating the dust and dirt from rugs, scrubbing the floors, and bringing water to the men in the field.

And then tonight's conversation about Seth. Charlotte had never seen Seth, his father, or the overseer on their land act aggressively toward the field hands, but it hadn't meant it hadn't happened. Last year, Charlotte had walked into the kitchen and overheard a conversation between Chloe and Hilda about the poor treatment Mr. Joed had shown one of his slaves. They'd stopped talking the minute she made herself known. If it was true, and she suspected it was, then she may never marry.

Charlotte moved her eyes from the window to the ceiling. Tears ran from the corners of her eyes. She was not blind to the slave pen in town, slave trades, or the fact that her father enslaved Negroes. Her position in society was clearly different from that of Negroes. Hilda was always in the kitchen, most days, with sweat on her forehead. Chloe spent hours washing clothes and bedsheets and hanging them on the line to dry. Rachel made the windows see-through and the silver shine. From planting to harvest, the work doubled with the needs of such a large garden and fruit trees. And the men—Lars, Tilby, Reedy, Willy, and Zeke—worked from sunrise to sundown.

Charlotte was unaware of what it cost to purchase a Negro, but Simone and Rachel had lived and worked at Huntington Manor for the past eleven years, and the others, besides Tilby, had been here longer. *Surely*, Charlotte thought. Her father's slaves had paid their debt.

Charlotte wiped her tears. She had a solution. *Tomorrow, I'll make things right.*

She closed her eyes and drifted off to sleep.

14

Huntington Manor, Virginia 1840

Thomas, Henry, Willy, and Zeke carved shallow furrows into the earth across the field, adding horse manure for the tiny tobacco plants. Simone and Rachel were in the garden, tilling the soil and preparing it for the spring plant. Hilda baked raspberry tarts. A lovely platter, one of Charlotte's favorite pieces of her mother's china set, was nearby for the cooled dessert. Rachel polished the silver and arranged the porcelain on the table. The set had been a wedding gift from Rosalie's mother for special occasions like Thanksgiving and Christmas. Still, Rosalie used it for birthdays.

"Happy birthday, darling," Rosalie said, standing near Charlotte's bed. It was around seven in the morning, and Charlotte was still groggy. Her eyes fluttered before remembering the night with Simone and Rachel in the servant's quarters.

"Thank you," Charlotte replied. She pushed the covers aside and swung her legs off the bed. "Mother? Can we invite Simone to share raspberry tarts with us tonight? After all, it is her birthday too. It's a lovely idea, and we should be honored to have my best friend join us." Charlotte didn't wait for a possible objection. "We are both eighteen," she emphasized, like this point may make a difference.

When Rosalie didn't respond, Charlotte busied herself, giving her mother time to see her point. She opened a trunk at the end of her bed and pulled out a new dress she and Mother had bought in town days ago. It was a beautiful soft shade of yellow with a high neck, long sleeves, and a bell-shaped skirt. Charlotte put it over a chair and reached in for her petticoat.

Charlotte's request surprised Rosalie, mostly because she'd expected this question five, seven, or even ten years ago, but not today, after this many years. Rosalie had been grateful it had worked out this way because situations like these undermined her unwavering poise.

When Rosalie was a child, she respected everyone, regardless of skin color. Her parents had instilled this kindness in her and her sister, Sarah. However, even her father, the fair man he was, would likely balk at Charlotte's request to have a Black girl share a dessert with them. Her father paid Negroes fair wages for their services and never spoke unkindly of them. He occasionally called upon the doctor and paid their fees. Her father employed Black and white workers for his business, but not once had a Negro been invited to their home for leisure, and it confused Rosalie for most of her childhood.

The fact that Rosalie fell in love with a slave owner was her undoing at these moments—accepting the life she lived and resisting something different inside her.

Charlotte went to the table positioned on the opposite side of the room. She looked into a handheld mirror. Today, Rachel promised to style her hair into beautiful cascading curls. She looked over at her mother. Rosalie was taking too long to answer her question, and if she didn't reiterate what she'd asked, it might be lost altogether.

"May I go and tell Simone she is welcome to have dessert with us this evening?" When her mother still didn't answer, Charlotte asked if she should ask her father instead.

"No, darling," Rosalie said. She sat on the edge of Charlotte's bed.

"No, I shouldn't ask Father, or no, Simone should not be invited?"

Rosalie patted a place on the bed so Charlotte would sit beside her.

"Tell me what's wrong, Mother."

"You may invite Simone," Rosalie said somberly.

What was wrong with everyone lately? First Simone, then Rachel, and now her mother. "Mother. Can I ask you a question?"

"Yes."

"Is Simone less of a person because she has dark skin?"

"Charlotte. That is an unfair question."

"I don't see how. You have always talked about how Grandma and Granddaddy Farnsworth taught you and Aunt Sarah to treat everyone kindly, and you've passed it on to Henry, Thomas, and me. Remember the bedtime stories you told us when we were children? There was always a hidden moral; when we couldn't figure it out, you found a way to explain it. On those particular story nights, I fell asleep thinking about showing kindness or gratitude or being of service the next day. But, I'm not blind, Mother. I live a different lifestyle from Simone and the other Negroes. For one, look at how I dress. Simone has never had a dress like this one, but that is not to say she doesn't have a heart or soul exactly like mine. And—"

Charlotte could not repeat what Simone said last night. That was between two best friends; her mother did not need to know everything. But she was curious what Mother thought of Seth and if they both disapproved of the Joeds.

"About Seth Joed."

"What about Seth Joed?"

"Well, if you must know. Seth is smitten—"

Rosalie interrupted. "Charlotte. I will not have Seth courting you."

"You needn't worry. I wouldn't dare, but may I ask why?" Charlotte asked because she saw her mother's reaction to the Joeds over the years—polite but distant.

Rosalie had not meant for the conversation to go in this direction. She'd only wanted to point out Simone's circumstances. Sitting around a table with the Worthington family after a lifetime of eating in the back kitchen might not be the lovely experience for Simone that Charlotte wanted.

Charlotte saw her mother's unrest and sensed hidden opinions—it happened in times like these, when Simone or Rachel came up in conversation, and it confused Charlotte at times—how aloof her mother was to the plantation's Negroes.

Charlotte didn't push. If Mother had an answer, then she would not hide it from her. "I apologize, Mother. I should have held my tongue. It's only—well, I thought maybe we agreed about the Joeds, but perhaps I needed a reminder of what you taught us as children. *Judge not according to the appearance, but judge righteous judgment.*"

Charlotte organized what she wanted to say next—what she needed her mother to understand. "Mother," Charlotte said in a gentle tone. "You and Father taught Henry, Thomas, and me that no matter if we plant an entire crop or a single fruit tree, we must work to secure its success, and, in turn, we will reap a profitable crop."

Charlotte's reminder stung. Over the years, Rosalie had strayed from the Lord's teachings.

"But these are people, Mother—not crops." Charlotte continued. "We must put aside our best and be better. Wouldn't you agree?"

"I do agree, Charlotte."

Charlotte hugged her mother. "May I be excused? I'd like to go tell Simone the good news."

Rosalie watched her daughter walk from the bedroom, happy to invite Simone to dessert and celebrate their birthdays. Her daughter had matured from a girl to a young lady, and Rosalie wanted to share with Charlotte the beliefs that lingered from her upbringing, but she would not impose on her daughter the strife she suffered. And Rosalie cast judgment on the Joeds because, at times, they mistreated their slaves, but wasn't owning another human just as immoral? How could she cast judgment or divulge to Charlotte her opinions when she and James partook in enslaving Negroes?

When Rosalie first came to Huntington Manor after the death of James's father, she knew the importance of fitting into this southern life. James was a businessman and in charge of his plantation, but when more than a year passed, Rosalie grew impatient and wondered when James would start paying his Negroes, like he assured her father he would do.

Rosalie remembered it so clearly. She had been pregnant with Charlotte and already felt immeasurable love for her unborn child. But it had been a trying seventh month, and with heightened emotions, Rosalie feared losing her child. It overwhelmed her so dreadfully that one day when she saw Hilda cleaning the nursery, she stopped in the doorway and talked to Hilda about it—just that once—but Rosalie still remembered it.

That next day, Rosalie set out to talk to James about making good on his promises. They sat in the parlor, James reading the paper before bed and Rosalie drinking tea when she asked the question. James looked up from reading the news and responded firmly that his slaves were treated fairly, which was payment enough. James's answer hadn't been abrasive that day. He'd only satisfactorily made a valid point. But her husband had marginalized her question so quickly that it surprised her. Rosalie was raised with an open mind and tenacity, and she wondered if the discussion was closed for good or if she should approach the subject later. It was hard to know what to do or think as a slave owner's wife.

Then, when Charlotte was seven months old, James returned from town with Reedy, *a strapping man, aged twenty and in excellent health.* Those had been her husband's words. Rosalie could not believe what James had said. It was one thing to carry on with the slaves already established on Huntington Manor before marriage, but blatantly purchasing another man against Rosalie's father's request was another. She was here, married to the man she loved because James had promised her father he would never purchase another slave.

Rosalie couldn't believe what James had told her. She stood from her chair where she was having tea, went to close the parlor's doors, and when she turned, found James staring at her, worried.

"James," she said, stone-faced. "How could you? You made a promise to my father, and in making that promise to my father, you made that promise to me."

Rosalie never heard James stumble on his words, but he had on that day. "Rosalie," he said, placing his hand on his forehead. "I need to think about this."

Today, Charlotte's eighteenth birthday, was a testament to how much precious time had passed.

What James implemented years ago was no mystery—he'd made it right by rescuing the two girls because Rosalie would not and could not send them away. James had saved Willy from near death and Tilby, a broken young boy, from cruelty and starvation. James had found a way to purchase slaves, ensuring his tobacco's success and impress upon Rosalie his love for her. And Rosalie went along with it because there was nothing she could do but accept her husband's answer.

However, the broken promises changed Rosalie. She hadn't returned home in years, except for the burials of her parents, because she hadn't wanted to face them or her sister and tell half-truths as she had through her correspondences. She respected the Negroes of Huntington Manor but avoided them. Rosalie understood the horrors of slavery on plantations, in town, or down south, but she put her abolitionist ideals aside and kept her opinions to herself.

Chloe was startled, almost dropping her oiling rag, when she walked into Charlotte's room and saw Rosalie sitting on the edge of the unmade bed. "Forgive me, ma'am. I didn't see you there."

Rosalie forced a smile in her troubled state. She knew little about this woman standing in front of her. She couldn't help but wonder what Chloe's life was like before Huntington Manor. Or any of the Negroes. She knew so little about them.

15

Simone and Rachel were using shovels to till the soil. There was much to do in the spring to prepare for planting seeds. Different plants needed extra care; if not done correctly, the large garden, about a quarter acre, would produce fewer fruits and vegetables. Simone saw Charlotte coming toward them from the house. She looked glowing with her wide smile, bright dress, and the sun behind her.

Last night, Rachel and Simone talked together long after Charlotte left their room. Simone felt wretched for the things she had said. She and Charlotte were friends. They had played tricks on her brothers and Tilby. She and Charlotte had worked together, sliding on the banister of the grand staircase, letting their skirts do the polishing, and they cheered in whispers with absolute delight. They sat under the willow tree, Charlotte reading from books and Simone learning. Simone loved touching the books and the words, and Charlotte had allowed her to, though when Rachel found out what Simone had been doing, she was beside herself. Rachel had fretted terribly, telling Simone that Ms. Rosalie couldn't ever know they could read. "My teaching and the Bible is all you need for learning," Rachel had told her crossly, but Simone had been unable to stop herself from reading with Charlotte.

She and Charlotte had hidden themselves in the garret, reading *The Legend of Sleepy Hollow* by the last light. The book had scared Simone stiff, causing many sleepless nights and sharing Rachel's bed for a week. Simone remembered when she and Charlotte sat under the willow tree on a pleasant afternoon. Henry was seated on one side of Charlotte and Simone on the other. Charlotte read the story of *The Three Bears* to her brother, tracking the text. Simone followed along, watching Charlotte's finger move under each word. Simone recognized many words, but porridge and bachelor were new to her. Simone asked about the two words. She wanted to know how porridge tasted. Charlotte said it looked like mashed corn cakes with added water, but she'd never tasted it.

Then Simone took a risk and asked Charlotte if she could borrow the book to show Rachel, and Charlotte handed it to her without any hesitation. Simone kept it hidden under her bed in a small trunk Charlotte gave her years ago when her father had brought a new one home from New York. Simone read that book a hundred times, hiding it under the dress she wore as a child—the one Mama had made for her, but Rachel caught her with the book and almost went mad.

"But Charlotte said I could," Simone said sturdily.

"And Ms. Rosalie could blame you for stealing, you hear me?" Rachel cursed, scared to death for the both of them. "Ms. Rosalie don't know we can read, and we got to keep it that way."

"Why, Rachel. Why must we keep it secret? Reading is a good thing." Simone was sure Rosalie knew she could read and never said anything about it, though Simone didn't dare tell Rachel about reading with Charlotte in the barn.

"Cuz you get a skill, and now you're worth money to someone. But reading gets you killed." Rachel didn't like to visit her past, but truth be told, sewing is what got her sold to Mrs. Brown. Her skills had paid off Mr. Sopley's debt. The only problem was she never got returned to her parents when that debt was paid. But Negroes learning to read was a sin to white folk. It hadn't been to Mr. Sopley, but that was unusual. Her parents could read and taught Rachel how to do it, but her mama said that Rachel had to pretend stupid around white folk. When Rachel asked her mama why, her mama only said because the white folk were scared of the Black folks' minds and left it at that.

When Simone oiled Charlotte's bedpost a few days later, she took the book from under her dress and returned it to the bookshelf. She wondered if Charlotte ever noticed it back in its rightful place. If her friend had, Charlotte never said a word about it. Simone could have taken a book, and she had wanted to, and hid it under her skirt on her way out of Charlotte's room. Charlotte would not have cared because that's the kind of person Charlotte was. But Rachel had a valid point. It was stealing to walk away with something that wasn't hers. And Ms. Rosalie, positively, would not tolerate stealing.

So when Simone thought back on her behavior toward Charlotte last night, she was ashamed of herself. She and Charlotte were friends. And yes, she was a slave, a fact Rachel wouldn't allow her to forget, but that's not how Charlotte saw her. Charlotte was more than a friend. She was like a sister.

Charlotte came and left the garden, leaving Simone worried and Rachel in awe.

"That girl's going to change this world. Maybe not in my lifetime, but she is going to do it, for sure."

"What should I do, Rachel? Sitting there with Mister and Ms. Rosalie will be awkward." Charlotte told Rachel she could join them to celebrate and eat raspberry tarts, but like a jackrabbit, Rachel uninvited herself, saying linens needed washing. But she thanked Miss Charlotte all the same. Simone didn't have the privilege of saying no like she wanted. Simone didn't belong with white folks acting all prim and proper. If word got around, there might be hell to pay later. Saying yes to Charlotte made her stomach ache, but it had been the right thing to do, and she couldn't deny it.

"You're gonna sit there and be respectful and polite. It's the person you are besides, Moni."

Simone liked when Rachel called her Moni. She only did it when they were alone, like a secret code between two girls once chained together. Rachel lifted the shovel inches off the ground and pushed it into the earth. "The soil ain't gonna till itself."

Simone brought the shovel high and heaved it hard into the ground so it stood upright on its own doing. She went to Rachel and hugged her.

"What's got into you, baby girl?" But Rachel wasn't expecting an answer. She let her shovel drop and embraced this child who'd grown into a beautiful young woman and friend, who Rachel loved more than life itself.

16

Huntington Manor, Virginia, 1840

The sun was hot. It was the last days of July, and James was out in the field overseeing his crop. Like most days when James was in the field, Thomas and Henry were with their father. Thomas looked over the crop with pride. The roots of the tobacco plants took a strong hold in the earth and were maturing to dark green. Thomas stood looking at the outstretched number of growing plants. It was a magnificent sight. The field slaves were topping the plants, pruning the seed clusters, and assuring better leaves for harvest.

James inspected one of the plants, checking for any infestation that could destroy a crop in days. "Thomas. Henry." James called to his boys. Thomas and Henry made their way over to their father. James broke off the center bud of a plant and inspected it before he spoke. "We've got work to do."

Seventeen-year-old Thomas took his place alongside the rows of tobacco—Henry to his left and Reedy to his right—and got to work.

That night at dinner, the conversation was business. James told his boys he was proud of their hard work on the land and said it had paid off. "If the weather cooperates for another month, we will be in the clear for one of our best crops.

"And if it doesn't?" Charlotte piped.

James looked at his older son. "Well, Thomas?"

Thomas replied to his sister, but he stated the information for the family. "We do everything humanly possible to save those plants. We all get out there and work twice as hard."

"That's right, Thomas. And Henry, I heard from Reedy that you have been watching for hornworms with eyes like a hawk."

Henry's face lit up. He was fourteen now. He'd grown inches this past year, and his voice had changed, but a young man or not, he adored a compliment from his father. "Yes, sir, Father."

"Well, I didn't see a single worm on those plants today. That's good work, son."

Thomas's insides swelled with envy. Undoubtedly, his father was proud of him, but his little brother had received the compliment, and it irked him.

"Henry," Charlotte alleged. "If you have a jar of worms somewhere hidden, waiting for the right moment to scare me, I'm telling you right here and now—I'm too old for such nonsense." Charlotte threw her brother a side eye and a tight-lipped grin.

"Why, sister," Henry jokingly mocked. "Whatever could you mean by that?"

"Henry." Charlotte stretched his name and crossed her eyes.

Henry burst out laughing. Charlotte smiled.

Charlotte and Thomas were a year apart in age, but Charlotte and Henry, four years between them, had a closer relationship. Rachel once told her that she and Henry were like milk and honey. They both resembled their father too. Their hair was the same golden color, and their eyes were sky blue. Their personalities had grown closer, also. They saw daily simplicities as opportunities, like sliding across a patch of ice just for fun.

Charlotte remembered when she and her brothers were on the porch with their studies. Lars tripped over a rotting tree stump, and he let out a holler that sounded much like a mad dog. Henry ran to Lars, sprawled on the ground, his face in the dirt. Henry was about nine or ten and a small boy. Lars was a big man, making his fall all that much worse, but Henry saw only a man who needed a hand, and her younger brother had been right there to lend it.

It's not to say Thomas hadn't cared about Lars's fall, he had, and it had shown. Thomas's body had straightened. His eyes focused on Henry and Lars, watching to see if he needed to assist Henry. Lars had fared well, so he returned to his geography lesson. Thomas was like Father in this way—waiting for the right moment to act and seeking the best plan. The main difference between Father and Thomas was that Thomas sometimes waited a moment too long.

Simone heard Henry's laughter coming from the dining room as she dried the last remaining pots in the kitchen. The Worthington family had a splendid time in the evenings, and Simone wished she could have that for her own someday. Tilby was on her mind, and if Rachel was right—that it was possible to change this world, then Simone wished it would hurry up and happen. She and Tilby could get married and have a family without fear of something terrible happening.

Simone finished the day's work and went upstairs to bed. It was late, and she was exhausted, but the excitement of seeing Tilby tonight kept her awake. Within minutes of dowsing the lamp, everyone was sleeping. On nights like these, when she was sneaking around, Simone was grateful for Hilda's gurgling snores coming from the other room. She quietly withdrew from her bed and tiptoed from the room, down the stairs, and out the back door, careful not to make a sound.

The air was thick and sultry. Simone slipped inside the stable. Summertime's gentle brown eyes summoned Simone to her. The horse lifted her head, and Simone stroked Summertime's face. The horse was Simone's favorite of the five horses inside the stable. They swished their tails and stamped their hooves, trying to rid themselves of the flies and their relentless biting.

Simone heard the barn door creak. She froze until Tilby whispered her name. "Simone? You there?"

Simone giggled. "I see you fine from where I'm standing."

Tilby smiled as he placed his eyes on her. He went to her, and they kissed.

17

It had been a remarkable growing season. Harvest was in full swing, and if all continued to go as planned, the plantation's tobacco should sell at a high price. Buyers from far and near referred to James's crop as the best.

James came down with a cough in the previous weeks that continued to worsen, and he'd struggled to get out of bed for the past two days.

"Where are Thomas and Henry?" James coughed between his words. He slowly pulled the bed covers off his body.

"What are you doing, James? Dr. Bishop said to stay in bed."

"The hell I will," James spewed. "There is business to attend to."

"Thomas and Henry are in the field. And Charlotte has gone for the doctor."

Another coughing spell slowed James's argument.

"You are in no shape to get out of bed, James."

James sat back on the bed, trying to calm his breathing.

Last week, when Rosalie sent for the doctor, James complained that she worried about a runny nose from harvesting the plants. Rosalie disagreed. Her husband coughed for a week prior, and it sounded like it had worsened. However, Rosalie was relieved when the doctor had little concern for what ailed James and said he only needed to rest. Unfortunately, James had balked at sleeping during such a busy time.

Harvesting the tobacco plants was tiring for everyone in the family. A portion of the crop had already been harvested, but plenty needed attention. Rosalie took over the books and record keeping during this time so that James and their boys could focus mainly on the crop. Everyone, including the house slaves, worked in the field. Charlotte managed the ripened fruits and vegetables in the garden during the tobacco harvest. Drying, curing, pickling, or canning foods in preparation for the winter took weeks past the harvest. By late autumn, Charlotte, Simone, and Rachel would fill the root cellar with beets, carrots, turnips, potatoes, and squashes.

It was too late for regrets, but Rosalie wished she had insisted James take it easy last week.

Chloe entered the room. "Ms. Rosalie. This be the willow bark tea you askin' for." Chloe put it on the table near James's bed. She didn't mean to stare, but Mister looked awful.

"That will be all for now, Chloe. Please bring the doctor in when he arrives."

"Yes, ma'am."

Rosalie offered James tea. He swallowed and spewed most of the liquid through a series of coughs. He held his chest, trying to ease the pain with each gasp of air. He struggled to sit up, so Rosalie helped him. She patted his back to help loosen the phlegm.

Rosalie became frightened. "What in the world has taken hold of you?"

Finally, a knock on the door and Dr. Bishop entered. He went to James and touched his forehead.

"He's burning up," Rosalie said.

Dr. Bishop confirmed the fever. He removed the blankets. Underneath, his patient shivered with chills. "We need to cool his body." Doctor Bishop told Rosalie to remove James's stockings. "And bring cool water right away."

Charlotte stood frantically by her parent's bedroom door. "Mother. What's happening?"

"No fretting, Charlotte. The doctor said to get cool water. Go now, darling."

Charlotte took the stairs by two on the way down. "Chloe," she yelled into the kitchen before she got there. "Come, please. We need to bring water to Father."

The two girls filled buckets of water from the pump, carried it upstairs, and placed it by the bed.

"Very well," Dr. Bishop said to Charlotte. "You there," he motioned at Chloe. "Close the door behind you."

Charlotte stood tall. "Her name is Chloe, Doctor."

"Very well."

Charlotte's voice softened. "How is he?"

"Your father will be fine but needs plenty of rest and medication."

Dr. Bishop waited for James's last coughing spell to subside. He listened to his lungs by placing a wooden tube on James's chest and his ear at the other end. Raspy sounds came from James, especially from the right lung.

"What is it?" Rosalie demanded to know.

James, whose coughing had subsided, reached for Rosalie's arm. "Rosalie. Let the doctor speak."

"It's winter fever. Some call it pleuropneumonia," Dr. Bishop said. "There is fluid in the lungs. The best solution is to rid the body of this excess fluid."

James kept his voice calm, hoping to avoid another coughing fit. "Doctor Bishop. If you are about to suggest bloodletting, please leave my house."

"Let me explain—."

James stopped the doctor by fronting his hand. His lungs wheezed, and phlegm was building. He needed to make his wishes clear. "They tried that on my uncle, and he's now been dead for ten years. There's no science behind the practice, and I refuse to let you cut me and have my blood spill over the floor."

Dr. Bishop looked thoughtfully at James. He pulled a bottle of Calomel from his bag, opened it, and gave James a large dose. With no other options, James swallowed the medication.

James vomited for the next twelve hours. Coughing spells exhausted him, and he endured bouts of diarrhea. The following morning, he lay on his bed, his head collapsed on a pillow. Doctor Bishop had stayed the night, administering opium to decrease James's pain.

Rosalie did not want to ask the next question, but she must while the children were still in bed. The sun was rising, and they would come to their father at first light.

"What should I be expecting?"

"James is strong-willed, so there is hope he will recover. Keep him comfortable."

Doctor Bishop handed Rosalie a bottle of medicine and instructions. "I'll be back to check on him in a day, but send for me if he worsens before then."

Rosalie spent most of her time at James's bedside. Most hours, Charlotte sat with her father, quietly begging him to open his eyes and show her he was alright. Rosalie stared out the bedroom window, scanning the trees in the distance. She spotted speckled reds and yellows in the hundreds of changing treetops.

Two days passed, and James remained with closed eyes and irregular breathing. His skin lacked warmth. Henry and Charlotte kneeled at James's bedside, whispering to God. Rosalie watched as she held James's cold hand. Her children needed their father. She needed her husband. It was impossible to fathom how James, robust and filled with life a week ago, was lying in their bed withering away.

James gasped. Henry and Charlotte stopped praying and looked at their father. "Mother," Charlotte fretted, searching for an explanation.

Rosalie knew the end was near. "He's alright, darling, but I want you to go for the doctor. Take Thomas with you."

Charlotte followed her mother's instructions immediately.

Henry was afraid. "Is he going to live, Mama?" It was a boyish tone that Rosalie had come to miss in the last year.

Henry was the spitting image of James, and Rosalie noticed it more than ever. She motioned Henry over to her. She pulled her son onto her lap. He'd outgrown her lap by years, but he softened, allowing it to happen."

"I don't know, Henry." Tears blossomed in the corners of her eyes.

When Dr. Bishop arrived, he leaned in and listened to James's lungs. Despite their round-the-clock care and medical intervention, James was dying.

"Henry," Dr. Bishop said at James' bedside. "I want you and Charlotte to fetch warm water. We can wipe your father's forehead." The two immediately left. Thomas and Rosalie remained.

"He's still with us, but not for long." Dr. Bishop said.

James gasped for air. It lasted more than a minute. There was nothing anyone could do for him. Thomas bowed his head and prayed it was over soon. Rosalie lay James's hand by his side, went around the bed to Thomas, and held her son. Tiny prisms stilled on the far wall by the sun's reflection of the diamond ring on her motionless hand. Rosalie felt James in those colors—his love for her and their children. Tears Rosalie had been holding back for the sake of her children let go and finally spilled from her eyes.

The doctor listened to her husband's lungs for a final time. James was dead.

18

James was buried on a Thursday. On Friday morning, Henry took his place among the plants. Reedy went to him. "Master Henry, sir. I come to pay my respects. Your father was a good man."

Henry's face swelled like he held back the River Jordan. He stood there, his head down, tears striking the soil.

Reedy put his hand on Henry's shoulder to let it comfort the young boy. "You'll be alright, Henry."

"Reedy," Thomas called.

Reedy turned. Thomas and Seth Joed walked toward him. "Yes, sir."

"Mr. Joed sent Seth to us to help with this year's crop. We must continue as usual if we plan to eat this winter."

"Yes, sir," Reedy said, lowering his eyes.

Reedy returned to picking the tobacco leaves closest to the ground and spearing them with a stick. He side-eyed Seth when the two men walked past, discussing the curing of the leaves.

"Father said the marketplace is changing. Vendors are selling their product on the street instead of in a warehouse—and without inspection."

Seth nodded. "Agreed. My father and I were discussing this change. Though, it will be a few years before it mainstreams into the streets of Alexandria."

Thomas disagreed. His father would disagree, also. Thomas was different from Seth. Seth was a university man.

Thomas had been working in the business for years alongside his father. The crop produced on their plantation was top quality, and the state inspectors confirmed it every harvest for the last decade. But without inspectors to assure quality, high prices could diminish sales. Thomas had had this conversation with his father several weeks ago.

Thomas and Seth inspected the rows of tobacco past Lars and Willy. Reedy could no longer hear the conversation but kept an eye on both boys. *Boys.* That's what they were, and without the guidance of Master James, things could go very wrong for him and the others.

Tilby and Simone cuddled under the blanket in the barn's garret. They were exhausted from the day's work of stringing leaves and hanging them to dry in the tobacco barn.

"It isn't fair," Simone said. "Thomas won't ever give us permission to marry."

Tilby wondered what Simone had overheard inside the house. Nobody told him anything. Only that Master died, but Charlotte and Simone were friends. Simone was bound to have news.

"Charlotte isn't herself. She's been carrying on for weeks, and I can't blame her. Her father was good to her. He was good to me a few times too. He brought us lemon drops once from New York."

"So nobody's talkin'?"

"Rachel says Ms. Rosalie is in charge and that Thomas is acting like he knows better than anyone. Rachel overheard Ms. Rosalie tell Thomas and Henry that their business would continue to prosper. But then Thomas said something about the leaves not being inspected at the market, so they should regard all leaves as saleable."

Simone looked into Tilby's eyes. She was happy to inform Tilby of what she knew. "Ms. Rosalie was mad like a rabid possum."

Tilby smiled. "Ms. Rosalie? Mad? Nah, not Ms. Rosalie."

Simone continued. "She said Thomas was never to produce anything but the best for selling. She would not have years of his father's work go in vain."

Tilby's eyes widened.

Simone continued. "When Ms. Rosalie says that to Thomas, Rachel whispers to Chloe and Hilda that Ms. Rosalie has it wrong. We are the ones producing the best tobacco out in that field."

"We sures is," Tilby said.

Simone settled in by Tilby's side.

"Simone?"

Simone watched the night sky through the window of the garret. "Hmm."

"We don't needs permission to marry. We love each other, don't we?"

"Mm-hm."

"Then let's confess we's love right now. Hold hands and say we is married."

Simone turned toward Tilby and stared. "I want to marry you, Tilby."

"And I's want the same."

"Should I be scared? What if we get sold away from each other? What if Thomas sells us south? Then what happens?"

"Thomas ain't in charge. And Ms. Rosalie—she gots a kindness in her."

"Can I ask you something, Tilby?"

"Sures."

"Rachel told me once that Ms. Rosalie was between two worlds, but when I asked Rachel what she meant, she couldn't explain it. But what she said makes sense to me, too, though I could never describe why. What do you think it means?"

"You and Rachel is the only two slaves on the whole plantation that can read, and if you ain't sures, I's ain't gonna know."

"But you agree?"

"I do. Ms. Rosalie is respectable but in a different way from Mister."

"What do you mean by that?" Simone asked curiously.

"Well, maybe I is wrong on Mister never sellin' us. My bet is Ms. Rosalie had her hands in it someway. Mister's a good man, but he's 'bout profits. If one of us ain't good for the business, then I's can't say what he'd do with us. Sell us, I's suppose. But Ms. Rosalie—I's gets the feelin' she wouldn't have it. She ain't so keen on thinkin' 'bout us as slaves. I's don't knows why I's thinks it like that, but I's do."

Tilby and Simone settled further under the blanket.

"So, we is husband and wife?" Tilby whispered.

"We won't be able to live together, Tilby. There's no other cabin we can move into; besides, we can't live together without Ms. Rosalie or Thomas noticing."

"Hows 'bout the shack down yonder, by the creek?"

"You call that livable?"

"I can fix it real nice."

Simone held onto Tilby. His skin was warm against the cool autumn air. The stars flickered in the blackness. Simone wanted more than anything to become Tilby's wife. She only needed to say the word, which she finally did, holding Tilby's gaze. Tilby rolled to his side and passionately kissed his bride.

19

Huntington Manor, Virginia 1840

Rosalie woke hours before dawn. Christmas without James was heavy-hearted, especially last evening. Caroling and decorating without him were the hardest. In the past, James led the singing of "Silent Night." This year, Rosalie and her children had muddled through.

Rosalie gave the slaves the week off. Reedy stared with wide eyes, like he hadn't heard correctly. Having two or three days to themselves at Christmastime was familiar, but a week was unusual.

Thomas had complained at the idea. "The tobacco needs to be stripped and sorted." He said to his mother, but Rosalie said it could wait a few extra days, to which Thomas replied that Father would never jeopardize the business in this way. Rosalie had scolded her son. Thomas was only doing what he thought was right—what Father would expect from him as the man of the house, and maybe he tried to avoid Christmas altogether—but Rosalie reminded Thomas that these were her decisions and she would not change her mind.

Rosalie held the curved railing as she descended the staircase. Her children were still sleeping, and possibly the house servants, too, because not a sound came from the kitchen. Christmas was a time for peace on earth, and with all the quiet this morning, Rosalie felt it.

She closed her coat around her and went to gather wood from the outside wood pile. Rosalie built a fire in the kitchen first because she assumed Hilda would rise soon and come down to the kitchen. The drawing room and parlor were next. Today, her children and the servants would wake to a warm house. Rosalie steeped hot tea, poured herself a cup, and entered the parlor.

The decorated Christmas tree stood in the corner of the room. She would light the candles when the children arose, but now she enjoyed the smell of fresh pine. Last night, she'd placed two gifts on the mantel—a new hat and mittens for Charlotte. And for Thomas and Henry, there was a chess board game. James had purchased it in New York on a business trip. Rosalie had asked him to save it for a Christmas gift. He'd agreed and said it would be a relaxing day of teaching the boys to play. It was hard to believe it had been three months since his death, and now her children would learn how to play the game through her teaching.

"James," Rosalie whispered into the silent room. "We miss you very much."

Rosalie sipped her tea. Mrs. Joed had invited her family for Christmas dinner, but Rosalie had politely declined. Today, after Christmas service, she and Charlotte would prepare a simple dinner. She'd regretted never teaching her daughter how to cook, like Mother had taught her, and there wasn't a better time than now. Charlotte was eager to learn when they first discussed it. She'd studied recipes from Hilda's cookbook, and she prepared a few meals in the last weeks with the help of Chloe. It had been a great distraction from James's absence.

Rosalie heard soft footsteps on the back staircase from the servant's quarters. Though it was still early, someone had woken upstairs and entered the kitchen. The servants would make their Christmas dinner earlier than her family.

Rosalie had told Hilda that she needed the kitchen by three, and she'd be much obliged if she and Charlotte could have the space at that time.

Rosalie heard the back kitchen door squeak open. She assumed Hilda or Chloe went outside, *but for what?* There were several water jugs in the kitchen. The barrel outside would perhaps be topped with a layer of ice. It had been cold, dropping below freezing for several days in the past week. Hilda could be gathering fire logs for later. Rosalie placed a warm blanket over her legs and stared at the blaze in the fireplace. At least, whoever ventured outside would return to a warm house.

Rosalie took another sip of tea. It had lost its steam and was lukewarm, but she didn't mind. It tasted better this way. She again thought of James. Her husband had finally agreed to discuss wages for the house servants and field hands before the next crop. James had died before he'd put anything into place, and now it was impossible. The well-being of her children and the business's success was her responsibility. Rosalie had no choice but to protect her family and ensure Huntington Manor could survive financially. She would not allow ruin to come to what she and James had built.

Simone took notice of the fireplace's warm glow when she crept through the kitchen. She figured Ms. Rosalie was in the house somewhere because she had left Rachel, Chloe, and Hilda upstairs sleeping. She tiptoed to the door, closed her coat, and entered the cold air. Scattered snowflakes drifted quietly to the ground in a serene background of a full moon and diminishing dark. It was a beautiful Christmas morning, but today she'd decided to face what she'd known for over a week.

Simone crept through the yard, entered the stable, and whispered into the dark. "Tilby. Tilby."

A soft glow came toward her. "O'er here, Simone."

Tilby held the lantern outstretched, letting it guide him to his wife. They met and kissed.

Simone smiled and held her husband close. Her belly would soon prove they truly belonged to each other. Simone feared Rosalie's reaction when she discovered her pregnancy. She would keep her growing belly secret until she couldn't—about four or five months, she figured. But for now, she was safe in Tilby's arms.

"Tilby," Simone said. "We don't have much time. Ms. Rosalie is awake in the house. The kitchen fire was going, and a pot of warm water was on the hearth. We don't want anyone to get suspicious."

Tilby raised his eyebrows. "Rachel knows 'bout us, and I's thinks Hilda and Chloe do too."

"They don't know that we are married, and Rachel—she'll call it unofficial and keep us apart for the rest of my life."

"She won't, Simone."

Simone pulled Tilby into the tack room. "Come. Hurry."

The small room where the saddles were kept and bridles and reins hung on nails was quieter and warmer than the rest of the stable and far enough from the horses to keep them quiet. Simone feared Summertime might greet her with a whinny when she entered the stable. Ms. Rosalie was awake in the house and would investigate any unusual noise.

Tilby detected Simone's urgency. "What, Simone?"

Simone let the situation spill into the room through a stutter. "I—I am with child."

Tilby stared, befuddled.

Simone's cheeks reddened from angst and the cold.

"We—we gonna have a baby?"

"We are in real trouble, Tilby. I can't have a baby. Nobody knows we're husband and wife. What if the baby gets sold? What if Ms. Rosalie says I can't keep it? I'll die. I will, Tilby." Simone covered her face with cupped hands. Her cheeks were wet with tears.

Tilby wrapped Simone in his arms. He tenderly hushed her. "We gots time before anyone knows you gots a baby in your belly. You sures you gots a baby?"

"As sure as the sun will rise."

"How?" Tilby stumbled for the second time tonight. "I mean—"

Simone interjected for Tilby's sake. "At least a month. I was supposed to bleed last week."

Tilby sat on a nearby bench and pulled Simone to sit beside him. Neither spoke for a moment.

"Are you happy or scared, Tilby?"

Tilby pulled Simone to his chest. "I suppose both. But mostly happy," he whispered.

Simone froze when she saw Ms. Rosalie's shadow cast on a wall from the dying fire inside. *What was she doing?* Simone worried. She'd been gone too long, and Ms. Rosalie must have discovered someone left the house and had not returned. It had only been twenty minutes, but that was long considering the early time. She quickly grabbed two logs for burning.

Rosalie went to the back door and opened it. She was sure she had heard someone leave but not return. Rosalie looked into the obscured outside. She saw a figure and called out. "Hello."

"It's me, ma'am. Simone."

"Simone? You've been out in this cold for some time. Is everything alright?"

"Yes, ma'am." Simone tried her hardest to sound confident and prayed to God her shaky voice would not reveal her panic. "I needed some wood for the fire. That's all."

As Simone walked closer, Rosalie saw Simone holding the logs. "Gathering two logs would not have taken so long."

"Sorry, ma'am," Simone said, quickly telling a fib and stumbling through it. "It's just that—it doesn't usually snow on Christmas." She needed another lie. "It looks pretty against the moon. I guess I got caught up in it."

"Well, come now. Get inside."

"Yes, ma'am," Simone said. She followed Charlotte's mother inside the kitchen.

Rosalie turned and looked at Simone before she left Simone to tend to the fire. "Happy Christmas, Simone."

"Happy Christmas, Ms. Rosalie."

20

Rosalie worked at the desk that sat near the bottom of the staircase. She reviewed the plantation's budget for the upcoming growing season. James's death had shortened Thomas's and Henry's childhood, and years of James's teachings allowed her boys to become business-savvy young men. Seth had stayed on until the first of the year before returning home, and within less than a half year that had painfully passed, her sons had managed the production of tobacco on their own.

This upcoming season would be the first her boys would manage without their father. The same went for Rosalie. She had taken over James's finances within weeks of his passing. She was meticulous about Huntington Manor and ran their business as her husband had, but this past year, she'd only finished what James had produced. The next crop, without James, would prove her success or failure.

Today, Rosalie sat at a small desk adjacent to the curved staircase. James seldom worked at this desk, but Rosalie enjoyed it here. The morning sun brightened the stunning curved staircase ascending to the second-floor landing, giving it a magnificent view of its beauty. Rosalie pulled the ledger from the desk's drawer. Laying it flat on the desk, she opened it and studied purchases and sales over the last few years. Their crop made a hearty net worth. Buyers trusted their tobacco at the market because James refused to sell leaves that produced less than the best quality even when unforeseen circumstances had nearly destroyed their crop. This promise had paid off. Solid buyers had sought out James Worthington's tobacco for years.

The cultivation of seedbeds happened in January. This second week in March, the tobacco seeds were ready for sowing. Rosalie had faith in her family to move forward without James, though it would be challenging. Thomas was well-versed in the business, but he was only seventeen.

Simone was oiling the staircase spindles when Rosalie glanced toward her from where she was seated. The sun shined brightly through a window above and onto Simone's dress. Rosalie noted the girl's protruding belly. Then Simone bent over, and her belly disappeared inside her draped dress. Rosalie was sure of what she saw because she had three children and knew the look of a swollen abdomen caused by a growing baby.

Rosalie called to Simone, who startled and turned around. Rosalie's voice hadn't been shocking, but Simone had not expected Rosalie to call her either. She'd oiled and polished this staircase many times and hadn't ever been summoned while Rosalie Worthington worked on the books.

Rosalie was concerned. "Come here, Simone."

"Yes, ma'am." Simone pushed the oiled rag into a pocket.

The two women stood a foot apart at the bottom of the staircase.

"What can I do for you, ma'am?" Simone said softly, trying to hide her alarm. She knew this moment would come, but it should have been another month before anyone noticed her growing abdomen, and she thought Charlotte would see it first.

"Are you with child?" Rosalie asked.

If there were a prayer Simone could recite to keep her standing upright, she would pray it, but her mind fell blank.

"Simone," Rosalie said curtly. "Are you going to have a baby?"

"Ma'am." *Oh, Lord.* She couldn't get the words out.

Rosalie had not meant to scare the girl, but if someone on this plantation had forced their way with her, Rosalie would make sure they were gone by dusk. She used a softer voice. "Simone. Do not be frightened, but tell me, who did this to you?"

"W-we did it together," she stammered. "We love each other."

Men and women lived here, in and around this house, but for some unknown reason, Rosalie had not considered that love had made Simone's unborn child. Simone would turn nineteen next month. She was no longer a little girl.

Simone stood there, contemplating what to say, when she finally spat out the truth. "I love him, ma'am."

"Who?" Rosalie replied.

Simone's eyes looked to the floor. "Please, Ms. Rosalie, don't send him away."

"I'd have no reason to send anyone away if what you've told me is true. But let me remind you, Simone, you are not united in marriage."

There was silence. Rosalie was not going to stand here much longer without an answer. "Simone," she said. "I don't condone getting pregnant before marriage, but what is done is done. Being a mother is a tremendous responsibility."

"Black babies are taken from their parents and sold. It's true, Ms. Rosalie," Simone's voice cracked, "because it happened to me. A man pulled me from my mama's arms. She was screaming and throwing a terrible fuss until—"

Simone covered her mouth and gasped. "Ma'am, forgive me. I should keep quiet."

Simone went weak in the knees. Rosalie caught Simone by the arm and eased the girl onto a step of the staircase. Simone had refused to speak of her life before Huntington Manor. Shortly after she arrived, she gravitated to Charlotte like a bee to sweet water. Rosalie remembered trying to get details from the little girl, but Simone had refused to say a word about anything.

Rosalie was genuinely concerned for Simone. The girl had grown into a beautiful young woman, but now, there was an intensity to this woman that Rosalie had never noticed before today. "Dear child. What happened?"

Simone patted her heart. "My mama is here, but I can barely remember what she looks like." Simone cupped her face and wept.

Rosalie could do little to comfort the girl. She'd let that job fall on the older servants. It was wrong. There simply were no words to express how sorry she was.

Simone held out long enough. She must know right this minute. "Can I keep my baby, Ms. Rosalie? I will die if my baby and I can't be together."

Rosalie gently took hold of Simone's arms and held her firmly at arm's length. James was gone. Huntington Manor was her plantation. She could not let foolish emotions take hold, or there would be chaos on these fields and in this house. She was sorry for Simone and ashamed of herself, but now was not the time for feebleness.

"Simone, don't go getting yourself into a downright tizzy. I've known you since you were a little girl. You will keep this child, but I insist you tell me the father's name."

Simone lifted her eyes. "It's Tilby. We professed our love for each other before making a baby. I promise we did."

Charlotte was upstairs, waking from an afternoon nap, when she heard crying. Approaching the staircase and following the cries, she saw her mother and Simone on the floor at the bottom. "Mother! Simone, what's happened?" she screeched and stumbled toward them, hanging onto the railing to stop herself from flying. Charlotte's panic lessened when she saw Simone and Mother on the third stair, not the floor as it had appeared.

"We are fine, darling," Rosalie said.

"Well, what on earth are you doing? You both nearly scared me to death."

"Simone has told me some interesting news that I guess you are already aware of." Rosalie stood and straightened her skirt. Her daughter's confused look took her aback.

Simone stood and faced her friend. "I'm going to have a baby."

Charlotte stood frozen. How was she supposed to react? She suspected it was Tilby's. The two had been lovebirds for far too long not to notice, but how did her mother know of this pregnancy before she had? She and Simone were best friends. Why hadn't Simone told her? "Simone—." Charlotte wanted to ask a question, but her mind went blank.

Rosalie kindly interjected. "Your friend is well. There is more to discuss, but it can wait."

Rosalie left the two girls. She needed a moment before venturing to the barn to speak with Tilby.

Charlotte shrieked in surprise when her mother was not within earshot. "A baby! Why didn't you tell me?" Charlotte did not wait for her friend's reply. "I'm going to be an auntie, and you a mama."

Simone saw how happy Charlotte was, but being an enslaved mother called for angst, not happiness.

"What's wrong, Simone?" Charlotte asked her friend. "You'll be alright. I promise. We're in this together."

Simone nodded weakly.

Charlotte tried to ease Simone's worried look. "What will you name your baby?"

"Well, if it's a boy, I'm naming him after Tilby. And if it's a girl, I'll call her Hanah. That was my mother's name."

"Hanah," Charlotte repeated. "It's a beautiful name. Simone? Why didn't you tell me? I would have been happy for you."

Simone hadn't told Charlotte of the baby or that she and Tilby promised their love for only each other. Charlotte was her best friend, but their differences were too many to say everything she wanted. Charlotte had an upbringing that was a world apart from hers. Simone took notice of these differences because white folks could strip Black people of any privilege, no matter how small, and at any time, unlike Charlotte. It wasn't her friend's fault. It was just the way it was.

Simone looked at her friend. Charlotte had always been good to her, and they had told each other almost everything for the last ten years. If anyone had ever said they would become friends, they might not have believed it, but they were.

Simone was overwhelmed by sadness.

"What is it, Simone?"

When Simone didn't answer, Charlotte took her friend's hand. "Simone, I may live in a big house and have nice dresses and the opportunity to learn how to read and write, but since the day I met you, we have been more alike than any other two people. I don't talk about how it's different for us because what could I say? How could I explain except to admit I was raised a certain way? It sounds like an awful excuse, and I didn't want to use it. But my father's death forced a new awareness for me. We are so similar and treated very differently, which isn't right. I love my mother and would do anything for my brothers, but I also cherish our friendship. I want to make this right, Simone. I do. I am unsure how, but I will always be your friend. And I hope that you will be mine."

Simone wanted to speak, but she could not. Heavy tears dropped from her chin.

"Don't cry. It's alright that you didn't tell me."

"Tilby is the father. We're married. I'm sorry, Charlotte, for not telling you before today."

"You did nothing wrong, Simone. It was your secret, and I tried to expose you and Tilby. I am the one who should be apologizing." Charlotte smiled, "Let's make things right."

"How?" Simone asked, wiping tears from her face.

"You should not live upstairs away from Tilby, and Tilby should not live in the cabin with the men. You and Tilby need a house to call your own and raise a baby."

"I have an idea," Simone said.

"What is it?"

"The cabin by the creek. We could live there. If it's alright with your mother."

Charlotte furrowed her eyebrows. "That's barely held together with planks of wood. You would freeze in the wintertime. Even a spring day like today is chilly."

Simone's excitement bubbled, picturing the possibilities. "Tilby can fix anything, Charlotte. And he can make the repairs before the baby arrives. It would be so nice to raise our child together."

Charlotte was pleased. "Well then, I guess it's settled. I'll talk to Mother and make sure that Thomas gets the materials needed."

The two girls hugged.

"Now, let's go to the creek and see what needs fixing."

"Thank you, Charlotte. You've been such a good friend to me."

"And you for me, Simone."

21

In the early evening, Rosalie strolled to the barn. Simone torn from her mother's arms was an image Rosalie could not dislodge from her brain. She saw how other slave owners had beaten their slaves, which disgusted her and James. James had never used a whip. Her sons were required to work in the tobacco fields. "There is no job a man can't do," James had told them more than once. "Working the fields amongst the slaves will allow you to know what your slave is capable of."

Running the plantation hadn't been easy for Rosalie, but there was no other choice. Thomas and Henry were mature teen boys. Their father had prepared them well by working and harvesting on a plantation, but owning land differed. All three of Rosalie's children were well-educated but still needed guidance. Business connections respected her son's hard work. Still, Rosalie's savvy business mind got them through, and now, with another growing season, other factors crept back into her consciousness with James gone. She could no longer redirect her guilt of owning slaves onto the decisions of her late husband.

She'd never wanted to own slaves.

James had saved the skins of men, women, and children from a horrific alternative when he purchased them, but had that been enough? Could James turn his back on an entire race if he saved a few? James was a kind man, and Rosalie loved him, but she and James offered these people nothing if they turned their backs on the reality of what was happening down the road at the next plantation or in town at the jailhouse. James had taught their children to work alongside enslaved people to know their value, *but what came next?*

Loo Loo, Hilda's little sister, was an example of the horrors of slavery. Simone was another. Simone's fear of being separated from her baby was real. The kindness that she and James had shown to their slaves stood for very little. Hilda and the others still regarded themselves as property because it was precisely what they were. The third example Rosalie conjured in minutes was the back-breaking work of their slaves, and they had not a penny to show for it. There was so much to do, and exactly how Rosalie would work it out was beyond any solution for the time, but something had to change.

Rosalie approached the barn. She deferred her thoughts for now. She was in charge of this plantation, and she would not appear any less than a leader.

Tilby pitched hay down from the garret. His forehead beaded with sweat, though the evening air was brisk, on the brink of a possible frost by dawn. Tilby worked feverishly to finish before heading to the cabin for supper. Sweat soaked the bandana wrapped on his head. He took a rag from his elongated pocket and wiped the sweat from his face.

Rosalie stood at the barn's open door with the descending sun behind her. Her face was shapely, with high cheekbones and a sharp jawline. Rouge lightly coated the sides of her face and rose colored her soft lips. Rosalie kept her brunette hair gracefully swept back into a low knot on the back of her neck. Wisps of curls left unbound bounced freely near her shoulders. She wore a simple black dress. Five small buttons streamed down the middle; the skirt flared large pleats. Rosalie had worn a black hat and veil once, on the day James was buried, out of respect for her husband. But here on the plantation, she'd seen no sense in wearing it.

In a tone that commanded respect but without threat, Rosalie told Tilby she needed to speak with him.

Tilby descended the ladder and walked over the dirt floor strewn with straw. Simone's pregnancy worried him. "Ma'am," he said, lowering his eyes.

Tilby stood six feet and some inches tall, but his head hung low. Having a mid-five-foot stature compared to such a tall man, Rosalie could see Tilby's sad face and worried look.

Rosalie kept an even tone. "Are you the father of Simone's child?"

Tilby shifted his head slightly. "Yes, ma'am. I is. I's beg you, ma'am." Tilby's pleading eyes made contact with Rosalie's. "Please lets Simone keep her baby."

"This baby will need care and supervision."

"Yes, ma'am."

"This is a tremendous responsibility, Tilby. How do you and Simone expect to manage a child and work?"

"I promise, ma'am. I's love that sweet little thing. If he be a boy, I's teach him how to be a good worker."

"You will, Tilby. You've never let Mr. Worthington or me down. You've been an advantage to Huntington Manor. You and Simone and your baby are safe here. There is no reason for alarm."

Tilby nodded graciously.

Rosalie turned to leave. Looking at the main house from where she stood, she couldn't help but think of many things. It was where she and James had raised their children. Fond memories filled the rooms. Rosalie taught reading and arithmetic to her children on the veranda on lovely mornings. Charlotte, Simone, and the boys had played in the yard, chasing and tagging one another. They had all matured so quickly.

She wondered how James would have handled the news of Simone's pregnancy. He would have accepted the situation, but James would have considered the Negro baby another slave he owned. It wasn't an unfair justice to James. It simply was the way it was. He was raised this way. Her father, on the other hand, despised slavery. Rosalie was trapped in between.

Rosalie's father forbade Rosalie to marry a slave owner's son and only changed his mind after realizing James was young and impressionable. Her father had believed he could change the course of James's reasoning for owning slaves versus hired help. And he had, but the death of James's father returned James to his roots, unraveling agreements for a different life. Rosalie supposed the only saving grace was that her father died believing she and James had kept their promise. In truth, it hadn't fixed Rosalie's struggle with the deception she felt.

She hadn't told untruths, Rosalie justified. Huntington Manor was not different from any other Virginia plantation regarding owning slaves. Sure, her father had employed colored people, treated them kindly, and had taught her and her sister Sarah that Negroes deserved respect as any fellow man, but not once had she seen her mother or father share a meal with a Negro or pray at the same church.

Rosalie approached the steps to the front of the house. She turned and looked past the darkening fields. The first stars were glimmering. The fact that she'd defended James's position years ago had been a truth she'd pushed from her mind. Simone's and Tilby's pleading had brought it to the forefront. Instead of celebrating the upcoming birth of their child, Simone and Tilby begged to spare their baby from separation and outside treachery.

What kind of person was she if a Negro man and woman feared the birth of their child? Did the color of his skin make Tilby less of a man? Less of a father? Simone, less of a mother? Was this the thinking of slave owners? But what could she do? She was responsible for all of this. Rosalie looked out into the silhouetted land. Huntington Manor could not profit without the slaves, and still she knew a change needed to happen. *But what?*

In the distance, she saw a dark shadow. By the tall stature, Rosalie assumed it was Tilby walking across the field toward the cabin after a long day of work. He'd have supper with the other men instead of inside the tiny back kitchen where the women ate. Rosalie and James hadn't forced this meal separation; the slaves had. Chloe and Hilda liked to eat in the small back kitchen. After Rachel and Simone arrived, they'd known nothing but eating and sleeping in quarters inside the main house. James's death left Rosalie lonely. She wondered if Tilby felt the same about living separate from Simone.

Tilby had long disappeared into his small home. Chill took hold of Rosalie. She turned, climbed the stairs, and went inside.

22

Huntington Manor, Virginia 1841

"Oh, my Lord." Rachel fell to the bed. She would have fallen to the floor if the bed hadn't been behind her.

Rachel called from where she sat. "Chloe. Hilda. Please come in here now."

Simone stood confident, but she couldn't stop her hands from quivering.

Chloe entered the room first. "What's this about?" she said.

Hilda wore a frown. "My eyelids were about to close. What's so important it couldn't wait until morning?"

Rachel scolded. "Pipe down, Hilda. Simone's got somethin' to say, and we need to listen real good."

Simone nervously stood in the bedroom with Hilda and Chloe staring at her, waiting.

Hilda was impatient. "Well, go on. I need my sleep, and your hesitation won't stop the sun from rising."

"Pay no attention to her," Chloe said of Hilda's brashness. "You be in trouble, Simone?"

Simone stumbled. "Tilby and me are married. I didn't tell you because we promised ourselves to each other, me and Tilby. And it was only for us."

The words were difficult for Simone, and she had yet to get the most challenging part of this conversation into the open. It didn't help that Rachel was eyeing her to move her story forward.

"Promising yourself to a young fellow don't mean you're married," Hilda said. "That thinking can get you into some real trouble, Simone." Hilda turned on Rachel. "Don't you take care of things like this? Simone should know what kind of trouble comes from a man who promises all sorts of things without even jumping the broom."

"Blazes Hilda." Simone cursed.

The three women stared. Simone didn't curse, no matter how angry she sometimes got.

Simone huffed. "Tilby is kind and sweet, and you know it. Me and Tilby are married, so you better get used to the idea. We did it right after Mister passed. Tilby was going to ask Mister to make it official, but he died."

The silent attention was staggering, and it wasn't about to improve with what Simone was about to say.

"But that's not the news I wanted to share."

Hilda's exasperation was growing. "Well, then. What are you holding back?"

"I'm having a baby. In August."

"Oh, Simone. What if—." Chloe put her hand over her mouth after a gasp, unable to continue speaking.

"What if what?" Hilda spewed, annoyed with Chloe's reaction.

"What if the baby be taken from her?"

Simone let out a cry. Her knees buckled. *Should she have believed Ms. Rosalie's word?*

"Before feathers get all ruffled," Rachel said, trying to disarm the tense situation.

Hilda interrupted before Rachel could finish. "I ain't got ruffled feathers. And I don't take kindly to you insinuating I do."

"What I meant to say—."

"You meant what you said," Hilda interjected.

Simone's eyes moistened. "Don't blame Rachel for speaking her mind."

"I'm not blaming anyone," Hilda said. "It's about time we have a youngling to bring some life into this place. And Simone—you'll find it best to stop all the sniffling and blubbering. You don't want your baby thinking she's got a babbling brook for a mama."

Simone, Chloe, and Rachel stared at Hilda.

"Didn't expect that from me by the looks of you— mouths hanging, like I'd gone and burst into flames or something worse."

Chloe was baffled. "None of us be expectin' it for sure."

Hilda asked Rachel. "How long have you and Simone been here now?"

"Eleven years real soon."

"Well, I've been here long before Ms. Rosalie, and I'm saying so long as that woman is running this house, Simone's baby is staying put."

Simone was not convinced. A man stole her right from her mama's arms. "How can you know for sure?"

Hilda looked at all three women in front of her. She spent most of her life avoiding friendships because she understood the pain when evil came for a loved one, how the hurt was unbearable. Hilda had seen Loo Loo in Simone when the little girl arrived at Huntington Manor. She'd wanted to take Simone into her arms and squeeze her with love, and dry her tears, but she knew what that kind of love could do to a person.

She'd come to Huntington Manor with her mama when she was five. Her sister Loo Loo was three. No other slave on this plantation knew of her mama, except Lars. Hilda kept Loo Loo for herself for all this time.

Simone spoke. "Hilda. Are you feeling alright?"

"That's all I'm saying, Simone. You'll keep your baby. Nobody's getting sent away if that's got you worried."

"But how—"

Hilda interrupted the girl, "Because I've grown old here."

Hilda took a step further into the room. "Sit down. I've got something to say, and I ain't going to say it twice."

Chloe and Simone sat on one bed. Hilda sat next to Rachel on the other bed. "I owe you something, Simone. You needed your mother when you got here, and I didn't bother with you much. I left the responsibility to Rachel because she needed you. You needed each other." Hilda looked at Rachel. "But you were young, and I should have known better than to leave you with such work."

Hilda took a moment before speaking. Simone needed solid facts proving she and her baby would be safe from separation, and the only way to make it real was to start from the beginning. Hilda could do this. *She must do this.*

"Me and my mama got purchased by Senior James when I was about twelve. Master James was a boy, maybe four or five. My job was to make sure James stayed out of mischief. It was no easy task because he was always into something he shouldn't be into. His older sisters were sweet as peach pie, but young Master James was a real handful. But even with all that mischief inside him, Mama said something was different about that boy. Said he had a genuine goodness in him that she ain't never seen in a white boy before. I couldn't sense it when I was young and running after him all the time, but the truth is, I grew fond of the boy."

Hilda shook her head. "It's hard to believe they are both dead now. Father and son, both gone so young."

Hilda looked at the faces following her every word.

Chloe said in disbelief. "Your mother? She be here on this plantation and I ain't know?"

"Cuz I never told you, Chloe."

"But I be workin' here all these years with you. It ain't right.

"Maybe so, but you're hearing it now, and that's all that matters."

Simone was desperate for the truth. "Chloe. Please. Let Hilda finish."

Hilda's shoulders sank. "I had a sister too." Hilda looked at Chloe. Her eyes softened. "You're hearing about her now. Only this one time."

Chloe and the other two nodded.

"Me, Mama, and Loo Loo lived in Mississippi picking cotton for Ol' Jacobs." Hilda looked down and shook her head. "May God have mercy on that man's soul before the devil takes him to hell.

"We had a bad life, and Ol' Jacobs made it worse, standing over me and Mama, kicking us, telling us we were lazy whores. So one day, Mama woke Loo Loo and me and told us to get out of bed without making a noise. We followed Mama's heels until Loo Loo tripped and stumbled to the floor, knocking a pan from its place.

"You can figure out how that played out. Ol' Jacobs caught us less than ten feet from the door. My mama swore she was only taking us to relieve ourselves, but that devil of a man chained her to a tree and whipped her unconscious. He came after me, and I took six lashes, and poor little Loo Loo took three for the number of years she was on this earth. That was Ol' Jacobs's reasoning."

"Poor little Loo," Hilda moaned. "She did nothing wrong but love Mama and me.

"Months later, Ol' Jacobs drug all three of us to auction to get us sold. When the time came, a white man pulled Mama and me from the jail cell to face our fate. Mama cried and begged that Loo Loo be with us—she said Loo Loo was too young to be alone. She pleaded like I had never heard no one beg in my life—on her knees, looking like a starving dog. And that man went and smacked her and told her to shut up. My mama didn't, though. She got right back to her knees and kept begging. That ugly man was going to smack Mama again, but another man caught that man's arm and told him to leave Mama be. He had a ring of keys that jingled, and I swear it was the sweetest sound I ever did hear.

"Mama could sense the man's kindness. She looked into his eyes and pleaded for Loo Loo, giving it everything. He told Mama a nice lady already bought Loo Loo, and he couldn't help her."

Hilda swallowed hard and tightly pursed her lips to keep from crying a river of tears. "Mama hung on to those words for the rest of her life."

Silent tears ran down the faces of the three women listening to Hilda's story. Rachel sniffled and pulled a cloth from her pocket.

"I've taken the roundabout way to answer your question, Simone, but you should hear the whole story. It's the only way to ease your mind."

Simone nodded and sniffled.

"For the next many years, Mama and me imagined Loo Loo living her best life, like baking a cake or making a nice soup. We imagined the loveliest lady in all the land who took her in and cared for her. One day, Master James enters the kitchen and overhears us talking about Loo Loo. Master James was about nineteen, or maybe a bit older. You see," Hilda said," "He'd been gone for months, living in Syracuse, working for the father of a girl he'd fallen in love with and told me more than once he was going to marry her. We didn't even know he was in the house, let alone in the kitchen."

"Ms. Rosalie," Simone whispered. She hadn't meant to say it aloud, but it had escaped her.

"Yes," Hilda said. "Rosalie Farnsworth was the girl from Syracuse.

"So James had come home for a short visit, and he was coming into the kitchen to say hello and to ask Mama if she could make his favorite onion soup. He overheard us talking and asked who was Loo Loo. He said he liked the sound of it like words in a song or something like that. At first, my mama and I were shocked. We never talked about Loo to nobody. Mama said she was our secret until we found her and were together again. I didn't believe in miracles, but Mama did, and I wanted her to keep on believing

"Master James was waiting for an answer, so I finally told him. Then, Master James asked Mama if she wanted to know where Loo Loo was. It sounds so foolish of a question, but Master James was young then. He said people remembered names like Loo Loo's.

"Master James came to me first when he got word about Loo."

Rachel, Simone, and Chloe hadn't needed confirmation of Loo Loo's death. Hilda's face showed them.

"She be in Heaven now," Chloe said. "And I be guessin' your Mama too since I never did saw her."

"Mama died two months later. The man with all them keys lied about Loo being sold to a nice lady. Mama believed the jail cell's mold grabbed Loo Loo's little lungs after nobody wanted an extra mouth to feed. Mama and me had been living a decent life here, and little Loo never saw daylight again. Mama slipped away after that. I think all that pretending buckled inside her. I prayed to God to take Mama's grief from her, but he took her body instead. Mama came down with something, letting it grab hold like that nasty mold did to Loo Loo.

"Senior master called for the doctor, but Mama would have none of the doctor's medicine or my nursing. She lay in bed for four days, staring at the ceiling and growing weaker. I climbed into bed next to Mama each night and held her tight. I listened for every breath, and it stopped just like that. Mama didn't groan or fight or have last words. She slipped into the night and was gone."

Hilda gave herself a moment, and in doing so, she heard Rachel whimper and Simone sob. She must continue, so she did.

"Master James got word Mama was dying and traveled home only in time for her burial. We stood there, Lars, Senior and Mrs. and Master James, watching Mama lowered into the ground. Then the oddest thing," Hilda said, wiping a lone tear. "Master James put his arm around me and let me cry. Men shoveled dirt on top of my Mama's box. I was thirty years old, and I suppose Mama was right about all that genuine goodness she said Master James had inside him.

"Before Master James was about to return to Syracuse, he told his father he would marry Rosalie and stay in Syracuse working for Ms. Rosalie's father—for some construction business or something like that. Senior James was hopping mad and forbade Master James to go—said he couldn't manage the plantation alone, but Master James would have none of his father's bullying." Hilda smiled, "That boy was in love from here to Canada. He walked like there was air under his shoes—and a smile a mile wide."

"What happened," Simone said. "What changed Mister's mind? Why'd he come back?"

"Senior James had himself a heart attack right in the middle of the tobacco, so Master James came back with his new wife to run the plantation."

"But my baby," Simone said weakly to Hilda. "If it's because you say Mister had genuine goodness, he isn't here anymore."

"No," Hilda interjected. "It's not Master James. He was a good man, but he was a businessman. And I been here long enough to know he has got his father's mind for growing and selling tobacco. The plantation was far smaller when I arrived. Three other fellows who ain't here no longer worked it. Mama and I cared for the house and kitchen like Chloe and me do now. But Master James, when he came back, his head was for business."

"Then how—"

Hilda stopped Simone. "It was Ms. Rosalie. She was the change. I'll admit, she's a hard nut to crack. When she got here, she barely said two words to me. If our eyes met, she looked the other way, like I had a bad omen about me or something worse. But eventually, she kindly asked me to bring her tea or a coat, always saying please and thank you. If I'm being honest, it spooked me.

"Then, one day, I'm in the nursery getting ready for Ms. Rosalie's baby coming—baby Charlotte—that's the baby who was growing inside her—and Ms. Rosalie enters the room and says she's sorry about my mother's passing.

"I didn't know what to think, so I went about dusting, but before Ms. Rosalie turned to leave, she said my name. 'Hilda,' she says. I turned to look at her. I wasn't spooked this time because there was a kindness in those eyes I could never forget. Can't say I ever saw it again—not in that way—but it was there, and I know it still is."

"Did she say somethin'?" Rachel asked.

Hilda looked out the window. The dark sky held millions of twinkling stars. She looked at her friends—that's what they were—friends. Before now, she hadn't wanted to admit it, but at a half-century old, it was darn time she did. So long as Ms. Rosalie was here, she and the others weren't going anywhere.

Hilda's eyes glistened with tears. She swallowed hard. "Ms. Rosalie says, 'And Loo Loo too. Your mother was deprived of her youngest child. She didn't deserve to suffer such a burden—no mother does.'"

Hilda gazed at Simone sitting across from her on the opposite bed. "Simone, Ms. Rosalie won't separate you from your baby. You'll stay right here and raise that little thing. I swear on Mama's grave."

Chloe did not like Hilda making one-sided promises. "Swear on your mother's grave? How can you be sayin' such things, Hilda?"

Hilda took unkindly to Chloe's accusation. "Am I the only one who notices things around here?"

"What is it?" Simone said, hurrying Hilda.

"I can't be sure, but things changed when Ms. Rosalie came to Huntington Manor. I noticed every one of you got here when Master James came across real grief, like he was trying to save us slaves or something. Tilby was half dead. Simone and Rachel were chained together and mistreated. Willy was nearly hanged."

Chloe quickly interjected. "But we all mistreated, Hilda. Every single last one of us be. Maybe we ain't be hit with a stick, but we slaves."

"I know that, don't you think? But it's different. Since Ms. Rosalie got here, not a single slave has been sold. And if I'm being honest, I don't believe she wanted any of us bought. I got the feeling she'd be fine without us. The fact none of us have been carted away says something."

"There ain't no right situation," Chloe said. "I don't care what you be sayin'. I'm grateful I haven't ever seen a whip here, but if Ms. Rosalie and her boys fall into bad times, we all in trouble. None of us ever be safe, Hilda, and fillin' Simone's head with such nonsense ain't right."

Chloe had reasons for what she was spurting. "How you be sittin' there knowin' of my mama and how she watchin' her children sold in a week's time? One week," Chloe erupted louder. "Our life be not great, but we had each other until our master goes and dies and his chil'n sell us all. My mama cried and shook so hard, it be hurtin' just to think it. It be a pain that never heals, but I be holdin' Mama in my arms anyway and told her everythin' be alright, just like you be spoutin' to Simone. But you know it, Hilda—it was horrid. Nothin' in this world ever gonna be alright. I lost my entire family in a week, and none of them went without cryin' and hurtin'."

Simone sobbed. Rachel tried to comfort her.

Chloe realized what she'd done, but the words had come so fast and furious. She felt ashamed to scare her friend so horribly, but it was true. "I be sorry, Simone. I pray you be able to keep your baby. I do." Chloe got up and returned to her room.

Hilda held Simone's hand. "Listen to me, Simone. I swear on my mother's grave."

23

Huntington Manor, Virginia 1841

It was hot already for an early June morning. Rosalie woke but lay in bed. There was the budget to balance and chores to complete, yet she couldn't pull herself from under the thin blanket that covered her. She and James were married on this day twenty-one years ago. James never forgot—not once. He'd wake, gently kiss her on the cheek and remind her how long they'd been married.

Loneliness filled Rosalie's heart. She needed to get up and busy herself. The men would already be working in the field, *and Thomas*, she thought, had taken on so much responsibility. He was certainly in the field inspecting the tobacco. Thomas yearned to emulate his father, but Thomas differed from her husband. He was a hard worker like his father—and respectable, but he lacked James's charismatic personality. Henry was more like James than Thomas, and it came so naturally for her younger son. There was no doubt Thomas would someday run Huntington Manor like James, but Thomas would have to work harder at it.

Rosalie sighed. Charlotte hadn't come to see what was keeping her. Though, these days, her daughter was fascinated with Simone's pregnancy. Sometimes, she checked on the girl in the late evening and early morning, ensuring Simone's comfort and health. Perhaps, Charlotte was with Simone now—in the kitchen talking about baby names or the progress on the new cabin. Tilby had plenty of work besides fixing up his and Simone's new home, and Rosalie doubted Tilby would finish it before the baby arrived.

Rosalie worried about the birth. She'd seen Dr. Bishop in town and told him she'd send Henry when the baby came. He slightly frowned and told her not to worry, "Negroes have been birthing babies for a thousand years." It was an odd statement, and Rosalie questioned if she should call upon Dr. Clay instead. He'd been to the plantation for Lars and Tilby, but it was Dr. Bishop who they'd relied on for James.

James hadn't kept his promise about enslaving Negroes, but there had been some changes that Rosalie was grateful for, and one of those changes was sending for the doctor if one of the men or women of the plantation were ill. It was uncommon for a plantation owner to spend good money on their enslaved workers, but Rosalie had asserted herself to her husband, and James had adhered to her request. Now she wondered why James had called on Dr. Clay for the Negroes instead of Dr. Bishop.

Rosalie sat up, moved her legs off the bed, and planted her feet on the cool wood floor. She took the diamond ring from the bedside table and slipped it on her finger. Prisms spread over the wall. The ring was such a simple yet complex reminder of who her husband was. Gentle and yet shrewd.

Rosalie dressed, exited her bedroom, and descended the curved staircase. Thomas was in the field. Henry was there, too, working alongside Reedy. The plantation thrived on the labor of the men and women who cultivated, cured, and processed the crop. The business, and her family, could have been lost without them. They deserved compensation. She'd worked on James for years. They'd been so close to employing their slaves before he passed on. Rosalie was left with guilt, but things had to stay the way they were until she was sure her family was safe from losing everything.

As Rosalie got closer to the kitchen, she heard Charlotte and Simone. She admired her daughter for the love she showed toward all people. Charlotte was so much like her sister, Sarah. Rosalie and Sarah had always been close sisters. During sleepless nights, Rosalie thought of Sarah and their lives together in Syracuse with their parents. When Rosalie first moved to Virginia after James's father's death, she and Sarah had corresponded often. Still, eventually, letters got few and far between because Rosalie had grown weary of writing half-truths.

In response to one of her mother's letters, Rosalie wrote that she and James had employed workers to help with the crop. Rosalie told herself it hadn't been a lie. James had occasionally hired men from town when there hadn't been enough slaves on the plantation to ensure the crop's health, especially during seasons of drought. The tobacco would have died if not for hiring extra men to help with watering the crop. Rosalie had wondered what the slaves had been thinking. It must have been awful to see white men get paid for the back-breaking work they did every day. The same angst she felt when she wrote to her mother returned now, as it had many times over the years. Her parents would have been disappointed in the life she lived.

Rosalie left Charlotte conversing with Simone and went outside to wait for her daughter, where they'd eat breakfast together before beginning their daily chores. Her children had quickly grown into adults after their father's death. She was proud of who they'd become in such adversity. It was these undertakings Rosalie told Sarah in letters now. Since James's death, Rosalie and her sister reconnected through correspondence.

Rosalie sat in a chair on the front porch and looked out over the plantation. After she and James were married, she'd called this place home, but it never felt right to Rosalie. It belonged to James and her children, but something perpetually was out of reach for her.

"There you are," Charlotte said upon seeing her mother. "I apologize, Mother, but you won't believe this? I felt the baby kick inside Simone's belly. It makes it so real."

Charlotte sat at the table opposite her mother.

Rosalie wanted to support her daughter's enthusiasm. "Is Simone excited about the birth?"

Charlotte smiled. "Mother, how nice of you to ask. She's terrified, but Chloe's mother birthed eight babies, and there was nothing to it." Charlotte raised in her chair and lifted her brows. "Mother. Did you know that Chloe had so many siblings?"

It was precisely what Rosalie was thinking. It reminded her how little she knew of the people who gave her family so much.

Charlotte hadn't waited for an answer. "Well, I had no idea, but I told Chloe I'd like to learn more about her family someday." Charlotte sat back, more relaxed than a moment ago. "She didn't respond, though."

"Let her come to you, darling. When she's ready."

Charlotte agreed but considered doing the exact opposite.

The two sat quietly, listening to the sounds of the cicadas growing louder in the day's rising temperature. Rosalie knew the risks of childbirth, but for the sake of Simone and her child, she hoped what Chloe told Simone was right.

24

Charlotte was washing floors for Simone. Simone rested on the second step to the bottom of the staircase. She tired quickly from the baby growing inside her.

"I shouldn't be letting you help, Charlotte. Rachel will go mad if she discovers you're doing my work." Simone pursed her lips and lifted her brows with wide eyes, "and your mother—" Simone stopped herself. "I don't think either will find it proper."

"Stop, Simone. Everyone is in the field, and Mother and Thomas are in town. Anyway, I offered, and I want to help. Nobody's getting in trouble."

Simone's belly was the size of a watermelon, and washing floors on her hands and knees was hard on her back. She tried to be comfortable on the step, but with the baby's every movement, it was difficult to get comfortable anywhere—this hard surface was worse.

"Remember we used to slide down this railing?" Simone said, leaning against the spindles.

Charlotte sat back on her heels, a scrub brush dripping water from her hand. "It was so much fun, Simone. Remember, we tricked Rachel and used our dresses as dust rags."

Simone laughed. "I sure do, but Rachel caught on when she found dust in the corners."

Charlotte grinned. "True, but we got away with it long before she discovered our deceit. And then Mother scolded me. We weren't allowed to catch fireflies the night she found out. But we had our fun and used our dresses again."

"How about when we fooled your brothers by putting currants in their beds."

Both girls laughed. Charlotte said. "They deserved it."

Charlotte leaned forward, dipped the brush in the soapy water, and continued scrubbing but quickly sat back on her heels. "I think our best prank was on Tilby."

Simone's smile widened. "There was flour everywhere. He was coughing powder plumes for days."

"Was he?"

Simone nodded, a huge grin blossoming.

"We have so many good memories."

"My favorite," Simone said, "Was reading *The Legend of Sleepy Hollow* in the garret. Remember how scared we were? We ran like wildfire back to the house. I don't think I ever told you, but I had to sleep with Rachel for a week after reading that book."

"You did not."

"I did. Cross my heart."

The baby moved. Simone grunted and held her stomach.

"He's an active baby," Charlotte said.

"He or she," Simone corrected light-heartedly.

"What do you think it is?"

"A girl." Simone hoped it was a girl so they could spend their lives together. She was afraid if it was a boy, he'd be put to work in the fields too young.

"Me too," Charlotte said. She moved the bucket and cleaned another patch of the floor. She sweated on this hot July day and wondered how Simone had managed to carry an extra twenty pounds for so long.

"It looks nice."

"Not as nice when you wash it, but nobody will complain."

"Charlotte. Can I ask you a question?"

Charlotte gave a silly face. "We're friends, Simone. Best friends. Remember? Kindred spirits. You can ask me anything."

"How did you know Tilby and I were together? The evening before our birthday, you hinted that Tilby and I were sweet with each other."

Charlotte let the scrub brush fall into the bucket of water.

"It was by accident," Charlotte admitted.

"How?"

"It was late, maybe around ten o'clock. I woke up and got out of bed to close my bedroom window because the temperature had dropped and it was too cold inside my room. I saw you walking toward the stable. Don't laugh, but I opened my window wider to call out to you."

"Are you fooling me, Charlotte?"

Charlotte shook her head, trying not to giggle at Simone's loopy expression. "But then I saw Tilby. The two of you held hands and went inside the stable."

"What were you thinking?"

"Honestly, Simone. I wasn't surprised. Initially, I was dumbfounded, but when I returned to my bed and thought about it, it was obvious you two belonged together. Tilby is so nice. And so are you, along with so many other qualities. If anyone should be together, it would be the two of you."

"I am sorry I never told you about Tilby and me. Or about the baby."

"You had your reasons, Simone, and who am I to judge your decisions? Best friends. Remember."

Charlotte was on the last square yard of the floor. Murky water soaked the bottom of her skirt, but she could tolerate another ten minutes to complete the task.

"Charlotte," Simone said softly. "I would like to tell you about my mother."

Charlotte stopped, left the brush on the floor, and went to sit next to her friend.

25

The baby was coming. The room's two four-paned windows offered almost no light from the quarter moon. Hilda held an oil lamp. Chloe held another.

Rosalie glanced at Chloe. "Come closer."

Chloe obeyed.

Rosalie had never birthed a baby, but she would not tell Simone how nervous she felt. She pushed her sleeves to her elbows. "Your baby is almost here, Simone."

Rachel saw the look on Rosalie's face. "You sure, Ms. Rosalie?"

Hilda, who assisted Rosalie by keeping Simone's legs steady with her free hand, shot a sharp stare at Rachel to hold her tongue in front of Simone. "Rachel. Get us cold water and rags."

"Go on," Rosalie added when Rachel stayed put, too scared to leave her friend. "Quickly now."

Rachel was Simone's protector, and to leave Simone in a bad way was wrong, but she ran from the slaves' quarters, leaving the bedroom door wide open. She ran past Charlotte and down a narrow set of stairs to the kitchen, jumping over the last three steps and landing hard at the bottom. She wasn't a child anymore, and the impact stung her feet, but there was no time to waste.

Nineteen-year-old Charlotte called into the room. "Is everything all right, Mother?" She wanted to be near her friend, but Rosalie said she must wait for the doctor and hurry him into the room when he arrived.

Chloe called back. "Simone's gonna be alright, Miss Charlotte."

Charlotte stood stiffly against the wall with worry. *Where is the doctor?* She cursed. She'd watched her father die nearly a year ago. A baby coming into this world was supposed to be joyous, and this didn't feel right. There was too much hurriedness and chaotic commotion in the room.

Tilby was outside the kitchen door when Rachel burst through it.

"I is worried, Rachel," Tilby said, distraught. "Is Simone okay? Is there a baby?"

Rachel put the bucket under the spout, and Tilby pumped as hard as he could. "I don't know, but it ain't look good. Ms. Rosalie is trying real hard to help Simone."

Rachel and Tilby hurried back to the house. Rachel took the heavy bucket from Tilby, went inside, and left Tilby standing outdoors alone.

Rachel took the stairs quickly, careful not to lose a drop of water, entered the room, and closed the door, leaving Charlotte alone again.

Rosalie plunged the rags in the cold water, wrung one almost dry, and placed the cool cloth on Simone's belly. Rachel wrung another rag and put it on her friend's forehead. "You're gonna make it, Moni. You got to listen to Ms. Rosalie. And when this baby is born, I will make it a dress if it's a girl."

Simone regarded Rachel. She tried to smile but grimaced instead and screamed as she pushed.

Rosalie glanced up from between Simone's legs. "Stop! No pushing, Simone! Do not push."

Wrenched in pain and her eyes closed tight, Simone stopped the baby from coming.

"The baby needs turning," Rosalie said. Grave concern followed her words.

The air was thick and sultry. The windows allotted poor circulation on such a hot August night. Blood-soaked rags heaped on the floor. Simone cried out. It was unbearable for Rachel. She wanted to save her friend. She wished she could bear Simone's pain, but prayer was her only option.

"Where is the doctor?" Rosalie angrily muttered, but she knew exactly his whereabouts. Dr. Bishop went to Mrs. Whitman, an older woman five miles in the opposite direction who didn't need looking in on any more than a hornet in its nest. Rosalie knew the truth. The doctor wasn't here because he didn't tend to Negroes. Henry had argued Simone's case, but it hadn't mattered. After this, she would tell Dr. Bishop never to step on her property again. Never.

In Simone's final push, Rosalie pulled firmly at the baby. Simone moaned in pain, too weak to scream, but it was over. Her baby was out.

Rosalie placed the infant near Simone's bosom. "You have a baby girl.".

Simone patted her baby, cradled the infant in her arms, and spoke softly. "She's beautiful." Simone's movements slowed, and she looked at her baby with weary eyes.

Rachel's skin prickled. Something was wrong. Simone went limp, and her arm fell to one side. Her eyes blinked heavily.

Rachel grabbed for the baby so it wouldn't fall. "Ms. Rosalie," she panicked.

"Sweet baby Hanah." Simone barely got the name out. "Don't take her away. Put her near me."

Hilda and Chloe propped Simone's head slightly upward on the bed. Rachel placed Hanah on Simone's chest.

Simone's eyes rested on Hanah. "My sweet, sweet baby," she whispered, her eyes closing for more extended periods at a time. She opened them again, but only slightly. She stared at her healthy baby, sleeping, lungs filling with air as hers deflated with every breath. "The Lord is taking me home, baby Hanah. Be good for Mama." And with that, Simone closed her eyes for a final time.

Rachel cried out. "No! Simone. Take a breath, Moni. Open your eyes."

Simone lay motionless. Rachel took Hanah to her bosom and held her tight. Chloe and Hilda bowed their heads, tears falling silently toward the stained floor.

The doctor hurried into the room for Rosalie's sake, but it was too late. The blood-soaked sheets informed him of this before seeing Simone's lifeless body.

Hanah was nearly an hour old when the sun rose on August 17, 1841. By the afternoon, Reedy, Zeke, Willy, and Henry lowered Simone into the ground and shoveled earth into the vast hole as Tilby watched his sweet Simone disappear forever. Rachel was inconsolable and took to her bed hours later. Hilda and Chloe covered for their friend, going unnoticed with their extra chores. Hilda let regret sit heavy on her soul. She wasted years keeping a distance to avoid feeling love, and love prevailed anyway. Hilda cried for Simone, and she cried for Mama and little Loo. But mostly, she cried for herself.

In the barn, Tilby cradled Hanah in his arms. He'd sing to the little thing if he could, but his crying didn't allow it. "I's love you, baby girl," was all he could summon. Tilby saw Rosalie walking toward them. It wasn't long ago when he'd promised her he'd care for this baby, but without Simone, he needed help.

Rosalie didn't know how to face Tilby, but she must for Hanah. She'd done everything possible to save Simone, but words like these would not soothe Tilby's pain.

Tilby's voice was barely audible, but he greeted Ms. Rosalie when she entered the barn.

Rosalie felt the sting in her chest, and her heart ached. James's death was unbearable, and she empathized with Tilby's grief.

Tilby forced back his tears and swallowed hard before he spoke. "Ms. Rosalie. My baby needs a mama's breast. We needs help." Tilby kissed Hanah on her head. "I is always here, baby girl. Yo'r papa is here." He held out his baby to Ms. Rosalie, his heart breaking as Rosalie took Hanah into her cradled arms.

"Tilby," Rosalie said. "I promised Simone she could keep her baby. That promise extends to you. You have my word."

Tilby watched Rosalie walk to the big house with Hanah. When his baby disappeared behind the closed door, he began cleaning the horse stalls. Summertime, the chestnut horse, gently nudged at Tilby's shoulder. Tilby looked into the horse's tender eyes. At this, he leaned against the wooden planks of the stall and sank to the dirt. Tilby took beatings from Mr. Lester so many times he thought he'd die under the whip. He'd been starved and so deprived of water that he'd prayed for death. He'd looked down the barrel of a loaded rifle. Losing Simone and letting go of his child was far worse.

Tilby lay still on the ground and wept until sleep finally came for him.

Charlotte sobbed violently in her mother's bedroom. "First, Daddy. And now Simone."

Rosalie sat on the edge of the bed. "These days aren't easy, but we'll get through.

Charlotte held Hanah at the large mahogany desk in her mother's bedroom. "She's so beautiful. She looks like Simone, don't you think so, Mother?" Charlotte tried to smile but again broke down into sobs.

Rosalie took Hanah from her daughter and placed the sleeping baby in a bassinet near her bed. She opened the window to let the summer's cool air settle into the warm room.

Rosalie took her daughter's hand. "Hanah will be alright for a while. Come, Charlotte. You need rest." The two women walked down the hall and into Charlotte's room. Rosalie helped her daughter into a nightgown and bed. There was nothing more she could do, but to hold her daughter's hand and let her cry.

Rosalie returned to her room after Charlotte was asleep, sobs lingering in the dark. A bassinet near her bedside held the tiny baby, whom Simone managed to maintain for minutes before her strength vanished. Rosalie swiped at her cheeks, clearing the streaming tears away. She must be strong, she told herself, *if not for myself, then for my family.* She watched Hanah's belly fall and rise with each breath. Hanah Smith knew nothing of this world she'd been born into only a day ago. She was unaware her mother, named Simone, died in childbirth. She didn't know her father was enslaved. Hanah did not conceive the idea of sadness or understand Rosalie's tears. These burdens hadn't yet entered her world. Hanah Smith would cry when she was hungry and sleep when tired.

Rosalie again wiped at blooming tears. She had a day-old infant who needed tending. She lay awake listening for Hanah, ensuring the baby lived through the night. How could Rosalie ever forgive herself? Hanah was motherless, and Simone was dead because of her inept skills as a nursemaid.

26

Kiki, a Negro woman from a neighboring plantation with three children, the youngest only five months, was volunteered by Mrs. Joed to feed Hanah until Rosalie made further arrangements. Rosalie accepted. She didn't particularly like Mrs. Joed's involvement, but Hanah was more important than pride. She owed this baby the warmth of a human breast and Simone for everything she'd ignored years ago.

Rachel's grief for Simone lingered. The first week, she avoided Charlotte's room. Hearing the girl's sobs brought Rachel to her knees on several occasions, but crying would neither get housework done nor meet the needs of an infant. Charlotte said she had lost a sister, but Simone had been like a daughter to her. Had anyone considered her heartbreak?

Two weeks after Simone's death, Rachel decisively went into Charlotte's bedroom with fierce conviction. "C'mon now, Miss Charlotte. You cried enough tears to water all of Heaven's flowers." She removed the blanket from Charlotte's lap. "The men need our help in the field. We can't sit 'round sniveling all day." Rachel half pulled Charlotte from the chair and helped dress her. "You got to make your mother proud. We got to keep this plantation working, or we will surely all be lost to the world."

Rachel was right. The world didn't stop for those lost to it, not for her father or Simone. Charlotte wept, but stood there and let Rachel help her.

Charlotte found solace in the garden. She snapped green beans and peas off their vines. She thought of the many times Simone cared for these plants. Her friend would never again reap the reward of her hard work. Tears bubbled in the corners of her eyes before the first large tear cascaded toward her chin. She missed her father and her friend.

Rachel was on her hands and knees, pulling beets from the rich garden soil.

"Look at this one." Charlotte showed Rachel a very long string bean that had been overlooked and hidden by leaves.

"That sure is a fine one, Miss Charlotte."

Charlotte worked alongside Rachel before but felt out of place without her best friend. *How could God let this happen after she'd lost her father?* She and Simone knew one another better than anyone else. They played, read, laughed, and wept together. They'd shared the same birthday. They kept each other's secrets. They made amends for arguing. Charlotte sat and listened to Simone tell her what had happened to her mother. Simone had cried, and Charlotte had held tight to her friend.

Charlotte sat back on her heels, only wanting to recall happy memories, like when she and Simone ran outside past the garden chasing Thomas and Henry around the willow tree. She remembered when she and Simone stole flour from the kitchen to play a trick on Tilby and how they had giggled and watched the prank play out. They'd been fifteen and perhaps too old for such a trick, but it had been part of their friendship and a fond memory. But these days,

Tilby slept in the barn. He said it brought him comfort. He ate with the other men, but in the darkness, before Huntington Manor settled for the night, Tilby solemnly walked back to the horses, through to the barn, and climbed the ladder to the garret. Everything and everyone seemed different without her father and Simone.

Rachel was turning the melons so their underneath wouldn't rot. When she saw Charlotte's body convulse from sobs, she stood and brushed off the beads of dirt hanging onto her dress. She moved closer, took Charlotte in her arms, and held her close.

27

Eight months had passed since Hanah's birth and Simone's death. It had been more than a year since her father's passing. Spring announced its arrival in Alexandria, Virginia, in late March of 1842. The plantation had seen the last chilly weather over a month ago, and thousands of green leafy sprouts poked through the dead layer of last year's harvest, reaching for the warm sun.

Charlotte woke early. It was her twentieth birthday. And if Simone were here, it would be her birthday too. Rosalie knocked and entered Charlotte's bedroom carrying little Hanah swaddled in her arms.

Charlotte went to her. "Hi, sweet girl."

Hanah batted her arms and gave an open smile, showing off two teeth poking through her bottom gums.

Rosalie smiled at Charlotte, who seemed to have grown into a woman overnight. "Happy birthday, darling."

"Thank you, Mother."

Charlotte tickled Hanah's belly, and the baby smiled again. "I suppose it is a happy day," she added in a high-pitched voice to appease Hanah. The baby batted her arms and giggled. Charlotte kissed Hanah's forehead.

"Mother. Can we have tea on the porch? I have something I'd like to talk to you about."

"Of course. Get dressed. I'll have Rachel prepare tea right away. Is everything alright, darling?"

"I've been thinking about some things and would like your opinion."

Rosalie left the room with Hanah. She, too, had been thinking of so many things over the past year. Rosalie suggested Charlotte visit Aunt Sarah and Uncle Warren in Syracuse for a year to help her daughter's melancholy. She hoped this conversation was the one on Charlotte's mind.

Rachel doted on Hanah in the kitchen while Chloe prepared tea and bread. After breakfast, Rachel would take baby Hanah to the stable to see Tilby and the horses. Rosalie and Charlotte sat on the front porch, the sun warming their faces. Charlotte gazed past the tobacco fields. Her beautiful pale skin glowed, and the long golden locks past her shoulders glistened with each tiny breeze.

Rosalie noted her daughter's reserved composure. James's and Simone's death had changed everything, and Rosalie saw the profound change in her daughter.

Rachel brought tea to the table and half-filled two porcelain teacups. "Would you like a fresh corn cake? Chloe's got them comin' from the oven."

Rosalie smiled. "Yes. That would be fine, Rachel."

"Butter, too, please," Charlotte added.

"Right away, Miss Charlotte."

Rachel returned and placed the corn cakes and sweet butter plates on the table.

Charlotte leaned forward in her chair. She sliced the butter and placed a pat on the warm corn cake. It melted and ran down the sides of the rich yellow sponge. "Mother. I've been thinking about Syracuse. Perhaps I should go. Do you think Aunt Sarah and Uncle Warren would allow me to stay with them?"

"Yes. Your Aunt Sarah would love to have you."

"Then, I will write to her if I have your blessing. I'd like to go soon. Maybe next month?"

"You've made a good decision, Charlotte. And considering Syracuse has seen the worst of winter, next month will be the right time for travel."

Charlotte met Sarah and Warren when she was a child. Her mother and brothers traveled from Virginia to New York by train and wagon to help Sarah tend to Rosalie's ailing mother, but Charlotte's grandmother had died by the time they arrived. It was the only time Charlotte had seen her mother weep. When Grandma was laid beside Granddaddy, Aunt Sarah took Charlotte by the hand, and Uncle Warren watched her brothers while their father wrapped his arms around their mother. They'd spent two weeks in Syracuse after the burial. Charlotte and Aunt Sarah had gotten along beautifully, and she hoped this decision to leave for a year would prove beneficial like Mother had suggested.

"Look," Charlotte pointed out. Tiny prisms of blues and purples danced on the wall made by the reflection of Rosalie's wedding ring.

Rosalie moved her hand ever so slightly so the sprinkled spots moved along the porch, from the wall to the railing and floorboards.

Charlotte reached across the table for her mother's hand. She never tired of the ring's beauty. Rosalie held her hand flat on the table.

"Your father was so proud when he slipped it on my finger, but mostly, he was proud of what this ring represented. His love for me. Our love for each other. Love for the family we would eventually have. This ring will be yours someday, darling. When you're ready."

"I'll never be ready, Mother. I'm two years older than you were when you were married." Charlotte leaned back in her chair from the proper position she'd been accustomed to when having tea with her mother. "I'm not sure I want to marry." Charlotte sighed, "I don't know what I want. It seems like marriage is almost a travesty with all this talk of women's rights. Is it wrong to say I agree? Being the wife of a plantation owner seems—oh, I don't know, Mother. For you. For the time. It was right. But things are changing."

Rosalie looked at her daughter with admiration. "I don't have answers for you. You'll have to sort these questions for yourself, but answers will come." Rosalie sat back, mirroring her daughter, setting her hands in her lap. "You've made an excellent decision to visit Aunt Sarah. I can't imagine a life without you here at home, but it won't be forever.

"I was scared to leave Syracuse when I first moved to Virginia, but travel changes a person, Charlotte. Syracuse will give you a sense of a different world than here. The city has much to offer. The people are different. In time, you will make your own opinions."

"Thank you for letting me go. Are you sure you'll be alright without me? You've already lost so much."

Rosalie could not stop her daughter from finding what she was to become. Though, inside, she was afraid. Some affairs would need discussing before Charlotte's departure.

Charlotte took another bite of corn cake. "Who is that?"

Rosalie glanced in the direction her daughter was looking. Thomas and a Black man—a very young Black man—walked toward the field, the man a step behind her son and his eyes to the ground. Thomas had gone to town on an early errand for supplies. Rosalie had expected him home over an hour ago, and before she sat with Charlotte had wondered what was keeping him.

A sick feeling crept into Rosalie's stomach. Thomas had asked to see the books yesterday. It was not unusual. Thomas had asked a handful of times, after James's death, before going into town for supplies, but now Rosalie wondered if Thomas had viewed the ledger for extra money to purchase a slave.

She tried to keep her composure in front of Charlotte. Her daughter had decided to leave Huntington Manor, and Rosalie would not add to any lingering trepidation Charlotte might have to change her mind.

"Excuse me, Charlotte," Rosalie said politely. "I would like to know who is here with your brother."

By the time Rosalie made it halfway across the front yard to the field, Thomas was on his way in from the far end of the plantation where he'd left the Black man with Reedy. Thomas was not yet nineteen, but he'd managed the plantation and slaves without James or Seth Joed for a year. Henry worked alongside Thomas, but Thomas was older and in charge, a point he made clear to Henry on several occasions. If what Thomas had done was what she thought, her son was about to learn who was in charge of Huntington Manor indisputably.

"Mother." Thomas tipped his chin in greeting.

"I need a word with you, Thomas."

"I was coming to you to tell you about Jim, our plantation's newest slave."

Rosalie's cheeks burned. She could not be sure who was within earshot, though visually nobody, even Charlotte, had retreated into the house, but still, she needed to keep her calm while she talked to her son."

"Thomas James Worthington," Rosalie said with half-closed lips. "What have you done?"

Thomas's expression fell flat. His manner changed from satisfaction to unease. "I bought Jim. In town. At auction." He stumbled through the events of his morning. "We had enough money."

"You don't purchase slaves, Thomas. Ever. You did not ask my permission. Had you, Jim would not be here on this property."

Thomas was confused. "Mother," he tried.

"I am not finished," Rosalie cut in. "This plantation—the entirety of it belongs to me. So long as I'm in charge, you are never permitted to purchase a slave."

Thomas shook his head and shrugged his shoulders in disbelief. "I apologize, Mother. I was being sensible. Father is no longer here to help, and Lars isn't getting any younger. A young field hand would be of great use to us—the production of the crop."

Rosalie softened with her son's explanation. Thomas wasn't at fault. She was. Her son was only following in James's footsteps because she'd never shared with her children or family back home the agreement James had with her father years ago, and Rosalie's regret for breaking those promises. The same affairs that needed discussing before Charlotte left for Syracuse.

Part II
1844-1854

28

Charlotte adored her aunt and uncle and their lovely home, but soon after she'd arrived, she found Syracuse overwhelmingly different from her home back in Virginia. She concluded she'd made a terrible mistake and expressed her loneliness in her weekly letters to her mother. *"Nighttime is the worst,"* she'd written in the first few weeks. *"Last night, I lay on my bed, looking at the blank ceiling, thinking of Simone and Father. Traveling here hasn't lessened my mourning as I hoped.*

"Furthermore," Charlotte added, *"I miss you terribly, Mother. And Thomas and Henry and baby Hanah."* In another letter, she'd complained, *"I have forgotten the sweet aroma of tobacco and cut hay."* And in another, *"I miss Chloe's freshly baked corn cakes for breakfast and gardening with Rachel in the early afternoons."* And in yet another, *"How are Tilby, Reedy, and Lars getting on? I do miss them."*

Rosalie's response in her letters came through with understanding and encouragement. *"In due time and patience, you may find your tireless efforts to have the opposite effect of what they seem now."* And in one letter, Rosalie reminded her daughter, *"In a year, when it's time for your return, you will be glad you stayed."*

Her mother's reassurance had turned out well. Charlotte prospered after the first lonesome month and soon found Syracuse alluring. She walked to the marketplace and bought fresh fruits and vegetables from nearby farms. She liked the people she met along the way. They greeted her with pleasantries. The storefronts displayed the current fashions, and the restaurants served delicious cuisine. Depending on the location, the nightlife could be rowdy, but she was happy staying home after dinner. Letters home became less frequent, one or two in a month, and by the time the cooler weather of autumn arrived, Charlotte Worthington relished it all. She came to love the hustle and bustle of the city.

Her uncle and aunt, Warren and Sarah Hayes, lived on Chester Street in the southwest neighborhood. Dozens of windows, each with twelve panes of glass, surrounded the house. The four bedrooms upstairs were small, much smaller than back home in Virginia, but the coziness of the modest space comforted Charlotte.

The front of the house had a large wrap-around porch with a well-crafted handrail Uncle Warren had carved to match their Greek revival house. The front yard was smaller than the home's layout, which was unlike the vast acreage on the plantation. Here, neighbors were in plain sight of each other, waving as they strolled by on their way to town or stopping to visit on an evening stroll. On a warm summer night, her favorite pastime was sitting on the front porch, watching children play, climbing trees, or tossing a ball. When Charlotte was a small girl, before Simone had come to Huntington Manor, she'd been envious of the children in town who played together.

When Charlotte lived with her aunt and uncle for nearly a year, she knew her mother expected her home. The most recent letters from Mother were difficult for Charlotte. *"It's hard to believe you've been gone nearly a year. I'm sure you are anxious to get home. I, for one, cannot wait for the moment when I see your precious face. You will not be able to comprehend all Hanah has accomplished. She's walking everywhere and has a large vocabulary for such a young child."*

Charlotte didn't want to leave the city. Aunt Sarah and Uncle Warren were thrilled and told their niece she could stay, but only with Rosalie's blessing. Charlotte finally wrote to her mother, asking permission to stay in Syracuse. It was one of the most challenging letters she'd ever written. Two weeks later, the letter Charlotte had nervously awaited arrived. Rosalie replied, *"How delighted I am that my daughter has found her place in the world."* Charlotte wept, reading the letter, knowing how difficult this must have been for Mother to accept her decision without a single complaint.

Sarah noticed Charlotte's tears and said, "It's a mother's love, sweetheart."

Another year passed. In Virginia, Hanah was three, and she had been in and out of every room in Huntington Manor, mostly with Rachel scurrying after her.

"Miss Hanah," Rachel animated with her hands on her hips and a silly face. "Your mama was my friend, and I'm supposed to be looking after you, but you are gettin' so fast I can't keep up."

Hanah smiled and laughed at Rachel's performance of acting silly when she talked. "I'm gonna get you." Rachel wrinkled her nose and stepped toward Hanah. Hanah turned and ran through the kitchen, squealing with a mix of excitement and dread.

Hilda scolded Rachel as the two ran through. "There is no room for play in my kitchen."

Rachel caught Hanah and pulled her in for a hug. Hanah screeched playfully, trying to escape, but she was no match for Rachel and gave in to her reassuring embrace.

Rachel rarely reprimanded Hanah for her noisy enthusiasm in the kitchen. The room was in the back of the big house, and if anyone had heard Hanah's giggles, they hadn't ever spoken to her about it. Rachel supposed, though, that Ms. Rosalie wouldn't protest as long as it didn't get out of hand. Rosalie treated Hanah like her own child. She was too busy during the day to care for Hanah, but near dinnertime, she wanted the little one bathed and fed so she could read to her before bedtime.

Rachel had passed by the nursery often on her way to turn down Ms. Rosalie's bed sheets or to close windows when the night air became increasingly cooler than comfortable sleeping weather. Rosalie told little Hanah stories, sang nursery rhymes, and read books. Hanah's eyes would slowly close as Rosalie rocked her to sleep. Then, Rosalie gently walked across the hall and laid Hanah on the soft pillow mattress once belonging to Charlotte.

Rosalie retired to her room after tucking the little girl in for the night. She sat at the mahogany desk and pulled a piece of parchment paper in front of her. She missed Charlotte terribly. She'd been gone almost three years now. Sometimes, she blamed herself for suggesting Charlotte live in Syracuse, but there was no room for regret. She and her daughter were alike, and Charlotte had always been ambitious. She'd known in her heart when she'd first suggested to Charlotte to travel North that there was more than a probable chance her daughter would want to stay. Rosalie's heart ached. Syracuse was her childhood home, and now with Charlotte there, she longed to return.

Over the past year, Rosalie considered visiting Charlotte at her sister's home, but the time never seemed right. She had Hanah, and though her boys managed the plantation, producing tobacco, and nice profits, she still was in charge of this family and the books. James had been gone almost four years now. Their slaves were trusted and hard-working men and women. Leaving Virginia now for a visit would be an unnecessary disruption.

Rosalie adjusted the lamp's wick to brighten where she sat at the desk. When she reached to dip her pen into the inkwell, the diamond on her ring caught the light, and strands of prisms produced an elongated brilliant star-like sparkle. It reminded her of James. Rosalie moved her hand ever so slightly, making the flash appear and disappear like twinkling stars. She noticed her thumb trembling. It was the strangest thing. It had a mind of its own before it finally stopped.

Rosalie dipped the pen in the inkwell.

September 3, 1844

Dear Charlotte,

I find it a blessing you are doing well in all your endeavors.

How are your studies? It is most impressive that you are preparing for your teacher's examination. You will be an excellent teacher, Charlotte. As you are aware, I wanted to be a teacher, but your father came along and stole my heart instead.

Everything here at home is well cared for by your brothers, Rachel, Tilby, and the others. Hanah is adorable. She is wise beyond her years and reminds me of you in many ways. Though, she's not as mischievous. I tell her stories about you. She sits in my lap and listens, and when she's about to fall asleep, her eyes widen, and she begins with questions.

She asks many questions about her mother because Rachel and I talk freely of Simone to Hanah. Maybe we shouldn't have, but there is no turning back. Hanah especially enjoys Rachel's stories of Simone. Last week, Hanah asked where her mama was. Explaining Simone was in Heaven was difficult. But little Hanah only danced and twirled in circles, like she does all day. She doesn't understand death, and that's a good thing.

I love reading your letters, so don't stop sending news of all your undertakings in Syracuse. Please tell Aunt Sarah and Uncle Warren hello and thank you for taking good care of my daughter. I'm sure they are thrilled you are with them.

With Warmest Regards,
Your Mother

Rosalie folded the letter and left it on her desk. Henry would post it this week when he traveled into town. Their home was five miles from King Street, the town's center. Henry usually ventured there once a week or twice, depending on the time of year. Rosalie dressed in her nightgown, removed her ring, and placed it in the jewelry box on the bedside table. The hour was late, almost eleven when she crawled into bed. The moon rose high in the sky. She drifted to sleep, thinking of her children, Hanah, and James.

Rosalie woke early. She'd had a terrible night tossing and turning, which was becoming more common these days. It wasn't unusual during the summer when the upstairs temperatures quickly reached eighty degrees, but it was mid-September. Nighttime had settled into cool breezes flowing through the windows and filling the rooms with the sweet smell of hay and the fragrant aroma of tobacco. But lately, neither had been noticeable to Rosalie. She'd asked Thomas weeks ago if the crops were anything but ordinary, and he'd indicated production was never better.

Henry confirmed. The looks of the plantation confirmed it too. Rosalie had an eye for what the crops would equate to financially, a skill James had taught her many years ago.

Rosalie walked to her window and looked out at Huntington Manor. Men emerged from the cabin as the sun rose. Rosalie heard Chloe and Hilda in the kitchen below. Rachel would already be dusting and making the window glass see-through perfect. It was another beautiful day in Virginia.

Rosalie jolted when she turned around and saw Hanah standing behind her. Hanah's puckered lips surrounded her right thumb, and her left hand held a stuffed dog by its ear.

Rosalie put her hand on her chest. "Where in the world did you come from?"

Hanah lifted her arm, the one with the dog, and pointed toward her bedroom. The stuffed animal swung from beneath her hand.

"Did you have a good night's sleep?"

Hanah nodded, unwilling to remove her thumb from her mouth.

Rosalie put her hands on her hips. "Now, I don't see anyone else around here with their thumb in their mouth, do you?"

Hanah turned and looked. When she found no one, she shook her head no.

"Well then, I'm sure it will take two hands to make bread today, but you only have one. Rachel won't allow you in the kitchen with only one good hand."

Hanah threw her arms above her head. "Two hands. See?"

"Well, I guess you do. Rachel will be glad about that."

Hanah twirled about the room.

"First, we must get dressed for another lovely day."

Hanah twirled again. "Play with Papa," she said, overlooking the possibility of making bread with Rachel.

Rosalie laughed. "You may."

Hanah ran to Rosalie and swung her arms around her skirt.

29

Huntington Manor, Virginia 1847

"They call themselves stationmasters—and can help us get from one hiding place to the next. We're closer to Canada than most slaves," Jim discussed at suppertime.

"Get that out of you's crazy head, Jim." Lars hissed at him.

Tonight, Jim was at it again. It had been years since he stirred this conversation, but the fervor had not changed from the first time.

"Slaves are escaping by foot and waterways for freedom." Jim looked specifically at Lars. "Don't you want that, Lars?" Jim didn't wait for an answer. He only ignored Lars's scowl and continued to the group. "Negroes and white people called abolitionists are helping fugitive slaves along secret routes and transportation to safe houses."

Chloe rolled her eyes. "We be knowin' 'bout abolition, Jim."

"Well, then you know they'll help us get from one place to the next until we're free."

"Go then, why don't you?" Willy said.

Lars grunted. "Don't be puttin' bad ideas in his head. If he goes, what happens to us? Did any of you brilliant brains think of that? Thomas is already on the edge of thinkin' we nothin' but slaves. He different from Mast'r James, I tell you."

Jim disregarded Lars's insinuation. He was tired of being told he was wrong. Jim had the attention of the group, so he quickly continued. "Virginia is closer to freedom than South Carolina or Georgia. Don't you see? We have a real chance."

Hilda ladled possum stew onto their plates. "You see those windows," she whispered angrily. "Don't you think no one is listening from behind them walls? Now all of you, not another word."

Jim's shoulders slumped. He looked around the table. He didn't have a chance with these people. He was on his own.

Tilby wondered if talk of the Underground would ever be discussed if not for Jim. He and Rachel loved Hanah too much to run. Hilda and Lars were too old, and Reedy seemed satisfied with his role as head Negro. Maybe Willy, Zeke, and even Chloe would run if given a chance, but they hadn't ever made a move. But Jim would run if one other slave on this plantation agreed.

What nobody knew, not even Simone, was Tilby knew what running meant. He'd done it, but only once, unlike what Mason Bolsom led Mister to believe when sirs came upon him chained to Bols's wagon. He'd been caught alright, but not by Lester or any of those devil overseers on the cotton plantation in Mississippi where he'd lived his whole life before being sold to Mister Worthington.

There were about twenty slaves on Lester's plantation. When Tilby's aunt died, Kendra, a mother of two children, a boy named Hector and a girl named Rhi, kept a watchful eye on Tilby—mostly from others blaming him for things he never did. When Hector and Rhi were five and six, Kendra feared separation from her children when a rumor surfaced that she was being sold. Tilby never saw someone cry so hard in his lifetime as Kendra had. The thought of never touching her babies again nearly killed her.

A week later, Tilby, only around thirteen, helped Kendra and her children escape from Lester's plantation. They slept mainly during the day for three months, hiding in brush or vacant barns or safe houses. Under the night sky, Tilby got them to the Mighty Mississippi River after days of trenching through the thick of forests. From there, they walked, ran, and sometimes crawled on their bellies, finding shelter where good folks allowed them to rest, eat, and drink.

Then one night, a man in Kentucky offered his root cellar as a place of refuge for the night. There they learned they were twenty-five miles from Indiana Territory. They would make it. The man gave them good food and blankets to sleep and told them to stay for a day or two, but Kendra insisted they leave the following evening, after sunset.

Tilby woke to a rifle pointed at him. Kendra woke in the commotion. She screamed and scrambled to the corner with her children when she saw what was happening. "Please, mister, sir," Kendra begged.

"Shut up, woman!" the man snorted. He pulled several flyers from his pocket. "This you?" he showed the wanted poster to Tilby. "Boy, you bring a reasonable price, and I plan to cash in. One for you also," he said to Kendra.

"Please, mister. Let us be on our way. We've caused you no harm," Kendra pleaded.

"Marshals are on their way. I can do nothing for you now, even if I change my mind."

Tilby hoped he was right in thinking it was one against one until the law showed. A fifty-fifty chance was better than none. He'd be dead or alive in the next seconds. Tilby shifted his eyes at Kendra. The woman sprang into action and screamed. When the man with the rifle turned, Tilby grabbed his ankles and jerked his feet from underneath him. The man fell, and Tilby lunged for the gun and pointed it at the man's head.

"Go," he yelled to Kendra and the children. "You gots to go, Kendra." And when she stood frozen, Tilby barked at her for a second time. "Run!"

Kendra, Ria, and Hector ran.

Tilby waited ten minutes before he heard horses and men closing in on him. He knew what he had to do. The man was frightened by the look in Tilby's eyes and begged for his life.

"I's never kill nobody, mister."

Tilby ran for the tree-lined woods carrying the rifle. He got into the trees, raised the gun to the sky, and pulled the trigger. The marshals turned their horses in pursuit. For nearly a day, Tilby led them on a wild goose chase in the opposite direction of Kendra and the children. He surrendered only when three rifles were pointed at him, but whether he died in those trees or was hanged from one of them didn't matter. For sanity's sake, he told himself Kendra, Hector, and Rhi had made it to freedom.

In the months Tilby and Kendra had been on the run, a handful of abolitionists had helped them, but it had been the man who'd betrayed them who he couldn't remove from his mind. The marshals handed him over for the man to collect the reward money from Mr. Lester, but instead, he sold him to someone else, along with the wanted poster, so he didn't have to do all the work of transporting him back to Mississippi for his prize money. Tilby changed hands four times, all for less than what Lester asked. He'd made his way to Norfolk to Mason Bolsom, half-starved and near dead by the time Master James purchased him from Bols.

Tilby suspected Lars and Willy had run at one time or another, but he wasn't sure. He was convinced, though, Lars and Willy, like him, fared better at Huntington Manor than any place before. Sunrise to sunset meant fifteen hours of work in the summer, but it was better than most plantations of eighteen year-round. And here, Tilby and the others had a bed and food. He wouldn't run. Not for now.

30

Tilby was in the stable the next afternoon when he heard Hanah chattering endlessly to Ms. Rosalie. Tilby imagined they were hand in hand. His little girl was coming to see him like she did every afternoon. Sometimes, Hanah came by herself. These were the times Tilby liked best.

Hanah was six now and reading simple sentences. She pointed to each word in her reader like Rosalie showed her. When Hanah carried a book to the barn, Tilby sat with her for fifteen minutes while she read. He began recognizing words like *the*, *my*, and *I*, and for the first time, Tilby wondered if he could learn to read. Hanah was missing her two front teeth, which made Tilby smile when she said thank you or Summertime, which came out like *fank you* and *Shummertime*.

Hanah gathered pieces of hay and long grasses outside the fenced area of the pasture and fed them to Summertime, her favorite horse. Summertime reached for the fresh grass, and Hanah petted the horse's face.

"Hello, Papa," Hanah called when Tilby came from the barn. She waved and ran to her daddy.

Tilby lifted her and threw her a foot above his head. He placed Hanah down. He bowed his head in respect. "Ms. Rosalie. Ma'am."

"May I stay with you, Papa? Please, may I?"

"Sweet baby girl, that's for Ms. Rosalie to decide."

Hanah looked at Rosalie.

"You'll get your pretty dress so filthy even Rachel couldn't pull the stains from it."

"Please, Ms. Rosalie. I'll be careful."

Tilby intervened for the sake of a squabble from his daughter.

"Now, look here, Hanah. I is busy, and po'r Summertime might not gets fed if we is off playin'. How 'bout you listen to Ms. Rosalie, and we play another time?"

Hanah folded her arms across her chest and stamped her foot. She was going to hold her ground. Tilby and Rosalie's eyes made contact for a split moment, each sporting a small smile.

"Come, Hanah. Your father and I will have none of this nonsense."

Rosalie was wrong. Tilby would have every bit of nonsense from his little girl. He longed to have Hanah here with him, pitching hay and Hanah brushing the horses or reading her books. His heart ached for Hanah with him here, now, and for every moment, but he stayed quiet because he wasn't a free man, and in these moments, Tilby agreed with what Jim was talking about—running north to freedom.

Tilby considered Rosalie clever. She managed the plantation like nobody's business, even better than her sons. And still, before Hanah, maybe if given a chance, Tilby would have run. However, Hanah changed things. He'd never leave his little girl. Never. Huntington Manor was a safe place for his baby, and it overshadowed everything Tilby might have done in the past.

Rosalie gave a soft smile, tightening the cloth bonnet on Hanah's head. She hugged the little girl into her side, and they turned back toward the house. Hanah didn't hold a grudge. She ran back and hugged her daddy, skipped back to Rosalie, and reached for her hand. The two separate motions, walking and skipping, caused her and Rosalie's arms to swing wildly.

When Rosalie came to the steps leading to the front porch, she let go of Hanah's hand and held onto the railing. Her left foot didn't always cooperate. Not enough for her sons to notice, and she wanted it unseen. She was forty-seven and capable of hard work. The railing helped her stability. She climbed the five steps and turned to view the entirety of the plantation. Rosalie's boys and the Negroes were tilling the earth in the fields. The last harvest brought a tall price to the market. Rosalie was proud of her boys, who'd grown into fine young men. They'd followed in their father's footsteps. The plantation had proven their hard labor and success.

Rosalie set her eyes on Simone's beautiful little girl. Hanah danced on the grass with outstretched arms, twirling round and round, singing "Brother John." She didn't know what being born Black meant to white people of slave states. Last year, Hanah had asked about skin color and why she and her daddy looked the same, but Rosalie looked different. Rosalie had explained to Hanah "that we are the paler or darker colors of our parents. Henry and Thomas are pale because I'm pale," she explained. "You have darker skin like your father." Hanah had been satisfied with her answer. She was five then.

It was only a matter of time before answers wouldn't come by so quickly, but Rosalie was now grateful for the child's inexperience.

31

The conversation between Hanah and Rachel came from necessity. Hanah had seen mice in the barn where her Papa slept. She'd never seen mice in her bedroom. Her face, forlorn, had looked to Rachel, needing confirmation of what Rachel reckoned Hanah had already figured. There had been no other option other than to tell Hanah why she slept in a beautiful bedroom with a soft bed and her papa slept in the barn atop hay piles. Rachel sighed, knowing Simone would do the same if she were here with her little girl. For far too long, Rosalie had denied Hanah the truth, and Rachel would set it right.

"Well, baby girl. It's time you learn who you are. Who we are."

Hanah's eyes emitted every ounce of love in the girl's body, which melted Rachel's heart. Hanah was six, older than most Black children when they learned of their fate and the cruel truth of their bigoted place in the world. However, Rachel considered Hanah's age. Rachel's mother had sheltered her from the horrors of slavery. Tilby wanted the same for his daughter, and Rosalie had, too, but Rachel knew firsthand how fast one's life could change. Her parents kept her safe for eleven years, and within an hour, she was sold and never saw them again.

Hanah needed to learn why Papa didn't live in the big house like she had every night. A minute ago, Rachel might have said Ms. Rosalie owns us like a master owns a dog, which was true. Tilby lived without his daughter because he was enslaved, and his place was not in the comfort of the big house. Every Negro on this plantation was enslaved. They were not indentured servants with a buyout to one day be free. She and Tilby and the other Negroes were slaves forever. Rachel was not sure of Hanah's place. When Hanah was born six years ago, and Simone died, Rachel never suspected what would happen. Hanah should have been considered a slave, who would eventually cook, clean, and work in the field, but when the newborn slept in a bassinet in Rosalie's room, it changed things. Since that fateful day, Rosalie had shown Hanah nothing but love, honest-to-goodness love—love Rachel sensed with all her being—the same tenderness she felt for Hanah, like a mother to a child. So to tell Hanah she was like a dog to Ms. Rosalie was a monstrosity and a cruel perception.

Hanah's question had come when Rachel was brushing Hanah's hair. She placed the brush on a table, took Hanah's hand, and guided her to one of the beds in the slave's quarters. They sat together, side by side.

Rachel sighed. "Baby girl, all us Negroes on this plantation was purchased. We was for sale, and Master James bought us all up. Your papa sleeps in the barn, and Hilda, Chloe, and me sleep here," Rachel said, motioning her hand to indicate the slave quarters, cuz we're not part of Ms. Rosalie's family, but cuz we're owned like that washtub." Rachel pointed to the copper bin in the corner of the room. "Only difference is, that washtub over there don't got a soul like we do. It ain't right, baby girl. God never intended for His souls to be purchased, but certain people don't think they got to listen to God.

Hanah's eyes widened in disbelief. "But Ms. Rosalie and Henry and Thomas are nice."

"They sure are. And that's why you can't ever tell Ms. Rosalie what I'm sayin'. She don't want you to know cuz you are white to her. She don't want you to know you are a slave like us. She treat you more like you are her child."

"But," Hanah crossed her arms. "I belong to Mama and Papa." Tears flooded her eyes. "I want to live with you in this room."

"Now, don't you get angry," Rachel said crossly. "Ms. Rosalie treat you like you are white cuz she loves you. And Ms. Rosalie respects us some cuz of you. She may own us, but she and her boys never lift a hand to us. We are lucky. An evil overseer beat your papa before Mister bought him. You keep that in mind. There's no better life out there for us than this one. We got food and beds and a warm place to sleep."

Hanah wiped at the tears beginning to stream. She grabbed a handful of her bright and yellow pleated dress. "I want clothes like you and the other slaves. I want you for my mother."

Rachel knelt by Hanah. She was afraid she'd said too much. If it got back to Rosalie, she could be in serious trouble. "Listen, baby girl. You can pretend Ms. Rosalie and me are your mamas, but you only got one mama, and she loves you. She's in Heaven but wants Ms. Rosalie and me to care for you like she would've done."

Hanah threw her arms around Rachel's neck.

"Hanah, do you love Ms. Rosalie?"

Hanah hesitated. She didn't want to hurt Rachel's feelings, so she lowered her eyes and softly nodded.

"Then you go on loving her. There is no doubt she loves you. I do believe Ms. Rosalie is learning somethin' 'bout herself in raising you. Try and remember Ms. Rosalie and her boys got a soul too. It ain't Thomas and Henry's fault.

That's all they know is to own slaves, but Ms. Rosalie knows better. You are changing her, Hanah. You don't know it yet. And she don't know it yet. But Ms. Rosalie ain't the same person from years ago."

Hanah didn't want to hurt Ms. Rosalie or Rachel, or Papa. She wanted to keep living in the big house with Rosalie. She wanted to continue working alongside Rachel, polishing the staircase spindles and hanging washed linens from the wicker basket on the line out back. She wanted to work in the fields and the stable with Papa. She wanted everything to remain the same because she was like Thomas and Henry. It was all she knew.

The sun shone brightly in the mid-afternoon, but the last several nights had seen frost. Winter was approaching. Rosalie watched Hanah in the field with Thomas and Henry from a front window. Henry swung Hanah around, holding her underneath her armpits, letting her legs jut out and whirl about. Henry returned to work moments later, and Hanah ran to the stables to find her father. She disappeared into the barn. Rosalie imagined Tilby in a tight hug with his child, lifting her to the sky and bringing her back for another embrace. Maybe, she was atop his shoulders, a favorite of Hanah's.

These days, Thomas and Hanah walked hand in hand on mornings when Hanah insisted on having breakfast with her father before the sun scarcely reached the horizon. At first, Rosalie had intervened, telling Hanah that little girls stayed in bed for at least another hour, "and the fields," she explained, "will simply ruin your beautiful dress and soil your shoes." Still, Hanah could be downright persistent and with a good point, "But Ms. Rosalie," Hanah had explained. "Papa's smile widens when he sees me comin' to him."

"When he sees me coming." Rosalie corrected.

"Because Papa loves you, too, Ms. Rosalie. He said so."

Rosalie had meant to adjust her little girl's grammar but instead admired Hanah's innocence.

Rosalie left the window, sat in a wingback chair, and opened the newspaper.

There was no denying things were changing. Talk of slaves running north toward freedom was spreading around the country. Charlotte sent clippings from penny papers, like the *New York Sun* and *Herald*. Rosalie read the news in the *North Star*. In town, Rosalie listened to conversations between men and women from other plantations. More and more slaves were seeking freedom and risking their lives as fugitives. White and Black people were helping Negroes escape by hiding them and leading them to safe houses until they reached free states or Canada.

Henry Brown was one story in the penny paper that had made its way to southern states. Brown was mailed to freedom in a three-foot box to Philadelphia. "Cheap postage," *The North Star* paper referred to the escape. Federal and state governments proclaimed the privacy of packages, and anyone who mailed them was assured delivery without tampering. It was why Rosalie and Charlotte had willingly sent clippings from papers that were damning to the South. The Adams Express Company was ideal for abolitionist groups. Charlotte trusted that her letters and packages would remain private, so she wrote about abolition in several of her letters. Henry Brown's escape heightened people's belief in the mail delivery system in the North. The South, especially the thousands of slave owners, was enraged.

Rosalie and her sons believed an uprising was already underway. Enslaved Negroes fled to free states and into Canada from every slave state, near and far. Rosalie wondered if Chloe, Reedy, or the other men and women here would risk becoming fugitives. Huntington Manor wouldn't survive without them. But Rosalie couldn't deny her truth either. She was raised with the notion that every man should be free.

Before Charlotte had traveled to Syracuse to stay with Aunt Sarah, Rosalie told Charlotte that Uncle Warren and Aunt Sarah were against owning slaves and would not care to understand enslaving the less fortunate didn't always contain the wickedness they believed it did. The subject had remained unspoken for many years, but lately, Charlotte's letters were reading differently. In her most recent letter to Charlotte, Rosalie wrote, *your father was a good man, and he had saved Negroes from worse fates had he not purchased them, but I believe it will be difficult for Aunt Sarah and Uncle Warren to stretch their minds to understand your father's actions.* Rosalie had written those words in response to Charlotte's belief that Warren and Sarah should know the truth about the slaves they owned.

The internal conflict bubbling inside Rosalie was getting more difficult to ignore, especially with Charlotte's letters wreaking havoc on her thoughts. If an uprising came for Huntington Manor, Rosalie could not stop it.

32

Rosalie sat on the front porch drinking a cup of tea. Hanah was in the near distance picking wild tulips and daffodils, which she did so often that Rosalie wondered how thousands remained outside the pasture. Hanah stayed an hour in the barn beforehand, most likely brushing Summertime and talking nonstop with her father. If Hanah asked a question, Tilby stopped pitching hay or feeding the horses and answered his daughter, but mostly he simply enjoyed Hanah's company and listening to her every word.

Hanah waved as she got closer to the house.

"How was your visit?" Rosalie asked.

Hanah thrust her arms toward Rosalie, bunches of flowers held tight in her fists. "Papa makes me laugh," she giggled. "These are for you, Ms. Rosalie." Hanah handed over one bunch of flowers. "These are for the kitchen, so Rachel, Chloe, and Hilda can share them."

"You are lovely to bring us flowers."

Hanah placed the flowers on the table and sat across from Rosalie. She brushed at the front of her dress. "I barely got dirt on me."

"You did well to care for your clothing."

Hanah spurted, "Can Rachel make me slaves' clothes?"

Rosalie was taken aback. "Slaves' clothes?" she repeated, stunned at what she heard. Rosalie never used the word slave in Hanah's presence. Her voice sharpened. "Where did you learn such a phrase?"

Hanah looked at Rosalie in surprise at the abruptness, but it didn't stop her from answering Ms. Rosalie's next question.

"What exactly are slaves' clothes?"

"Clothes for work in the barn with Papa or in the kitchen with Chloe. I want to wear plain clothes like they do. May I, sometimes? Please."

Rosalie suspected Rachel told Hanah what it meant to be enslaved, and she was furious. The girl had better not appear with the kettle to refill her cup because Rosalie needed a moment to think. If Rachel came into the room, she might snap at her. "Think before you jump in a river," Rosalie's father instilled in his daughters, "and you'll be spared from drowning." She had remembered this childhood advice frequently in her adult life, and adhering to it in moments like this one was crucial.

Hanah detected displeasure in Ms. Rosalie's silence. She spoke softly, keeping eye contact, unlike her papa's response. She looked at Ms. Rosalie when they conversed, so why wouldn't she now.

"Papa is a slave. Every black-skinned person here is a slave. Rachel is too."

Hanah waited patiently for Rosalie to respond, though she didn't know why it took so long. Dressing properly when she was with Rosalie and in loose linens with Rachel and Papa made sense. It was a perfect solution, and eventually, when Hanah told Papa and Rachel, they'd agree. She was seven. *And seven-year-olds were good at making decisions.*

Rachel remained in the kitchen. It gave Rosalie a much-needed moment to process what Hanah had just asked. Questions were inevitable. Her children were the same, especially Charlotte, who'd summoned endless inquiries.

But slaves' clothes? How in the world was she supposed to answer this, especially with Hanah looking at her with big, appealing eyes?

Rosalie had handled disrespect with her children. When young Thomas said to Hilda, "Bring me my coat." he got a sharp swat to the bottom and an immediate correction. She handled young Charlotte's inquiry, "Is white skin better than black skin?" by reading from the Bible, which was so uncommon for Rosalie to do that all three of her children remembered it and referred to it often over the years. She'd gathered them in the parlor, opened the Good Book, and read John 7:24: *Judge not according to the appearance, but judge righteous judgment.*

Rosalie regarded Hanah sitting across from her. Hanah was undoubtedly like Charlotte—inquisitive, stubborn, and determined. Rosalie must carefully choose her words. This little girl needed something to satisfy her satiable disposition, like when she'd asked about skin color.

Rosalie's eyes were kind. "I suppose you are old enough to decide what you wear occasionally. And I suppose Rachel would love to make clothes for you other than fancy dresses." Rosalie furrowed her eyebrows to let Hanah know what she said next was stern. "However, you should never call your new dresses slaves' clothes. Understood?"

Hanah nodded.

"Now, go on. You may ask Rachel politely."

Rosalie nearly forgot the unopened letter from Charlotte laying on the table. She'd planned to read it when she saw Hanah coming with flowers. Then, she was bothered by the conversation she'd just had with Hanah. Rosalie broke the letter's seal and unfolded the paper. She couldn't help but think the letter inside would be another jolt.

October 12, 1848

Dear Mother,

I hope this letter finds you well.

Aunt Sarah and Uncle Warren, and I are doing well. My teaching duties keep me busy during the week, but I make a point to help Aunt Sarah with the cooking and cleaning. Besides, I enjoy house chores. Sometimes, I help Uncle Warren with the inventory at his hardware store.

Saturday evenings are becoming fond memories for us. We three talk about current events over coffee and biscuits. Auntie says Grandma and Granddaddy, and you did the same thing growing up.

Aunt Sarah and Uncle Warren loathe what the South promotes by owning Negroes. They say it's appalling; therefore, your concerns are valid. I've kept my promise, Mother. I don't mention Father's broken agreement with Granddaddy or Huntington Manor's enslaved Negroes.

Honestly, Mother. Sometimes, I want to tell Aunt Sarah how our family treats our slaves. We're not like the white folks they depict in our conversations, but being here, I've come to agree with the abolitionists. People should never own people. This is of no disrespect to you, Mother. You and Father have always been kind to the plantations' workers, as have Thomas and Henry, because you and Father raised us to be kind. However, I don't think I can stop at kindness.

There are movements to bring justice to Negroes, particularly further south. The streets of Syracuse are busy. Conventions are held to voice the concerns of Confederate states. Maybe, in some small way, I can be helpful.

It is so lovely to hear Hanah is doing so well. I'm happy she keeps you company while Thomas and Henry are in the fields. It's been eight years since Father died. I think about him often. He and you were so lovely to Thomas, Henry, and me. However,

Father, I presume, would never have let me stay on with Aunt Sarah. Thank you for allowing me to live here. I miss you.
    With Love,
    Charlotte

33

Warren, Sarah, and Charlotte sat on the front porch. It was a warm Saturday summer evening. The fireflies were abundant, and it reminded Charlotte of Simone.

Sarah was writing a grocery list when she looked at Charlotte, who was quiet this evening. "Is there something on your mind, Charlotte?"

Charlotte said. "I am quiet, I suppose."

Simone was on her mind. Hanah was nine years old today, and the anniversary of Simone's passing. Age gave way to maturity, and it kneaded at Charlotte's insides. She had convinced herself for years that she and Simone were the same below the surface of skin color, but in truth, their experiences made them vastly different. Simone lived with a reality that Charlotte had never fathomed. Her friend had endured hardships unimaginable to her, but all aside, perhaps Simone's greatest strength was befriending Charlotte. It meant trusting a white person after another did the unthinkable to Simone and her mother. Simone had chosen Charlotte for a friend, not the other way around like Charlotte had believed her entire life.

The Negroes of Huntington Manor were enslaved people, a truth engraved in her mind since the dreadful argument with Simone. Her friend had pointed it out with unwavering clarity. It was funny how she remembered what the sky looked like, but she had all these years later. She'd looked at it from her bedroom window, repeating

185

Simone's words. *I'm not only a Negro, Charlotte. I'm a slave. I'm your father's slave.*

Charlotte wanted her aunt and uncle to know that her father was indeed a slave owner, but he was a kind overseer of their plantation, but Mother said it unwise to give up such information. Her aunt and uncle never inquired about their slaves. Charlotte figured it was because they were under the pretense that the slaves of Huntington Manor were employed servants like many of the Negroes in Syracuse. Otherwise, her aunt and uncle would not talk as candidly about the monstrosities of owning another person if they knew what her family was part of. Nonetheless, Charlotte wouldn't believe her aunt and uncle would love her family any less.

There was always so much more Charlotte wanted to write in the letters she sent to her mother in the past two years. She agreed with the ideas of abolition, but how could she put into words her opinions without implying Mother and her brothers were wrong in what they were doing by owning slaves? She'd lived on the tobacco plantation for nineteen years and hadn't ever thought she had been in the wrong, but living in Syracuse had changed her.

Warren lowered the newspaper. "I do say you are quiet tonight, Charlotte." Warren light-heartedly laughed. "It's not like you."

"Oh, Uncle. Do I talk that much?"

"Don't believe a word he says, Charlotte. You know how your uncle likes to tease."

"Well, I've been thinking about Simone."

"Simone?"

"For Heaven's sake, Warren. Charlotte's childhood friend from back home. Hanah's mother—remember? Simone died in childbirth."

"Yes. Yes."

Warren went back to reading the paper, and Sarah said to Charlotte. "What about Simone?"

"It's the anniversary of her death. And Hanah's ninth birthday."

"Charlotte. Sweetheart. I'm sorry I forgot."

"I wish I could have been a better friend to Simone."

"A better friend? In what way?"

It was evident that Aunt Sarah was interested, like she always was, and Charlotte adored her for it. But without revealing her mother's secret, Charlotte wasn't sure how to divulge what she wanted. "Simone once asked me if I thought she and I had the same kind of life. I was so angry with her Aunt Sarah because I thought she was using the difference in our skin color to convince me that we were more like oil and water than kindred spirits."

Charlotte blushed. At twenty-eight, she felt foolish disclosing this childhood memory, but she knew her aunt would understand. "Simone needed me to understand how our lives differed deep beneath our skin color. How foolish to think sharing a birthday and lemon drops meant we were the same." A contrite look blanketed Charlotte's face. "Simone knew so much more than I ever had, and I was too naïve to grasp what she desperately wanted me to understand."

Sarah moved her rocker chair closer to her niece and held Charlotte's hand. "No soul on this earth hasn't looked back at regrets and wished they'd done or said things differently."

"I cannot go back and rewrite my regrets, but I can secure a better future. I mean, maybe, I can. I don't know. I believe in what the abolitionists do for Negroes, and

187

perhaps, I could be useful to the cause, but where would I begin? It's so confusing at times."

Warren closed the paper and laid it in his lap. "You know what this family needs? A few days somewhere other than here. Just the three of us. How about we go to Cazenovia?"

Charlotte had no idea why Warren chose Cazenovia; however, there was a beautiful lake there, but there were beautiful lakes here too.

Sarah understood Warren's choice, and in time, Charlotte would understand, but for now, for the sake of Charlotte and maybe for her and Warren, they would stumble upon the convention by chance—nothing more than a bit of luck.

34

William and Mary Ward hadn't planned on attending the convention, but it was neighborly. And William hadn't planned on spotting Warren in the crowd. Cazenovia was nearly twenty miles from Syracuse. He considered this his lucky day and pushed through the crowd toward Warren Hayes.

"Mr. Hayes," William said, addressing his former boss when he reached Warren. "It's me—."

Warren extended his hand. "Of course. William Ward. How are you?"

"Very well. And you?"

"Wonderful, as well." Warren turned to Sarah and back to William. "You remember my wife, Sarah."

"I do, sir." William slightly tipped his cap. "How do you do, ma'am? Good to see you."

"I'm well," Sarah said. "And there is no need for formalities. Please. Call me Sarah."

Warren introduced Charlotte. "And this is my niece, Charlotte."

"Hello, Miss," William smiled. He pulled Mary into his side. "And this is my beautiful wife, Mary."

"Wait!" Warren exclaimed. "Are you the same Mary—" he paused, rethinking his words. Sarah would scold him if he messed this up. There were many girls named Mary in the city.

William laughed, covering Warren's trepidation.

"I should have known," Warren laughed and said to Mary. "For the two years this young man worked for me, he spoke of you often. It sure is good to meet the infamous Mary Foster finally."

Mary Ward smiled. Her face was thin. Her lips were narrow. She wore wire-rimmed glasses tightly pressed to the top edge of the bridge of her nose. Mary had short, auburn hair with loose strands she constantly tucked behind her ears. Her shoulders were narrow, and her petite frame sturdy. She turned to Sarah and Charlotte. "Are you staying with anyone while you're here?"

"No," Sarah replied. "We plan on heading back to Syracuse tonight."

"Have dinner with us. Please. We have plenty of food and plenty of room. You can get a fresh start in the morning."

The day listening to Fredrick Douglass and Gerrit Smith led to an evening of discussion into the late hours of the night. Eventually, the women retired to their rooms. William Ward and Warren Hayes, each with a cup of coffee, furthered the talk of the convention.

"This Fugitive Slave Act has everyone riled," William commented. "I agree with Douglass. We should oppose it."

Warren agreed.

William sat forward, gesturing his hands in a frustrated manner. "Imagine handing over a free man. How absurd. Here these people risk their lives, sometimes spending weeks without food and shivering from cold to cross over into a free state, and now that isn't good enough. Ludicrous, I tell you. Ludicrous."

"So, what would you do if a runaway came to your home?" Warren asked William. Warren hoped his friend provided insight to ease his unbinding thoughts.

William sat back in his chair, exhausted. "I don't know, Mr. Hayes—Warren. I'd want to help, but if the Fugitive Slave Act becomes a law, what choice do I have but to obey the law?"

There was a long moment before William spoke again. "May God help us," he whispered like he hadn't meant for it to slip off his tongue. "May God help us."

35

Huntington Manor, Virginia 1850

When Hanah turned nine in August 1850, Rachel baked a two-layer cake. "This is for you, beautiful girl. Your mama would be so proud of you." She bent down and whispered in Hanah's ear. "Not so sure she'd love those fancy dresses you's wearing, but we won't talk 'bout that."

Hanah hugged Rachel around the neck before Rachel stood. "What was my mama like? Tell me."

"Baby girl. I've told you 'bout your mama a hundred times. What do you want to know that I haven't told you already?"

"Was she pretty?

"You know she was."

"Did she love me?"

"She loved you more than anything in this world."

Hanah became teary-eyed. "Why did Mama have to die?"

"It was her time, baby girl. The good Lord decided it was her time. There ain't no changing what the good Lord wants." Rachel put her hands on her hips. "But today is your birthday. No crying. Do you hear me? Besides, you got Ms. Rosalie and me for your mamas. We love you more every day."

Hanah was small for her age. She weighed fifty pounds and was skinny with knobby knees and elbows. Unlike what Rosalie remembered when Charlotte was little, Hanah fit into the same shoes for the past year. For Charlotte, it seemed new shoes were necessary every few months.

Though Hanah looked much younger, her vocabulary and ability to read and write made her seem much older. Last year, when she and Papa were feeding the horses, Hanah told her father he talked funny and that he should pronounce his words. She hadn't meant any harm, but Hanah had seen the hurt in her father's eyes.

"I'm sorry, Papa," she'd apologized. She hugged him tightly, wrapping her skinny arms around his firm waist. "It was unkind of me."

Her papa knelt and pulled her chin into his hand. "Hanah," he spoke in a gentle tone. "You ain't learnin' like we's kind. You is learnin' from Ms. Rosalie. You is learnin' to be white."

Soft tears wet Hanah's face. She looked at her black arm. "I'm not white, Papa."

Tilby smiled. "No, you is not white, Hanah. I is just saying, you is learnin' from Ms. Rosalie. But you is got to be respectful of all folks —if they is your papa or your foe."

That same night Rosalie and Hanah were reading quietly in the parlor. Hanah closed the book by Hans Christian Anderson and placed it firmly in her lap. "Am I like the ugly duckling?"

Ms. Rosalie looked up from reading. "Of course not."

"All the other ducks and geese teased the ugly duckling because he didn't look like his family." Hanah pointed to her face. "I don't look like you. You are pretty," Hanna told Rosalie. "That must mean I'm ugly. Are you my foe?"

"Foe?" Ms. Rosalie questioned. "Where did you hear that word?"

Hanah shouldn't tell Ms. Rosalie she heard the word from Papa because she didn't know its meaning. Papa had used it like it was the opposite of him. Ms. Rosalie was opposite him because Ms. Rosalie was white, and she and Papa were Black. Wasn't that what Papa meant? Now she'd wished she'd asked her daddy instead of Ms. Rosalie.

Hanah had never lied. She only knew what bending the truth meant because she heard Rachel and Chloe twist stories to keep Ms. Rosalie happy. "Bending the truth won't hurt nobody," Rachel told Hanah. "But make sure you ain't tell Ms. Rosalie 'bout the extra lemons they'd squeezed for the lemon cake they'd baked for Chloe's birthday because it might make Ms. Rosalie sad forgetting such a special day. You hear me?" Hanah had promised because she knew it would make Rosalie sad to know someone had a birthday go unnoticed.

Hanah's eyes fell to the floor with the lie she was about to tell Rosalie. "I read the word foe in one of my books."

Rosalie was not fooled. "What is upsetting you?"

Hanah didn't respond. She sat there staring at the floor.

"Come here, Hanah," Rosalie said when she heard the girl sniffling.

Hanah stood and slowly laid the book on the chair's seat. She turned and ran across the room to Rosalie. She clung to her and cried.

"I hurt Papa. I didn't mean to. I told him he doesn't speak properly, and he said I was learning to be white." Hanah cried harder. She looked at Rosalie. "I want to be like Papa and my mama, but I love you too."

Rosalie pulled Hanah onto her lap. "Quiet now," she said gently. Hanah buried her face in Rosalie's bosom. Rosalie rubbed Hanah's back, noticing her thumb's odd movement. It was trembling.

"Love is love, Hanah, and it doesn't make an inch of difference who that love comes from so long as it's there.

Your papa loves you, and your mama in Heaven, Rachel, and I all love you. Imagine. Three mothers. Promise me you will remember this," Rosalie said.

Hanah gently pushed herself from inside Rosalie's sleeve. "What should I remember?" she sobbed.

"A mother is made of so much love it could fill the entire earth. There is nothing you could ever do to change our love for you."

"Really?" Hanah sniffled.

"Come now. You are a beautiful girl." Rosalie gazed into Hanah's eyes. "And, you have grown too big for my lap. How will I ever get you to stop growing?"

Hanah half-laughed at this. "Do you think Papa knows I'm sorry?"

"I do, but I suggest you go and give him another kiss good night so you can be positively sure he's fine."

Hanah flared her nightgown. "In this?"

"Yes. Now scoot. Go tell your papa how much you love him."

Hanah, Rosalie, Rachel, Tilby, Chloe and Hilda, Thomas, and Henry celebrated Hanah's birthday with cake and lemonade on the front porch in the early evening.

"When did you go and grows up?" Tilby said. He patted Hanah's soft hair. "My baby girl ain't so little anymore."

Hanah laughed. "You said that last year. Remember, Papa?"

Tilby pointed up. "Well then, you is gots to stop growin' toward 'em clouds."

Chloe served the cake and tea. Hanah received a red coat with raccoon fur around the neck.

"To keep you extra warm this winter," Rachel said.

Hanah tried it on. "It's perfect. Thank you."

"Reedy got the raccoon for it, so the gift is from both of us."

"I have to thank him before bed. May I, Ms. Rosalie?"

"Yes, you may," Rosalie said. She handed Hanah a box wrapped in blue paper. "It's from your brothers and me."

Inside was a doll with the most beautiful china face Hanah had ever seen. Hanah held her close. "She's so delicate and beautiful." She eyed Rosalie and her brothers. "I love her. Thank you."

"Don't thank me," Henry smiled. "If Mother thinks I want any part of that, she's half out of her mind. Sorry, Mother. This one is from me." Henry handed Hanah a wooden peg and three wooden rings.

"What is it?"

"Look." Henry placed the peg on a base a few yards from Hanah and the group. "You've got to get the rings around the peg. Try it."

Hanah missed all three. "That's not fair. Let me try again."

"Oh no," Henry said. "My turn." Henry rang all three rings around the wooden peg. He clapped once in excitement. "Looks like I'm up by three points. Anyone else?"

"Give me those," Thomas said. "It would have been nice to mention you had something for Hanah. I'd rather not be part of giving Hanah a doll either." Thomas grinned. "Sorry, Mother."

Rosalie took part in her sons' playfulness. She knew it was for Hanah, and by the looks of it, their sister was thrilled.

Thomas scored zero. "You've been practicing, Henry. That's all this is."

"Quite right, brother."

"Papa. You do it." Hanah pleaded.

"Is it alright, sirs? Should I's gives it a go?" He asked Thomas and Henry. His eyes lowered momentarily.

Hanah took notice. Had she done something wrong?

"Of course, Tilby." Henry laughed, giving Tilby a friendly slap on the back and saving everyone from the short-lived awkwardness.

Tilby took the rings. The first ring rang the wooden peg. The second one fell onto the stationary peg without ever touching its sides.

Hanah clapped. "Papa's going to get all three," she said, cheering, but Tilby missed the third peg.

Hanah jumped in excitement anyway but downplayed it a bit. Her father had rung two rings, but she'd seen how he changed his throw when he played the third. Hanah was sure her father could have rung all three. He had missed on purpose.

Chloe cleared the cake plates away and served more coffee to Rosalie. Thomas took his pipe from where it lay on the table and prepared it with sweet-smelling tobacco.

Tilby pulled something small from his pocket. "Happy birthday, Hanah." He held out a wooden spool, much more extensive than what Rachel used for sewing.

Hanah took it from her father and looked at it from different angles. The spool was split in two, and between the two halves was tightly wrapped twine around the center.

"I's made it for you."

"You carved this?" She ran her hand over the softness. "It's beautiful, Papa. Thank you." Hanah pulled at the loop at the end of the string.

"Lets it fall," Tilby said.

Hanah let go. The wooden spool ran down the twine, and when it got to the end of the string tied around a middle peg, the spool floated back toward Hanah's hold, twirling the line back in place.

"It goes up and down."

"Please show me, Papa." Hanah handed it to her father.

Tilby wrapped the twine tightly around the middle peg between the two spools. He held tight to the loop, let the spool fall, and when it fell to the bottom, he jerked it upward, causing the spool to return to his hand quickly. He did this three times before stopping.

"That is a splendid toy," Henry said. "May I try?"

"Yes," Hanah said excitedly. "Try it!"

Henry gave it a try. The spool returned to his hand several times before it lost its momentum. "Fantastic," Henry said. "Very ingenious, Tilby."

Thomas added. "I do believe Henry has found himself a new toy." He looked to Hanah. "Sorry to inform you, sister, but it may be possible you have lost your birthday present to Henry."

Laughter floated around the room.

It was a wonderful birthday celebration. Hilda and Chloe departed to wash dishes. Rosalie retired upstairs. Thomas read the newspaper by the oil lamp. Rachel, Tilby, and Hanah walked to the cabin to thank Reedy for his gift and give the men the leftover birthday cake.

"Baby girl. You will die of heat in a coat on this hot summer night." Rachel told Hanah. "Look. The icing on this cake is melting right off. You and this cake will be nothin' but puddles on the dirt."

"But I've got to show Reedy how wonderful my new coat fits, especially since you both made it for me."

Rachel laughed. "Mercy. You got a mind of your own, that's for sure."

Hanah smiled. She looked at her father, who was holding her hand. "Papa. Do I have a mind like Rachel says I do?"

"You sures do," Tilby replied in a gentle voice. "And it has me lovin' you more every day."

36

Huntington Manor, Virginia 1850

August 26, 1850

Dear Mother,

I am most hopeful this letter finds you well. I took notice of your penmanship in your last letter. The slanted strokes seemed messy compared to your beautiful and most distinctive handwriting. Have you been ill?

Mother, I have much to write, and I will speak candidly.

Frederick Douglass was in Cazenovia to oppose the Fugitive Slave Act. Aunt Sarah and Uncle Warren, and I attended. The trip was long, and we often rested the horses, but we made it without a hitch. Uncle Warren ran into a man who once worked for him when he opened his hardware business. He and his wife Mary were delightful. William Ward. Does the name ring a bell? Aunt Sarah said there was a slight chance you'd remember him. They offered us a stay at their home to rest the night before returning to Syracuse.

The meeting place was moved from the Free Congregational Church of Cazenovia to an orchard on Sullivan Street because there were so many people. Hearing Douglass speak has me wanting to help free the slaves. Douglass was once a slave, Mother. His voice gives hope to so many people, especially Negroes. Enclosed is a clip from the paper.

Ms. Rosalie put the clip aside on a small table. The paper shook in her trembling hand, unlike a moment ago. She held it with both hands to keep the words from moving about Charlotte's letter, but it didn't help. She sealed her elbows to her sides. The trembling almost diminished, except for a thumb and index finger on her right hand. She continued reading her daughter's letter.

Fugitive slaves attended the convention. Honestly, Mother, I'm not sure I'd be so brave. The Fugitive Slave Act says we must return escaped slaves to their rightful owners. It says it is against the law to keep another man's possession. Likewise, it allows federal marshals to arrest slaves and punish anyone who harbors them in their attempt for freedom. But Fredrick Douglass says no man is a possession. No man can be owned, so we must stand against such a senseless act. We must protect the freedom of any person, even if it intrudes on our liberties.

There was another great man at the convention. His name is Gerrit Smith. I'm sure you've heard of him. He's been working for human rights for many years past. He believes people can change their views and realize slavery is wrong. Like Douglass, he says no man can be owned. He's a brave man, Mother. He uses his wealth for good. He purchases freedom for fugitive slaves and aids them in arranging safe routes into Canada, where slave owners have no rights to claim people as their possession. It is a cause worth fighting for, Mother.

Please hug Hanah and tell her a happy birthday. I've sent her a book. I suspect it will arrive a few days past this letter. I thought about her on her birthday. Did she enjoy her cake? It's hard to believe she is nine years old. I can't imagine how grown she must be. It's been so long since I've been home, but I love my work here. I am useful. Please give everyone my love. I hope Thomas and Henry are doing well.

With Love,
Charlotte

When the book arrived from Charlotte, it became Hanah's favorite bedtime read-aloud. Rosalie sat on the edge of

Hanah's bed, reading. She finished the chapter and closed the book. "That's enough of *The Swiss Family Robinson* for now." She smiled at Hanah, who had been attentively listening to the story.

"Can someone live in a treehouse and tame wild jackals?" Hanah asked.

"I suppose if you were intelligent people like the Robinsons. They had their wits about them. William prepared his family for survival. Being shipwrecked and forced to live off the land wasn't easy, but the Robinsons didn't give up. They used their heads to solve problems. They gathered supplies from the ship and built a safe place to live."

Rosalie sighed, "Now, it's time for sleep. I want you bright-eyed tomorrow morning at the break of dawn. It should be another beautiful day, but we must complete our work before it gets too hot."

"Tell me about Charlotte." Hanah used her pleading eyes to coerce Rosalie. Sometimes her convincing expression worked. She hoped tonight was one of those times.

When Hanah asked about Charlotte, Rosalie had difficulty resisting, no matter what they were doing. Hanah knew this and used it strategically. She loved hearing stories about Charlotte. Besides, it brought her closer to Charlotte, as sisters should be.

"How come she liked to play tricks on Thomas and Henry?"

"You are like her. She was capable of evading bedtime like you." Rosalie smiled. "One short story."

Hanah pulled a thin cover to her chin and snuggled deeper into her pillow.

"Your mama is included in this one."

Hanah shimmied into the mattress. "Hurry, and tell me what happened?"

"Well, I believe Charlotte and your mother were twelve or thirteen. That would make Thomas eleven and Henry eight. One day, the boys ran about, scaring the girls with the dead mice they found in the barn. They'd caught them in traps, and later when the girls were unsuspecting, Thomas and Henry sneaked behind Charlotte and Simone, each holding a mouse by its tail, and lowered it like a spider in front of their face."

Hanah's face grew worried with excitement.

"The girls screamed and ran away fast, leaving Thomas and Henry laughing. So, one day Charlotte decided to give her brothers a taste of their own medicine. She and your mama collected about twenty beetles, kept them in a jar, and hid them in Charlotte's room."

Hanah's eyes grew wide like saucers. She hung on Rosalie's every word.

"The next day, before dawn, the girls entered Thomas's and Henry's room. Your mother and Charlotte gently lifted a blanket off each boy, one at a time. And they placed hundreds of currants all around. Then, they emptied the bugs onto their pillows."

"What happened?" Hanah squealed in anticipation.

"Thomas and Henry were roused by the bugs crawling on their faces. They sleepily brushed them off at first, but it became too much. Henry woke at dawn, scratching his neck and seeing creepy crawlers on his bed. He quickly jumped from the bed, pulling his blanket with him. That's when he saw hundreds of what he assumed were bugs in his bed."

"But it was the currants?" Hanah shrieked in a whisper.

"That's right. Henry screamed, waking his older brother, who saw a large cricket on his pillow. His reaction was much like Henry's. They hollered for their father and me. When we got to them, they were wriggling like wild monkeys trying to rid themselves of bugs."

"Where was my mama?"

"Well, your mother and Charlotte hid in Charlotte's room waiting for their prank to play out, but eventually, they came smiling from the bedroom."

"Did you and Mr. Worthington scold them?"

"Heavens no. Mr. Worthington had himself a mighty laugh. He told the boys they deserved every bit of it. We even made the boys clean the mess—told them it would do them some good. Thomas and Henry thought twice before pulling pranks on Charlotte after that, but it didn't stop Charlotte. She put salt in their oatmeal and glue in their shoes. Your mama, though, tamed herself. I sensed she liked pranking the boys for Charlotte's sake, but left to her own devices, she'd be out in the fields bringing water to the men or feeding the horses. You are like her in this way, Hanah."

"How, Ms. Rosalie? Please tell me."

"Mostly, your sweet disposition. The way you want to please everyone. You have such a good heart."

Hanah smiled and clasped her hands together like a dreamy girl.

Rosalie, her eyes warm with love, bent forward, kissed Hanah on the forehead, and tucked her darling girl in for the night.

Rosalie walked across the hall from Hanah's room and entered her bedroom. She sat at the mahogany roll top desk where James had worked while she read a book in bed. It was a fond memory.

Rosalie placed a clean sheet of thin paper on the desk and dipped a pen into the inkwell, tapping it to rid the point of any remnants that might spoil her paper with thick blots. The pen trembled as it neared the paper. *What is this?!* She had no control over her trembling hand. She put the pen aside and placed her hands flat on the desk. Neither trembled. On her left ring finger was the beautiful 5-carat diamond ring James had given her on their wedding day. The diamond reflected the light from the oil lamp directing rainbow prisms to the ceiling. She lifted her hand to watch the prisms dance, and though she held her hand steady for what was in her control, the flecks of lights moved vigorously from the ceiling onto the wall.

Charlotte's concern for Rosalie's penmanship was on her mind. She'd noticed it too. Something was wrong, but she would not have Charlotte worrying. This letter was to encourage Charlotte to focus on her teaching and avoid potentially unfavorable events, for Rosalie knew that conventions and protests could quickly turn into riots. It was a difficult letter to write when Rosalie and James had always encouraged their children to work hard and be helpful. Now she was scared for Charlotte.

Rosalie pressed her forearm on the desk's edge to help steady her hand.

September 8, 1850

Dear Charlotte,

I'm fine, darling. Please do not worry. Hanah and your brothers take care of all my needs. I wished Hanah a belated happy birthday for you. She received your gift a few days later, and we've been enjoying the story at bedtime. You may have received her thank you letter by now. She is such a bright and cheery girl. She reads and writes very well and enjoys learning. I continue to use your school books from childhood to teach her.

She is interested in knowing about our family. After receiving The Swiss Family Robinson, she asked me to tell her stories of when you and Simone were little girls. I haven't held back on the pranks you and Simone played on your brothers and our...

Rosalie was about to write *slaves*, but how inappropriate this seemed now. She wrote *plantation workers* instead.

Though I only met him occasionally, I remember William Ward. If I remember correctly, he was a nice young fellow.

Your ambition is admirable, Charlotte. Your Aunt Sarah has always been remarkably ambitious, as well. Our father (your grandfather) allowed his two little girls to speak openly. He listened to our viewpoints on newsworthy events. He never skewed the facts of what was happening in our society, as our mother had hoped he might. At times, this meant seeing the best and the worst of humanity.

With the mention of your travels to Cazenovia, I presume Sarah has followed in our parents' enthusiasm for humankind. According to your recent letter you seem just as enthused.

Rosalie's hand was growing tired. She stretched her fingers before she dipped her pen in the inkwell for the third time. Her left hand was trembling less than her dominant hand, shaking relentlessly. Perhaps from the pressure of keeping her forearm pressed against the desktop to help steady the pen.

She reread her letter, not for accuracy, but for elegant penmanship. If she could prevent it, Charlotte would not notice any flaw in the sweeping letters, but to continue tonight meant worrying her daughter by possibly forming imperfect cursive. Sleep seemed to help. Her hands worked best in the mornings. She laid the pen down, slid the letter onto one of three shelves inside, and rolled the top of her husband's desk closed. Rosalie would finish the letter tomorrow morning. For now, she needed sleep.

The following morning, Rosalie woke with Hanah pressed into her back, and her arm and leg lay over Rosalie's side like a snow-capped mountain. Hanah had had a bad dream last night and stormed into Rosalie's bed and climbed under the sheet to lessen her fear of monsters and to get Rosalie's protection. Hanah was a jumpy sleeper, twisting and turning until she found the right spot to nuzzle closer to Rosalie.

Rosalie stayed quiet and stared out the window from her bed. Hanah's breath warmed the back of her neck. She thought about how best to continue her letter to Charlotte. Last night she'd wanted to tell Charlotte to keep to her teaching and avoid trouble elsewhere. However, a restless night and this precious girl beside her, looking for protection from monsters, changed her mind. Rosalie protected Hanah. She and James had protected their three children. Together, they'd raised Charlotte, Thomas, and Henry to envision their goals, work hard, and stay vigilant on achieving success. Rosalie could not turn her back on this realization.

James had been dead for a decade, but Huntington Manor still enslaved Negroes. They were her property. Hanah, if she was being candid, was considered property. James had known nothing different than owning slaves, but Rosalie had, yet she let it carry on long after his death. She tried to pinpoint when she had made the switch, accepting what was for the sake of her family and plantation. James no longer had a say in the matter, though Rosalie had carried forward his ideals. The implication of such a thing was a disgrace, but she had grown to accept it.

Hanah stirred again, loosening her grip on Rosalie and shifting, heavy with sleep, toward the other side. Dawn was about to break. Rosalie sat on the edge of the bed, giving herself ample time before fully trusting her left leg to work correctly. Rosalie covered Hanah's leg where the girl's movement had pulled away the blanket. "You are so precious," Rosalie whispered. Rosalie stepped onto the cool floor and walked steadily to James's desk. Charlotte would have her blessing.

Rosalie took a clean piece of paper and practiced her handwriting. No trembling. She reread last night's letter she wrote to Charlotte. *Ambition resonates from love. She* reminded herself. Charlotte was in love with humanity. She continued the letter to her daughter with a new perspective.

You are a wonderful daughter and a kind friend. It only seems plausible the path you are shaping is in the best interest of humankind. I would expect nothing less.

You will always be my sweet Charlotte. Follow your heart. Act for truth. Love thy neighbor.

With Warmest Regards,
Your Mother

37

Huntington Manor, Virginia 1851

Rosalie opened the jewelry box on the bedside table. Inside, each facet of her diamond ring glistened. She slipped it onto her finger like she had every morning for the past thirty years. The ritual was her daily reminder of James. He would be getting ready for another new day, straightening his tie or tucking a bulky handkerchief into his pocket, depending on his day's business, and then kissing Rosalie on the cheek before he left the bedroom.

Today, she was in her room alone. Rosalie had a busy day ahead, but thoughts of this evening were on her mind. There were matters to bring into the open, and tonight Thomas and Henry would be made aware of her plan. Broken promises had fallen far from her mind for too long. She would no longer ignore what should have occurred years ago. Rosalie prepared for her boys' objections. She was in charge, and there was no room for negotiation.

Rosalie went down the curved staircase, holding tight to the railing and watching her footing. Her left leg was getting worse. She couldn't seem to make it do what she wanted. Descending stairs meant each foot should easily lift from one step and lower to another below. Her foot wanted to drag instead of raise. Rosalie hated needing to focus on the stairs after a lifetime of never having it enter her mind. If she wasn't careful, she could stumble like several evenings ago, when she tripped over her own feet, stumbled, and fell to her knees before grasping the porch railing. The fall had caused no harm. However, Henry had seen it happen and ran to her aid. Whatever was exploiting her once proper form had Rosalie worried. She needed to take extra care. This staircase would be less forgiving if she tripped.

Rosalie sat at the desk near the staircase curve, opened the plantation's ledger, and got to work.

It was seven in the evening when Rosalie made her way to the parlor on the main floor. She smelled the tobacco of Thomas's pipe, and it reminded her of James. Her two sons were seated in wingback chairs. Henry was reading the *Alexandria Gazette*, one leg crossed over the opposite knee. James had blessed him with a fine-looking face and broad shoulders. Rosalie marveled at the similarities—how Henry's blonde hair curled at the ends, the color of his ocean blue eyes and fair skin—all like James's. Henry was twenty-five but looked much older. He'd grown taller than Thomas from when the boys were teens.

Henry heard his mother approach. He placed his paper on a nearby black walnut table and left his chair. "Evening, Mother." He went to her, and linking arms, he accompanied her to the lounge couch.

Convening in the parlor had been a nightly ritual before their father died. Back then, she had neither worried about steadying herself nor had her son taken her arm to assist her. And though it had been years since Charlotte joined them, Rosalie still missed her daughter's presence by the fireplace, reading another favorite novel. Rosalie treasured the memories of her family together in this room, talking about their day and drinking tea or coffee and James smoking his pipe. And especially Christmas mornings with gifts around the eight-foot tree, illuminated by candles and decorated with plenty of glass ornaments and her family singing carols. These were Rosalie's fondest memories of inside this parlor.

A puff of smoke encircled Thomas's head. "Evening, Mother. How are you feeling?"

"Very well."

"Mother," Thomas said. "Yesterday, you disregarded my and Henry's concern."

Rosalie sat quietly and spoke. "And today, I shall also disregard it."

"We're worried, Mother. We've spoken to Dr. Clay. He'll be out tomorrow morning to have a look at you."

Upon hearing this, Rosalie wanted to scold her boys. But she'd known with her last tumble she no longer could deter her sons' actions. They had noted her trembling hands more times than she liked to admit. "Honestly, boys, I was going to suggest we call on the doctor. I wish you had left the decision to me. I'll see him tomorrow, but we will not talk or worry about me until then.

"There is something I'd like to discuss with both of you, and now, seeing that we need to get our minds off my health and back to business, is the perfect opportunity."

"What about the business?" Thomas spoke. "Tobacco has never been better."

"That's true. And it will further the point I'm about to make."

Henry smiled at his brother and mother. "Mother. Does your point mean more work for us?"

"Hard work reaps success. Does it not?" Rosalie went silent, thinking of so many things. Her health. Her family's wealth. The plantation. She had often organized this decision in her thoughts and on paper before this moment.

Thomas and Henry presumed the business on their mother's mind was serious. It was rare that Mother managed what they were undertaking, but it had happened on occasion, like when she insisted the slaves' fieldwork be done by sunset, even in the colder months when their work could continue well past dusk. Rosalie had been adamant, and there was no room for argument.

Thomas and Henry stared at Rosalie. She was about to change how her sons handled business around Huntington Manor.

"The Negroes who we enslave will be paid for their work."

Rosalie let what she'd said hang in the air.

"I'm not speaking of tomorrow or next week, but soon. Of course, we must discuss the logistics before we unfurl my plan."

Thomas disagreed. "Mother, we can't afford—."

"No," Rosalie interrupted her eldest. "We will discuss when to move forward. Do not presume for a moment there is a chance I'll change my mind because, boys," she said to both her sons, "if you do, you will be dolefully disappointed."

Rosalie's presence here tonight was short-lived. She'd planned to refuse any argument from her boys, give them time to receive her request, and perhaps speak with each other.

Rosalie stood and steadied herself. Henry went to his mother for a second time this evening. "Let me help you on the stairs."

Rosalie linked arms with her youngest child. Evenings were tough on Rosalie's body, and she appreciated his assistance. What bothered Rosalie was the realization she needed Henry's aid.

38

Huntington Manor, Virginia 1851

The following day, Rachel came from the kitchen when she heard a knock on the front door. Hanah followed her. Visitors were uncommon on a Tuesday afternoon.

Rachel and Hanah saw it was Dr. Clay. "Please come in, doctor." Rachel opened the door wider and motioned Dr. Clay into the front foyer. "Hanah, go call on Thomas and Henry."

"What's wrong?" Hanah asked. She remembered Dr. Clay from last year when she had a terrible cough. At first, she'd been afraid of him with his black bag of instruments, but he'd been kind and eased her fear.

"Don't worry yourself, Miss Hanah," Dr. Clay interceded in a solid but temperate voice. "I'm only looking in on Mrs. Worthington."

Rachel gently swatted at Hanah's backside to help turn her outside. "Scoot. You go and get Thomas and Henry."

Dr. Clay's calm demeanor and smile hadn't fooled her. Hanah knew Rosalie wasn't right, but she did as Rachel said and ran for her brothers.

"Thomas," Hanah yelled across the field, running toward him. Hanah saw Papa peering from the barn, watching her run, wide-eyed and perhaps wondering why she hurried. She wanted to wave, but Rosalie was on her mind. Someone else had finally noticed her trembling fingers and shaky walk. Dr. Clay was going to make Ms. Rosalie well.

Reedy was sowing the field when he saw Hanah running past him like a spitfire. "What's got you out of breath," Reedy hollered.

Hanah yelled as she ran by. "I'll tell you later, Reedy. I've got to hurry."

Hanah reached Thomas. Thomas whistled to Henry, who was farther in the field than he. Henry looked up, and Thomas waved him over. "I supposed Doctor Clay is here," he said to Hanah. Hanah breathed heavily and nodded in agreement. Thomas put his hand on Hanah's back, and they walked toward the house together.

"Is Ms. Rosalie going to get better?" she puffed.

"Mother isn't ill, Hanah," Thomas said. "Dr. Clay is only checking in on her, nothing more. You needn't worry." Thomas wanted to tell Hanah the truth, but Mother was adamant Hanah was not informed of any health issues.

Hanah stopped stiffly.

Papa had a no-nonsense respect for Thomas like Rachel did for Ms. Rosalie. "We're the help, Hanah. We're not family. Don't ever forget that." Rachel had told her just last week, and though Hanah never disrespected Rachel's advice, she considered Huntington Manor her home. Ms. Rosalie, Thomas, Henry, and Charlotte were family, like Papa and Rachel. She'd told Papa what Rachel said, and Papa said Rachel was right—that his little girl should watch herself. He didn't want to see her get into trouble. Hanah hadn't believed Papa either, and she would finally prove it.

Hanah turned sharply toward Thomas, backing away a few steps to see all of him standing tall. "I don't believe you, Thomas," she said sharply. "Something is wrong with Ms. Rosalie. She shakes morning and night. And nods her head when the time ain't right."

Henry reached Thomas and Hanah. "Why are you standing here?"

Thomas looked from Hanah to his brother. "Hanah knows about Mother. There's no point in keeping her in the dark on the subject any longer. Come. Let's go."

Henry stopped Thomas with the back of his hand. "What are you crazy in the head? None of us know anything. That's why the doctor is here."

Thomas flung Henry's hand away from his chest. "I'm saying we've known something is not right. We've been stupid to think Hanah hadn't noticed. She spends more time with Mother than the two of us combined. Maybe if we'd inquired, Hanah would have told us sooner. Maybe, she could have prevented Mother's ailments. By the looks of her last night, I think whatever has a hold of her has manifested itself so deeply there's no returning from it."

Hanah had never seen Thomas and Henry this angry. It scared her, and she wondered if Rachel and Papa had been right.

"Please, Thomas. Stop being the big brother for once. We know nothing yet. Keep your thoughts to yourself until we do." Henry handed Hanah a sweaty handkerchief. "Wipe your tears. You don't want Mother seeing you upset."

Thomas walked ahead of Henry and Hanah.

"He's upset, Hanah," Henry said. "He feels responsible for everything and everyone here."

The two continued behind Thomas without a word until they neared the front entrance. Henry turned to Hanah. "When we get inside, I want you to stay with Rachel."

Thomas knocked on his mother's bedroom door. Henry stood behind his older brother.

"Come in," they heard Mother say.

Dr. Clay was listening to Rosalie's lungs. He took the stethoscope earpiece from his ear. "Your mother's lungs and heart are properly working. There is no problem there."

"For Lord's sake, boys," Rosalie said. "I told you there was nothing to worry about."

The doctor checked Rosalie's reflexes, spending more time on this part of the examination. He took hold of Rosalie's hand. "I'd like you to stand, Rosalie."

Rosalie gently pulled away from Dr. Clay's assistance. "If you don't mind, doctor. I'm perfectly capable of standing on my own two legs." She pushed herself up, tightly gripping the chair's armrests for support. She let go and stood upright. "See, there. Sometimes I tremble a bit, but I manage fine."

Thank goodness Dr. Clay was there early when she was at her best. Rosalie wondered if the doctor suspected this.

"Please hold your hands out in front of you."

Rosalie followed the doctor's request but with a learned approach. She tucked her elbows firmly into her sides. Her hands trembled, but barely.

Dr. Clay gently pulled her elbows away from her sides. "Now, with your elbows relaxed."

The three men watched Rosalie tremble. She shook her hands, like ridding water from them, and steadied them again. The trembling returned.

"And walking? Please walk across the room or to your bed if it's easier."

Rosalie flared with anger. "Doctor Clay. You're here for the sake of my boys, who have better things to do than watch this nonsense, but since they are in our presence, address me as an adult and not a child."

"Mother, please," Thomas spoke.

"Hold your tongue, Thomas." She stood confident and turned to Dr. Clay. "I don't doubt I will wobble. Maybe I must tell you I've fallen a few times. My left leg doesn't always cooperate, but I manage."

Henry stepped aside. "Let me help you?"

"With all due respect, Henry," Dr. Clay advised. "To best diagnose your mother, I need to see her manage on her own."

Rosalie seldom riled, but right now, she was furious. "Diagnosis!" she said bluntly. "You've got me in the grave before I've walked across the room. Don't be so quick to jump to conclusions, doctor."

"Pardon me, Mrs. Worthington." Dr. Clay was not disturbed by Rosalie's candor. She was an intelligent woman, and he figured she may have already inquired through reading if this was shaking palsy. He'd never heard of the affliction in someone so young, but in medicine, anything was possible. If this were the onset of the disease, Rosalie would eventually need assistance in her everyday routines.

Rosalie walked across the bedroom without shaking.

"And back to the chair," Dr. Clay requested.

Walking was one thing, but turning direction was another. Still, Rosalie did so with conviction. She stumbled, and Thomas jumped to her aid.

Rosalie sat back on the soft mattress with her son's unwavering assistance. And then lay flat on her back at the doctor's request.

Dr. Clay poked and prodded at Rosalie's legs. "Elevate your leg by a few inches, please."

Rosalie followed orders. She lifted her left leg and felt its weakness.

"Good. Now, the other leg."

Thomas, Henry, and Rosalie stayed quiet and let Dr. Clay finish his examination. Outside the bedroom door, Hanah stood silent, listening to every word.

Hanah waited for two days, hoping Rosalie would come to her and explain what Dr. Clay said, but when she hadn't, Hanah took matters into her own hands and asked Rachel. "What is shaking palsy?"

Rachel stopped dusting the fireplace mantel in the front parlor and stared at Hanah. "Where did you hear such a thing?"

"Outside Ms. Rosalie's bedroom when Dr. Clay was here."

Rachel toughened, her hands on her hips, the feather duster pointing toward the ceiling. "And what was you doing outside Ms. Rosalie's room?" she said sternly.

"Listening."

"Hanah Smith. I got a mind to whip you. You could get in a heap of trouble sneaking 'round where you ain't invited."

Rosalie came into the room unannounced. "Shaking palsy is as the name says."

Hanah looked over Rachel's shoulder. Rachel turned quickly on one foot, almost losing her balance. She reached for the chair's wingback to steady herself. She stood straight and pressed wrinkles from her skirt before she clasped her hands loosely below her waist. "Sorry, ma'am." She lowered her eyes. "I didn't see you there."

"Rachel, there is no harm done." She looked at Hanah standing near Rachel, at almost the same height. "Unless you still plan on whipping Hanah, I'll step aside."

"No, ma'am. I mean, yes, ma'am. I mean, she sure deserves it."

"Well then. I'll speak with Hanah afterward."

Hanah straightened, looking directly at Rachel, ready to take whatever was to come, but a whipping didn't make sense. No one had ever whipped her.

Rachel smiled at Hanah and turned to meet Ms. Rosalie's patient gaze. "Ma'am. Maybe we can excuse her mischievousness just this once."

Hanah walked toward her adopted mother. "Explain it to me. Please, Ms. Rosalie. Are you going to die like Mama did?"

Hanah's worried face spoke volumes. "Rachel. Please leave Hanah and me to talk."

"Yes, ma'am." Rachel turned, leaving Ms. Rosalie and Hanah in the front parlor.

Ms. Rosalie held out her hand. "Come sit with me, Hanah."

They sat on the dark lavender velvety couch. "It's called shaking palsy. Like the name says, my muscles are shaking without my control. I'm not the only person with this illness, but I'm the only person who you know who has it, so it might seem scarier than it is."

"Will you die from shaking palsy?"

"I won't get any stronger from it. And my trembling will get worse in due time, but I will not die from it. You have nothing to worry about."

"Do you promise me?"

Rosalie smiled. "I cannot promise I will never die. Everyone dies sooner or later, but I promise my tremors have nothing to do with dying."

"I'll help you, Ms. Rosalie. You can hold on to me all the time. You will never fall again."

"I suppose you heard me tell Dr. Clay I fell?"

Hanah looked at her shoes. "Yes."

Rosalie lifted Hanah's chin with her finger and willed their eyes to meet. "Child," Rosalie smiled. "I love you."

Hanah flung her arms around Rosalie's neck. "I love you too."

39

Syracuse, New York 1851

Charlotte received her teaching credentials and obtained the summer teacher position in Eastwood within two years of her mother's permission to stay in Syracuse. For six years, she taught girls and boys, primarily ages six through twelve, all the mandatory subjects, including history. Her pupils were mainly girls and younger boys too little to work the land. The older boys, beginning at age ten, usually attended school in the winter months under the tutelage of Mr. Wooden. Charlotte could teach year-round and queried the school board for equal wages like Mr. Wooden, but the township disagreed. She'd complained to Aunt Sarah after a tough day and a three-mile walk in frigid spring weather that being paid less because she was a woman was wrong. The learners under her tutelage advanced in reading, writing, and arithmetic more than those under her colleague's teaching.

"But you wouldn't want those unruly boys when they have nothing better to do than cause trouble." Uncle Warren stated clearly at the dinner table when Charlotte voiced her opinion on the matter for a second time.

"I can handle those boys. No trouble at all."

Sarah agreed. "She could, Warren. She's Rosalie's daughter."

During the winter months, when Mr. Wooden took over the schoolhouse, families interested in Charlotte teaching their children employed her as a private tutor once a week

221

so as not to digress under Mr. Wooden's teaching. Charlotte charged a dollar a day. She taught her pupils new lessons, assigned each child proper homework, and expected it to be completed by the following week on her return.

She had a different family each day. Jacob and Casey Tallson on Mondays. Tommy, Homer, and Alicia Peters on Tuesdays. Wendy, Gertrude, and Eleanor on Wednesdays. And Frankie Fredrickson and Negro twins, Jack and Raymond, the sons of Mrs. Fredrickson's cook, on Thursdays.

Raymond and Jack had such a love for learning. When Frankie behaved poorly during their studies, one of the twins would guide him back on task. Their enthusiasm fascinated Charlotte. When she was a child, she'd wanted to learn to read and write much more than her brothers. And even still, her love for learning didn't compare to that of these twins.

Nearing the end of one of her tutoring sessions with Frankie and the twins, Mrs. Fredrickson leaned in toward Charlotte and whispered, "With the way the world is changing, Frankie needs to learn how to work alongside Negroes." Mrs. Fredrickson covered her heart, pretending it ached for the two boys who were less fortunate than she. "We're a Christian family. I figured it would be saintly to let our Frankie be a role model, like civilized folk." Mrs. Fredrickson waved her head toward the table for Charlotte to follow her gaze to where the boys were computing mathematical equations on slates. "Manners can be taught, I suppose, but learning's not for everyone." Mrs. Fredrickson gave a broad smile like she and Charlotte were in cahoots. "I'm only sorry you have to waste your time. You know what I mean, don't you, dear?"

Charlotte saw right through Mrs. Fredrickson's insincerity. "No. I do not understand," Charlotte candidly stated.

Charlotte found Mrs. Fredrickson's comments atrocious. Simone had become an excellent pupil and hadn't learned reading until she was almost ten. Mrs. Fredrickson did not hire Charlotte to side with her beliefs. And if her employer didn't like what she was about to say, she would consider herself fired.

"On the contrary, Mrs. Fredrickson. I believe it is Frankie who is learning from Jack and Raymond. They've guided your son in his studies many times. Now, if you don't mind," Charlotte said, gathering her books, "I've got chores to do at home. I'll be here next Thursday."

On Fridays, Charlotte tutored the O'Malleys, an Irish-Catholic family of seven children who lived on Clinton Street, the farthest walk from her home. Charlotte charged the O'Malley's a dollar-and-a-half. She often sang their names while walking to their farmhouse, hoping she'd finally get their names straight. Meghan, Mary, Michael, Patricia, Elizabeth, Patrick, and Margaret. All seven were born within ten years, and five with red curly hair only added to the confusion.

On Saturdays, Charlotte and Aunt Sarah baked bread in the morning and cleaned the house in the afternoon. When Uncle Warren was home from work, they visited with friends or gathered for other evening celebrations. And Sundays, Sarah, Warren, and Charlotte attended service and enjoyed a hearty midday meal of fresh-baked cornbread, stew, and a lovely plum pudding.

Warren retreated to the French room with a full stomach. He sat on the sofa and reached for the newspaper.

"Uncle?" Charlotte said upon entering the French room.

"Yes."

"Have you read the news about Daniel Webster speaking at the Courier building?"

Warren pulled his paper away from in front of him. "So, it was you reading the paper. I wondered who'd gotten to it first."

Charlotte smiled. "I always read the news first. So, have you? Read the article?"

"Yes."

"Shall we go?"

Uncle Warren looked over the top of his reading glasses. "I anticipated your interest in this sort of thing."

Charlotte's wide smile showed anticipation of her uncle's agreement. Her rosy cheeks and primrose pink lips on her alabaster skin revitalized the room. Charlotte Worthington was a beautiful girl with confidence and persistence people could not undermine. Her uncle often found himself supposing the same point his niece was making. Warren simply could not disagree. Charlotte reasoned opinions by backing her viewpoints with an intelligent argument. His niece had gumption, not common among girls from the South, and it made him proud. *A true northern girl.* However, today was not most days, and Warren had no intentions of letting his niece roam the streets of Syracuse to listen to Daniel Webster.

"Now, wait for a second, young lady. We will not be attending. Every marshal from Onondaga County will be there, looking and waiting for abolitionists to crawl from the woodwork. Individuals who oppose Webster's viewpoints will be considered Negro lovers. Trust me. It's not safe. We'll stay put and read all about it in the paper."

"Oh, Uncle Warren. We'll be fine," Charlotte explained, trying to coerce her uncle. "This is more than a speech we can read about in the paper. It's how Webster responds to the people of Syracuse. We've got to see for ourselves if he is for or against slavery."

Sarah entered the room. "What about Daniel Webster?"

"Your niece wants to hear the man speak—among crowds. No, I take that back—amid hordes of angry people. She wants to know if the orator is for or against slavery." Warren sat straighter to make his point. "He's for the Constitution. We've heard enough from him to know he won't change his views."

Sarah leaned into the conversation. "Warren," Sarah said thoughtfully. "I don't see any harm in finding out firsthand."

Warren, eleven years older than Sarah and much like a father to Charlotte, said to his wife in disbelief, "You mean to tell me you agree with her?" He turned his eyes to Charlotte. "Sweetheart, I love you, but I am not sending my only niece into harm's way."

"I love her too, Warren."

Warren scratched at the skin under his graying beard and elongated his disagreement. " Dear. It is not—"

"We're going, Warren. With or without you." Sarah insisted.

40

Charlotte, Sarah, and Warren squeezed through the crowded streets to get closer to the Courier building in downtown Syracuse where Mr. Webster was to speak from a second-story balcony. The orator strolled outside. He looked like a giant overlooking his feed. It was a cold day in May, and if anything, his cheeks should have been rosy, but instead, they were flushed, and he appeared ill.

The crowd stayed tame. Charlotte spotted marshals and deputies everywhere. The three stayed inconspicuous, moving about the group. Charlotte smiled, of course, and apologized when she bumped another spectator.

Uncle Warren insisted they not react to either side, opposing the Fugitive Slave Law or agreeing with it. They were there only to listen.

Charlotte's anger flared when Daniel Webster insisted abolitionists committed treason and violators of the law would be punished.

"I don't stand with either side of the law; I stand only with the law," Webster yelled into the crowd from the balcony.

How could Charlotte or anyone argue his point? Charlotte couldn't deny Mr. Webster was the right man for the job. His speech scared people into turning over any Black man, fugitive or not, which infuriated her even worse.

"Let them punish me," she retorted when they returned home.

"Just hold on here," Warren said. "We can believe in anti-slavery all we want, but if you start voicing an opinion outside this home, you'll find yourself in trouble."

"I don't plan on saying anything outside this home, Uncle Warren, but we can't sit back and watch injustice happen around us. Maybe, we can—."

"Stop, Charlotte. You cannot be part of this revolution."

"Why not?" Charlotte went to her uncle, who leaned forward, sitting on the edge of the sofa with his morning paper strewn to the side of him and his reading spectacles in his hand. "Why shouldn't I get involved in something I believe in? I've been living here for nine years, and you and Aunt Sarah have taught me to go beyond my capabilities to help others—to be a good citizen. Those are your words, Uncle. Helping others is important to me."

"Praying for sick friends and bringing food to the church for less fortunate people is one thing. Abolition is another." Uncle Warren countered.

"Uncle Warren. You've done more than bring cakes and bread to the poor. What about the men you have working for you at the hardware store? You employ men based on their skills, not their skin color. Isn't this right, Uncle?" Charlotte didn't wait for an answer. "That in itself is a far cry from doing nothing. And how about Claudia and Abigail? You hired them to occasionally keep the house tidy and work in the garden when you know I like to do both. They needed work, and you gave them a job."

Warren waved away his credit due. "Well, now. That's being a good Christian."

Sarah sat quietly in a corner chair, listening to both sides of the discussion between her husband and niece. It had been a long day. Everyone was tired, but Sarah couldn't stay quiet any longer. She must handle this right. She loved her husband, and Warren loved her and adored Charlotte and undoubtedly saw to it that they were safe. Warren fought long and hard to keep his niece from the truth, but Charlotte was determined. Their secret needed unveiling because today, Mr. Webster stirred an unwavering passion in her niece. Sarah made up her mind. It was the right moment. Here and now.

"Warren. Charlotte believes in this cause. We can't keep her safe forever."

Warren threw Sarah a desperate look. "Sarah, don't say such things. Charlotte is our niece and Rosalie's daughter. It is our job to keep her safe."

The expressions of her aunt and uncle alerted Charlotte.

Sarah went to her husband, overlooking Charlotte for the moment, and sat by his side. "She's an adult. And we should consider ourselves lucky that our niece wants to be here with us. Charlotte's done more for our spirits in the last decade than we ever had before she came to live with us. We love her like a daughter and want to protect her, but it doesn't give us the right to stop her from choosing what's right for her. Slavery is wrong, and to deny Charlotte the opportunity to fix a wrong and make it right is no better than if we enslaved people ourselves."

Charlotte's heart leaped hearing what her aunt had just said. All these years, she'd kept her promise to her mother, never to mention they owned slaves at Huntington Manor. Her gut twisted with angst. Was she a fraud to be the niece of objectors and the daughter of enslavers?

Charlotte wanted to remind her aunt and uncle that she was twenty-nine years old and deserved to know whatever they were discussing, but she thought better of it. "Please, Aunt Sarah. Uncle Warren. What are you not telling me?"

Warren sighed. "Your aunt is correct. It's a crime to do nothing."

"You agree with the abolitionists, then?"

"You need to understand," Warren said regretfully to Charlotte, "Hiding and helping fugitives escape into Canada is treason, as Dan Webster said. Those harboring fugitives, if found out, could be imprisoned or worse. It's a steep price to pay for another man."

Charlotte held her gaze, willing her uncle to continue, unbelieving what she was hearing. When he said nothing more, she couldn't wait any longer. "Are you telling me you would let one man die because you fear imprisonment?" Tears pooled in the corner of her eyes. "How could you, Uncle Warren? How could you believe this?"

Sarah interjected. "That's not at all what your uncle believes."

"What is going on—." And then Charlotte directed her words to her uncle. "Are you—?"

"Yes." Warren looked to his wife and his niece, "We are breaking the law."

Sarah and Warren told Charlotte of a home in Auburn owned by William Seward, miles from where they lived. "It's a beautiful home. William and Frances have been hiding fugitives below the main floor in a cellar for the past year. They provide rest and food to slaves on their journey to freedom. Some of those men, women, and children find their way here and—"

"Station?" Charlotte interjected in a whisper, unsure if what they discussed might be heard outside their home. "As in a safe house? As in the Underground?"

Warren nodded, but only slightly, like he might at any second change his mind and say this was all a practical joke.

"Why have you kept this from me?" Charlotte gently demanded. "Does Mother know?"

"No!" Sarah said boldly. "What we are doing can't be written in letters. To speak with your mother in person, if she were here, she'd most likely be part of what we are doing, but to write such things in a letter could be damning to fugitives and us. Promise me you will not write such things."

Charlotte agreed. "I want to help. Tell me what I should do?"

"We will go about every day without a change." Warren said.

"How will that help?" Charlotte asked.

Warren softly gripped Charlotte's shoulders so they faced each other. He spoke intently. "It's the only way, my dear niece. Your aunt and I have been transporting some of the food meant for the church to Negroes in hiding. I've transported a few fugitives from the boats using boxes of construction material to conceal them. Nobody's the wiser when you go about life like nothing has changed."

Charlotte was in shock. Her aunt and uncle had pulled it off right under her nose. She'd help cook the food and deliver it to the church. She sometimes wondered where the extra loaves of bread or dried meat had gone when she'd sworn they'd prepared more than what they had delivered, but there was never enough missing to make a point of it. Her Aunt Sarah was kind and generous and had always delivered loaves of bread and cakes to neighbors. Charlotte's eyes widened. "The convention in Cazenovia? Did you know there would be a convention there?"

"You had been upset about Simone. You were looking to find your way in this world. I saw an opportunity to possibly lessen the confusion you were feeling about abolition and justice for Negroes."

Charlotte remained awed. "And William and Mary? Was it your plan to meet with them?"

"No, Charlotte," Warren said. "That happened by chance, but it goes to show how life brings opportunities. You must be open to them."

41

Huntington Manor, Virginia 1851

It was a beautiful June morning. Temperatures, usually hot and humid by mid-morning, had been mild all week. A cold front rolled in by supper, and the temperature dropped ten degrees.

"Storms a-brewing," Reedy said to Lars, looking toward the sky. He wiped his sleeve across his sweaty forehead. Henry was coming toward him. He covered his head with his tattered hat and got back to work.

Henry looked toward the horizon as he walked toward the men in the field. Rolling dark clouds blanketed the sky.

"Afternoon, Reedy," Henry called out.

"Afternoon, Henry, sir."

"Before sundown, fetch the men and come to the house. My mother, Thomas, and I are gathering everyone for a meeting."

"Yes, sir." Reedy was puzzled. He waited until Henry turned toward the main house before walking toward his fellow men. "Zeke, Willy, Jim," Reedy called and waved the three men over. "Meeting at the house. Master Henry wants us there before sundown."

A few of the men looked at each other accusingly. Lars slouched. Nearing sixty with a permanent scowl, he was the first to ask. "Which one of you did something? You know we stick togetheh. There ain't nothin' betteh out there."

Reedy put Lars at ease. "Henry ain't bothered. He was nothing but calm. It has to do with Ms. Rosalie. Tilby says

Hanah told him Ms. Rosalie is sick with the shakes. Maybe she's dying."

"That bad news fo us, then," Lars snorted. "Henry be respectable all right, but what if Rosalie dies? Maybe Henry and his brotheh ain't gon' be so fond of us."

"Heck, Lars." Reedy insisted. "Those boys ain't got a cruel bone in them, and you know it, so stop talkin' like you don't."

Jim spoke. "Don't be so sure. White folks got hearts of stone."

Lars shook his head in disgust and turned his scowl on Jim. "You be young, Jim. Huntington Mano be you's only stompin' ground. It much worse out there."

"You don't think I know that." Jim raised his voice to Lars. "This ain't my first place, besides. I was in Carolina until I turned fourteen, and the overseer sold me."

"Yeah, but you lived inside, like Hanah. You learned how to read. They sold you 'cause their white girl took a liking to you."

"Shut your mouth, Lars!" Jim snorted. "You said we're in this together. I told you about the Railroad when I got here nine years ago." Jim looked around at Reedy and the other men. "We should have fled then, but no, is what you all told me, that this plantation was the best in all of Virginia for slaves. I said I didn't wanna be nobody's slave. None of you did. I was willing to escape alone, but you said it would cause trouble for the rest of you. I stayed 'cause you talked me into sticking together, and now you're accusing me of being privileged." Jim looked sharply at Lars. "That I don't know a damned thing about how slaves live? Working fifteen hours a day without a penny to my damned name and living in a cabin with the likes of all of you." Jim looked around at the men. "Have all of you convinced yourself this is a good life?"

"Keep your head, Jim," Reedy interjected. "This meeting has got us upset. If Thomas sees us standing around 'stead of working, we might find ourselves in a heap of trouble. Besides, the rains are comin'. C'mon, now. We got work to do."

The men separated and went back to work. Jim raged inside, much like the strong wind pushing at his back. He didn't care about this meeting or how good he had it here. Jim was going to be a free man. He was going North.

Rosalie and Henry sat in the parlor on two wingback chairs facing the large bay window. Thomas stood. A strong wind was beginning to work at the large branches of the oaks. He listened to his mother, but he kept an eye on the workers in the field. "You're sure, Mother? Because now, Reedy and the others are discussing something when they should be working. Giving them wages might have an ill effect on the plantation."

Rosalie spoke in an even tone. "We've been over this, but since you are bringing it to my attention again, to which concern are you referring?"

Rain sprinkled the window. Thomas turned toward his mother. She was right. The three of them had mulled over this conversation a handful of times since the night she first brought it to their attention in this same room, but this was his last chance. "We've given our slaves a nice life. We don't beat or disrespect them, and they give us the privilege of hard work. They're fed good food. They have beds to sleep in, and we don't work them to the bone. But paying them for their work? It's like pulling a trigger on a rifle. Once the bullet is out, there's no reeling it back in. We don't get a second chance, Mother. We can't undo what we will tell them if this doesn't work. We'd have a rebellion on our hands."

"Thomas. It is the right thing to do."

Thomas accused. "Or is it Charlotte who thinks this is the right thing to do?" Like the pulled trigger, as it rolled off his tongue, there was no reeling it in. He'd been bothered by Charlotte's letters, and this was the first he'd ever voiced his opinion about it.

Henry gave his brother a sharp stare.

Rosalie sat poised. Her head trembled, but her confidence remained intact. "Your sister has nothing to do with this. She and Aunt Sarah support the abolitionists like many other people.

Rosalie remained calm. This decision was not easy for Thomas, and she anticipated resistance.

"I'm going to tell you something that I'm ashamed of," Rosalie began. "Grandfather Farnsworth allowed me to marry your father on a few conditions. One, your father pays wages to our slaves. And two, we never purchase or sell another Negro. Your father agreed, and we were married the following day.

"Father was a good man, Thomas, and loved us very much. You, Henry, and Charlotte know this. Your father lived in Syracuse for thirteen months. He worked with free Negroes and understood what freedom meant to them. We planned to marry and stay in Syracuse and raise a family eventually."

Rosalie held both sons' attention. "When Grandfather Worthington suddenly died, our plans swiftly changed. If not for his death, you would have been born and raised North in a free state, but life didn't turn out as planned. My father, Grandfather Farnsworth, regarded James as a respectable man who kept his promises. It was the only reason I was allowed to marry your father. We married, and a few weeks later, we moved here to run the plantation and make it our home. Then one day led to another with very few changes to how Grandfather Worthington ran Huntington Manor. It is difficult to change one's upbringing, especially when they return to their roots. It is the reason you are struggling so much, Thomas. Enslaving people was familiar to your father as it is for you. Father began to justify his promises. He and Grandfather had always treated slaves respectfully and provided a good home, so your father concluded it would be acceptable to run the plantation as it had been.

"I have lived with this regret for years."

"That was about to change, boys," Rosalie said. "Before your father passed, he'd agreed to pay our slaves wages. After he died, the blame was mine. I was afraid of losing the business. We needed to be fed and clothed, so I kept the plantation going the only way I knew how. But now, we must move forward. I must do what is moral and for the good of others."

"Why didn't you tell us this months ago when you first told us of this plan?" Henry asked.

Rosalie saw Rachel coming with tea. "I hadn't thought I needed to. Our plan was in place, and until Thomas's inquisition a moment ago, there was no need for further discussion. Hopefully, my further explanation has eased your minds, but regardless, we are moving forward on this."

"Tea, ma'am," Rachel said.

"Yes, thank you."

Rachel placed a tray on the table and poured tea into the three tall glasses.

"Will there be anything else, ma'am?"

"Yes, Rachel. Please find Hanah. The last I saw, she was upstairs reading. I would like Hanah, Hilda, Chloe, and you to join us in the parlor in fifteen minutes."

"Yes, ma'am." Rachel lowered her eyes and backed out of the room.

Thomas frowned. "Hanah?"

"She's part of our family," Henry said.

"But to learn your father is a slave?"

Rosalie held the half-full glass of tea with both hands, brought it to her lips, took a sip, and shakily directed it back to the table. "She knows, Thomas. She's known for years."

"Who told her?" Henry asked.

"I suspect Rachel, but only because Hanah figured it out. She's an intelligent girl. She's figured out many things over the years."

"It's because you share letters from Charlotte with her." Henry paused. "Will you be writing to Charlotte about these wages?" Henry did not give Rosalie time to answer before quickly adding, "And Mother, don't you agree we've kept Charlotte in the dark long enough about your condition? It's high time she knows."

"No. A letter about my condition will bring Charlotte running home. I do not want to disturb my daughter's happiness. You boys chose to stay and run this plantation, and your sister has made her choice. If she returns home, it will be of her own doing."

Henry lowered his eyes.

"What is it?" Rosalie questioned. "Henry," she demanded when her younger son hesitated.

Henry had already written the letter. He'd asked his sister not to mention a word to their mother, that he must be the one to own it. Henry was sure Charlotte had received the letter a week ago and read it a handful of times. He didn't know if Charlotte could wait. She may have already posted a letter asking a hundred questions. There was no turning back.

He peered into his mother's eyes. "I wrote to Charlotte about your health concerns."

Rosalie was deliberate in what she said next. "Very well, then. I expect you to write another letter to your sister about this evening's discussion."

Henry nodded.

"Henry," Rosalie specified. "I will decide when to divulge my health concerns from now on. Is this understood?"

"Understood," Henry replied.

Lightning split the sky. Thunder boomed. Hanah came running into the parlor and jumped into Henry's lap.

The men arrived as the sky opened. Rain pelted the house.

"Come in quickly," Thomas said. The Black men and women quietly shuffled into the crowded front parlor.

Hanah peered around the chair before bounding toward Tilby. "Hi, Papa."

Tilby seemed unsure how to react in the big house. It wasn't the first time he'd been inside. He'd repaired broken cabinets and sanded doors and floorboards, but to be here like this—waiting for news of Rosalie's sickness was uncomfortable. He took Hanah to his side, squeezed her tight, and let her go. He worried about their future together. If Rosalie was going to die, what would happen to them?

Thomas took charge. He still was not convinced this would reap anything but disaster, but he needed to present the news with certitude. If he was to remain in charge of this plantation, then his workers would regard him as a decisive and confident overseer.

He respectfully cleared his throat. "I will be straightforward on why we called you here. You will earn two dollars a week for your labor from here on out."

An awkward silence filled the room. This matter was not about Rosalie or her illness. This matter was not about money or saving coins 'til a jar was full. This thing Mister Thomas was talking about was freedom.

Hanah looked at her father. His face was shallow, and his eyes watered. He wiped away a single tear.

Later that evening, the men were in the cabin. Reedy said, "Does it mean we're free? Can we wander off the plantation without permission?"

Lars smirked. "Try it and see if you get a bullet in you's head."

"We ain't free," Jim said. "We're earning money to keep us working. Don't think Thomas can't sell us because he can. Any white man can beat us for no good reason. Would we be allowed in the big house to sleep and eat? Nah. We ain't free. We're nothing but slaves to white folks—even to Rosalie Worthington. The only thing wages will do is to make us thieves."

"What are you talking about?" Reedy said. "Not one of us got it in us to be thieves."

"Jim's right," Lars barked. "Nobody eveh thinks they be thieves o murderers until they be about to lose somethin' they love. That's when a man risks everythin'. Fo once, Jim is makin' plenty of sense."

239

42

Syracuse, New York 1851

The leaves turned weeks ago. Elms, maples, and oaks were preparing for a cold winter. Reds, oranges, and purples filled the neighborhoods and lined the streets. Evergreen needles turned brown, and pinecones fell in abundance.

Charlotte had two weeks remaining before turning her class over to Mr. Wooden. She'd proposed a full-time position to the township board for the second time but could not change their minds. Mr. Wooden had no intention of leaving his teaching position. Charlotte, who loved teaching too much to see the children deprived of an education, made it relatively easy for the board to deny her request again.

Today was a beautiful Wednesday. Her pupils were outside eating lunch. Charlotte was inside preparing her afternoon history and geography lessons but was immensely distracted. Inside her cloak's pocket was the letter from her brother. It arrived last week. Since then, Charlotte had read it many times, mulling a course of action. Henry told her not to worry, but it was impossible. She wondered if Henry had been sincere, or had he skewed the facts of Mother's health to keep her from returning home? She had searched the letter for clues on what to do next.

Charlotte couldn't concentrate. Trying to plan a geography lesson with the letter on her mind wasn't helpful. She went to the tiny closet where her cloak hung, took the note from the pocket, and opened it.

October 15, 1851

Dear Charlotte,

Hello from your little brother. It must be a surprise to receive a letter from me. Please don't be alarmed. All is well here at Huntington Manor.

However, Thomas and I called Dr. Clay for Mother. Believe me when I say she resisted our involvement in the situation, but Thomas and I thought it necessary.

Dr. Clay has diagnosed Mother with shaking palsy. Mother is experiencing weakness in her legs and tremors in her hands because the disease affects her motor abilities. There wasn't much Dr. Clay could tell us other than he's treated two other patients with shaking palsy, and through research, he says there isn't much we can do to stop its progression.

I'm writing to inform you only because Mother will not mention anything in her letters. She's been clear with Thomas and me that her illness be kept from you and Hanah because she's afraid it would cause unnecessary worry. Except Hanah, unbeknownst to any of us, was listening outside Mother's bedroom while the doctor examined her.

As Mother explained to Hanah, and I am telling you, there is nothing to worry about, but I felt Mother was wrong in her position that you needn't know because if it were I on the receiving end, I would want to be made aware.

Mother is getting along well, mainly because Hanah is so helpful. Mother's ailments were on Hanah's mind long before it was for Thomas or me. Hanah is the life of Huntington Manor. She brings water to everyone in the field. Then she skips off to the barn to assist Tilby in cleaning the horses' stalls, so she says, but I can hear giggling a mile away. She's doing more playing than helping. We all love her dearly.

241

I'd like to end by saying, please don't tell Mother I've told you about her illness, but I'll assume this will be nearly impossible for you because even though I've said not to worry, you will. It will be difficult, Charlotte, but please let me tell Mother that I've notified you before you write. Can you do that for me?

Tell Uncle Warren and Aunt Sarah I say hello. One of these days, I hope to make it to Syracuse for a visit.

Sincerely,

Henry

Charlotte placed the letter on the desk and slumped in the chair. Then, it came to her. She straightened. Her eyes widened, and her mind raced. Henry's correspondence was her opportunity. It was what her uncle had meant—in this letter, staring at her through her brother's words.

Charlotte rang the bell, and the children filed quietly into the schoolroom. By afternoon's lesson, Charlotte had wished it over. There hadn't ever been a time she could remember in all her years of teaching that she wanted to shoo her pupils from the schoolhouse and run home.

When Charlotte arrived home in the late afternoon, breathless and worn out, she quickly sought out her aunt and uncle.

"This is it, Uncle. Don't you see?" Charlotte waved the letter toward him.

Sarah rushed to her niece. "What has got you so riled?"

Charlotte saw the confused looks on both their faces. "The letter." She repeated, waving it once again. "It's my opportunity. Remember Uncle?"

Warren was processing. Charlotte took his reaction as needing clarification.

"Uncle Warren," she insisted. Her brows lifted. "You said life has opportunities. And I should be open to them."

Charlotte turned her attention to her aunt. "I want to go home, Aunt Sarah. You can understand. I want to see Mother, Hanah, and my brothers. And ..." she could barely get the words out.

"And what?" Sarah said, flustering herself with her niece's position.

Warren took the letter from his niece and reread it. Maybe he'd missed something earlier when Charlotte brought it to their attention days ago. "What has got you so flustered?" He said.

"Huntington Manor is a perfect safe house for fugitive slaves. It's near the railroad and the Potomac." She looked at her aunt and uncle in desperation. "I have no idea how it might work, but this is the opportunity."

"But your tutoring obligations begin next week," Sarah said. "How will you explain your absence to the families who employ you during the winter months?"

Charlotte pointed toward the letter. "Anyone would find it normal to leave a job and travel home if their mother was dying."

"Your mother is not dying, Charlotte," Sarah said.

"But we can bend the truth like the six of the thirteen loaves of bread we took to the church, pretending six was all we'd baked." She looked questioningly at her aunt and uncle. "And the remaining beets and turnips we pulled yesterday? You pickled less than half of what came from the ground."

Warren wanted to tame his niece's impulse, mainly because the arrest and rescue of a Black man named Jerry. "It's getting worse. We can all see that," Warren said. "Jerry's arrest is a perfect example."

243

Jerry was a runaway slave who fled from Missouri, evaded capture, and made Syracuse his home by 1850. He was a free man. When The Fugitive Slave Law was passed, Jerry's owner intended to reclaim him. The community of Syracuse took Jerry's arrest as a personal attack on their liberties, and planned to free him from the authorities. Gerrit Smith and other prominent abolitionists headed up the plan for Jerry's rescue and a passage from New York into Canada.

Charlotte had Sarah's and Warren's full attention. She dialed down her frenzy by a few notches and used her uncle's example to her benefit. "Federal marshals and police can arrest a hard-working man because he's colored. Jerry is no more a thief than we are—and they lied to him to get him in shackles with little fight. He only went mad after the authorities told him he was under arrest according to the Fugitive Slave Law. Any man would resist. I've gone mad thinking about it. Don't you see? We can't let this continue right under our noses. We've got to do more than what we're doing. When they arrested Jerry, I was teaching, but honestly, I wished I'd been in town helping the rescuers."

"Don't say such a thing, Charlotte," Warren protested, straightening in his chair. "People got hurt. Some will go to jail. We must be careful not to bring attention to ourselves."

Charlotte waved the letter between them. "I utterly understand. That's why this letter about Mother's health is the perfect excuse. No one will suspect I'm leaving for any other reason than to be with my mother. We've got to help."

"And how, young lady, do you know your mother and brothers will be willing to share this idea."

Aunt Sarah stood from the chair. "Warren, this is Rosalie we're talking about. She is no more for slavery than us. Charlotte should go. If the plan does not work, she will return, and if our friends and neighbors ask about Rosalie's health when Charlotte returns, we say she's feeling well enough. No harm in this, is there?"

Warren sat back. "Of course not. But let me say this for the last time. What Charlotte is suggesting implicates a much greater risk." Warren turned to Charlotte, his face filled with worry and caring eyes. "You are like a daughter to us. However, you are more like Sarah every day, and I am certain there will be no stopping you." Warren brought his hand to his forehead. "I'm to blame for this."

Charlotte went to her uncle and kneeled by his feet. "We don't even know if my mother will agree. Can we see what comes of it?"

"Your mother will agree. I am sure of it," Warren said. "You have my support. We'll do what we can, but Charlotte, you must understand. If your family gets involved, there is no stopping what we are doing until every slave is free. It isn't slight, Charlotte. It's immeasurable. There will be no stopping trouble from coming for any of us."

43

Rosalie brought the letter to her heart. Her face brightened. "Charlotte is coming home for Christmas."

Hanah jumped with excitement. "I finally get to meet my sister?"

Rosalie tilted her head, elated that Hanah had called Charlotte her sister. "Yes. Your sister's coming home."

"Read the letter. Please, Ms. Rosalie. I want to know everything."

Rosalie smiled again. "Your eagerness is like Charlotte's when she was a girl. When a letter arrived from grandma and granddaddy, she'd jump with excitement."

Ten-year-old Hanah smiled because she and her sister were similar. She sat on the floor in the parlor, her legs crossed and her hands in her lap, ready to listen. Rosalie instinctively placed the letter in her lap, and to help stop her trembling hands, she tightly grasped her skirt.

November 27, 1851

Dear Mother,

I hope this letter finds you in good spirits with the holiday approaching. I imagine you have decorated the house with wreaths and garlands. Another Christmas will soon be upon us, and this year I plan to celebrate at home with you and everyone at Huntington Manor.

I have missed the warmer temperatures of Virginia. Syracuse saw over a foot of snow here last week. It stopped the whole city for the day. I've enclosed several clippings from The New York

Times. Yesterday, the newspapers reported Binghamton got eight inches. The canal has a continuous thin layer of ice. If this continues, ice may immobilize the boats and delay the mail.

If the weather does not improve, I will delay my trip until spring, but for now, I plan to be home soon and stay until after the New Year.

With Love,
Charlotte

Hanah wondered if Rosalie's tremble worsened because of her excitement that Charlotte was coming home. Sometimes, Rosalie shook for long periods, especially in the evenings, but today it seemed worse. Hanah went to Rosalie, took the letter from her lap, and put in aside.

They linked arms on the couch. "Won't it be wonderful, Ms. Rosalie—to have Charlotte here with us?"

Christmas finally arrived. Charlotte had not made it home. Winter had proved much worse than the states had predicted. It was a disappointment for Rosalie and Hanah, but there was nothing they could do but wait until spring for Charlotte's arrival.

Alexandria, Virginia, hadn't seen snow like this in decades. Snow had fallen through the night, and large flakes floated peacefully toward the earth by Christmas morning. Hanah crept downstairs when she woke in the early morning. The outside was dark, and the house was silent. The Christmas tree, with all its decorations reflecting the moon's light through the window, was the most beautiful thing she'd ever seen. Presents encircled the tree. She couldn't wait. She turned, ran upstairs into Rosalie's room, and flung herself onto the bed.

"Ms. Rosalie. It's Christmas. Santa's been here."

"Are you sure? I've heard Santa does not come to houses where little girls rise before dawn."

"Aw, Ms. Rosalie. Santa would never pass our house. Besides, you told me last night what a good girl I've been."

"Well ..." Rosalie blinked, trying to force her left eyelid open to its full extent. "I suppose you have a point."

Hanah wanted Rosalie to hurry instead of doing everything that could wait until they opened presents. Rosalie splashed water on her face and patted it dry with a hand towel. Hanah sat on the edge of the bed impatiently.

"Can we open presents? Please?"

Rosalie did not say a word. She took her wedding ring from the jewelry box and slid it onto her trembling finger. "Oh dear," Rosalie said. "I've misplaced my house slippers. Can you please look in the closet for me, Hanah?"

Hanah jumped from the bed, skipped to the closet, and looked inside. When she did not find them, she looked under the bed and desk. She could never remember a time when Rosalie misplaced her slippers. She suspected Ms. Rosalie was taking her sweet time on purpose. And when Rosalie said, "Oh, goodness gracious, here they are, behind the bedside table," Hanah was sure Ms. Rosalie was procrastinating with purpose. There was nothing she could do but wait patiently.

To Hanah's surprise, Papa was waiting for her downstairs. A wide smile brightened his face. Hanah ran to him. "Happy Christmas, Papa."

"Happy Christmas, Hanah." Tilby swept her off her feet and tightly embraced his child.

Hanah hugged her brothers and Rachel, and over Rachel's shoulder, Hanah spotted the sled underneath the tree. Hanah shrieked and ran to it. "It's beautiful!" She turned around to face her family. "Santa remembered me!"

There was no Santa Tilby ever heard of when he was a child, and he was happy his little girl got to believe in something so magical. He'd made the sled for Hanah. It took him weeks to get the wood smoothed and the runners placed evenly.

Hanah handed a gift to each person in the room, and watched excitedly as each present was opened. Chloe was an expert bow maker and helped Hanah wrap each gift with white paper and a red bow. Inside the packages were socks for Papa, Thomas, and Henry.

"Did you make them?" Papa asked.

"Yes. Rachel helped me. I also have a pair for Reedy, Lars, Willy, and Zeke."

"She's useful with a set of knitting needles." Rachel smiled. "And darning needles, too, ma'am," she added, looking over to Rosalie.

Rosalie pulled a woolen scarf from the wrapping. "My goodness, Hanah. It is beautiful. Thank you."

"There's one for Charlotte too." Hanah lowered her voice so Chloe and Hilda wouldn't hear her. They were in the kitchen, fixing a special breakfast. "I made one for Chloe and one for Hilda."

"What is this?" Rachel said when Hanah, smiling wide, handed her a package.

"It's for you."

Rachel untied the bow and folded back the paper. She stared at it before she could speak. "A Bible. It's perfect, Hanah." Rachel opened her arms, and Hanah flung herself into them.

"Henry helped me. He took me to the mercantile, and we ordered it from the catalog."

Henry took off his slippers and replaced them with his new socks and lifted his feet off the couch. "I'll be warm until summer."

Hanah laughed, and so did the others. Hanah eyed the sled, wishing to use it.

Henry snagged Hanah into his arms and gave her a tight hug. "I'll tell you what, little sister, get your coat. We'll take it outside right this minute."

Rosalie intervened. "You'll do no such thing. We've got Christmas service this morning."

44

Huntington Manor, Virginia 1852

January 16, 1852
Dear Charlotte,
Though we missed you terribly for Christmas, I'm thankful you delayed your trip home. The weather may be one of the worst winters in history for upstate New York. The New York Times reported Buffalo is experiencing "the most violent snowstorm ever known." I've sent you the clipping from the January 14 issue. I've read repeatedly that the cold continues to dip into negative readings. Though I'm sorry you couldn't make it home, knowing you are safe with Aunt Sarah and Uncle Warren has made it possible that I needn't worry about your safety.

Is it fair of me to say had you made it here, the inclement weather would have extended your stay home? The Times reported ferries could not get across the water. Passengers cannot continue their travels by train if they cannot get from one depot to the next. However, the city will solve the problem. Businesses are not keen on losing revenue. I learned this all too well growing up. Granddaddy said when problems get in the way, people pull together and fight back with solutions.

Have you heard the South is faring as poorly, especially the Deep South? Six inches of snow fell in parts of South Carolina. We've seen colder temperatures here at home and plenty of snow, but less snow than I remember as a child in Syracuse. Hanah and I were hoping for more. Henry, Hanah, and Tilby sledded Hick's Hill with the sled Santa left under the tree on Christmas morning.

It was difficult for Hanah to steer, and she kept falling off. We all had such a great laugh.

Tilby did not disappoint. He got on with Hanah and raced down the hill. We stayed out for nearly an hour until the cold and wind were too much. Rachel prepared hot chocolate for our return, and she and Tilby joined us for a cup. It made for a beautiful Christmas afternoon.

Our Christmas dinner was delicious. Hanah made the plum pudding and plenty of it—enough to feed a small army. She was very proud of herself.

Rosalie included details for reasons she wasn't sure about. Maybe she considered herself a better person knowing Tilby and the others were earning wages.

She had prepared for repercussions before Thomas informed the slaves of earning wages. "Changes bring on problems," her father told her, "but people can solve problems." Rosalie had been right to prepare. Jim had fled the following day. Rosalie worried for Jim because his fate would be uncompromisingly unpredictable, but Jim had made his decision. After Jim, Rosalie expected repercussions for not sending Thomas after him. She figured by the next day or maybe a week at most, the other slaves would follow, but nothing since Jim's departure had happened.

Tilby's dilemma was easy to understand. He was a father and would not leave his daughter. Rosalie's heart ached for Tilby because Tilby perhaps lived with the idea that Hanah would never go, and it didn't matter if he longed for freedom. Tilby loved his daughter too much to leave without her. Rachel, too, was a mother to Hanah. And Lars was too old and crippled. He wouldn't last a day if he decided to walk away, but the others were strong.

Hanah whispered the letter thus far to ensure she'd made no mistake. She loved reading about Papa and Christmas. She'd sped down Hick's Hill many times since with Papa, Henry, and Rachel.

Hanah dipped the pen into the inkwell and held it over the top so drips would not splatter on the parchment paper. She looked at Rosalie, whose eyes were focused on the wall and looked as if a handful of thoughts were mulling around inside her head.

"Ms. Rosalie," Hanah said. "What else should I write to Charlotte?"

Rosalie cleared her throat and dictated the rest of what she wanted to tell her daughter.

I miss you, Charlotte, but I never want you to think you must come home for anything but a visit. I'm proud of you. You have such admiration for humanity. Your granddaddy would be so proud. And though your father fostered a different life for us, he would be proud too. He was willing to live in the North because he loved me. Had we stayed, he may have become an abolitionist himself.

We will see you in springtime. Tell Sarah and Warren hello from all of us here at Huntington Manor.

With Warmest Regards,

Your Mother

Postscript: Mother said I could tell you it's me, Hanah, writing this letter. I cannot wait to see you. Ms. Rosalie and I read the paper every week. I pray winter will end soon so you can hurry home.

I love you, Charlotte.

Your sister,

Hanah

Hanah had two things on her mind after she ended the letter. One, was she a sinner because she told a teeny lie? She wanted Charlotte home, but she did not want winter to end. She wanted the snow to keep coming so she could race down Hick's hill forever. Rachel would tell her she was only bending the truth, which put Hanah at ease.

And two, what was an abolitionist?

Hanah asked Rosalie that night at bedtime. "Is Charlotte an abolitionist?"

Rosalie had helped Hanah spell the word for Charlotte's letter. She was surprised Hanah hadn't asked immediately what the word meant and wondered if Rachel had already told her.

Hanah crawled under the covers. Rosalie tucked the feather blanket under Hanah's chin and placed her hand on Hanah's cheek. She looked into the girl's eyes, remembering when this precious child was small and safe from harsh truths.

"Yes, Hanah. Your sister and Aunt Sarah and Uncle Warren are abolitionists."

"What is an abolitionist?"

Rosalie evaded the truth from reaching her father many years ago that, indeed, James had purchased and enslaved Negroes. And if that hadn't been bad enough, she'd continued to run the plantation with slaves for years after James's death. She'd convinced herself there had been no other way. Without extra hands, they would have lost everything. First the tobacco fields, then the reputation James had worked so hard to achieve, and eventually the house. James had purchased slaves against her father's wishes, but she had gone along with it. And now this beautiful girl with cinnamon eyes was looking deep into Rosalie's soul and asking questions deserving of answers.

"Abolitionists are people who want to end slavery."

"Is Papa a slave?" When Rosalie didn't answer immediately, Hanah continued. "He says he isn't," Hanah said. "Papa says earning wages can set him free. He says you didn't send Thomas and Henry looking for Jim because Jim is free. Is what Papa is saying true?"

Rosalie had suspected Tilby would keep Hanah from the truth, and until this moment, she believed he had, but his daughter was growing up. There was no keeping her from the truth. Hanah read the news, though Rosalie often scanned the lines first and kept some information from her by clipping articles.

Rosalie spoke softly. "Your papa is a good father, Hanah. He will always protect you."

Hanah smiled. "He protects you too."

"How's that?"

"Papa says you're the nicest person besides Mama and Rachel. He says you love me. And I need to keep a careful watch so you don't fall. He says I should practice writing words every day to help you write letters to Miss Charlotte."

Rosalie laughed. Hanah was growing up, but some innocence remained intact.

"Am I smart like Charlotte?"

"Of course you are."

"Am I as pretty?"

"You're beautiful, Hanah."

"Am I a slave, Ms. Rosalie?"

Rosalie was mindful of how to answer. Hanah deserved the truth, but she needed to handle specifics appropriately. "Moments ago, you said your father was not a slave. And you're from your papa's being. So no, you're not a slave, Hanah."

Hanah looked at the ceiling thoughtfully. "I don't understand. So, when Papa was enslaved, I was too?"

"This talk doesn't do any good before sleep," Rosalie said. "I don't want dreams waking you at night and sending you running to my bed."

Hanah did not take the bait. "It doesn't make sense, Ms. Rosalie." Hanah took her hands from underneath the blanket. "Papa and Rachel and I, and even Jim and the other workers, are slaves because our skin is dark? But if I am beautiful and smart, why does my dark skin make me different?"

Rosalie was stunned by Hanah's reasoning. Moreover, how was she supposed to answer her sweet little girl? How might Rachel or Tilby explain the ugly truth? Hanah, born of an enslaved person, meant she became a slave at birth. Having a white adopted mother hadn't changed the fact Hanah was Black. If left outside Huntington Manor's walls, the society she belonged to would condemn her little girl like any Negro.

Rosalie hadn't cried since the day Hanah was born, but tonight her eyes teared. "Hanah," she said softly. "The world doesn't make sense. Because you have black skin, white folks see you as different from them."

"But you don't see me as different, Ms. Rosalie. You love me like a daughter."

"I consider you my daughter, Hanah. And I will never stop loving you. Promise me you will never forget how much I love you.

45

Huntington Manor, Virginia 1852

Charlotte arrived home at Huntington Manor on the afternoon of April 5, 1852, after spring had finally come to Syracuse. Hanah was with Rosalie on the front porch and had not taken her eyes from the front gate. She saw the wagon and caught sight of her sister and Henry. She jumped over the steps to the walkway and ran to greet Charlotte.

Henry stopped the buggy at Charlotte's request.

"It's still a distance to walk for someone awake all night." Henry teased.

Charlotte grinned. "Look at her run. She'll be here before I step foot on the drive."

Henry laughed. "She doesn't have a single shy bone. She's like you in so many ways. Daring, bold, and sharp, to name a few."

"Why are you buttering me up, little brother?" Charlotte said. "You were never so quick for kind words when we were kids. What's gotten into you, Henry Worthington?"

"Glad you're here, that's all. You better meet our sister halfway before she keels over like a sick horse."

Charlotte hopped from the buggy and walked quickly to meet Hanah. When the two were close enough, Hanah flung herself toward Charlotte and into her arms.

"You're the most beautiful sister. You're prettier than the pictures Ms. Rosalie has in the parlor."

Charlotte laughed. "We're going to get along wonderfully."

Charlotte's face had rosy cheeks and fuller lips than years ago. Her long blonde curls, loosely pulled back and secured with beaded hair combs, hung down her slender back, bouncing about. She stared at Hanah. "You are an absolute image of your mother. You have her beautiful eyes and gorgeous hair."

"Rachel and Papa tell me all the time."

"And look at you," Charlotte continued, flabbergasted. It was like she was looking at Simone herself. "You are filled with her same eagerness too."

"Do I have any Papa in me?" Hanah giggled. "He tells me I have his big appetite."

Charlotte smiled. "And his big heart. You and your Papa have enough love to share with all the world."

They turned toward the house. The two sisters walked together, hand in hand. "You take good care of Mother, don't you?"

"Yes," Hanah said. She looked at Rosalie sitting on the chair, waiting for them both. When they got close, she would stand and greet them, but Hanah knew Rosalie was saving her energy. She told Hanah the tremors were less evident if she rested between chores, but Hanah didn't see how it helped. Rosalie's trembling didn't differ if she relaxed, but she kept quiet about it.

"Thank you, Hanah. It means a lot to me that you take such good care of Mother."

"We take care of each other."

That evening, Chloe and Hilda served a pheasant for dinner. The trimmings were so grand it seemed like Christmas. Rachel spent the day washing the china and polishing the

258

silver. Tonight, the pieces sparkled on the table. Chloe and Hilda prepared winter squash and turnip soup. The desserts included tapioca pudding topped with cream, and butter cake served with coffee.

The room buzzed with laughter. Hanah asked so many questions of Charlotte, and she answered with her version of many stories. Thomas and Henry debated a few, and several times they'd turned to Rosalie for an accurate account of a childhood memory. Rosalie was in awe of her grown children. They'd matured into responsible and hardworking adults and yet enjoyed the animation of their youngest sibling.

The adult world enthralled Hanah, and Rosalie marveled at Hanah's good qualities. She was intellectual, zealous, and radiated compassion. Tonight, Hanah held the room at attention. Rosalie had always considered Hanah so much like Charlotte, but tonight she saw this in a different light. After Simone had come to Huntington Manor, Charlotte had become like Simone. Not the other way around. Watching her family together, Rosalie realized how much Hanah was like Simone.

Charlotte retired to the guest quarters by nine. She was exhausted but lay under the sheets staring at the ceiling instead of sleeping. Being home after ten years reminded Charlotte of her first night in Syracuse. Not uncomfortable but somewhat misplaced. Something wildly unexpected entered her thoughts. Until now, Charlotte had considered Syracuse a place she was visiting, a city she'd leave someday and return to Alexandria and settle near her mother and brothers. However, Charlotte had not expected another realization. Huntington Manor was no longer her home. Syracuse was home.

Her lids were heavy. There was so much to discuss with Mother and her brothers. She was here for more than a visit, and tomorrow, she'd announce her plan.

46

Huntington Manor, Virginia 1852

After breakfast, Rosalie, Thomas, Henry, and Charlotte proceeded to the parlor to deepen their conversation. And Hanah skirted off to help Hilda in the kitchen before attending to the horses with Papa.

Thomas spoke. "I was willing to employ slaves, but to take part in housing fugitives is unimaginable. It's beyond—."

Charlotte interjected. "Negroes have a right to freedom like you and me. You can't tell me you want a slave's life for Hanah."

"Of course not," Thomas exploded under his breath. "It is Hanah who I speak of. I don't want her to get hurt because, sister, believe me when I say if someone will get hurt in this mixed-up mess, it will be Hanah. You've been living North for far too long. Free states are different."

Charlotte was poised and confident. "You're wrong, Thomas. New York is as free as a flightless bird. Negroes aren't free like white men. Colored folks must have papers proving their freedom. And most often, that's not enough. They work for pathetic wages to barely feed their families. And now, because of the Fugitive Slave Law, folks who are anti-slavery are obligated to return Negroes to their owners or fear the consequences. Think about this, Thomas. Negroes must be returned to their owners. Owners!" Charlotte repeated for the third time. "No man has the right to own another man."

261

"This is Virginia. It's perfectly legal," Thomas argued.

"Legal doesn't make it right," Charlotte shot back.

"The law was written because the North keeps poking its nose in our business. Let the South prevail in the South."

"Are you agreeing with the law?" Charlotte said accusingly.

Thomas sighed heavily, feeling like he'd lost a battle against reasoning. "I don't agree with chasing down slaves, but the law is the law."

Rosalie was the matriarch of this family. It was in her control to keep this conversation progressing in a civilized manner.

"Listen," Rosalie said to all three of her children. "We are either in this together or not at all. If we decide to become part of this Underground Railroad, there will be no changing our minds after the fact. What is done will be done."

Rosalie directed her following comment to Charlotte. "You need to hear what Thomas has to say. You want this desperately, Charlotte, but Thomas can voice his opinion without judgment. The same goes for Henry and every last person on this plantation because, without a consensus in its entirety, this plan will not work."

Rosalie turned to Thomas. "Please continue."

Thomas wanted to convey his argument so both sides, his and Charlotte's, could be received for the sake of Huntington Manor. His mother owned the land, but he was running it, and if Huntington Manor was to stand the test of time, he needed first to convince his mother of what detriment such a discussion of the Underground could have on this plantation.

"Mother," Thomas said, with sincerity, "If it's freeing our slaves you are requesting, then I will agree just as I agreed to pay their wages. Freeing enslaved Negroes is becoming quite common. Delaware and Maryland are essentially free states. Plantation owners are finding if they don't offer freedom by Deed of Gift or pay wages, their slaves are running and risking capture by escaping. And here in Virginia, so close to freedom, slaves are confident they can make it to the North.

"We are facing something far different from when Father was alive. Slaves need more than a bed and food, which we've given them. Henry and I have never lifted a finger to one of them." Thomas glanced at Henry, leaning against the mantel, arms crossed, and Charlotte listening with critical ears before turning back to Rosalie. "Charlotte has a valid point. Black folks want freedom. And no doubt they're willing to risk their lives for it. We've seen this firsthand with Jim. I'd also risk my life for liberty, but by God, I would not take my family's freedom and risk it for bondage instead." Thomas looked through the window and past the porch to the men bent over, sowing the fields.

Thomas was cross. "Look out there! We've enslaved these men for years and didn't think anything wrong. Now, I'm supposed to be disgusted by it." He turned back toward his family. "Plantation owners in the Upper South are freeing slaves left and right. But what then? Where are they to go? Guaranteed, some will beg their owners to stay on and work for not a dime because it's their place of security for them and their children. Some overseers will oblige. Some won't because machinery is replacing their labor. So freed slaves escape to the free states, but now that's not even good enough with the Fugitive Slave Act put into law. Slaves must get themselves and their families to Canada while having to trust white folks like us, who have enslaved them, or risk being caught, beaten, or killed." Thomas pointed at the window to the fields. "Those men out there are better off employed by us than hunted like animals."

"Who are you to say what they would choose!" Charlotte barked in return.

"Stop this minute!" Rosalie commanded. Her head trembled as her anger deepened.

Henry straightened from his lean on the mantle. "That's enough, Charlotte. You too, Thomas."

"A fine time for you to speak up, brother. You didn't seem to mind a moment ago when I was trying to save this family from ruin. Go ahead, Henry. Tell us how we are to pull this off," Thomas demanded. "Freeing our slaves. I'm okay with that. Hell. They can leave today. But that is not what Charlotte is proposing. She's suggesting that our property become a safe house. Charlotte wants us to partake in this secretive Underground Railroad, which means we," Thomas flared his finger at Henry and back at himself, "you and I become stationmasters. Can you not admit, Henry? How crazy in the head this is? If we get caught, you and I and Hanah and Mother will sit in prison. And for what? So, a few Negroes can flee North?"

"Thousands!" Charlotte blasted. "Thousands are escaping."

"And thousands are dying horrible deaths," Thomas said, glaring at Charlotte. He turned back to Henry. "Please, Henry." Thomas sneered sarcastically. "Indulge me."

"Keep quiet, Thomas. Let me speak for myself."

"Please." Thomas motioned with his hand to indicate Henry had the floor to himself.

"I agree with you, and I agree with Mother and Charlotte. We would be taking unimaginable risks. And I'll admit being the younger brother has its pluses. I don't have the responsibility you might, considering you took over

Father's duties to this family. And maybe you think I have less to risk than you, but that would be far from the truth. Let's look at the facts. Charlotte is committed to the cause. We have three women in this house who are more than willing to follow Charlotte's lead and risk it all. Imprisonment is a harsh reality. You, Thomas, said you'd fight for your freedom. But can you indeed be free if you don't fight for the rights of another human being?

"Hanah loves you, Thomas. If you haven't noticed, she's a Black girl. She isn't white. And we all love her. You are only trying to protect this family, but if we don't show Hanah she's our equal, we are nothing better than hypocrites."

Thomas shot back. "And it was fine to be a hypocrite yesterday and last year and our entire lives. And now it isn't!"

"We didn't know any better yesterday, but today we do."

Thomas sank into a chair, mumbling under his breath.

Charlotte empathized with her brother. "We're all imprisoned, Thomas," she said softly. "Every one of us." She pointed this out further. "Mother. Henry. Hanah. You. Me." Charlotte pointed toward the field. "Everyone here at Huntington Manor is imprisoned. It's our responsibility to do something about it. Enslaving Negroes is just plain wrong. Skin color should not condemn a person. Ever."

Thomas spoke. "I agree, but we can't change the world."

Charlotte's voice softened. "You may be right, Thomas, but on my deathbed, I want to believe I left the world a better place for all people."

Silence enveloped the room. Minutes went by before Thomas straightened. He pushed himself from the chair, went out on the front porch, lit his pipe, and looked over the land.

47

Huntington Manor, Virginia 1852

They were all committed. Rachel had reported back to Charlotte. Chloe and Hilda were ready and willing to do their part. Tilby reported to Thomas. "We's men is willin' to help. All of us."

Tilby left Lars's response unsaid when he'd heard of Miss Charlotte's plan. The cabin was dark, with only a sliver of a moon and one dimmed oil lamp so as not to attract attention. "I'll help any colored folk who come this way. Bah! I'll go down fightin' 'til I be dead if that what it takes to free a Black man, but you tell that boy," Lars said, referring to Thomas, "If he gets himself into trouble, I ain't savin' his skin. I swear, I'll turn my back on that boy."

Lars continued, mumbling more to himself than to the others. "Mast'r James. He found me half-dead in the woods and sent fo a docto to nurse my wounds. Fo days, I could do nothin' but lay in bed and pray to God to finish the job before Mast'r James returned and said to get my lazy self to the field. But it neveh happened. Mast'r let me mend." Lars looked into the lamp's light. The other men saw the wetness on his cheeks. "Yeah! I'd save Mast'r James if he got into trouble, but Thomas, nah! He ain't nothin' like his old man."

The six stood inside the barn. Rosalie. Thomas. Charlotte. Tilby. Rachel and Hanah. The door was open like every morning when Tilby cleaned the stalls, and the horses went to the pasture. It was April 8, 1852, a Thursday. The air was warm. Thomas recently purchased hay bales that lined the walls of the barn and stable, filling the space with a sweet fragrance. Rosalie steadied herself against a horse stall, away from being seen if a passerby were to stroll down the road. Light came in through the garret's open window. Charlotte, Rosalie, Thomas, and Henry meticulously planned every detail before this meeting.

Henry was in the field working with the men. Hilda and Chloe were in their garden, tending to the soil, getting it ready for the spring plant. Huntington Manor appeared as if nothing unusual was taking place. Slaves worked in the fields and the garden. Rachel was seemingly in the house, though she wasn't there. She was here in the barn with the others. On an ordinary day, she'd be inside cleaning and changing bed sheets. Typically, Thomas would be in the fields with Henry, but he was here too. His absence would be a glitch if, and only if, a passerby decided to take notice.

Charlotte handed Tilby and Rachel several papers before she spoke. "Anyone can leave Huntington Manor at any time. These are documents declaring your freedom. It's imperative to report what is discussed today to the others. If anyone on this plantation chooses to leave, they will be given necessities and led to the next safe place. Whoever decides to stay, and make things appear as they have been every day, will continue to earn wages and become part of something much bigger." Charlotte paused, letting the initial information settle on the room's quiet.

"You are free men and women." She let her words hang in the air. "But to the people outside of Huntington Manor, it will appear as if nothing has changed. If you decide to leave, we'll help you, but you'll be considered a fugitive to anyone poking around and inquiring. There will be little we can do but have you returned to us. If men decide to beat you in the process, we won't be able to help you until you're back on our land, where we can tend to your wounds in secrecy."

Thomas looked around at the four faces glued to Charlotte's words. *When did she become so persuasive?* Over the past days, she'd convinced him that everything he'd believed for nearly thirty years was wrong. And on this early morning in the barn, Thomas realized how proud he was to have Charlotte as a sister. There was something else. It was hard to admit, but Charlotte took on some of his responsibilities for the first time since their father's death. It wouldn't be for long. She would leave in a few weeks, but for now, still, on complete edge with what was to come, Thomas Worthington let his sister take charge.

Charlotte continued. "We will clothe and feed any fugitive who comes here looking for refuge. From here, the most likely path will be to stop at Darcy's Store, then toward Harrisburg. From there, I'm unclear. Most people are uncertain of the whereabouts of safe places until they've reached them. Once a fugitive gets to Cazenovia, Aunt Sarah and I will get word to Mary Ward. Mary hides escaped slaves in her attic through a secret passage behind the walls. She'll make sure they get proper food and warmth.

"We are all in danger. Every one of us is taking an enormous risk. If you stay, you will need to accept this fact."

Everyone agreed.

Hanah interjected. "How will slaves get here?"

"Conductors are people moving escaped slaves from one location to the next. Fugitives will arrive at night if they're coming on foot. Most likely, hidden in a wagon if they're coming by day."

Tilby spoke softly. "Where should my kin hide, Miss Charlotte?"

Rosalie looked at Tilby, who stood across from her. He stood straight, without a trace of slouch to his tall posture, unlike he showed on the day she walked to this very barn and asked him if he was the father of Simone's baby. The whites of his eyes were no longer clouded but precise, and still, anyone could see his gentle nature through them. *How old was Tilby? Rosalie thought. Thirty? Thirty-two?*

Charlotte answered Tilby's question with a request. "We need your help, Tilby. The closet in Mother's bedroom needs reconstruction. If we close off a portion of it with a wall, we can get at least one or two people in there. You could build a wall in the closet. We can use wood from the kitchen pantry, so it's the same color. It should barely be noticeable. We don't have a basement or attic like the Wards, so we'll need a few different places around the house."

"Yes, Miss Charlotte," Tilby said.

Thomas looked up. "There, in the loft. We can hide fugitives under the hay."

"Yes, sirs. I will fix it real good." Tilby said.

Charlotte turned to her sister, who eagerly awaited her part. "Hanah, I've seen you every day, right here in this stable, cleaning the stalls alongside your papa. You've got to work long hours until Tilby has built a few good hiding places."

"I will, Charlotte. I promise I will."

Charlotte looked at the faces looking back. These brave men and women of Huntington Manor. The family she loved. The plantation she once called home—the little sister who would become the most fearless of them all.

Everyone methodically left the barn and went about their day. Charlotte walked aside Mother with linked elbows, but still, Rosalie carefully watched her footing so as not to stumble. Hanah held Charlotte's free hand. They moseyed back to the house on this beautiful morning as if they'd been on a stroll. Nobody would be any wiser of their meeting in the barn.

Rosalie spoke. "Charlotte, I'd like to talk to you about something."

"Are you alright, Mother? You're not feeling worse, are you?"

Rosalie said in a gentle tone. "Heavens, no. It has nothing to do with me. It's about you."

"Me?"

"Well, I suppose the both of us. It's about my diamond."

"Your diamond ring?"

"Yes. I'd like you to have it before you leave."

"Mother, how nice, but," Charlotte hesitated. She didn't want to offend her mother. "Mother, I'm not ready for your ring. Someday, yes, but not now."

"What good is my gift if I can't see you wearing it."

"I won't have it, Mother. Father gave you that ring."

They were at the steps leading to the front porch. Rosalie unclutched Charlotte's arm and held onto the railing. She faced her daughter. "I suppose, it can wait."

They sat at the table on the front porch. Hanah ran to help Rachel bring tea.

Charlotte smiled at Hanah. "Sit with us."

Hanah sat in one of the chairs alongside her mother and sister, sipping tea from the tall glass. The air was growing warmer. It was indeed a beautiful morning.

48

The first year after Charlotte's visit, Tilby and Reedy led three men away from slavery and toward freedom. Hanah had been disappointed. She had envisioned droves of fugitives hiding in the main house and barn, fleeing from horrid masters and daring escapes with her brave father's assistance. However, with another birth of spring, the summer blossoms, and autumn's changing colors, things were shifting more inside the main house of Huntington Manor than outside. Rosalie needed Hanah's help more than ever.

Hanah was no longer a small child at thirteen. Her bosom blossomed, and her hips slightly widened.

"I'm telling you, baby girl," Rachel commented almost daily. "You look so much like your mama."

Hanah's face widened near her cheeks like a decorative vase, and her prominent eyes were beautifully round and cinnamon in color and could melt Papa's heart, which Tilby often told her. Hanah was slightly taller than Rachel, but her youth made her physique lanky to Rachel's slender figure.

"You's bumpin' and thumpin' 'round like a loose cannonball," Rachel laughed when Hanah tripped on her two feet.

Tilby was more sympathetic. "Don't you worry. You is only growin'."

Hanah woke each morning and stepped into her calico dress made of quality cotton, one of the two dresses Rachel had made for her for working in the stables. Rachel was a talented seamstress, and though it was popular to buy already made clothing for slaves, Rosalie admired Rachel's skill with a needle and thread and how competent she was with a sewing machine. Rachel was eager to learn and had mastered the contraption within days of its purchase. Rosalie provided Rachel with materials made from cotton and linen, the more delicate fabric for dresses and fine nightgowns, much more expensive than osnaburg cotton and coarse wool, which Rachel used for trousers and shirts worn by the field men.

Rachel wore a similar dress to what she sewed for Hanah, a calico made from cotton and protected with a linen apron. In the afternoons, Hanah changed into her alabaster long-sleeved bodice with a high neck and a matching long skirt, like Chloe and Hilda wore for kitchen and garden duties. Hanah wore this clothing when she brought water to the men in the fields.

At first, Rosalie objected to Hanah's permanent clothing change, but Hanah argued her point and explained the importance of being seen as a slave.

The reason had pulled at Rosalie's heart.

Hanah continued. "We all must play our part like Charlotte told us. I have got to resemble my own, Ms. Rosalie. It makes sense. Pretty dresses won't do me any good."

Since she was a little girl, Hanah went to the barn to visit her father. No one—not Thomas, Rachel, or Rosalie could have guessed how ideal it would become for what they were doing now. Everything needed to seem the same. Any passerby would usually see Hanah heading to the barn or the fields. But things were different, indeed. Details of fugitives were received from Papa to Rosalie through her.

As the months went by, Hanah visited Tilby less in the mornings, and eventually, it was more common to see her casually making her way to the barn in the afternoons while Rosalie rested. Running and skipping from the house naturally settled into walking. No one questioned the change. Hanah Smith was simply maturing from a girl into a young lady.

Part III
1860-1861

49

Huntington Manor, Virginia 1860

Hanah left her bedroom, walked to Rosalie's room, and knocked on the door. "Ms. Rosalie," she called softly, "Are you awake?" She entered the room without waiting for a response. "Good morning," Hanah said in a cheerful tone.

Rosalie was reading, propped by bed pillows supported by the mahogany headboard. The book rested on her lap so it wouldn't tremble in her hands.

"Good morning, darling." Rosalie closed the book and moved it to the bedside table near a half-full glass of water. Spilled liquid darkened the wood around it.

Hanah's eyes softened. She lifted the glass to Rosalie. Rosalie framed her quaking hands around Hanah's hands, guided the glass to her mouth, and took a long drink.

"Thank you, Hanah. You're always so kind to me."

"Of course, Ms. Rosalie. I'm your daughter, and you're my mother."

Rosalie smiled. "Well, now. No prolonging the warmth of my bed." She scooted toward the edge of the feather mattress. Hanah helped Rosalie stand until she could steady herself. Together, like mother and daughter, with arms linked, Rosalie walked to her cedar chest and pulled out a new dress, light blue with an easy fit. Fancy dresses and the idea of gracefulness had been impractical for years. Rosalie needed help to put on her clothes in the morning and take them off before bed.

When Rosalie sat at the desk so she could slip on her stockings and button-up shoes, Hanah opened the small jewelry box placed on the bedside table. She removed Rosalie's beautiful diamond ring and slipped it onto her mother's trembling hand.

"It's so beautiful, Ms. Rosalie."

Rosalie stared at the ring, quivering on her finger. The 5-carat diamond was stunning, and the memories it bequeathed were dear to her heart, but this ring represented so much more than she could have ever imagined forty years ago when James asked for her hand in marriage. *This ring,* Rosalie thought, would remain long beyond her lifetime and Charlotte's.

Hanah gave a soft smile and then spoke evenly. "Papa took Hugh and his girl to the Potomac last night. Papa stayed with them, hiding in the tree line until another man got them on a boat. He was back before dawn and reported that nobody followed him."

Hugh and his six-year-old girl, Ester, had arrived two nights earlier, starving and tired. The two runaways slept huddled together between hay bales in the loft. If anyone were to come sniffing around, two coughs, a five-second pause, and one cough would warn them. If this occurred, Hugh and Ester would silently climb inside an already burrowed hay bale and pull another by the attached ropes closing them inside the other bale. When done correctly, nothing looked out of the ordinary. Only two hay bales side by side.

The previous night, Tilby had told Hanah to inform Rosalie that he was taking them to the Potomac after sundown.

"Your father is a brave man, Hanah."

"And you're brave too, Ms. Rosalie."

277

"You've grown into such a beautiful young lady."

Hanah laughed. She held out her skirt. "In this old thing?"

"What you wear doesn't mean a thing. It's the person's heart that counts. You taught me that."

"Oh, Ms. Rosalie." Hanah batted the air. "You've known it your whole life. I didn't teach you anything of the sort."

"But you, Hanah, are beautiful inside and out."

"Promise me you'll never forget how much I love you." Hanah threw her arms around her mother.

"Never shall I forget." Rosalie planted her feet soundly on the floor. "Are we ready for another wonderful day?"

The two women, Rosalie in her late fifties, filled with tremors, and Hanah, nineteen today and vivacious, walked from the room. Henry met them at the top of the staircase. The three carefully took the stairs one at a time—Hanah and Rosalie with linked elbows. Rosalie gripped tightly to the railing with her free hand. Henry stepped backward, one step at a time, in front of his mother. If she were to stumble, he would be there to catch her.

At the bottom of the staircase, Henry helped his mother into a wheelchair, bid Rosalie and Hanah a lovely day, and headed outdoors.

"It's a lovely morning," Rosalie said to Hanah. "Let's have our breakfast outside."

"Oh, Ms. Rosalie." Hanah was surprised by the gift on the table. It was wrapped in lavender parchment paper and tied with a dark purple bow. Hanah positioned Rosalie's chair even with the table and sat down.

"Happy birthday, darling."

Hanah smiled at her mother. "You remembered."

"I could never forget your birthday. Nineteen today. My, how the time has passed."

Hanah opened the present. Inside was a journal with a hundred empty pages. "It's lovely, Mother. Thank you." She stood, went to Rosalie, and kissed her on the cheek.

"Now, the corn cakes are getting cold. We don't want Rachel complaining that we allowed her hard work to go to waste because of our emotions."

Hanah sat, held the journal, and looked at the blank pages. "I'm going to write everything in this book. Stories of the past and now and so many more."

Rosalie lifted a small piece of corn cake to her mouth. She carefully chewed small bites so the cake became almost liquid. Swallowing had become increasingly perilous with the progression of shaking palsy. She had nearly choked a few too many times to forget her crippling disease was affecting her throat. And not to argue with the doctor on the times he checked in on her, but she suspected this disease was more than what he understood, and it caused her to tire so quickly these days. Maybe she had a condition not yet discovered.

"Tonight, your father and everyone will be celebrating with us. Rachel has made your favorite—lemon cake."

Hanah laid her journal on the table and broke off a piece of the yellow corn cake. "I'm the same age as Mama when she gave birth to me."

"You are. It's hard to believe," Rosalie said.

Rosalie was reminded of Charlotte sitting here on her twentieth birthday, thinking of Simone's and James's deaths and planning to leave for Syracuse. The time had passed so quickly but seemed so slowly. She'd only seen Charlotte a handful of times over the past years, yet Rosalie considered their relationship closer than those years

Charlotte was a child. They'd since helped many fugitives, housing them on the plantation and guiding them miles away toward freedom.

Tilby and Reedy were considered conductors. They took fugitives from Huntington Manor to the Potomac, traveling miles under cover of trees to where a boat awaited the runaways on the river. Ship captains, sympathizing with the cause, transported men, women, and children on their ships. Fugitives continued to either Philadelphia or Trenton.

In Syracuse, Charlotte took in fugitives, primarily from Philadelphia. Some came from William and Mary Ward's farmhouse in Cazenovia. From there, by the light of a faint moon, William hid people in wagons or traveled by foot, leading Negroes of all ages for miles through woods, some thick with trees, others scarce, before turning back. Slaves looked for houses with flickers of candles shining through windows or lanterns hanging outside, indicating it was a safe place for resting and food. Syracuse was a distance but could be made in a full day if problems didn't arise, which was unlikely with slave hunters and politicians breathing down the backs of abolitionists.

Once in Syracuse, Uncle Warren hid Negroes in large crates otherwise used to ship supplies and tools to and from his hardware store. If there was a word of someone poking around or a ruckus or when someone entered the shop, fugitive slaves hiding in the back room slipped quietly into marked crates.

Warren and a couple of good men unloaded the crates onto cargo ships. Captain Smitter, and a select boat crew, specifically looked for boxes marked WH Cargo with faint lettering. Inside these boxes were escaped slaves, dependent on the assistance of a few good people and a God who they prayed would protect them. Once the boat docked elsewhere, someone would guide them toward freedom. Routes led to Rochester, onto Buffalo, and into Canada, where Negroes were safe from the capture of greedy slave hunters.

Rosalie hoped at least one or two fugitives who'd been here had also been helped by Charlotte or in the care of Mary and William. Maybe someday, she and Charlotte would discover they'd helped the same person. It connected her to the cause more than ever.

Hanah stood and went to Rosalie and guided her wheelchair from its place at the table. "It's a beautiful August morning. Let's take a stroll around the plantation?"

Hanah wheeled the chair down a ramp Tilby built alongside the house, so Rosalie's chair could move slowly and steadily into the grassy area and toward a favored willow tree. "Do you expect Abraham Lincoln to win the election?"

"It's hard to guess. Lincoln will be the first Republican to win the presidency if he does. Stephen Douglas is a powerful politician."

"We need change, and Abraham Lincoln is that change," Hanah said. "Charlotte agrees. If he's not elected, how soon before this madness of slavery ends."

"What makes you think Lincoln will end this madness?"

"Any man who wants to stop the spread of slavery would be willing to take it further and end it altogether. Charlotte said—."

Rosalie interjected. "Charlotte is perhaps writing things she should not. Putting one's views in a letter is careless. The same goes for responding to those views."

"I understand, Ms. Rosalie. I'm only hopeful."

"I am too, Hanah."

The conversation continued later that evening in the parlor.

Thomas spoke. "It's careless to speak outside of this house, Mother."

"It was only the two of us, Thomas. We were careful."

"But what about next time?" Thomas continued wearily.

"That's enough, Thomas. I'm well aware of what I was saying."

"Yes, but Hanah is impressionable. Why wouldn't Hanah assume the same if you're willing to speak openly outside this house? And Hanah might not be as careful. We've agreed. Any conversation we have about our illegal acts is done in this parlor only."

Hanah's sweet disposition left her. She was not a child. She was part of this family and Huntington Manor. "Thomas, we weren't discussing anything illegal," Hanah stated bluntly.

"But we cannot take any chances of bringing attention to ourselves."

"Having a picnic is bringing attention to us?"

"If you get absorbed in a conversation, and a neighbor you didn't notice coming for a visit is in the listening distance, then yes, it is.

"Don't forget last month we hid two fugitives from Mr. Jenson's plantation, only fifteen miles from here. These are neighboring plantations, Mother. If word gets around, even if to only slaves, law enforcement will be banging on our doors. We will be finished. Desperate people take desperate measures. No longer will slaves come secretly at night. If they are desperate, and they are, they'll come running midday to get away from their hell. We know the consequences if we're exposed. Neighbors don't take kindly to theft and treason."

That night, Hanah lay in bed, her eyes wide, staring at the ceiling. Thomas was frightened. There had been an incident last year that shook him. Rosalie had fallen and hit her head on a bedside table. The injury hadn't looked terrible, but Henry had called on the doctor to assure his mother's cut didn't require stitches.

Three runaways, a young couple, and their crying newborn had arrived moments before the doctor. Hanah had seen them by chance through Rosalie's bedroom window. And not more than fifty yards behind them, Hanah spotted Henry and the doctor. Without alarming Rosalie, Hanah pulled the drapes closed and excused herself. She ran for Thomas, who was overseeing the plantation for the evening.

"Get them to the barn!" Hanah demanded of her brother. "I'll make Ms. Rosalie's situation seem much worse. Now! Go!" She ordered in a frantic whisper and hurried the doctor into the house minutes later.

As she stared at the ceiling tonight, she sympathized with her brother, but Thomas's fear of the law could not deter her from helping enslaved people. Hanah sat up in bed, opened her journal, and quietly read aloud what she'd written before settling in for the night.

August 17, 1860.

Nineteen years ago, I was born a slave, and my mother died a slave.

Nothing could stop Hanah. Not Thomas. Not Ms. Rosalie. Not anybody.

50

Two disheveled girls slid behind a movable wall in the back of Rosalie's closet.

"You are not to make a noise," Rachel whispered.

The older girl's voice trembled. "Sorry, miss. We were so frightened. Somebody shouted at us from a distance. We shouldn't have come—."

Rachel spoke softly. "Hush. Not a word."

The pounding on the front door came as Rachel slid the wall into place. The younger girl, not more than ten, jolted with fear.

"Not a noise." Rachel reminded the girls, then quickly returned to the sewing room and continued darning socks.

The sky was darkening. Fugitive slaves were led here mainly during the darkest part of the evening and into the night, though it hadn't been the first time a runaway arrived before dusk. A few had come hidden beneath blankets, alongside supplies in Henry's wagon on his way back to the plantation in broad daylight, but tonight was different. Never before had anyone come pounding on the front door.

Rachel heard the second round of pounding, and her heart jumped. She knew her place in the house should this happen. Everyone knew their place, depending on the day and time. Hilda and Chloe would be clearing and washing plates in the kitchen if it happened near dinnertime. Tonight was this particular drill.

Thomas opened the door quickly. "Luke, is there a problem?"

"There is. I saw a couple of runaway slaves run this way not more than twenty minutes ago. I was on my way home from town." Luke Jansen pointed toward the road. "Saw two Black figures run across the path down yonder, like two turkeys missing their heads. I reckon they're Hank Davenport's slaves. He said they went missing last night. He's at the pub right now getting a posse to go after 'em before they get too far north. He's offering a $500 reward."

Rachel stretched her ear to hear every word. She and everyone in a fifty-mile radius knew of Hank Davenport. He was a wealthy and unforgiving master.

Thomas looked past Luke and, pretending alarm, called out to his brother, who was walking toward the front of the house. "Henry!"

"Evening, Luke. Is something wrong, Thomas?"

Luke turned and had to catch himself from stumbling.

"Luke says he saw two escaped slaves on our property twenty minutes ago."

Henry acted unruffled. "I don't believe so, Mr. Jansen. I've been checking on things for the past two hours, overseeing the barn and stable and checking our feed and hay. In fact, I've just come from the cabin. All the men are hunkering down for their dinner. There's no one on my land I don't know about. They'd need to be buried a foot under the dirt to hide. No, Sir. There isn't anyone poking around here."

"I saw them, I tell you. And it ain't men Hank's lookin' for. Two of his female slaves run off."

"No disrespect, sir, but you seem a bit off. Are you feeling alright?"

Luke Jansen snorted. "Don't go thinkin' I've drunk myself silly." He pointed hard. "I saw two colored runaways dart across the field over there headed this way."

"Like I said, no disrespect." Henry removed his glove and used it to gesture toward the tobacco fields behind him. Pine boughs covered the dirt to protect the fragile seedlings. "Take a look if you'd like. I'd be glad to show you around. You can question my slaves, but if you saw runaways twenty minutes ago, they're long gone now."

Thomas spoke. "This seems serious, Henry. Mr. Davenport is at the pub now, gathering a posse."

"This is serious," Henry said. "Is there a reward involved?"

Luke blurted. Droplets of spit discharged with his irritation. "Five hundred dollars, and I ain't sharin' if that's what you're insinuating."

"Not at all. Instead, I have a business proposition."

"Like what?"

"To be perfectly honest, Mr. Davenport and I have never seen eye-to-eye. Maybe if I helped you find these two slaves, you claim you saw—"

"I ain't claiming' nothing but the truth."

"Well then, this business deal will be better than I thought."

"Go on," Luke said stiffly.

"You get the reward, and I get Mr. Davenport's respect."

Before Luke could argue, Henry quickly walked toward the stable and shouted for Tilby in an unfamiliar and impertinent manner. "Boy, saddle my fastest horse. I've got business to attend to."

Thomas called after his brother, hoping to reassure Luke. "It's about time you earn Mr. Davenport's respect, little brother."

In truth, Thomas and Henry stayed clear of Davenport, like their father had done. He was a spoiled boy who'd grown into an evil man, living off his father and grandfather's hard work and wealth. Hank inherited established land and more than his share of enslaved Negroes to attend the apple orchards. Hank Davenport used young female slaves offhandedly to meet his sexual desires. Rumors surfaced that Hank raped young Black girls and sold the ones he impregnated.

After scouring Huntington Manor's barren fields and the cabin, the two men, Henry with his prepared saddlebag and Luke Jansen, rode off into the distance in the opposite direction of where Tilby would soon lead the two young girls.

Thomas had long closed the front door and made his way upstairs. Gathered in Rosalie's bedroom was Alyssa, ten, clinging to her older sister, Jane, seventeen, Rosalie, Hanah, Rachel, and Tilby.

"There is no time to think," Hanah said. "We need to act now." She pushed her father to get moving, take the fugitives, and run fast. "Go, Papa. Please go."

"No," Thomas said. "Always take a moment to think. You must keep your wits about the situation at hand."

"Master Thomas is right," Tilby told his daughter.

"They'll come for them," Hanah cried, turning to Papa and Thomas. "When Henry and Mr. Jansen return empty-handed, that stupid drunk will go straight to Mr. Davenport. We've got to hurry, Thomas."

"We will, Hanah! But first, these two girls and your father deserve a well-thought plan. Capture comes to those who run in haste. And then they come for us. You've got to see my point."

"Stop. Both of you," Rosalie said. She rested on her bed, propped against the headboard. Only now had anyone seen she was half-dressed. Hanah had been helping Rosalie slip into a nightgown when Rachel burst into the room with the two girls. Minutes later, Luke pounded on the door.

"Hanah. Thomas is right. In haste, everything will go wrong. However, we need to move quickly." Rosalie's voice quivered, not from fear but shaking palsy. Her speech and head seemed to mimic each other. Rosalie looked at Tilby. "Tilby, we are asking you again to put yourself in danger. The stakes are much higher now. There will be a posse of men looking for easy money. You are in great danger. Are you willing to help us?"

Tilby stared hard at Rosalie. "Ma'am," he paused. "Have you forgot what you is done for my sweet Hanah and me? You show me a kind of respect I's never know'd before comin' here." He looked at Alyssa and Jane, who were frightened and shaken. "They is my people, Ms. Rosalie. Theys freedom is we's freedom. Should I's die doin' what's right, may the Good Lord take me to His heavenly house where the color of a man's skin don't matter none."

Thomas stood still. Tilby was brave, and his willingness to die was a heroism he could only imagine. Hanah ran to her father. "I love you with all my heart."

288

51

Huntington Manor, Virginia 1861

The following evening, Thomas and Rosalie sat alone at the dinner table. They couldn't risk having Hanah join them in case their dinner was interrupted. The slightest indication they treated Hanah like anything but a slave might enhance Luke Jansen's allegations that, yes, indeed, he had seen two slaves run toward their property.

Furthermore, they couldn't risk skipping dinner or anything seemingly unexpected.

"Don't worry, Mother. Henry is on a wild goose chase, and Luke was drunk enough not to notice."

"I'm not worried about tonight, Thomas. It's tomorrow night and the night after that, I worry. Sitting around and waiting for the next time something happens is a death wish. It could have been anybody passing by, anyone sober and sure of what they saw. We were fortunate it was Luke Jansen."

Hanah entered the dining room. "Ms. Rosalie, please let me help you." Rosalie let Hanah lift the cup of milk to her lips. She wrapped her shaky hands around Hanah's one so she could drink without spilling.

Hanah lowered the mug. She spoke softly. "Word has already gotten around that no fugitive should come here until this settles down."

"What exactly do you mean, word has gotten around?" Thomas said.

Neither he nor Hanah had noticed Rosalie having trouble swallowing. Milk had dribbled down her chin. Rosalie tried to catch it with a linen napkin.

"Reedy and Lars. They have been sneaking around, talking to the other slaves on other plantations. They'll make sure not a slave in fifty miles of here comes this way for now. When it's safe again, word will get around about that too."

"Along with white people, Hanah. Every last set of ears will hear of what's going on here. You can't tell me you're foolish to believe some slave somewhere won't tell their white master everything. Put fire to their feet, and they'll talk."

"No, brother!" Hanah bellowed. "That's the difference between you and them, Thomas. You have everything to lose. They have everything to gain. Slaves are fighting to save their people. You're fighting to save yourself."

Thomas stood abruptly, almost knocking his chair over. "You and Charlotte have this notion that you can save the world. You can't, Hanah. Neither can Aunt Sarah and Uncle Warren nor Abraham Lincoln, for that matter. People are going to die if we keep this up. You must understand this."

Hanah shot back. "They are already dying, Thomas. It's you who needs to understand."

Rosalie's mug fell to the floor. Thomas and Hanah turned. They hadn't seen when Rosalie stood from the chair. Hanah grabbed for her, but Rosalie stumbled in the opposite direction. Thomas leaped over part of the table and caught his mother seconds before she hit the floor. Hanah ran for Rachel.

Hanah and Thomas were at Rosalie's bedside.

Rosalie argued. "For Heaven's sake, it was a tiny fall."

"We are sorry," Thomas said. "This would not have happened if we hadn't been cutting each other's throats."

"Perhaps. But I'm fine now."

Thomas stood from where he sat at his mother's bedside. "I'll leave you for now."

Rosalie spoke before Thomas turned to leave. "Thomas. I want you to know how proud I am of you. For everything you've done all these years to keep us safe."

Thomas only nodded. "We will discuss how we should proceed when Henry returns." Thomas went to Rosalie and kissed her on the cheek. "I love you, Mother."

Hanah took Rosalie's nightgown from the closet. The secretive wall crammed Rosalie's dresses and other attire.

Hanah carried the nightgown to her mother. "Ms. Rosalie, I am sorry about tonight. Truly, I am. I let an ache I cannot explain stand in the way. You and Charlotte—Thomas, Henry, and everyone here have endangered their lives. I should have reminded myself that we are in this together, even though we may have different reasons for supporting our cause. I blamed Thomas for only looking after himself when in truth, his burden is protecting this entire estate and our family."

Tears rolled down Hanah's cheeks. "Please forgive me."

Rosalie motioned for Hanah to sit next to her on the bed. "You and your sister are no different. You're not afraid to speak your mind and stand for justice. Your brother knows that, darling. If you're apologizing, it should be to him, not to me." Rosalie took Hanah's hands in hers. "Often, we don't discover how difficult something is until we're so deep that there is no turning back." Rosalie softly smiled. "Maybe, God wanted it this way. It keeps our souls searching for love and our bodies doing what is right."

It was strange when Rosalie mentioned God because besides making Hanah say nightly prayers, Rosalie rarely mentioned God or religion. Over the years, Rosalie's family had survived ruined crops and threatening storms. However, everyone worked harder to overcome any devastation standing in their way. Several summers ago, when heavy rains damaged acres of tobacco, Rosalie said that praying on one's knees couldn't tame any storm. A Bible rested by Rosalie's bedside, but had she ever read it, Hanah wondered? Perhaps after Hanah left Rosalie for the night.

On the other hand, Rachel read from the Bible passionately and shared stories with Hanah to raise her as a Christian. Hanah reminded herself of Rachel's lessons from over the years when needed.

Proverbs 20:11. *Even a child is known by his doings, whether his work be pure, and whether it be right.*

"God don't like lying little girls," Rachel told her. "When you lie, you get into a whole bucket of trouble, but telling the truth is pure and right." And little Hanah looked into Rachel's eyes and promised to be good.

But Rosalie let lessons derive from experiences, stories, and sometimes newspapers and Charlotte's letters. Rosalie went to church on Sundays until it was too much for her, but besides this particular duty, Rosalie rarely mentioned God.

"For goodness sake, Hanah. Clear your tears. I'm fine. Your brother is fine. You can discuss your apologies with Thomas in the morning. I'll tell you what I told Charlotte when she frowned. You will have fewer wrinkles with a lifetime of smiles than a lifetime of sorrows."

Hanah took a bulky handkerchief from her pocket and wiped her tears.

Rosalie griped when she saw the stained cloth. "You are more like your father every day. A lady should carry a delicate and embroidered hanky, not a cloth big enough to carry a sack of potatoes."

Hanah laughed light-heartedly and helped Rosalie into her nightgown and bed.

Rosalie motioned Hanah to sit by her side. "I have something I'd like to discuss with you." The two women held hands. Rosalie's cold hands enclosed Hanah's warm skin. "I want you to do me a favor," Rosalie told Hanah. "I'm not asking for your permission or an opinion. I'm asking you to do something for me. There will be no fretting or questions about a decision I've already made."

"What is it, Ms. Rosalie? Anything."

"First, adhere to my requests."

Hanah was perplexed. "Of course. You know I will."

Rosalie withdrew her hand from Hanah's. Her eyes focused on the magnificent diamond ring. She twisted at it, removing it from her finger. The flickering lamp directed prisms from each facet to the wall, where colors danced like fireflies on a summer evening. "I want you to put this ring behind the closet wall for safekeeping."

"You're silly, Ms. Rosalie. Those men are not coming for us if that is what you are implying. Nobody is taking your ring."

"You are."

"Pardon me?" Hanah questioned.

"If it comes time, I want you to take this ring and go to Cazenovia, New York. Find William and Mary Ward."

"Ms. Rosalie—"

"Go to Pompey Hollow Road. There's a red saltbox-style home there—the only one of its kind. A large willow tree practically swallows the front yard. There's a huge barn on the property and trees and fields all around. Mary Ward will notify Charlotte if you should find yourself there."

Hanah swallowed hard, trying to understand. She'd heard of the place several times in conversation but never in detail. "Pompey Hollow Road."

"Yes. That's right, Hanah."

"Then I've got a request, too," Hanah said to Rosalie. "That ring belongs on your finger. We'll see Charlotte soon enough because she will surely miss us. You can give her your ring then."

There was no raising this young girl any longer. Hanah had grown up. Rosalie hadn't known when it happened, but it had arrived. She only said again, but this time in a whisper, for she was exhausted. "Pompey Hollow Road."

Ms. Rosalie lay in bed, and her eyes focused on the mahogany desk. She wanted to write a letter to Charlotte or maybe jot down a few notes for the books, but the trembling in her feet continually worsened before bed. Besides, her hands trembled wildly these days. She hadn't written more than a sentence or two in over a year.

Rosalie had something far worse than what Dr. Clay called shaking palsy. This disease was different. She was experiencing more symptoms than mentioned by the doctor, like the tingling in her feet and fingertips or the way her throat closed when swallowing even small pieces of food. Rosalie hadn't eaten bread or corn cakes in weeks, explaining she'd come to like the texture of corn hash instead, which was a bit easier to swallow. An itch plagued her several times, but Rosalie could not locate its exact location. She scratched so hard in some areas skin had reddened and torn under the pressure of her fingernails. It was an agonizing affliction.

And then there was the fall tonight. Thomas and Hanah had assumed she'd only stumbled, but her eyes had troubled her. She'd blinked, and her eyelids had gotten stuck. She tried forcing them open for a few seconds by intensely raising her brow, but it was impossible until they lifted open on their own. Rosalie had stumbled not because of shaking palsy. She'd struggled because the room had gone black, and she'd lost her balance and couldn't see where to grab.

52

Huntington Manor, Virginia 1861

Henry returned to Huntington Manor with unpromising news.

"He's insistent. Nothing will stop Luke Jansen. He knows what he saw. And it's worse than we thought. Get a man drunk enough, and he'll tell you what you need to know."

"And what do we need to know other than Luke maintaining we're hiding fugitives?" Thomas asked.

It was late. Henry had come in after sundown so as not to be seen by anyone. He and his brother and mother were in the parlor. What Henry was about to tell them would change their lives. He didn't know how exactly, but news like this could only change things. There was no way out.

Henry crossed his arms across his chest, heavy from worry. "Mr. Davenport will believe Jansen. A couple of men have been watching our place. Six months ago, Mr. Davenport thought he'd seen one of his brothers' slaves passing by here with some white folks he didn't know. The Negro looked so familiar, but he disregarded the notion because the sun was low, and there had been a fair distance between him and the Black man." Henry looked at his mother and Thomas, who were heeding his every word. "Mr. Davenport hadn't thought about it again until his brother, a week later, mentioned his slave had run off. It was the night before Mr. Davenport spotted him near here."

Thomas barely sat in a wingback chair. He leaned forward. "Who's watching the place?"

"A couple of men. I couldn't get Luke to disclose their names. Honestly, I don't think he could remember. He only said Mr. Davenport is paying men as informants. And if they catch us in the act, they'll have enough reward money to drink themselves to oblivion. According to Hank, nobody was watching the place when the girls arrived. Hank seeing those two girls happened by chance."

Hanah stood in the doorway. "Where is Mr. Jansen at the moment?"

"How long have you been standing there?" Thomas asked.

"Long enough to know there is trouble brewing." Hanah turned to Rosalie. "Ms. Rosalie. I'm sorry. I should have announced myself, but please, may I stay?"

Thomas wanted to deter Hanah, but instead, he heaved in agreeance.

Henry answered Hanah's question. "Up north. More than sixty miles from here, I suppose. I got Luke good and drunk, but not before convincing him we should split up. He's traveling farther north if he remembered the plan. I left him in a stupor and headed here after Luke was out cold. I suspected it took ten or twelve hours before he woke up. It took me a full day and a half to get back here. If he heads north, we've got maybe a few extra days before he's back."

"Have no doubt, Mother," Thomas interjected. "Luke will be back. He's not backing down on his story. It's not safe. If we're discovered housing fugitives, jail is not out of the question." He paused. "It will be far worse for Hanah."

Silence filled the room.

"I'm not scared," Hanah said bravely. "I'll do what it takes—."

"No," Rosalie repositioned herself in the chair. Her eyes caught Hanah's. She sensed the desperation in her daughter's dark and fervent eyes. "It's over, Hanah. You and I will leave Huntington Manor. If we need an excuse, we'll say Charlotte is ill and needs us in Syracuse."

Hanah hurried to Rosalie's side and slid to the floor. "Ms. Rosalie," Hanah begged. "Please let me stay. Colored people are counting on me to help them. I can continue without you, Ms. Rosalie. I swear I can." In desperation, she turned to Henry, confirming Rosalie could not travel alone. "Henry, you can take Mother, can't you? I promise I'll help Thomas like I was you. Rachel can take on extra house chores. Everyone will be willing to make it work. Please, Henry. Tell Mother I can do it."

Thomas didn't wait for Henry to surrender to Hanah's pleas. If he lingered for a second longer, Henry would make a decision he couldn't live with. "No, Hanah. It's over. I will not place you or Mother or this plantation in harm's way any longer."

Thomas faced Rosalie like a tin soldier going into battle. "Mother, can you be ready by tomorrow? We'll send word to Uncle Warren."

Hanah acted quickly and challenged Thomas, confident and angry. "Sending us away just as a few townspeople are suspicious is not a good idea. What if marshals start snooping around Uncle Warren's hardware store or Aunt Sarah's home while we are there? Then they question why Charlotte visits Cazenovia so often. Now they focus on Pompey Hollow Road. What then, Thomas? After we've put three innocent families in jeopardy?"

Henry spoke. He could soften the blow of any conversation. "Waiting is worse. It will only be days before Luke stumbles back here. Men will watch Huntington Manor like a hawk on a field mouse. They will pounce on our mistakes, Hanah." Henry looked at his sister with regret. "Someone will make the smallest mistake. That's all it will take to bring us to our knees—your father, Lars, Reedy, Rachel, Mother—not a person will go unscathed if we're caught."

"I won't stay in Syracuse." Hanah turned from Henry to face Rosalie. "Mother. I love you with all my soul, but I will not abandon my post here with Papa. I'll take you to Aunt Sarah's, but I'm returning here. I'll make it on foot or by water, but I'll get back here."

Thomas stood and directed his frustration at Hanah. "I will not be part of this any longer. Unless you return with Mother, you will not be welcome on this plantation."

"Thomas," Rosalie scolded. "Huntington Manor belongs to me. I make the decisions for this family and this plantation. You may run it how you wish when I have passed, but until then, I will make the decisions."

"There won't be a darn thing left to manage or even be proud to call our own if this—this belief we can save the Black folk continues." He instantly turned the conversation toward Hanah. "Honestly, Hanah! What difference have we made? There are three million slaves. We've helped maybe forty. And we don't know how many made it to the next station after your father led them away from here. What if slave catchers captured them? Tell me. Do you really believe you've made even the smallest difference?"

"We've made a difference to thirty-eight people, Thomas. Thirty-eight. Twenty-two men, ten women, and six children. If it had been one person or a whopping one hundred thousand—we made a difference."

Thomas threw his hands in the air. "Talk sense into her, Henry."

Neither Henry nor Thomas, nor Rosalie could talk sense into Hanah. She had unearthed an overpowering determination. It began years earlier when six family members gathered inside the barn. On that early April morning, Hanah had discarded any remaining sanctuary. This outcome had been established then. There simply was no turning back.

53

Huntington Manor, Virginia 1861

The full moon shone brightly when Hanah came upon Huntington Manor. A mile back, the hairs on her neck stiffened. The skittering of field mice and shadows spooked her. A breeze whispered through the trees. Hanah turned quickly on her heel several times, terrified of what was there. If the forest could talk, it would tell her to go back, but Hanah kept coming like an animal to food, urging herself to heed every detail, especially on this moonlit night. It had been a motherly guide the last week. The sky had been nearly cloudless, and the moon was almost waning toward this full moon. Hanah used it cautiously as a guide because a bright moon could also uncover her whereabouts. Her shadow nearly scared her to death when she slipped away from Uncle Warren's home at night. Almost four weeks had passed since then—the moon told her so.

The big house of Huntington Manor was dark. Too dark. There was not a single oil lamp burning. Not in the parlor. Not in Henry's bedroom, which was visible from where she stood behind a line of trees. The cabin's door, if she guessed right because she couldn't particularly see it, banged against the side of the small house with the blowing wind. Bump. Bump. Bump. It was a faint thud, wood against wood, unfailing every five seconds. Nobody was living there. What had happened to the place? Had they been discovered?

Then a burst of fear entered her mind. "Papa," she whispered. Her eyes followed the fields to the barn. And there it was. The white handkerchief—a sign for runaways was barely visible in the darkness. Her papa had used it often, but the cloth wasn't enough. She would see the light if her father was here and if it was safe.

Hanah had seen dim glowing oil lights in upstairs windows on her journey home. She'd been fed by strangers and given a dry place to sleep, and the next evening she'd slip away into the darkness. She was a runaway now, not a fugitive. Nobody was combing the land and trees for her, hoping to cash in on a reward. There wasn't a reward on her head, but being seen without white folks could signify to slave hunters she was a runaway.

Charlotte and Rosalie knew of Hanah's plan. Hanah hadn't spoken about which night she'd leave but told her beloved sister and mother she would know when the timing was right. They'd arrived in Syracuse on April 11, the day before a shot was fired on Fort Sumter. The daily newspaper reports had worried Rosalie for Hanah's safety more now than ever. She had asked Hanah to stay, but only once, and Hanah told Rosalie she couldn't.

"We'll be together soon, Ms. Rosalie. I promise. When it's safe, Charlotte will bring you home." Rosalie had not responded. In the two weeks she'd stayed at Uncle Warren and Aunt Sarah's house, Rosalie rested more than usual. She'd assumed that travel had been too much for her mother, but after a week, she'd questioned if there was more to Rosalie's illness than shaking palsy. Hanah figured that deciding to slip away into the night was best for everyone.

Hanah dismissed the consequences of slave catchers or Confederate soldiers from her mind. She'd met Negroes in the passing days and weeks. She'd seen starved pregnant women and men whipped so severely scars raised from their spines like spiders. She'd seen Lars's back, and it scared her then, and now it scared her more, but fear was a reality she forced out of her way.

Cici, an old white woman, hid Hanah and two men with swollen feet in her barn. The men had run for thirty miles on nothing but the soles of their feet, which had grown to the size of melons with gashes and bruising. Hanah slathered the men's feet with pulverized roots and herbs Cici had made into a salve to soothe their sore feet before wrapping them in sterile cloth. One man whimpered through the process and groaned through the night. The other slept, only flinching through the worst of it.

Hanah met Thaddeus, a young man with scarred lips. She presumed some of his tongue was missing by the way he spoke. Some words were so difficult for him to pronounce that Hanah had to listen closely to understand.

"It happened when I was a boy," he'd told Hanah. "A white boy wrest'ed me to the grou'd and ho'd me while ano'ter poured hot coas in my mouth."

Hanah's face swelled when Thaddeus spurted the rest. The overseer told him the only way to save his mother from death was to swallow hot coals.

"I wa'ted to scream from the pain, but I only hear the sizz'ing of my skin—have the scars to prove it, but those bastards stru'g my mama besides. They said she was no good to them after she was't right in the head. But they the reaso' she was't right. They beat her almost dead."

He swallowed hard.

Hanah silently begged to hide her face and weep a lake of tears. She prayed for pardon from witnessing anything worse.

'I—." Thaddeus struggled desperately, willing the muscle in his mouth to work how he remembered his mama's words. 'Mama to'd me she loves me before they hanged her upside down from a tree.

"I'm going to ki'l them. You hear me right. I got myse'f a stream of information in Mayem Junction. I'm going North to join the Union. Mark my words, Miss, I'm goin' hunt Mr. Billiards and his kin and ki'l them for my mama's sake. And God won't blame me because it's okay to ki'l if it's war. Ain't that right, Miss?"

Thaddeus hadn't wanted an answer. He was too busy convincing himself that *Do unto others* didn't apply during wartime. Thaddeus hadn't looked at Hanah when talking about killing people, and she was glad. His scarred face could convince anyone he deserved the pleasure of killing the people who had tortured him.

Hanah thought of Lars and the raised scars on his back. When she was a child, she'd asked her father why Lars had puffed skin. Knowing what she discovered years later, how silly the words must have seemed to her father. Lars had been whipped almost to death several times before being sold and taken from Atlanta. Sympathetically, to help spare Hanah from the wickedness, Tilby said a cruel man had hurt Lars, but he was safe at Huntington Manor.

Later, when she was coming of age, Hanah asked Lars what happened. Lars first told her to mind her own business. She'd been so ashamed and begged for his forgiveness.

"Don't worry yourself none, Hanah." Lars sighed contritely. "Men whipped me so often, I stopped countin' after one hundred bouts. Now go on, and don't ax again."

Had Lars wished to kill his oppressors, like Thaddeus? If war took over this country, would all Black men go crazy and kill every white person who took a breath?

Hanah never stopped until she made it to another safe place to rest. Supporters told Hanah not to return south. "Freedom is in Canada, Hanah," Mr. Hastings, an elderly man, told her. He and his wife had been harboring fugitive slaves five miles from town since the day Daniel Webster, ten years ago, spewed the reality of the fugitive slave law. Mr. and Mrs. Hastings would have none of what the orator proclaimed. They prided themselves on living in the free state of Pennsylvania, but once the news from New York crossed their ears, Mr. and Mrs. Hastings fumed.

"Listen," Mr. Hastings said. "A few people around these parts, like us, are inclined to help runaway Negroes since that ridiculous law took hold of this nation. Slave catchers are trash—whisky in one hand, a chain in the other. They can go back and rot down south for all we care. You listen to me, young lady. You are going the wrong way. If they can catch you, they can kill you."

Hanah finished a warm bowl of soup and bread Mrs. Hastings had brought to the cellar, and only told the Hastings that she must get back home.

Mr. Hastings gave a weak smile, one of sincerity and understanding. "I'm not sure what is so important that you are willing to risk your life, but I suppose you have your reasons." He poked at the fire in the hearth. "Follow the river for about twenty miles. You'll see a white house. A two-story red barn stands about one hundred yards to the west with a pasture with plenty of horses. Bessie and her sons will help you. She'll have one window shade pulled. Light from the inside room will let you know it's safe to knock on the back door."

Before daybreak, Hanah thanked Mrs. Hastings for the bundle of food. Mr. Hastings handed her fifty dollars. Hanah looked at him. "Sir?"

"I'm the lawyer in this town. God knows it doesn't do a grain of good for folks of your kind, but I've seen it myself, two men freed on five dollars by a drunk passerby, if only they might untie the ropes binding them."

Hanah hugged both Mr. and Mrs. Hastings

"Use your head, Hanah. Haste makes waste. Remember that, and you'll be alright."

Mrs. Hastings hugged her twice. "God bless you, child."

Hanah ran through dense woods and alongside desolate roads. She hid under straw in wagons and once under a blanket in a rowboat. Most nights, she was running on her wits and trying to remember everything good people told her and what Papa had taught her about the moon and the stars. Rachel's teachings of the Bible came in handy too.

Deuteronomy 31:6. Be strong and of a good courage, fear not, nor be afraid of them: for the Lord thy God ... will not fail thee, nor forsake thee.

She wouldn't stop until she reached the only home she ever knew. And by the grace of God, she found her way, now hidden in the tree line, yards from where Papa and Henry and Rachel should be, except the only plantation she loved looked sad, like not a soul had ever loved her.

Again, Hanah's eyes caught sight of the white handkerchief flapping slightly in the breeze when unexpectedly, the moonlight spotted a glimmer of movement. Hanah was sure someone was in the barn. Her heart jumped with both unease and hope. She must be careful. Slave catchers set traps hoping to snag a fugitive and earn money—catch plenty of slaves, and they could make a living on it, which made slave hunters thirsty for blood.

Hanah's desire to run straight to the barn was agonizing. She observed from behind trees for any movement confirming her father was there. Twenty, maybe thirty minutes passed before she saw it—the lighting of the oil lamp. A black shadow of a hand darkened its light. The flicker again. And again, a hand masking its already dim glow. Then it was gone. It was the sign. She, Papa, and her brothers used this sign to communicate that the night was safe for a fugitive to hide there. Carefully, Hanah stepped from the shadows of the trees, and then, as if a violent wind was pushing her, she sprinted across the barren field.

Tilby's searching eyes spied his daughter coming at him from a distance. He took off running and called, "I is here! It's me, baby girl."

The embrace swallowed Hanah. Her father's tight hold released something she had not known existed inside her. The tears came with a reckoning that she was home. She let her father's arms hold her as they sank to their knees, both desperate to know they were both alive.

"Come, Hanah," Tilby whispered. "We is not safe in the open."

Tilby helped Hanah to her feet, and they ran to the barn. The inside looked oddly unfamiliar. The darkness crippled Hanah, but the strange ambiance troubled her. She didn't hear a snort or hoof kneading the dirt from the attached stable.

The questions came like a raging river. "Where are the horses? And Summertime?" Hanah had been gone only six weeks? Thomas would have never sold her favorite horse. He'd told her so when she was fifteen. She strained her eyes in the blackness, looking at each horse stall. Summertime and the other horses were not there. If Summertime was gone. Where was Thomas? And Henry? "Papa!" Hanah panicked. "Where are the others? Please tell me if they are safe. What has happened?"

"Hurry! To the garret. I's gots rifles there," was all Tilby said.

Hanah obeyed immediately. She quickly climbed, her father following close behind.

Tilby dragged the ladder onto the planks. Three of Thomas's rifles lay near the closed door where Hanah remembered her father pitching hay to the ground below not long ago.

Hanah removed her shoes and let her aching feet settle on a pile of wilted hay. She desperately needed sleep to stop her head from pounding, but she forced herself to hang onto this very moment, for if she slept, she might wake to realize being here with Papa was nothing but a dream. Tears swelled in her eyes. "Are you alright? Are they looking for you?"

"We is safe, baby girl. It may be only for a short time, but we is safe for now."

"Where are Henry and Thomas?" This separation was the unease Hanah felt since she reached the tree line of Huntington Manor, and it settled hard on her exhaustion.

"Reedy? Lars? The men? Oh, Lord! And Rachel? What's happened to Rachel? Chloe and Hilda?"

"They's all gone, baby. Only me and you now. I's know'd you'd come back like you say, but we gots to go soon. Once you and Ms. Rosalie left town, word gots 'round that Marshals was to raid the place. Negroes is smart enough to know that ain't good. Reedy, Chloe, Lars—everyone left that night. I's gots 'em all thirty miles from here before turnin' 'round and comin' back. I's suppose they is part of the fightin' now. Ain't much to do now but fight."

"Did they believe Mr. Jansen—" Hanah choked on her words. "Did they raid Huntington Manor?"

"Theys did, baby girl. And found nothing. Not this either." Tilby pulled a book from under a hay pile. "Rachel told me to gives it to you."

"Oh, Papa. My journal." She hugged it to her chest.

"How did you escape capture?"

"I's hid behind the wall in Ms. Rosalie's closet. Men was in the room tearin' things apart. When theys got near the closet, one man calls out to another man that there ain't nobody in the house. Then, theys was gone. I's pray to God to keep me hid all that night. I's swears, Hanah, God was watchin' o'er me. He save me because He know'd I is here to save you. And I is. I is right here, baby girl." Tilby's eyes swelled, his tears resisting release. "Ain't 'til mornin' when I's opens the slide door and sneaked from the closet. That's when I see dots of lights flickerin' on the floor."

"What kind of lights?" Hanah squeaked.

Tilby reached deep into a pocket and pulled Ms. Rosalie's diamond ring into the darkness. "This was with me all night, and I's never know'd it."

Hanah reached for the diamond ring. "Cazenovia. Pompey Hollow Road," she whispered. "We must get to Cazenovia, New York, Papa. Ms. Rosalie made me promise."

"We leaves tomorrow, Hanah."

"Tell me, Papa. Are Thomas and Henry part of the fighting?"

Tilby kept the worse from his daughter. Henry joined the Union Army, and Thomas the ever-growing

Confederacy, a fact Tilby couldn't divulge to Hanah, not now, after what she'd been through. All he said was, "They's part of the fightin' now."

"Oh, Papa. I cannot take it anymore. There is such evil in this world. So much more than I ever suspected. Ms. Rosalie. You. And Thomas. Oh, Thomas. He was only trying to protect me from horror beyond my comprehension." She covered her face. "I saw them, Papa."

Tilby was confused. "Who?"

Hanah shook her head, unable to speak. She'd asked God to spare her from worse than Thaddeus. He had not listened.

Tilby held his daughter, rocking her gently in his arms. "Tell me, baby girl. It's good to gets it from yo'r head to the outside. Lets the wind carry it off."

54

"There was a man and a woman. And a little girl—not more than five years old. A little girl, Papa. How could there be such evil?"

Her face swelled with redness. Her heart pounded, pulsating stronger for every second it twisted inside her. Her throat tightened, choking the life from her, like the noose in her memory.

"I'm not sure where I was, but I swear, Papa, the town radiated hatred. I saw at least two wagons go by a short distance from where the cries were happening, but neither stopped. I wanted to run the other way, ignoring the fuss like those in the wagons, but I couldn't. It sounded like an injured animal at first, but when I got closer, it sounded like a whimper, but more dreadful, so I followed where it was coming from to see for myself. I crept closer and stayed hidden behind a thick of trees. There was a small girl, but she wasn't the one crying. It was her mother. She was begging three men to have mercy for her little girl's life. But those ruthless men," Hanah gasped.

Tilby squeezed Hanah's hand, letting her know he was right there.

"The men didn't listen. They told the woman any colored running off ain't worth nothing—that they couldn't get any money for them. 'You'll watch your girl twitch 'til she's dead.'" Hanah put her hands over her face.

She couldn't bear to remember the noose tightened around the child's neck.

Tilby's voice cracked. "Go on, Hanah. Gets it out, or it'll eat you alive."

"Then I remembered the money. Two hundred and fifty dollars. Fifty from Mr. Hastings, a man who helped me get here, and $200 from Ms. Rosalie. I didn't want to take it from her, but she insisted. She knew I'd run off in the night. I don't know how she knew when, but she knew. Mr. Hastings told me to use my head, so I did. I stepped from behind the trees, pretending to be desperate for air like I'd run to them to save my skin from the whips of a master. 'Sirs,' I called.

"The three white men turned and stared at me."

"Well, looky here."

"My mast'r sent me," Hanah called hurriedly.

"Why? You need a whippin'?"

The men laughed at their crude joke.

"No, sir. My mast'r hears you got a woman and child. He wants them."

"How'd your master know we're out here."

"Their mast'r," I said, pointing at the woman and child. "That's when I noticed the man hanging from the tree above them."

In her father's presence, Hanah gasped, drawing in the air so deep it almost didn't release from her lungs, but when in the company of white men, she pretended she didn't care.

"I told them, 'My mast'r said to find these two and bring them back cuz they going to make good slaves. He don't care what you do to the man. Don't matter much anyway, I suppose. I can see he's dead.'

"I reached into my pocket and took out Rosalie's money pouch. I threw the sack, and two of the men grabbed at it. I told them Master said it was good pay for what he was asking for."

Hanah changed her tone like she was back in front of those horrid men. "My mast'r wants me to say that if I ain't back in one hour, he'll come lookin' for me. Says if I don't have his money, he'll come lookin' for you."

"Then one of the men taunted me. 'Who is this master of yours who thinks he's so fine and mighty?'"

"I told more lies, Papa."

"Mr. Green from South Carolina, sir. He's passing through and got word about these two."

"From the South? Hmm," the man sneered. "You're a liar. You don't talk nothin' like you live anywhere near the South."

"Mast'r bought me yesterday, sir. Down yonder in Alexandria, Virginia, sir. He's traveling through. He says this here is a test of obedience. If I run off, he'll hunt me down and kill me."

"Then, the man who'd done most of the talking counted the money for the third time. He told me, 'I ain't scared of nobody.' He looked over at the other men. 'Let's have a little fun before we get rid of 'er.'"

"The old man spoke. 'Deep South, boys. Those men will cut a leg off a colored for walkin' funny. God knows what he'd do to us for stealing his money.'"

"He grabbed the pouch, Papa, confiscated the money, and threw the emptied pouch at my head. 'Git,' he yelled at me. 'Tell your master if he needs slave catching done right; we're the men for the job.'

313

"'Yes, sir,' I told him. Then I thanked him." Hanah gasped. "I thanked him, Papa, for all the evil he was secreting. I thanked him."

The release was more than Hanah could handle without letting it pour from her stomach. She turned her head and vomited.

Tilby rubbed his daughter's back.

Hanah sat back. She wiped her mouth on her sleeve. "I got us to Bessie's place. Little Milly cried for hours before her mother could quiet her. Bessie's taking good care of them, but I run off the next morning, hours before the morning light."

Tilby pulled his daughter close and wrapped her in his arms. Before dawn, Tilby and Hanah would be gone from this barn. They'd be gone from Huntington Manor. They'd be gone from Virginia forever.

55

Cazenovia, New York 1861

William Ward had gotten word last week from a stranger traveling through from Ithaca. He and his wife, Mary, had been in the local store delivering fresh eggs to the storekeeper when on their way out, a stranger purposely bumped into William on his way into the mercantile. The stranger apologized, brushing William's worn farming jacket so he could slip a note into the open side pocket.

"You're very kind, sir. No harm done."

The Wards went on their way, and the stranger continued into the store. William and Mary read the note when they got far from town. Two slaves would be searching for their house. Tonight, the Wards would have a light in the second-floor window on the right. They'd both be on the lookout and remain inconspicuous.

William and Mary Ward had never planned to harbor fugitive slaves. They'd intended to tend to their land—raise chickens, milk two or three cows, and maybe plant a garden of vegetables and fruits. They weren't farmers by any means, but they liked the idea.

At fourteen, William worked for Warren Hayes at the hardware store, sweeping floors, taking inventory, and managing the register when Mr. Hayes was away on business. Later, William took a job at the Syracuse House, a prominent theater on South Salina Street, and eventually became senior ticketmaster.

William and Mary met at grammar school, a small, drafty one-room building in the center of town and a mile from their homes in opposite directions. The two had remained friends, married when Mary was eighteen, and in 1850, seven years after they'd married, they moved to a saltbox-style home on Pompey Hollow Road in Cazenovia for a life different from the city.

William worked five days a week at the general store, under five miles from their home. He enjoyed the quiet ride, the vastness of the open land, and the hundreds of trees. He and Mary moved here from Syracuse for this sole purpose. Eleven years had passed from when they'd moved to Pompey Hollow Road. They'd only lived here a few months when the convention took place, and William spotted Warren Hayes in the crowd listening to Fredrick Douglass.

William and Mary's quiet lives changed the night Warren, Sarah, and Charlotte stayed at their house before heading back to Syracuse in the morning. William and Warren discussed the Underground Railroad after the women retired to their rooms for the evening. The two men discussed a plan to stay vigilant—keep an ear out and an open mind—strive for the freedom of all men—but never once had Warren and William discussed harboring fugitive slaves. But one thing led to the next for William in Cazenovia and Warren in Syracuse until the house on Pompey Hollow Road and the back room of a hardware store eventually became safe houses for runaway slaves.

Mary and Charlotte had become confidants, and for the past six summers, Charlotte stayed in Cazenovia to help her friends. Mary told folks Charlotte was her cousin to disguise any notion of why Charlotte might visit.

They looked nothing alike. Mary was thin and wiry, a few years older and several inches shorter than Charlotte, who was stunningly beautiful with flawless skin and brilliant bright blue eyes, even at thirty-nine. There was no reason to question their physical dissimilarities. Cousins were different, despite their relations.

Neighbors, who'd inquired on a Sunday after church or a summer picnic, accepted their lies as fact. "Well, it feels delightful to get away from the hustle and bustle of the city," Charlotte mentioned when asked, or "My cousin's home is a wonderful place to visit. Country air is so fresh," she might say to another when stopped on her way into town. No one ever suspected Charlotte was in Cazenovia to help William and Mary get Negroes from one safe house to the next. Once, Charlotte had managed to get a family of three to Uncle Warren's hardware store in Syracuse by wagon in broad daylight.

Friends of Warren and Sarah were also easily fooled. They had no reason to question why Charlotte returned to her hometown of Alexandria, Virginia, for a summer visit. No one was the wiser when she boarded the train and headed home. Three stops later, Charlotte exited the train and went to Cazenovia. Neighbors believe Charlotte because she remained confident and poised when she fibbed, a necessary skill in harboring fugitive slaves.

Neither family, Mary and William Ward nor Sarah and Warren Hughes, ever imagined how vital Charlotte's routine visits would become when in June 1861, Charlotte learned of Hanah and Tilby's fleeing to William and Mary's home on Pompey Hollow Road in Cazenovia.

56

Somewhere near Cazenovia, New York 1861

A patroller pinned Hanah against a large tree. He'd sneaked behind her while she collected berries in the woods, a reasonable distance from where she and her father formed a small camp to rest before they continued their journey. She cursed herself. *How did she let this happen?* Within seconds of the shock, Hanah quickly organized her thoughts. She had to keep her wits like the Swiss Family Robinsons when they found themselves shipwrecked on a deserted island. She had no idea why this burst into her head. "Mr. Robinson prepared his family for survival," Rosalie had told her as she lay in bed listening to a chapter from the book. "They used their heads to solve problems, Hanah, as any intelligent person would."

So long as her father didn't come calling for her, she could escape. Run in the opposite direction of where he was now, soaking his swollen feet in a large puddle left from a recent rainstorm. Hanah was sure he was already worried she was taking too long. She wriggled, but the man only pinned her harder. A broken branch sticking out from the tree trunk stabbed sharply into her back and through the corset she wore to disguise her breast. She winced, afraid to cry out.

The man snarled, exposing his yellowed teeth. "Try that again, and you'll be sorry you were born." His lips curled, bringing shape to a heinous smile. "A young lad like you will bring a good reward." He spat a wad of tobacco, just missing her face. "Who's looking for you?" When Hanah didn't speak, afraid she might reveal her gender, he became angry. His breath reeked with such intense sourness she impulsively turned away when he got close to her face. "You a mute," he scowled. "Don't matter much what they call you. You're mine now." With a gun at his side, the man dragged Hanah to his horse, tightly secured her wrists, and tied the rope to the horse's saddle.

The horse pulled Hanah as she ambled along, but she could not regain an upright position when she stumbled and fell. The man didn't care, so the horse pulled her over tree stumps and rocks. Her head bounced. Hanah tried to keep it upright to lessen each blow. A root, sticking through the ground, tore at her face. Tree stumps thrust into her front. She let out a scream.

"Shut up!" The man hollered from atop his horse. "Or I'll put a bullet in your head."

Tilby heard the scream. Immediately alarmed, he sprung to his bare feet. He ran toward the cry in the direction it had come from when he heard a deep voice. They hadn't seen another soul in these woods for an entire day, but he was sure of Hanah's scream. Tilby hurried with caution. He would endanger both of them if he went wildly for his daughter. His wits could save them both.

Tilby jumped over a downed tree and landed on a sharp object, possibly a thorn, but he ignored the pain. He had to stay in earshot of the fading horse's hooves. If he didn't, the dire situation would worsen. Tilby wished Hanah would yell again to know if she was alive, but his daughter was clever. Hanah hadn't screamed more than once because she'd been afraid Tilby would have come running right into the barrel of a gun. Tilby stopped and listened carefully. He heard the horse snort. Tilby hurried in pursuit. Minutes later, he saw Hanah's lifeless body pulled behind a horse like a dead animal.

The sky was darkening. The thick of the trees and black clouds made the situation worse. Tilby found two good size rocks. When he was within aim, he'd kill Hanah's captor. He fought back the urge to do it now, in poor range, as he followed wildly at the horse's pace. Then, in a split second, with his eyes focused on the man's temple, Tilby plowed into a low tree limb. He fell back, stumbling before hitting the ground hard. Stars danced above him. He sat forward and shook it off. Seconds passed before he remembered he'd been following Hanah. He stood in a panic and fell backward again. He stood again, refusing to lose sight of his daughter. And then he vomited, trying desperately to keep his convulsing throat soundless. He stood silently, listening. Finally, he caught a glimpse of the horse. He raced toward his daughter. When he was close, the man stopped and looked in his direction. Tilby fell silent and watched from behind a large tree. His head throbbed profusely. The man dismounted his horse and walked farther into the woods.

Hanah lay face down in the mud and unmoving. Tilby knew he must act now. When Hanah's captor returned to his horse, Hanah would be gone if only Tilby could stay alert and resist the sluggishness he felt. He tried to focus on the trees where the man disappeared, but it was no use. His eyesight seemed to be fading. He could not waste another second. Tilby ran to untie the rope around Hanah's wrists and then fled, carrying his daughter over his shoulder. He ran and ran until he slowed, zigzagging and delirious. Twenty yards more, and he stumbled into a clearing. He was confused, and it was worsening with every step. Where was he heading? They'd been so close to their destination. *Cazenovia. Pompey Hollow Road.*

A ticking in Tilby's head, like a time bomb, forced him to lay Hanah on the side of the road. He saw a flicker of light in the far distance. Or was it Rosalie's ring casting colors onto the sky?

His memory eluded him. Tilby fished around in his pocket to show Hanah Ms. Rosalie's diamond ring, except there was nothing there. He clasped the absent piece of jewelry that Hanah secured before they ran from Huntington Manor. Before they prayed together. Before they gathered food. Before they ran into the woods under a fading moon.

He looked away from the imaginary ring he believed was there and stared into the distance. There it was again—the flicker of light. Tilby stumbled toward it. *Could it be someone willing to help?* The last person to hide them, Deek, said Pompey Hollow Road was less than fifteen miles away, "but you are fools if you don't go straight to Gerrit Smith's. One way or another, he'll get you to Canada."

Fifteen miles. Or was it fifty miles? Tilby couldn't seem to discern the difference. His semi-conscious world spun, and his thoughts became chaotic.

No, Hanah had protested to Deek. *We must get to Pompey Hollow Road. I promised Ms. Rosalie.*

Tilby spun around. Deek's voice echoed nearby. *Watch your back. There's patrol everywhere.* Chirping crickets exploded into song. Tilby heard thunder in the distance. Flashes of lightning brightened dark clouds. He couldn't let his daughter die. He ran toward the light in the window. His head pounded with a crack of thunder. Tilby was falling, but he believed he was flying. How wonderful it all felt, swimming above the trees. Then, his world went black.

57

William was traveling toward home in a hurry. The black clouds were rolling in quickly, and droplets of rain were beginning to fall. Lightning and thunder and heavier rains were evident.

William clucked, "Giddy up," and his ten-year-old Appaloosa, Trombone, changed from walking into a trot. The covered buggy turned onto Pompey Hollow Road. Ahead, he saw something lumped on the side of the dirt road. He came closer and saw it was a Black boy or a very frail man. He and Mary had been expecting runaways, but when weeks passed, and no one had shown, they figured plans had changed. It wasn't uncommon to reroute runaways. It meant they foresaw trouble and avoided it.

William hurried from the buggy and knelt by this person, who looked like an injured animal. Blood soaked his clothes, and fresh blood puddled around a deep cut on his forehead. William nudged him slightly and called out in a loud voice. "Son, are you alright? What is your name?" The boy neither answered nor moved, but he was alive. William carefully gripped him under the arms, dragged his limp body to the buggy, and lifted the boy's frail figure onto the seat. Still unconscious, he slumped forward. William crawled over him and grabbed Trombone's reins. He leaned the boy against his right shoulder and quickly looked around. If this was the person they'd received word about, there should be two runaways, not one.

William hurried home. Mary would be able to help.

Mary laid the boy on a soft bed. "Get some cool water, William. Hurry."

A low groan came softly at first.

When William returned moments later, Mary was cleaning a deep cut above the right eye with a towel. Mary said. "It's a young woman, not a boy. Hurry, get clean sheets from upstairs. I need to get her out of these wet clothes. She's burning with fever."

"Papa." Hanah moaned. She tried to lift her arm, but its weight was too much. "Papa."

Mary continued to wipe the blood from her face, neck, and chest. She spoke loudly. "My name is Mary Ward. I'm here to help you. Can you tell me your name?" There was no response.

Mary removed the girl's shredded pants. She unbuttoned the oversized shirt and pulled it from her feverish body. A tightly wrapped corset flattened the woman's bosom. Mary tilted the girl to one side and untied the string binding the piece together. When the corset separated from the tight hold, something secured inside it clinked on the tin washbowl on the floor and sank to the shallow bottom of the basin. Mary fished around in the bloody water for whatever had fallen to the bottom. Her fingers grabbed hold of something round and she pulled it from the water. It was the most beautiful ring she'd ever seen.

Hanah's eyes shuttered. The release of the corset triggered the pain. She wanted to scream out, but her lungs wouldn't allow it.

"My God," William barked when he saw the deep purple bruises and swelling on her chest and abdomen. "It looks like she's been—," William was about to say, *kicked by a horse*, but this girl was injured far beyond what a horse could do.

"She's calling for her father. Try to find him. And go for Dr. Fritz."

William stared. "Mary. We can't. He's mandated to report us to the law."

"I can't fix this girl on my own. I think she's got broken ribs, and maybe something ruptured inside. It's a chance we'll have to take. Go now."

"Are you sure, Mary?" William asked.

The moment the first fugitive arrived at their Cazenovia home, they'd been sure. It had happened so quickly after agreeing to help Warren and Sarah. They figured this moment would eventually come—when they needed help from someone outside their secret.

"Go! Now!"

Lightning lit the sky. Thunder roared. William unhitched Trombone and climbed onto the horse's back. William saw the girl's bludgeoned body. She needed Dr. Fritz immediately. There was no time to lose. He directed Trombone toward town and raced down the road.

"She's bad off," Dr. Fritz said, "but there are no organ ruptures. Her spleen is enlarged. She's got broken ribs and wrists. Something dragged this girl by the looks of the lacerations on her legs."

Dr. Fritz looked at the thermometer. It registered at 104 degrees. He turned to Mary. "We need to get her body cooled right away. She will be in pain when she wakes, but she's fortunate." The doctor examined the girl's forehead again. "Besides this bad gash, there's no other head trauma. No swelling of the brain."

"Will she make it?" Mary asked.

"I can't say for sure—"

William burst through the door, causing Mary to scream from fright. "Doc," he hollered over a crack of thunder. "I need an extra set of hands. I found the girl's father."

58

Cazenovia, New York 1861

Two days passed, and Tilby remained unconscious. The center of his forehead swelled to the size of a man's fist, and his eyelids were bluish and bulging. He'd hit the tree so hard that the tree bark left an imprint in two different areas. Dr. Fritz removed the cold compress. The wedge of ice underneath slid to the side of Tilby's head. "If we can't get this swelling down, we might not get him back."

The doctor carefully opened one swollen eyelid and the other. Tilby's bludgeoned eyes remained unimproved. "I honestly cannot believe this man is still breathing." The doctor slid the chair back from his patient's bedside. "Determination is a curious thing."

Dr. Fritz turned his attention to Hanah. She was faring better than her father, though her fever could prove far worse in time.

Mary said, "She hasn't been able to tell us her name, but she's awake sometimes. All she ever says is Papa. I've told her he's safe, but I'm not sure she understands."

"That's all you can do for now. Keep reassuring her." Dr. Fritz gently checked Hanah's casted wrists. He unwrapped the bandages on both legs to inspect for infection. There was none. He was relieved. Avoiding disease was crucial. Next, Dr. Fritz checked the girl's forehead. The area was puffy, but the redness had subsided.

Hanah stirred. "Papa. Papa," she muttered.

Dr. Fritz gently rubbed her arms, hoping to rouse her. "Your father is safe."

Her eyes fluttered. She moved her arms and lifted a hand toward her face.

Mary came closer. "My name is Mary Ward. The doctor is here to help you. Can you tell us your name?"

"My head hurts," Hanah whispered, reaching for it. Each spoken word felt like a hard thud inside her brain.

Mary stared at Hanah in shock. "She's talking. Praise the good Lord."

Doc assured his patient. "I know it hurts, but you'll be fine. You're healing nicely." He paused. "Can you tell us your name?"

Hanah didn't know if she could get the word into the open without her head exploding. Every word. Every grunt. Every movement traveled through her brain like thunder. The doctor was asking for her name. His words, too, drilled at her pounding head.

Hanah grimaced, knowing the simple task of speaking her name would send a thud through her brain, but she needed to divulge who she was. *Mary Ward. Isn't that what the lady said?* She had made it to Mary Ward. And Mary Ward would get word to Charlotte.

She needed Mary to hear her the first time. To repeat herself would be too much. She swallowed hard, causing another thrust of pain to rip across her forehead.

"Hanah Smith."

Mary stilled. "Oh. My. Heavens." A split second later, she ran for William.

327

Cazenovia, New York 1861

Hanah greeted Dr. Fritz at the side door. "Good afternoon," Hanah smiled at the doctor. Dr. Fritz had regularly checked on Hanah and Tilby for the past six weeks.

"Afternoon already?" Dr. Fritz pulled his pocket watch from his breast pocket. "Well, look at that. Twelve o'clock on the dot."

Hanah's smile widened. "Come in. Please."

"You look well, Hanah. How are you feeling?"

"Well. Thank you."

Dr. Fritz's kind eyes widened. "If you keep improving, what excuse will I have to come for fresh bread and Mary's jam preserves?"

Hanah laughed. She liked Dr. Fritz. He'd come three times in the first week, Mary told her. He'd been concerned the fever would not subside. Twice, he traveled here during the late evening, sneaking into the dark, avoiding detection. "And when I apologized for the late hour," Mary had said with unmistakable gratitude. "Dr. Fritz told me there was no such time in his profession. He laughed heartily and said, 'Babies are notorious for reminding me of this. Haven't had one come at a decent hour yet.'"

Charlotte came into the room. "You are always welcome, Dr. Fritz. I insist you stay for lunch today."

"A man would be a fool to pass on such an invitation." He looked to Hanah. "Ready?"

Hanah sat still on a chair.

"Take a deep breath," Dr. Fritz told her. He listened with his stethoscope to both sides of her lungs while he surveyed the closed wound on her forehead. Then, he probed her semi-healed ribs. "Tremendous." He continued by slightly shifting Hanah's head and examining every angle of what was, six weeks ago, a deep and jagged laceration. "You'll have a scar, but it is healing nicely."

Dr. Fritz unwrapped the snug bandage from Hanah's left wrist. The firm, long slat holding her arm, wrist, and hand in place fell away. Only the faintest bruises remained. The doctor gently manipulated Hanah's hand, feeling and watching the movement.

Hanah grimaced.

Is it painful?"

"It's sore, but I can manage."

Dr. Fritz smiled. "I don't doubt that. The bones have mended, but the muscles are stiff from being bound for six weeks. Give it time, and your wrist will strengthen."

Dr. Fritz turned his attention to Tilby. His injuries were far worse than his daughter's, though at first glance, when they first arrived, this was not apparent. Hanah's body had taken a tremendous beating, but in Tilby's case, his brain had taken the jolt of his injuries. He'd laid in bed unconscious for four days.

Tilby was seated in a wooden chair beside Hanah, listening to all the doctor said about his daughter, thankful for the excellent report. Dr. Fritz pulled his chair adjacent to Tilby's. He took a light from his bag and shined it in his patient's eyes. "How are you feeling? Any confusion?"

"I is doin' alright, sirs. Thank you kindly for carin' for my Hanah."

"The pleasure is all mine. Now let's take a closer look." Dr. Fritz palpated Tilby's neck for soreness. The doctor slowly turned his patient's head to the left and right. "Any pain?"

"No, sirs."

"Are you sleeping through the night?"

William spoke up. "He's been talking in his sleep, Doc. He's restless and moving about in bed like he's awake."

"Good to know." The doctor read his notes from prior visits. He looked from his report to Tilby. "Do you know the month and year?"

"Yes, sirs. August 1861."

"Good. Good. And how long have you been living with Mary and William?"

"Three years, sirs?"

"You've lived in Mary and William's house for three years?"

"Two years."

"Papa," Hanah said gently. "We've been here for six weeks."

"I's forgot."

"Fine. Fine, Tilby. I don't want you to worry." Dr. Fritz wrote something in his notes and returned his attention to his patient. "I'm going to give you three words to remember. I'll ask you to tell me those three words in a few minutes."

"Yes, sirs."

"Saddle. Apple. Bed."

Tilby repeated the words.

"How's your mood?" Dr. Fritz asked.

"Happy. I is glad Hanah is safe."

"Papa's building a table," Hanah interjected, widening her smile to let her father know how proud she was of him. "He was the best builder in all of Virginia."

Doctor mirrored the pleasantries. "Good to know."

"Do you remember the three words from a moment ago?"

Tilby stared at his shoes. His lips twisted as he tried to recall even one word. "Horse?"

"The first word was a saddle. What was the second word?" Dr. Fritz sensed Tilby's frustration after a moment. "Now, listen to me, Tilby. Healing takes time, especially when it's a person's noggin."

Charlotte spoke up. "Is there anything we can do to help his recovery?"

"Rest is key. Building a table is fine, but take long breaks. In the meantime, conversations, discussing memories, and asking questions have proven to improve memory when there has been a brain injury."

Lunch and a good conversation ensued for about an hour before Mary cleared the plates from the table. Dr. Fritz and William talked politics, and the women fussed around the kitchen, washing and drying dishes before placing them neatly back on a shelf.

Suddenly, Mary hushed the men. She heard the quick clop of horses in the near distance.

Charlotte hurried Tilby and Hanah down a wooden staircase and into the basement.

Two men outside dismounted their horses and headed toward the house, looking toward the woods and the open acreage before arriving at the door. Their leisurely stroll gave Hanah and Tilby the extra minute they needed.

William opened the side door leading into the kitchen. "Afternoon," William offered.

"Howdy, William. Doc." Carlisle tipped his hat. "Mary. Miss Charlotte."

"What brings you here?" William said, pretending concern.

Marshal Mealy handed William an official document before he spoke. "Here for a random check. Town's people are concerned about the fugitive Leonard Sully claimed he captured."

"That was weeks ago," William said. "Is there still a reasonable concern that Leonard might be telling the truth?"

"He's insisting. Now, he's twisting the story and saying he believes there was a gang of them."

Doc gave a hearty laugh. "I doubt that very much. I've been here for the last hour, invited for a nice lunch, and I can verify I saw nothing on my way here. Besides, Sully is always good for an elaborate story. I got absorbed in a couple of his tales myself. It's all nonsense."

"Perhaps. But it's our duty to check things out."

Dr. Fritz turned to Charlotte and Mary. "Don't you women worry yourselves any. Leonard Sully may have seen a deer in the woods."

"That's what I've told them," William agreed. "This is nonsense, but," William elongated, "go ahead and look around. Unless you need my assistance, I've got chores in the barn that won't wait all day."

Carlisle said. "It won't be more than five minutes. Then we'll be on our way."

John Mealy and Carlisle Burton stepped over the threshold.

"It's good to see you," John said to Charlotte.

"You as well, John."

Carlisle was already snooping around in a few closets.

"I am sorry. We realize this is an inconvenience." John said apologetically.

When Charlotte visited Mary six years ago, she'd met John Mealy, who quickly became smitten with her. And if Charlotte was not committing treason right under his nose, she may have been smitten with John. He was a tall, strapping, and attractive man dedicated to his work. When she returned to Syracuse, she voiced concern to her aunt and uncle. If John continued to pursue her, trouble could arise.

The following summer, she was ready to tell John she was uninterested. Several years before, after another appeal, the school board hired Charlotte for the permanent teaching position. Her job was too important, and she would not quit for marriage.

But when she returned, John was engaged to a girl. Charlotte used this to her benefit, telling John they'd remain lifelong friends, and she didn't blame him a single ounce for marrying a beautiful girl.

The two officers climbed the narrow attic steps and walked on the planks above where Hanah and Tilby lay. They lay sandwiched on the attic floor between two layers of longboards of wide pine planks. They hid here when strangers approached. Someone was always on the watch, either Mary or William, or Charlotte. Any approach in the distance, Hanah and Tilby hurriedly went to the basement. A thick rope ladder was positioned and ready on the other side of the basement staircase. They climbed into an uncovered hole and a space behind a mock broom closet. Tilby, always behind his daughter, pulled the rope into the small entrance and sealed the open space with a fitted board. They climbed a narrow wooden ladder that took them from behind the first-floor kitchen wall, behind a closet on the second floor, and onto the attic's original base. They scooted their bodies forward, using their arms and feet to inch between the two floorboards like a snake slithering underground.

Hanah and Tilby lay still, barely breathing. Hanah kept her eyes closed, needing to believe that if she couldn't see them through the thin floorboard slits, they couldn't see her. Though, she knew better. A twitch of a leg might catch an expert eye. The slightest movement from light to dark would uncover their secret. Hanah's right cheek lay flat and stiff on the floorboards.

John Mealy spoke gruffly to his partner. "We're going to find nobody here, Carlisle. There isn't enough space." He paused and quickly scanned the area. "Frankly, I believe it's a farce that slaves are hiding in these parts. Why would anyone come here when they can sneak to Smith's house? Negroes are lucky to get there and find freedom. Smith is so conniving, and nobody can touch him with a ten-foot pole."

Hanah and Tilby silently listened, their slowed breath synchronized. The first time under these planks, their injuries caused them pain. Before then, the risk had been grave, with Tilby unconscious and Hanah barely moving with broken ribs. William and Mary placed beds in the basement and surrounded them with crates and barrels. The makeshift arrangement was not promising, but it was all they could do to hide them with such severe injuries. They were fortunate nobody had come to the house but Charlotte.

Mealy and Burton descended the narrow attic stairs to the second floor and rounded the banister to a beautifully polished staircase at the front door on the first floor. Mealy called out. "We'll be on our way."

Charlotte rounded the corner from the kitchen. "Good afternoon, gentlemen."

John Mealy tipped his hat. "Thank you, Charlotte."

"Of course," Charlotte said. "Though I'll be honest, John," she said calmly. "You upset Mary so much with your visits. She thinks she's unsafe with a hoodlum running about the streets."

"Understandable. Please remind your cousin she's safe. Sully was perhaps mistaken. The night was pitch-black. There was no good reason to be in those woods during an electrical storm."

"I do agree with you, John," Charlotte said sweetly.

Carlisle Burton stepped outside and down the three concrete steps. He looked around outside one last time before walking toward the horses.

John Mealy took the opportunity while alone with Charlotte. He cleared his throat. He didn't want to sound presumptuous but couldn't help himself. "I noticed the ring on your finger. It sure does sparkle like an evening sky on a clear night. Did you marry?"

"Oh, Heavens no." Charlotte instinctively brought her hand forward for viewing. "My father gave this ring to my mother on their wedding day. My mother wanted me to have it."

John Mealy smiled, tipping his hat. "I hope your visit has been a good one. Are you here much longer?"

"I told Mary I'd stay on for another week, but I've got to get back home eventually. The school year opens in the fall."

60

Cazenovia, New York 1861

Hanah would not return to Syracuse with Charlotte as planned at the end of August. She could not leave her father, who was not well enough to travel. Tilby's memory was not returning as quickly as Dr. Fritz had hoped. Bits of non-relevant information surfaced in conversations. Hanah had asked her father if he wanted milk with his breakfast. And Tilby replied, "Huntington Manor." He hadn't understood why he had said such a place or what it meant. He tired quickly too. An hour or two outside in the sun or inside the barn scraping wood was enough for an entire day.

Staying on Pompey Hollow Road posed a problem. Hanah and Tilby couldn't just appear in the front yard without a neighbor inquiring or church folk gossiping and asking questions. So, William faked the help of his neighbors and friends around town—asking if they knew anyone looking for employment. "The farm's upkeep is too much," William fibbed. "And Mary needs help around the house." He and Mary could work to the bone for ten more years, but they'd established this plan so Tilby and Hanah could take permanent residence. It worked. From there on out, Tilby and Hanah Smith, father and daughter, came from Syracuse to work for the Wards, sent by Mr. Warren Hughes, Charlotte's aging uncle who no longer had a position for the pair. Tilby and Hanah had all the documents with false prior residence and reliable sources.

Eventually, the deceits didn't matter. Marshals and other law officers had lost interest in searching homes on Pompey Hollow Road and other parts of Cazenovia. War was at the height of four months, and there were more important issues than one man's account of one escaped fugitive slave. Black folks in every county were gathering in small and large factions, protesting the prohibiting of Negroes from enlisting in the Union Army.

In November 1861, five months after Hanah and Tilby arrived in Cazenovia and three months after Charlotte had returned to Syracuse, Mary Ward received mail from Charlotte. Inside the envelope was a letter addressed to Hanah. Rosalie was failing quickly from complications of her disease.

Part of the letter read. *–As you know, Dr. Clay diagnosed Mother with shaking palsy, but as her symptoms have advanced, several doctors here in Syracuse have admitted they cannot confirm what ails her. Mother has lost the majority of her muscular function.*

Hanah placed the letter on the table. "I must go to Ms. Rosalie right away."

Hanah and Tilby and Mary and William set out for Syracuse. Thick snow had fallen the night before, making the trip dangerous. They stopped and rested the horses and stayed overnight at Widow Grace Stoops's home, a friend of Mary's. The following morning, they boarded the train to Syracuse.

The train conductor asked for proof that the Negroes who accompanied William were not runaways. William handed Hanah's papers to the conductor. "They work for me," William told him

The conductor pointed at Tilby without eye contact. "And his."

"The man has a name," William grumbled. "Tilby is a free man, so if it's his papers you need to see, you can ask him yourself."

The conductor tipped his hat at Mary and spoke again to William. "My apologies, sir, but we must check, or I could lose my job." He looked at Tilby and held out his hand. "You got papers?"

"I's do, sirs." Tilby reached into his coat pocket and handed the papers to the man, whose scowl could make a badger retreat.

"Very well." The conductor said to William. "You and the Mrs. are welcome to sit in the car, but coloreds ride in the back."

"Shameful," William quietly said to Mary. "Thousands of Negroes are building the tracks for these trains, yet they can't ride on them."

The back of the train meant outside. It was November and cold, but Hanah and Tilby were prepared. They stood together in their warm coats, enduring much less than they had in the past.

61

When Rosalie saw Hanah, her weakened state grew a bit stronger. A slight smile curled her lips.

Hanah went right to her side. "I'm here, Ms. Rosalie. I'm here."

Rosalie formed her lips the best she could. "Hanah."

Hanah took Rosalie's cold and bony hand in hers. Tears bubbled up.

"I'm sorry." Rosalie slurred the two words together.

"Sorry? There's no reason to be sorry, Ms. Rosalie."

Tears glistened in Rosalie's eyes. She could barely blink them away. "Sorry."

Hanah gazed lovingly at Rosalie—her mother. Rosalie had raised her. She'd been a mountain of strength and a valley of deep love. And now she laid here bedridden, using every morsel of muscle to formulate a single word.

"Sorry for what?" Charlotte probed.

Rosalie took a deep, gurgled breath. "Mama."

Charlotte stepped to her mother's bedside. "Hanah," Charlotte said, speaking for Rosalie. "Mother is terribly sorry she couldn't save your mother." Charlotte looked over to Tilby, standing off to the side and tearful. "She wanted you to know how sorry she is that she could not save Simone."

Tilby let out a whimper. He remembered. Simone was his wife and Hanah's mother. "It's alright, Ms. Rosalie. You done everythin' possible. Me and Hanah know'd that."

Rosalie looked at the man who had come to Huntington Manor a mistreated and malnourished boy. Now, his hair greyed at the temples, and scars traveled across his forehead, but his brown eyes held the same benevolence as years ago. Tilby looked older than Rosalie remembered, standing in the corner like he was—*inconspicuous*, but more significant than most people realized. Tilby had risked his life for hers, his daughter's, and everyone on the plantation and for the greater good of all people. Rosalie wished she could walk across the room and hug him.

Hanah held tight to Rosalie's hand. "Ms. Rosalie—Mother. You may not have been able to save Mama, but you–" her chest tightened. Silent tears fell heavy. "You became my mother. You didn't abandon me or leave me to fate. You coddled me and loved me. You told me nighttime stories and taught me how to read and write. I love you, Ms. Rosalie. Mama's been in Heaven all this time, knowing you loved me. That's all she wanted—was for me to be loved. You and Papa, Rachel and Charlotte, and Thomas and Henry—you all loved me. So don't go believing you need to apologize. Please, Mother. Tell me you know you did well by me all these years."

Behind Rosalie's gaze, Hanah could easily read her mother. She had been able to since she was two years old. "I hear you, Mother. And you must keep those good thoughts." Hanah lovingly smiled at Rosalie. "You told me once that a mother is love. Do you remember?"

Rosalie's gaze once again told Hanah she did.

Rosalie's eyes shifted to her eldest daughter. Charlotte smiled, knowing what Mother was asking. Charlotte pulled the beautiful 5-carat diamond ring, wrapped in silk cloth, from inside the pocket of her skirt. Charlotte carefully unwrapped the gift and held it by the gold band. Prisms took to the wall and fluttered about like angels.

Hanah glanced at the ring.

"It's for you, Hanah. Mother and I want you to have it."

Hanah shook her head. "No, Charlotte. It belongs to you and Mother. Ms. Rosalie wanted me to bring it to you. And I did. From Virginia to Cazenovia."

"And now, we want you to have it."

Hanah was still holding Rosalie's hand. She felt a soft squeeze from Rosalie. She faced her.

Rosalie's mind went to that day so many years ago when Hanah was a child and asked if she was an ugly duckling. Rosalie had known something was wrong before the words ever came from her daughter. She'd been able to comfort her daughter back then and felt she was doing the same now. Rosalie rounded her lips to speak. If she concentrated, she could maybe get the words out.

Hanah sensed Rosalie's struggle to talk, and without thinking, she whispered, her chest tightening from both love and anguish, desperate to hold back an explosion of tears. "I love you, Mother." She leaned in and kissed Rosalie on the cheek, leaving tears wet on Rosalie's face. Hanah softly wiped them away and gazed lovingly into the eyes of the mother who loved her. "I will wear this ring close to my heart. I have the perfect chain to hang it from, and I will be reminded of you every day. I'll be reminded of us."

For now, Hanah slipped the ring onto her finger.

Rosalie's eyes met Charlotte's and then Hanah's. "Love," she whispered. She struggled to get the word out, but she'd done it. She loved her children—all four of them. Rosalie closed her eyes. She needed the rest.

Charlotte and Hanah held their mother's hands. An hour passed, and still, Rosalie slept. That evening, Rosalie opened her eyes to her girls still by her side. She maneuvered her lips into an open pucker. And as clear as a summer sky, Rosalie Worthington spoke one final word. "Home."

She died early the following morning. Sarah, Hanah, and Charlotte were at her side.

Acknowledgments

Thank you to my assemblage of first readers, Linda Peaslee, Jim Mahar, Candy Tumidalsky, and Daphne Tantalo. Thank you for carefully combing through the completed manuscript twice. Your insightful questions, comments, and suggestions made *Pompey Hollow Road* a better story.

Thank you, Jennifer Hasson, my talented website designer, media and events manager, and gifted social marketing expert. Thank you for always being on call, on time, and just on whenever I need you. I am incredibly grateful for your professionalism.

Thanks to my sister Lin for traveling with me to Cazenovia and Syracuse, New York, and Alexandria, Virginia, to research this book. The ten-day trip was one to remember. And special thanks to all the historians, museum personnel, and storytellers who answered my numerous questions and always pointed me in the right direction to further my knowledge.

Thank you, with gratitude, to my editor, Linda Surlak. Your research and attentiveness to the AAVE of the enslaved peoples of this story were remarkable. Thank you for your honesty and guidance with every draft, edit, and revision.

Thank you, J. Scott Wilson, for proofreading the final manuscript before publication. Your eye for detail is appreciated.

Thank you, Deborah C. Blanc, for designing the perfect book cover to convey the created world on the pages inside.

Thank you, Kevin Moriarity, for taking on the most challenging job of putting all the pieces of a novel together and making the final product perfect. I'm extremely grateful for your support and expertise.

Annie Hansen, my friend, neighbor, and accountability partner. You keep the crazy moving forward and sharing a good laugh when we need it. I'm glad to be on this writing journey with you—one story at a time.

Mike, my wonderful husband, for always believing in me, especially when I needed it most. And Bo—our golden chow who has captured my blog readers' hearts with his POV.

Elizabeth, my mom, who tried her darndest to hurry me along so she would have time to read my novel. It's here, Mom. You're here—so enjoy the story and memories of the house on Pompey Hollow Road.

I am incredibly grateful to Mr. Laurence 'Fritz' Sovik, who invited my sister Lin and me to his home in Cazenovia, New York, to explore first-hand the stories I'd heard throughout my childhood. Fritz spent the day with us, letting us explore every last detail of his house, barn, and land. Seeing the staircase, the basement, and the attic, key focal points in *Pompey Hollow Road* and future novels in the *Pompey Hollow Road Series*, was beyond awe-inspiring. And thank you to Mr. Sovik's daughter, Molly, who corresponded with me in connecting with her father, and Zoe, who invited my sister and me to sit for a while and visit Fritz over iced tea on a beautiful day in May.

To my wonderful readers and fans, to whom I owe so much. Thanks for inviting me into your hearts and homes. Without your support, my writing would only be a hobby. I'm happy this isn't the case.

About the Author

Julie Oleszek is a teacher, writer, and baker. She graduated with a bachelor's degree in Education from Northern Illinois University and later earned a master's degree in Education from National-Louis University. Julie has been teaching elementary school students for twenty-five years. She loves animals, midwestern thunderstorms, history, and vacations near water. Julie is one of ten children and the proud aunt of fifty nieces and nephews. Her first novels come from the heart of growing up with nine siblings in a house filled with constant commotion. She and her husband live in Chicago's western suburbs. *Pompey Hollow Road* is her fourth novel and first historical fiction novel.

Dear Reader,

Please consider leaving me a review on Amazon. Reviews can be as short as one word or paragraphs long. Whichever you prefer, every review will help *Pompey Hollow Road* get noticed.

If you enjoyed *Pompey Hollow Road*, check out Anna's story in *The Fifth Floor Trilogy!* Subscribe to my newsletter at JulieOleszek.com. You can also find me on Facebook and Instagram.

Best Wishes,

Julie Oleszek

Website:
https://www.julieoleszek.com/

Facebook:
https://www.facebook.com/novelsbyjulieoleszek/

Instagram:
Instagram.com/julie.oleszek.author

Made in the USA
Columbia, SC
11 January 2024

30320955R00212